DARK TOWN

A FANTASY LITRPG ADVENTURE

Tales of Temerity, Book One
Level One of the Dragon's Crawl

BY PALMER PICKERING

This is a work of fiction. All of the characters, organizations, locations, and events portrayed in this novel are either products of the author's imagination or are used fictitiously.

DARK TOWN, A FANTASY LITRPG ADVENTURE
Copyright © 2024 Barbara Palmer Pickering

ISBN 978-1-960530-01-1 (Trade Paperback – Amazon)
ISBN 978-1-960530-00-4 (Trade Paperback – Ingram)

FIC129000 **FICTION** / LitRPG (Literary Role-Playing Game)
FIC009000 **FICTION** / Fantasy / General
FIC009100 **FICTION** / Fantasy / Action & Adventure
FIC009020 **FICTION** / Fantasy / Epic

Cover art and design by Dusan Markovic at www.markovicdusan.com
Tales of Temerity wordmark and character logo by Zayan Waleed at www.instagram.com/graphics of zayan/
Interior art by Nele Diel at www.nelediel.com, Sebastian "Ghoters" Jara at www.artstation.com/ghoters, and Claudio "Vanharmontt" Vidal at www.artstation.com/vanharmontt
Interior design and layout by Gretchen Dorris at www.inktobook.com

MYTHOLOGY
→PRESS←

Published by Mythology Press
www.mythologypress.com
Follow Palmer at www.palmerpickering.com
10 9 8 7 6

DEDICATION
&
ACKNOWLEDGEMENTS

This book is dedicated to Daniel Wright, Mohan Sun, and Final Fantasy XIV for saving my sanity during the Covid shutdown.

Thank you to my phenomenal editorial team: Tracey Govender, Dom McDermott, Kate Cobb, Gwynevere Kipling, Rachel Marchesi, Laura Lawson, and Terri Brownfield. Plus, endless thanks to my beta readers and ARC readers. It takes a village to raise a book. Love you all.

Cover art by Dusan Markovic. Interior art by Nele Diel, Sebastian "Ghoters" Jara, and Claudio "Vanharmontt" Vidal. Tales of Temerity character logo and wordmark by Zayan Waleed. Interior design and layout by Gretchen Dorris.

No AI was used in the writing, art, or production of this book. Everything flows from the creative minds and souls of human creators.

TABLE OF CONTENTS

LIST OF ILLUSTRATIONS

BRIEF GAMING LINGO GLOSSARY

The language in Dark Town is largely accessible to a general audience. However, a few terms are specific to video gaming and might not make sense to everyone. In particular:

Attack – See DPS.

Boss – A major, hostile non-player character (see NPC) that players must beat, usually in order to progress through the game or move on to the next level. Often, it refers to a primary and very powerful boss ("big boss," "final boss"). "Mini-bosses" are smaller bosses that generally support the big boss.

DPS (damage per second) – A video game statistic that measures how much damage a player inflicts, calculated in increments of seconds. The more damage the better. Players whose main focus in combat is to deal damage are labeled "DPS." In Dark Town, this role is called "Attack."

Healer – A Healer's role is to keep their team members healthy and alive during battles. Often, if the Healer dies, the whole team fails. A Healer can regenerate health in himself/herself and others, and may be able to resurrect others from death under certain circumstances.

Mob (mobile, mobile object, or mobile entity) – A hostile non-player character (see NPC) that players need to fight in order to complete a quest or reach a boss. Mobs often attack in groups and usually appear in final challenges (aka trials, dungeons, raids) on the way to the final boss. Annoying mobs that appear in large numbers and are easy to beat are often referred to as "trash mobs."

NPC (non-player character) – A character that is a part of the game environment but not actually playing the game, versus a player who is trying to beat the game. Players may interact with NPCs in conversation, quests, or battles.

Positionals – A fighting style or damage calculation that depends on the location of the attacker relative to the opponent. For example, certain moves are best executed from the front, flanks, or rear of the opponent, and may garner additional points.

Rotations – Combinations of fighting moves that achieve the best results, the most damage, or the highest points.

RPG (role playing game) – This is a genre of gaming where the player assumes the identity of a character and adopts their associated attributes, roles, gear, skills, etc. The player explores the game world, engages in activities, quests, and battles. They typically gain power and skills as they progress in the game.

Shield – See Tank.

Tank – A Tank's role is to lead the combat team through the "challenge" (aka trial, dungeon, raid) by navigating the "map," attracting ("pulling") the enemies, and absorbing as much damage as possible in order to free up the rest of their raiding party to defeat the enemies. In Dark Town, this role is referred to as "Shield."

1

THE TIN ROOF

Temerity stood behind the bar of her family's tavern, wiping away the sticky rings left by mugs of ale. The pair of travelers had finally left, without giving her so much as a copper for a tip. Her feet ached from standing all day, but it was just her and her ma now. And Half-pint.

"Stop it," she hissed, stepping aside as dishwater sloshed onto her boot from where Half-pint was washing the mugs in his hiding spot under the counter.

He did it on purpose, like he always did, more to amuse himself than to annoy her, she had learned. She glanced down at the shadows behind the parted curtains that hid the underbelly of the countertop, where the house goblin worked during the day—whenever he decided to show up, that is, appearing suddenly and startling Temerity every time.

Many older houses and farms in the surrounding area had their own house goblin—a hobgoblin, in fact. The reclusive fae creatures usually worked at night and were rarely seen, but they expected a dish of cream for their efforts, else they would make more of a mess rather than clean up. And one should never be so bold as to ask them their name, or they would stomp off in a huff, maybe never to be seen again. So Temerity's family called him Half-pint, for his short stature and acerbic personality.

Mostly, the hobgoblin had appeared to members of her family in his cat form, but she had seen him a few times over the years in his goblin form, and most often at night. She was given the task of leaving him his cream every evening before she went to bed. It was when her pa and brothers had left to play the Dragon's Game that he began appearing as a hobgoblin during the day, helping her and her ma with the cows and the tavern, though Temerity saw him much more often than her ma did. In fact, he worked under the counter only when Temerity was tending the bar, and her ma praised her for how clean she kept the mugs and dishes.

Another splash of water hit her boot, and she nudged the curtain aside with her toe. Half-pint ducked his mischievous yellow eyes behind his cowl and showed her his rounded rump, his small, squat body robed with the old roughspun curtain he had nabbed from the front window. The window still stood half-draped with faded brown fabric, the missing panel making perfect garb for Half-pint to disappear into.

The hobgoblin was knee-high to her, not much larger than the tomcat he shapeshifted into on occasion—a brown striped tabby, peering down from atop cupboards too high for a normal cat to reach, or rubbing himself against her shins, nearly tripping her when she trudged out to milk the cows before the sun came up. In the barn, he would stare up at her with his big yellow cat's eyes, wanting some of the warm milk. She normally ignored him, and when she moved from cow to cow, he would eventually turn into his goblin form and tend to his chores. When she split wood for the daily fires, he would stack it neatly by the back door, then change back into a cat to chase the mice from the woodpile.

She sighed, hanging the damp rag over a rod, and stepped out from behind the bar to check on the few tables still occupied at this late afternoon hour—the lull before the supper rush, when people would line up for her ma's savory stew and fresh brown bread.

The Tin Roof was named for the corrugated metal roof her pa had put on the old wooden building, way back when he and her ma had married, before Temerity and her two brothers were born. Temerity and her ma, Hannah, had painted the roof a bright blue this past summer and stained the log siding a rust red. Half-pint had given the roof a second coat of paint one night, earning himself a whole jug of fresh cream and three honey cakes.

The tavern sat along a main thoroughfare that cut through cultivated fields and fenced pastures between two good-sized towns, East Haverly and West Haverly. The line demarcating the two townships was the Haverly River, a slow-moving waterway murky with brown sludge.

Situated on the west bank of the river, the Tin Roof was one of several buildings that clustered together to form a smaller town called Haverly Arms, named for the three smithies that competed for business from the surrounding farms, itinerant traders, and adventurers.

Travelers, traders, and adventurers used Haverly Road because it was relatively safe, even though it was the long way around to go between the major trading hubs of Port Maverick and Glistening City. Haverly Arms also had the best and most affordable tools and weapons forged outside of Port Maverick.

Four travelers at a table lifted their hands to prevent Temerity from taking away their nearly empty mugs, then asked for water instead of more ale. They were waiting for supper and wanted to keep their table, was Temerity's guess. She went to the cistern and brought them water, then waited on the next table of travelers. She finally made it to the back of the L-shaped room, where two tables of adventurers sat.

Temerity's ma often warned her not to fraternize with adventurers. "Unsavory characters," she would call them, even though her own husband and two sons had gone off adventuring, disappearing underground to try their luck in the Dragon's Game. Hannah would ask any adventurers who entered the Tin Roof if they had seen her husband and sons, gesturing to the charcoal portraits that hung behind the bar.

"Don't think so," was the regular response. Hannah would frown and then direct them to the tables in the back, so that she would not have to look at them and be reminded of her heartache.

It was Temerity's job to wait on them, and she didn't mind. She was more curious than heartbroken. It was rare for adventurers to be killed for good, or so she had heard. When they were slain, they normally got dumped back where they had started, as her pa and brothers had confirmed the few times they had returned from the game, scuffed-up and wild-eyed, before heading out to try again.

Adventurers were usually men, with a glint in their eyes and a faraway look, as though remembering places they had been and monsters they had slain in the labyrinths of the Dragon's Crawl, the first of three Dragon's Games.

"It's not a game," Hannah would tell Temerity whenever she dreamed aloud of joining her pa and brothers.

"They say it is," Temerity retorted. "With dragon treasure at the end."

"Ain't never seen no treasure," Hannah scoffed. "Only an excuse to abandon family and responsibilities."

The majority of the men in the Haverlies had been drawn into the Dragon's Game, leaving the women, children, and elders to take care of everything that needed taking care of. Temerity had encountered a few women adventurers, but they hadn't looked much different from the men, truth be told—gritty and muscled, wearing men's clothing and boots, and many of them sporting scars and tattoos.

"I want to try," Temerity had told her ma more than once.

"You will do no such thing, young lady," Hannah would say, snapping at her with the painful tip of a wet towel. "I need two of you around here, not none, and if I'd had any sense, I would have had another daughter to help me." Hannah would wipe at her furrowed brow and return to the cookfire, and Temerity would resume her chores, kicking aside Half-pint when he was in his cat form and asking for his help when he appeared in his goblin form.

"I am not your servant," he would claim tartly, his broad little chest puffed out. "I am a skilled laborer, worthy of respect. Unless you want me to disappear down my well and never return."

"No, no. Please don't go," she would beg, then leave out extra cream at night to soothe his slighted ego. Honestly, she didn't know what she would do without the little hobgoblin. He cleaned up the tavern after the last patrons left and mucked the barn in the mornings while she milked the cows, humming as he eyed the buckets of fresh milk.

She brought her attention back to the tavern and served more ale to a pair of customers in the back. The toughened men appeared to be seasoned adventurers, while another pair of adventurers at a nearby table looked wide-eyed and green.

"Get any treasure?" she asked the older pair, always trying to pry information out of adventurers, who normally guarded their secrets more tightly than a dragon guarding its gold.

"Hmpf," was the only response as they lifted their mugs

to their lips. A broadsword hung from the back of the larger man's chair, and a recurve bow and quiver of arrows were splayed across the table at the elbow of the thinner man.

She sniffed loudly and went over to check on the younger adventurers, who were in their late teens, about the same age as Temerity's brothers, and looked to be fresh off the farm. One was tall and lean, in loose-fitting, roughspun clothes with sleeves that didn't quite cover his bony wrists. He had pale skin, dirty-blond hair tied in a messy ponytail, and a wispy moustache and goatee. A scythe leaned against the wall behind him. She supposed he intended to use it as a weapon, considering his bright but nervous eyes that marked him as a first-time adventurer. The other one was just as tall but more heavyset, with a broad, friendly smile, swarthy complexion, and unkempt black hair and beard. He had a woodsman's axe hanging from a strap off the back of his chair.

"More ale?" she asked, noting the pitifully small pile of coppers sitting on the table.

"No, thank you kindly, miss," the smiling one said. "I hear you serve food here?"

"Yes, at sundown," she said.

The men glanced at the still-bright windows and then gazed at her with pained eyes, as though they were close to starvation. They reminded her of her brothers, who could eat all day long and still scrape the stew pot clean and then raid the larders for more food. She wiped her hands on her apron and sighed. "Smells like some bread just came out of the oven." She peered over her shoulder at the steaming loaves on the butcher block. "I'll get you some bread and butter, to tide you over."

"Thank you kindly, miss," they said in unison.

She returned with thick slices and a pot of butter, placing the basket in front of the grateful young men, who tore into the warm bread. She then took her time wiping down the empty, neighboring tables while she eavesdropped on the conversation of the older adventurers.

"My cousin swears there's an entrance in this cursed backwater," one of them grumbled. "He says it's safer than the one in Glistening City."

"But the Tower's in the city," the other replied.

"Don't matter none, you still have to get through all the levels and traverse the entire godsdamned dungeon labyrinth to climb the Tower anyway. Don't matter where you start—under the Tower or all the way in Port Maverick—they all end up at the same place. At least an entrance this far out in the middle of nowhere won't be staked out by every thief, hooligan, and scalawag in the lower realms."

The thinner, gray-haired man shrugged and grunted his reluctant agreement. "So, he says it's below a tavern, eh?" he asked in a hoarse whisper.

Temerity did not wait to hear the other man's reply but hurried back to the bar, her pulse racing. The locations of Dragon's Crawl entrances were not to be shared with strangers. Information about the game passed in whispers among networks of adventurers, who took vows of silence lest their hard-earned experience help outsiders who might beat them in the game.

No maps existed of the Dragon's Crawl, and no Haverly Arms native would reveal to outsiders the location of the entrance under their feet. Even Temerity did not know the exact location. Nor had anyone ever confirmed to her that there was an entrance at the Tower in Glistening City, though talk of the Tower was always laced with awe and trepidation combined with unreasonable excitement. So she had always suspected as much, but now she had finally heard it confirmed by actual adventurers.

Not five seconds after she had slid to a stop behind the long wooden counter, one of the men slammed his mug on the table and bellowed, "More ale, girl."

Temerity drew in her breath and filled the two clean mugs Half-pint handed her. She returned to the back corner, setting down the foam-topped mugs in front of the older pair of adventurers and noting that their other mugs were still half full.

"You got a cellar down here?" the burly one asked, taking a loud slurp of ale and stomping his boot on the wooden floorboards. His long red moustache curled into his mouth and was rimmed with white foam, and some yellow ale had dribbled down into his bushy beard. "We might need to rent some cold storage space, you know, if you have any spare room in your cellar." He cocked his eyebrows meaningfully. "Goin' boar hunting later on. Might catch two."

"Or a whole herd," the thin one with the pointy nose and long stringy hair added, earning an annoyed glare from his partner. The pointy-nosed man patted his bow, as though to confirm the veracity of their story.

"Nothing but a crawl space down there," she said. "We have a root cellar out back, but it's not very big and it's full of ale kegs. Sorry." She escaped back to the bar, making it safely behind the wooden counter and stubbornly ignoring the loud grumblings of the middle-aged men.

Half-pint's large yellow eyes gleamed up at her from underneath the countertop. The hobgoblin tossed back his cowl and waggled his large imp ears, which stuck out from below a grimy leather cap he had fashioned from a cast-off blacksmith's apron to hide his bald spot and receding patches of thin gray hair. His skin was leathery, and his chin and jawline were fringed with stubble. Under his robe, Half-pint wore a simple shirt and short pants he had made from burlap feed sacks, with the red imprint of East Haverly Feed printed diagonally across the chest. He used a rope for a belt, his hairy legs stuck out below his shorts, and his feet were always bare.

She had learned that Half-pint's hearing was as good as a cat's, so she was sure he had overheard the conversation. "They must mean Lucy's Tavern," she whispered excitedly.

"Of course," Half-pint whispered in return. "Your brothers told you as much."

She bobbled her head back and forth. "Sort of. Hinted. Let slip. Before Ma shushed them up."

It was a well-kept secret for such a small town—where everyone knew everyone's business—where exactly the entrance to the Dragon's Crawl tunnel labyrinth was hidden. Temerity had always suspected Lucy's Tavern, given the constant stream of adventurers who frequented the place—many more than the Tin Roof. But Temerity had never gone down into the cellar herself, and Lucy and her dogs guarded the door as if the dragon's treasure itself lay buried down there. And her brothers had not actually revealed their secret. They had only said that Lucy knew where the entrance was—and that didn't confirm anything.

"I may have to pay Lucy a visit," Temerity muttered softly, so that Hannah, who was stirring the pot over the fire, would not hear.

"*Tsk, tsk,*" Half-pint said, wagging his finger and shaking his head.

"What, no," she hissed. "You ain't the boss'a me."

"Well, well, well," he whispered insistently.

"Well?" she echoed, rolling her eyes.

"No. *Well!*"

She scowled at him, then understanding slowly dawned, and she smiled.

2

THE WELL

Temerity's two rat terriers snuck in the back door of the Tin Roof and went straight to the curtain that hid Half-pint underneath the counter. One dog growled, and the other wagged its tail. The hobgoblin was used to this daily ritual and beat the growling mutt over the nose with a wooden spoon and pelted it with spiny nuts. The dog carefully picked up a spiny nut with its teeth and went out back to gnaw it open and eat the sweet chestnut nestled inside. The other dog responded best to kindness and happily left with a dried pig ear clutched in its jaw.

The tavern hadn't yet opened for the day when the Cartwright twins from down the road pushed the heavy door open and waved cheerfully at Temerity. The two young women were fifteen, a year younger than Temerity's sixteen years, and they were almost like sisters to her, the three of them having grown up together since they were little. The twins sat at the bar, facing Temerity with identical smiling mouths, freckled noses, and hazel eyes. Only their copper-colored hair set them apart from one another: Shannon's was always twisted up in a bun, and Siobhan's was always worn long in a tangle of loose curls. Temerity was plain compared to them, with dark brown hair and eyes to match; but she was tall and strong, and well-fed.

"Want to help me with the honey cakes?" Temerity asked.

They nodded and accepted mugs of tea sweetened with honey and cream that Temerity set down in front of them. The twins had been showing up most mornings lately to help make the honey cakes and had even offered to help with the milking. Temerity knew it was because they were hungry, but they were too proud to say so. The twins' father had gone off adventuring like most Haverly men, but unlike Temerity's mother, who had the good fortune to run a thriving business, their mother was a spinner and a weaver—skills every woman in town had, and so her services were not in high demand.

Temerity gathered the ingredients, and they each grabbed a large bowl to mix the batter.

"Let's make extra today," Temerity said, fetching additional pans from the rack. "You can take some home to your ma."

The twins nodded and smiled shyly. "She's making new curtains for your front windows," Siobhan said, glancing behind her.

Temerity regarded the windows. She had long since stopped noticing the faded curtains. In addition to the half-draped window, the two other windows were framed with the same brown curtains that must have been as old as the tavern's tin roof. "My ma would like that," she said. "We haven't had time to weave since my pa and brothers left."

Temerity and the twins exchanged gossip while they mixed the batter and poured it into pans, slid the pans into the stone ovens, and then chopped almonds and pecans and set them aside with the honey to pour over the tops later.

Hannah whisked in through the back door, bringing a gust of cold air with her, and set sacks and baskets of supplies from the farmer's market onto the countertop. The three young women helped her put everything away.

Shannon turned to Hannah. "Our ma said we should come help Temerity milk the cows and clean the chicken coops." The young woman tried to keep her expression casual and cheerful, but Temerity could detect the shame and desperation in her eyes and noted that the twins' faces were growing gaunt, their normally pudgy cheeks hollowing beneath pronounced cheekbones.

Whenever they had offered before, Temerity's ma had politely declined their help, having her own daughter to feed. Temerity caught her eye with a pleading look before she could decline again. Hannah closed her lips, and the crease between her eyebrows deepened. She sighed. "Well, I suppose we could use a little help around here. Our hobgoblin seems to nap more often than not, and we have been getting more and more adventurers coming through as of late."

Claws dug into Temerity's hose at her ankles, and she surreptitiously kicked away Half-pint the cat. "The goblin is a good helper," Temerity said quickly, "but he is so small." More claws and another kick followed, and she bent down and placed a small dish of cream under the counter, swatting at his head as his long, tufted ears pressed back against his feline skull.

The cows and chickens had already been tended to that day, but after Temerity and the twins helped Hannah chop vegetables and meat for the midday stew, the sisters stayed on, serving customers and cleaning tables. Hannah stirred the stew and chatted with the regulars, and Temerity and Half-pint the cat sat behind the counter and grew bored.

Half-pint yawned and stretched, then sauntered towards the back door, his long tail standing up like a flagpole, and glanced over his shoulder for Temerity to follow him. She trailed behind him out the back door, past the root cellar and working well, through the herb garden and their small apple orchard, behind the blackberry brambles and the ancient oak, to the old dry well where Half-pint lived.

"This is the entrance to the Dragon's Crawl?" she asked skeptically. The cat flicked his tail and purred.

Temerity and her brothers had climbed down inside the well as children, fastening a thick rope to the iron bar, which used to turn with the old well crank, and dangling it down into the dark pit. One time, her older brother, Mathias, had pulled up the rope, leaving their other brother, Hamish, in the well all day. Pa had been furious, and Mathias spent the entire next day on his knees with a bucket of water and scrub brush, cleaning the two chicken coops until they were spotless. But she had never seen an entrance to the Dragon's Crawl down there. It was just a cavern that used to have a stream running through it, which had since dried up.

Half-pint hopped up onto the stone rim of the well, then with a lashing of his tail and in the blink of an eye, transformed into his goblin form, clothing and all. She always wondered where his clothes went when he turned into a cat, sometimes imagining him padding around in his cat form wearing a little cap and cape, but instead, the clothing disappeared with the fae magic and then reappeared again when he turned back into a goblin. The little hobgoblin scrabbled down inside the well, clinging to the rough stones with long knobby fingers and bare hairy toes.

The rope was still there, where her brothers had left it, tied to the iron rod that spanned overtop the well, its length coiled up in the leaves and covered with moss. Temerity uncoiled the slimy rope. The fibers still seemed strong enough, and the old knots were still there, spaced out at regular intervals to make the rope easier to climb. She tossed it down into the dark hole and heard its end hit the bottom. She hopped up onto the well's rim and tugged at the rope. It would probably hold her weight.

Temerity glanced around at the blackberry brambles, then stepped off the rim and clung to the rope. Her feet scrabbled for a hold on a large slippery knot as the rope swayed gently. She climbed down into the darkness and landed on the uneven stone floor. Her eyes slowly adjusted to the dim light. She should have brought a lantern, she realized, but she was familiar with the layout of the cavern, which extended under the fields for a ways before narrowing into rocky crevices too small to squeeze through.

"Now what?" she asked Half-pint, whose yellow goblin eyes glinted up at her.

"This way," he said, waving her forward. He turned and headed north, using his hands to scramble over the rocks, resembling his cat form as he hurried away on all fours.

She followed reluctantly. He had lived down here since before she was born, supposedly, so she trusted that he knew where he was going. She couldn't see anything more than smudges of gray against black as she left the narrow shaft of light behind and felt her way over the rocks, crouching and using her hands as Half-pint had done.

"I can't see," she complained as she slipped on a wet rock and bumped her knee.

"*Tsk, tsk,*" he said. "Blind as bats, you trolls."

"I am not a troll. You are a freak with cat's eyes."

"Pfft," he said dismissively.

A green glow suddenly dispelled the darkness. Half-pint held a small glowing orb in his palm, illuminating his weathered face from below and casting his hooked nose and pointed chin in ghoulish shadows.

"Oooh, an aurora stone." She approached him with wonder. "Let me see."

He curled his fingers around the glistening orb, quenching its light.

"Alright," she grumbled. "Be that way."

His fingers uncurled, and the light crept across the cave again.

"Where are we going?" she asked.

He turned his back to her, and she followed him in a crouch. Deep in the shadows, where the low ceiling forced her onto her knees and elbows to crawl along like a lizard, they came upon a rusted, round metal grate that she had never noticed before. Half-pint produced a skeleton key from his robes and opened a rusty padlock, then swung the grate open on squealing hinges.

They crawled into a low, man-made tunnel paved with river rocks on all sides. A trickle of water ran down the center, and water dripped from above. By the time they exited the tunnel through another locked grate, the fronts of her skirt and apron were soaking wet, and her hair hung in damp strands across her cheeks. She was able to stand up on the other side, and looked around at the low cavern, her head brushing up against the ceiling. The dank space was silent except for a steady *drip drip* and was filled with the eerie green glow of the aurora stone. She plaited her long hair into a quick braid and looked down at Half-pint.

"I never knew this was here," she said. "Where are we?"

"Lucy's," he said, hopping gleefully on his bare feet, as though thrilled to have shown her something new.

"Ah," she said. The far side of the small cavern ended at a stone wall, which had a drainage archway blocked by another metal grate. Half-pint opened it. They crawled through and were confronted by stacks of wooden crates. They stood up and edged around them, squeezed between a collection of empty ale casks and dusty tavern chairs, and found themselves in a proper cellar. Half-pint held up the glowing stone, illuminating the musty space. Shelves and crates lined the walls, a large oak table stood in the center, and a brass chandelier holding a half-dozen unlit candles hung from a wooden beam over the table. The room was cluttered but clean, with a closed wooden door at either end. Faint creaks overhead hinted that they were standing below Lucy's Tavern.

Temerity knit her eyebrows together. "So, this is the entrance to the tunnel labyrinth? Which door goes to the tavern, and which leads to the labyrinth?"

Half-pint gestured to one of the doors and then suddenly transformed into a cat as the doorknob on the other door jiggled. The light from the green aurora stone was instantly extinguished, and Temerity flailed around in the dark until she felt the edge of the table. She crawled underneath and held her breath as the thick wooden door swung open, letting in a shaft of light followed by heavy footsteps.

3

LUCY'S CELLAR

"Recite the honor code."

Temerity recognized Lucy's voice as the tavern keeper neared the table, the lantern illuminating the cellar in a golden halo. Temerity peered out from underneath the table, examining three pairs of feet: pointy women's boots dyed a deep purple, and two pairs of scuffed and muddy men's boots.

The two men spoke in unison, one voice gruff and the other gentle. *"The dragons' eyes are everywhere, and so that I shall not lose my way for all eternity, I place a piece of myself in your keeping to guarantee my safe return."*

Temerity tilted her head—the men's voices sounded vaguely familiar.

The toe of a purple boot tapped impatiently on the stone floor. "And the rest?"

One of the men cleared his throat, and they resumed speaking together. *"I shall not violate the safe haven of the entry portals, and I swear upon my honor that I shall not steal from my fellow adventurers their homing amulet, or I shall be barred from the game forever and die a horrible death."*

"Well said," Lucy praised them, then her voice became firm. "In the barrel."

Two loud clunks resonated in a barrel by the second door.

"Good luck," Lucy said, friendly again.

"Thank you kindly," the soft-spoken man said.

"Luck ain't got nothin' to do with it," the other man scoffed, and Temerity realized the voices were from the two older adventurers she had served in the Tin Roof the day before. The gruff voice belonged to the barrel-chested man with the bushy red beard, and the gentle voice belonged to the thin, wiry man with the long gray hair.

The door at the far end of the room opened. The men passed through and were gone in a flash of blue light.

Lucy closed the door behind them and walked across the floor, standing near the table where Temerity hid.

"Why are you sneaking about?" Lucy asked, and Temerity froze.

A flash of movement caught Temerity's eye as a large scruffy cat leapt from a shelf and landed with heavy paws on the table above her head. A moment later, Half-pint's nasal, raspy goblin voice replied, "I do not sneak. I was merely observing at a respectful distance."

"Hmpf," Lucy scoffed. "Thank you for cleaning up down here. The last crew that passed through acted like they owned the place."

Half-pint muttered a reply, but Temerity was not listening. She was surprised and confused and more than a little hurt. Did Half-pint help Lucy, too? And all this time, Temerity had thought Half-pint was *her* hobgoblin. Well, at least the hobgoblin of the Tin Roof, though Temerity's ma only paid him any attention when he was a cat.

"And who have you brought with you?" Lucy asked. Long purple braids came into view and then two shiny, violet eyes peered under the table, bright against dark skin. Lucy squinted into the shadows. "Is that Temerity? What are you doing here, darling?"

Temerity huffed and climbed out from under the table. "How did you know I was here?" she asked, brushing off her damp skirt and work apron.

"I smelled sour ale."

"Ah," Temerity said. Her clothes were indeed overdue for laundering. "So, you know Half-pint, I see," she continued. "We got bored, so he showed me his well, and next thing I knew, here we were, in your cellar."

It was almost the truth. She turned up her palms in a shrug and gave Lucy a half-smile, relieved that the tavern keeper did not appear to be angry.

Lucy placed her hands on her wide hips and tapped her toe on the floor, narrowing her eyes curiously. "Are you thinking of going adventuring?"

"Oh, well, I … uh …" Temerity faltered. "No. Yes. Maybe. My ma doesn't want me to."

"But what do *you* want?" Lucy asked.

"I think it would be kind of … I don't know. An adventure?" Temerity tried to smile confidently but felt awkward and clumsy all of a sudden. "It's not something women really do."

"Pfft," Lucy scoffed. "I've gone a few rounds in there."

"You have?" Temerity's eyes widened. "I didn't know that. How come nobody told me? But, anyway, I'm still too young."

"Nonsense," Lucy said, her full brown lips curling into a smile. "I was only your age when I first ventured into the labyrinth. And so was your brother Hamish, if I remember correctly. Age doesn't matter in there. Cunning matters. Wile matters. Patience and smarts. Bravery and ... *temerity.* See?" Lucy laughed. "You have exactly what it takes." The tavern keeper laughed harder, slapping her knee at her own joke.

"My ma would be upset," Temerity said, the prospect of actually doing what she had been talking about for years chasing away her courage.

"No more upset than she was when your pa and brothers left," Lucy said with an arched eyebrow. "Why should you stay behind just because you're a girl? Huh? Why does it usually work out like that?"

"Yeah, why?" Temerity echoed. "Doesn't seem fair."

"Not fair at all," Lucy agreed. "You've got no little brats to take care of. Your ma's got a good business to keep her going. You're strong and intelligent. You should do it while you can."

Temerity swallowed and glanced at Half-pint.

"It is but a tunnel," the little goblin said, waving at the portal door. A wide grin split his face, revealing his myriad of small, yellow teeth.

Temerity frowned at Half-pint. "Don't tell me you've played the Dragon's Game, too?" His impish grin brought an indignant flush to her cheeks. "And you didn't tell me?"

"It was a long time ago," he said, raising his hands defensively and putting on a guilty face. "Besides, what happens in the game stays in the game. Isn't that right, Lucy?"

The tavern keeper bobbled her head in tacit agreement, then she and Half-pint fixed their gazes on Temerity.

Her heart was suddenly pounding, and thoughts bounced around in her head like corn on a hot skillet. Something welled up in her chest, and the best she could figure was that it was an unfamiliar feeling of excitement, as though something big and important hovered just beyond her grasp. All she had to do was reach out and take it.

She took in a deep breath and exhaled slowly, then asked, "What do I need to know?"

4

GEAR

Temerity followed Half-pint back through the underground passage that connected the two taverns, climbed the rope out of the dry well, and began gathering the adventuring supplies Lucy had recommended.

First, she needed suitable clothing. Her family's small cottage adjoined the tavern, with a living area in the front and sleeping quarters in the back. Temerity rummaged around in a wooden chest of her brothers' clothes. She found a pair of Hamish's old canvas pants, the color of dirt. She pulled them on over her stockings, removed her tavern serving dress and apron, and fastened the slightly large pant waist with her belt. They would do just fine—comfortable and worn-in from use, with plenty of pockets. She pulled on the sturdy leather boots she wore when she did her outdoor chores, then tucked the long pant legs into the tops. She dug into the chest again, removing random articles of clothing until she found what she was looking for.

She shook out Mathias's green suede vest. She had helped her ma dye the hide with a sorrel and pine needle bath, turning it the color of moss. She put on the hip-length vest over her camisole, fastened it closed over her smallish chest, and admired her outfit in the polished-tin mirror. She could pass for an adventurer, she supposed. A first-timer, for sure. She made a face at herself. *Is this a good idea? Maybe this is really stupid.*

It was not too late to change her mind. Only Lucy and Half-pint would know the difference, and they would never tell anyone about her hare-brained idea.

Temerity frowned at herself, then removed the vest and tossed it onto her bed. After pondering her next move for a few long moments, she finally crossed the room to her clothing rack. She grabbed one of her long-sleeved linen shifts and cut the bottom third off. She pulled it on and tucked it into her pants, then put the vest back on. The long, cream-colored bell sleeves were slightly dramatic but gave the outfit a bit of flair that she rather liked—confidence, with a small dose of *devil-may-care*. She nodded at herself with a playful smirk and went in search of the remaining gear.

A thick leather belt of her pa's could work as a weapon belt, she figured, thinking of the belts she had seen some adventurers wear, filled with hooks and loops, from which hung all manner of weapons, tools, and other gear. She slipped her sheathed knife onto the belt, then tightened the belt over the vest. Her knife was a hunting knife, but she needed something bigger. Two knives were better than one, she guessed. Besides, everyone knew you needed to enter the game with three weapons, which Lucy and Half-pint had confirmed. After pulling a loose smock dress on over her adventurer's attire, she sauntered casually into the tavern. Her ma barely spared her a glance from her spot at the cooking fire as Temerity stepped behind the counter. The red-headed twins were busy cleaning tables, and the floor had been freshly swept.

Temerity opened the knife drawer and casually grabbed a blade from the back that hadn't been used in recent memory. It was a long boning knife with a narrow steel blade, tapered from years of use. She sharpened it on the whetstone, searched the drawer for its leather sheath, and slipped out the back door. Hiding in the barn, she tied the knife sheath to her belt with a leather cord, then snuck around the side of the building and headed down the road towards a clattering of competing hammers.

The three blacksmiths were all located near one another. Temerity went directly to the third and smallest smithy and entered through the front door. The heat from the forge hit her as she stepped over the threshold, and the ruddy-faced blacksmith turned to greet her with a broad smile.

"Temmy!" he said with delight. Only her pa and the blacksmith, Pauly, ever called her that anymore, the two men having grown up together, closer than brothers.

"Hi, Uncle Pauly," she said, returning his grin.

"Need something repaired?" he asked, scanning her quickly. Not seeing a hoe or oven hook in her hands, he raised his eyebrows.

"I, um … I was wondering," she said, bringing an index finger to her chin. "Do you think you might have some spare swords? You know, old ones. Bad ones. Seconds."

His eyebrows arched further up on his sooty forehead. "I don't make bad swords. You know that, Temmy." He narrowed his eyes at her. "What kind of mischief are you up to?"

"Me? Mischief?" she asked, bringing her hands to her chest and feigning affront. "Never."

"I recognize that look," he said, putting down his hammer and shoving the glowing rod back into the fire.

"What look?"

"The look of all wannabe adventurers. What's gotten into you all of a sudden?" He folded his thick arms across his chest and gazed at her, holding her eyes.

She shrugged. "Bored, I guess. This little town is so … little."

"True," he said. "But half the kingdom passes through here. They bring the world to us."

She held his gaze, unswayed.

He sighed. "Does your ma know?"

"No, not yet."

"Who are you going with?" he asked.

"Um, nobody. Just me." She tried to brave a smile, but Pauly met it with a concerned frown. She hadn't really thought much about companions. All her girlfriends thought she was crazy whenever she broached the subject. Besides, she'd have more freedom if she went by herself.

"It's dangerous in there, you know," he said.

"I suppose," she said, tilting her head. "But you can't die, at least." She laughed, but he did not. "I'm going to look for my pa and brothers."

He frowned. "I hear it's pretty big in there. Easy to get lost. I don't know how you would find them."

She steered the conversation away from herself, not wanting to find an excuse to change her mind. "How come you never played the Dragon's Game?"

They stood in the open doorway, where a breeze beat back the suffocating heat. "I'm afraid if I go in there, I'll like it too much and become obsessed, like your pa and brothers." Pauly shook his head. "Nah. Tilly would kill me. Besides, I do a good business off all the starry-eyed adventurers." He grinned, then looked at her sideways. "What kind of sword you looking for? Do you even know how to use a sword?"

"A little bit," she said, following him into the back room.

He looked through a rack of swords and chose a relatively short one and handed it to her. She clasped the leather-wrapped handle and swung the blade around. It was lighter than it looked, and when she held it straight upright, she could barely feel the weight at all.

"This is too fancy," she said, admiring the wave-patterned steel. "I can't afford such a nice one as this."

"Nah, that one was quick and dirty. Had some spare slag I needed to use up. Besides, you won't hang onto it for too long, if things go well in there."

"What do you mean?" she asked, striking a defensive pose and pretending to parry the blade of an imaginary foe.

"You'll want to trade up as soon as you can," he said. "Take one, leave one, that's the rule."

"Really?" she asked. "But I wouldn't want to leave this behind. Can't I hang onto it and get another sword, too?"

"If you have something else to barter for it, I guess. Any loot you find is a trade-in policy. Or so I heard. You get to take three weapons into the game, you know."

"Yeah, I know. I have two knives," she said distractedly, holding up the sword and examining the blade's double edge. "I'll keep this as long as I can."

"Don't worry, someone else will make good use of it when you leave it behind. It all comes back around, you'll see." He gave her another toothy grin. "Here, come on out back." He grabbed another sword and followed her into the yard. They faced off and crossed steel with a sharp ring. He went easy on her, but his blow still sent a painful shudder through her forearm. She hopped back into a ward position, and he ran her through the same drills her pa used to do with her and her brothers.

"Seems your pa has been teaching you," Pauly said, relaxing and wiping off his blade. "Here, let me sharpen that for you." He took her sword, and they went inside.

"Pa used to teach us with wooden swords, before they left," she said, catching her breath and watching as Pauly touched up the edges and ran a polishing cloth over the sparkling blade. "He always said I was too careful."

"Can't be too careful," Pauly said. "My pa was a master—trained me and your pa—and he said technique beats strength any day."

"Well, I don't know how good my technique is anymore," she said. "I haven't practiced in two years. Once, I got mad at Hamish and won that fight handily. I forgot all about technique that time, but my pa said if I always fought like that, no one could beat me."

Pauly laughed. "You are pretty strong. You gave me a workout."

"Ha ha," she said with a half-grin, eyeing his massive blacksmith's arms. "It's all those mugs of ale I've been carrying. And wrangling ale barrels and lugging sacks of grain, repairing fences and chopping firewood. All the chores my brothers used to do."

Pauly nodded somberly and asked if she wanted him to sharpen her knives, and she unsheathed them both.

"Ah," he said, taking the boning knife. "My pa made this one. Looks like it's had a lot of use. Still holds an edge, though. And this one, Griffor made," he said, handling the hunting knife and speaking of another blacksmith in town. "Not half bad, for someone who churns out blades faster than Tilly churns butter."

Pauly showed her how to sharpen the knives and sword and gave her a pocket-sized whetstone and a small tin of oil.

"I can't pay you much," she said. "Don't you have any swords that are more plain? You know, made of regular metal? Not this fancy, wavy steel."

He laughed. "Don't worry about it. I owe you."

"Why do you owe me?" she asked, returning his infectious grin.

"Sally."

"Oh." She had accompanied her ma to attend Tilly when she was birthing little Sally. "That was nothing," she said. "Tilly's stronger than a cow, and Sally came out screaming."

They laughed together. "Anyway," Pauly said, picking out a sheath, "it's my good luck gift to you. May you discover the dragon's lair and find favor with him. Or her. I hear the fiercest dragons are female." He slid her blade into the sheath and handed it to her.

"There aren't really dragons," she said, her smile fading.

Pauly threw her a cryptic look and walked her to the front door.

"I'll bring by a tray of honey cakes and a couple tankards of ale later on," she promised.

"That'd be mighty nice," he said.

"Thank you for the sword, Uncle Pauly. Say hi to Tilly and the baby."

"Will do. Hope you find your pa and brothers. Tell that stubborn old father of yours to come home one of these days."

She grinned and gave him a small bow, hid the sword in the folds of her dress, and stepped out onto the road.

5

THE DOOR

Temerity brought Pauly a tray of honey cakes and two tankards of ale as she had promised. She spent the rest of the afternoon and evening at the Tin Roof checking on Siobhan and Shannon, who were still there, bustling around the tavern and waiting on customers, eager to please Hannah. Half-pint must have appreciated the help as well, for he was nowhere to be seen.

The twins' timing was perfect, Temerity reflected. Her ma would have no cause to resent Temerity for leaving her to manage the tavern by herself now, and the twins needed the work. She slipped away to the cottage, gathering supplies. She found an old canvas travel sack and packed some underclothes, an extra pair of Hamish's pants, and one of his work shirts. She dug around in another chest and found her pa's old leather cap and Mathias's festival shirt with the puffy sleeves that she had always liked. Then, she took the linen scraps from the shift she had shortened, rolled up a wool blanket, and packed some toiletries. She paced through the cottage, worrying that she had no idea what she was getting herself into, and started grabbing random items: a small slate tablet with three soap-stone pencils, needles and thread, a ball of twine.

She recalled the items Lucy had told her to bring. Light. She needed light. She snuck into the supply closet off the main tavern room and nicked a half-dozen taper candles, a brass candle holder, and a tinderbox. Next, she went out to the storage shed and grabbed a small spool of copper wire, a pair of pliers, wire cutters, a jar of torch cloths soaked in tallow, and then sawed off a length of a stout linden branch for a torch. Finally, she filled a waterskin and surreptitiously raided the larders for food for the road.

A fair amount of room remained at the top of her travel sack, which she would need for all the loot she would collect down in the tunnels, if she understood the game correctly.

She couldn't think of anything else she might need, and so when the tavern closed for the night, she left a bowl of cream by the hearth and then fell into a fitful sleep. The next morning before dawn, the twins were waiting for her in the dairy barn, and Temerity watched as they did all the work. Then she watched as they opened the chicken coops, put out feed, changed the chickens' water, and brought in the eggs.

Temerity helped her ma bake the morning bread while the twins mopped the tavern floor and hung the new curtains their ma had made, dyed a bright indigo blue to match the tin roof. Temerity took one of the old, drab-brown curtains, retreated to the cottage, and stuffed the faded fabric into her travel sack.

She checked the barn for any last-minute items she may have forgotten and grabbed a coil of rope and her work gloves. Not finding anything else useful, she scratched the ears of each of the cows and the two rat terriers, then clucked goodbye to the chickens. Finally, she returned to the cottage and left a note on her ma's bed, carefully shaping her letters on a piece of parchment with a sharpened quill: "I went looking for Pa, Mathias, and Hamish. Please don't worry. I will be back soon. Love you, Temerity. PS: Don't forget to leave cream out for Half-pint."

She left out the back door of the cottage, slung the travel sack over her shoulders, and walked down the road to Lucy's Tavern.

———————◆———————

"Remember," Lucy said, facing Temerity in the cellar, "you can leave the game at any time by finding a homing spike and pressing your hand against the glowing blue spiral. You will return to this cellar as your home portal, as long as you still carry the matching piece of your homing amulet."

"What should I use as an amulet?" Temerity asked, looking into the open barrel by the rear door. Inside was a collection of broken swords, half of a busted stone goblet, scraps of fur capes, a broken medallion, and all manner of other junk.

"Something very important to you," Lucy said. "Something that resonates deeply within your heart. Those are the most powerful items and will ensure your safe return."

Temerity wrinkled her brow. She did not want to part with anything she had packed, particularly not the sword, even if she could break it. Her hand flew up to her throat, where a locket hung. She sighed and unclasped the silver chain. She slid her fingernail along the edge of the small round pendant and the locket opened. Staring up at her was a miniature etching of her ma, and on the other side of the locket was one of her pa. Wincing, she bent the two discs backwards and snapped the delicate hinges. The loose piece, unattached to the chain, was her ma's face. She grimaced with guilt and tossed the tiny silver disc into the barrel, listening to it clank and rattle through the junk and settle to the bottom. She gazed down at her pa's face, then clasped the chain around her neck.

"There," she said, and Lucy nodded.

"What if I lose this?" Temerity asked, grasping the necklace at her throat.

"Then you will exit into wherever the homing spike leads. Could be anywhere in the real world. Could be a long walk home," Lucy said with a crooked grin.

Temerity tried to look unconcerned as she tucked the pendant under her vest.

"Now, you must recite the honor code," Lucy said. "Repeat after me, *'The dragons' eyes are everywhere, and so that I shall not lose my way for all eternity, I place a piece of myself in your keeping to guarantee my safe return.'"*

Temerity recited it back to Lucy.

Lucy continued, *"I shall not violate the safe haven of the entry portals, and I swear upon my honor that I shall not steal from my fellow adventurers their homing amulet, or I shall be barred from the game forever and die a horrible death."*

Temerity repeated it, then Lucy made her recite the entire thing again, then once more until she had committed it to memory.

"Okay," Lucy said. "Now, like I told you before, when you get in there, the first thing you need to do is navigate the tunnel labyrinth and come out the other side. Then you will need to collect three dragon jewels to pass to the next level, so don't let anyone steal them. Got that? And try not to die."

"I don't plan on dying." Temerity curled her fingers around the hilt of Pauly's sword. She was not much of a fighter, but she was good at hiding and sneaking around. Most adventurers she had encountered were brash men, loud and overconfident. She had grown adept at avoiding such men while working in the tavern. "How do I find dragon jewels?" she asked. "What do they look like?"

Lucy replied, "They are nearly the size of chicken eggs, but they are jewels. And they glow. They come in various colors. Red is the best, but any will do. They do different things, but anyway, the important thing is to collect them."

"Like Half-pint's green aurora stone?" Temerity asked. "Is that a dragon jewel?"

"No, you can't take dragon jewels out of the game. What does his aurora stone look like?" Lucy's eyebrows knit together. "Does it glow?"

Temerity described it, and Lucy's mouth puckered somewhere between disbelief and wonder. "He has an end-game jewel?"

Temerity shrugged. "What's an end-game jewel?"

Lucy did not answer, but a confused and calculating look passed over her features before she straightened and focused on Temerity again.

"Where do I find dragon jewels?" Temerity asked.

Lucy turned up her hands. "I can't tell you where to find them because they are always in different places. *But never fear, they shall appear, when all hope is lost, and the end is near.'* That's an old faery rhyme. Anyway, good luck!" Lucy smiled, her gold front tooth glinting. The tavern keeper hugged Temerity and then opened the heavy oaken door.

Temerity nodded with nervous anticipation and stepped through the doorway.

◆

A flash of blue light blinded Temerity for a moment. When her vision cleared, she found herself standing in a cold, dark, musty cavern. A hollow silence echoed around her, and a shiver ran up her spine. An eight-foot-tall standing stone towered next to her. A swirl of blue light twice the size of her hand glowed at waist level. A pointed capstone in the shape of a four-sided pyramid also glowed blue. She glanced behind her, but instead of the wooden door she had entered through, the cavern wall was smooth, unbroken rock. She hesitated for several panicked heartbeats, then pressed her palm to the blue spiral. The stone flashed, and the next moment, she was standing in Lucy's cellar, blue dots swimming across her eyes.

Lucy stood there with arms crossed and a smirk on her face. "Everyone does that the first time. It works, don't worry."

Temerity grinned sheepishly. "It's dark in there."

Lucy laughed. "Did you bring candles like I told you to?"

Temerity nodded.

"Good. You'll be fine, then. Ready to go back in?"

Although Temerity wanted to climb the stairs to the warm, cheerful tavern up above, pride made her turn and step through the doorway once again. The same flash of blue light greeted her, and the same dark cavern wrapped its cold fingers around her.

She turned and examined her surroundings. Shadowy walls faded into murky blackness beyond the light of the glowing pillar. She took out a taper and tinderbox from her pants pocket, knelt down, and struck the flint against steel until the char cloth ignited. Holding the candle with a trembling hand, she lit the wick. The yellow flame flickered and then steadied. She stood up and held the candle aloft. Facing her was a single arched opening in the stone wall, gaping black and sending shivers up her spine. She held her breath and stepped through it.

More stone walls surrounded her on every side, with a narrow passageway stretching to her left and right. She chose the left branch and followed the passageway as it curved gradually until the arch disappeared from view behind her. A low ceiling pressed down from above, and every step echoed back at her, making her jump as though someone were following her. The air was deathly still, and she imagined this was how a tomb must smell—of bones slowly turning to dust. She stood still and examined the flickering shadows. She was alone. She trod carefully forward, cupping the wavering flame with her free hand.

Another arch appeared, and after she stepped through it, she chose to turn left again. At the next juncture, she did the same, and the next. Every stone wall and archway looked identical, and tendrils of panic crept up her throat. She hadn't asked how big the labyrinth was, but after several more left turns, she was bathed in cold sweat and struggled to steady her racing pulse.

In a fit of panic, she turned on her heel and retraced her steps, turning right, and right, and right again, until she emerged into the entry cavern with the homing spike. The luminescent blue spiral swirled slowly, and the pyramid-shaped top of the standing stone seemed to pulsate. She sat heavily on the stone floor and dropped the taper, the flame guttering out. Maybe she should have found a traveling companion. The sound of her heartbeat thundered in her ears, and she took long, slow breaths, trying to calm her shaking limbs.

"Come on, Temerity," she whispered. "You can do it." She lit the taper again, stood up, and turned her back to the swirling blue spiral. She gathered her courage and stepped through the dark archway.

This time, she turned right at every arch. She got farther this time before turning back and trotting through the maze, sighing with relief when the familiar blue spiral lit the cavern. She shrugged off her travel sack and sat down on the cold floor, leaning back against the stone pillar and pinching out the candle flame.

A soft, rumbling thrum came from inside her travel sack, and she scrambled to her feet. A scruffy cat's head poked out from the top of the canvas sack, and with a flutter of whiskers and fur, Half-pint transformed into his goblin form and waggled his ears at her.

She let out a burst of surprised laughter as he climbed out of the sack and glared up at her with his bright yellow eyes.

"How many times are you planning on turning back?" he asked grumpily, resting his long-fingered hands on shapeless hips. "We'll never get anywhere at this rate."

Relief washed over her, and suddenly her fear was gone. She picked up the chunky little hobgoblin and clutched him to her chest. "I could kiss you," she said as he squirmed in her arms and swatted at her head.

"Put me down! What in a rock troll's name has come over you, Miss Temerity? Why, I never ..."

He hopped down from her arms and straightened his brown cloak, then marched over to her travel sack and pulled out a little canvas sack of his own, hoisting it on over his shoulders.

Temerity squinted at a flash of steel glinting from the top of his sack. "What have you got there?" she asked.

"What," he said, reaching back and grabbing a wooden handle. "My axe?" He pulled out the little weapon, and Temerity laughed.

"That's Ma's favorite meat cleaver," she said, eyeing the wide, curved blade. "It does fit you quite well, though." The large blade was nearly half his size, a great battle-axe in the hands of the stumpy hobgoblin.

He tucked it back into his sack, and as she knelt to light the candle, he pulled out his glowing green aurora stone, casting a bright orb around them. "Don't waste your candle in the tunnel labyrinth," he said. "This casts enough light for now."

She slid the candle and tinderbox into her pocket and pulled her travel sack onto her shoulders. "I wish I had an aurora stone," she said as he led the way through the first archway.

"It's a dragon jewel," he said proudly.

"Aha! Lucy and I suspected as much."

"You told Lucy?" he asked with a scowl.

"Yeah, why? Is it a secret?" She ignored his stormy glare and admired the glowing, faceted jewel. "You got one already? Great, now we only need five more." She suddenly felt lighthearted and courageous, and wondered why she had ever been afraid.

"We need six," he said. "This one is special and doesn't count for leveling."

"Why so special?" she asked as he turned left and waddled down the curved passageway. "Is it an end-game jewel? Lucy thought maybe it was."

He responded with an exasperated huff.

She was accustomed to his grouchy demeanor and asked, "What is an end-game jewel?"

When he did not reply, she pressed him. "You can tell me. We're inside the game now. 'What happens in the game, stays in the game.' Right?" She gave him a bright smile, which he ignored. "Did you get the extra cream I left out last night?" she asked sweetly.

He rolled his eyes and grunted, then finally said, "You can only carry a dragon jewel out into the real world after you win the game. One per win. Then if you go back in, it's used as a power jewel, not for leveling."

"You won the game?" she asked, incredulous, and hurried after him as he crossed through another archway and turned right.

"Yes, but only once. And that was a long time ago. I only

beat the first game, though—the Dragon's Crawl. There are actually three games in the Dragon's Game, that I know of. Each game has several levels. But I didn't want to devote another decade to beating the others."

"A decade? Is that how long my pa and brothers will be gone?" She was momentarily stricken and thought guiltily of her ma.

"The first game doesn't take that long, usually, unless you want it to. But the next two are longer. Or so I heard."

"This is great," Temerity said, her good spirits returning. "It's going to be really fast and easy with you, since you've already beaten the game."

Half-pint peered over his shoulder at her, gazing down his long nose, then faced forward and passed through another archway and turned right again. "I can help a little bit, maybe. But things always change in here, so you never know how it will go."

"You seem to know where you're going," she said, her voice bouncing off the stone ceiling as he turned left at the next juncture.

"I'm just taking random turns," he said lightly, holding up his dragon jewel and inspecting the walls. "There's no rhyme or reason to this place. It's just dumb luck."

Her buoyant mood deflated a bit. "Well ... if you don't know where you're going, then mightn't we get hopelessly lost?"

"Quite so, Miss Temerity, quite so. Getting lost in the labyrinth is the only way to get out."

6

THE TUNNEL LABYRINTH

The farther they went into the labyrinth, the more Temerity feared they would never get out. She had not thought it possible for the passageways to grow any darker, but soon she lit a candle to dispel the disturbing sensation of floating in a green bubble on a black sea. The flickering candlelight did not really make her feel any better, as it only exposed the endless circuits of ancient stone walls that curved between one archway and the next, leading them deeper and deeper into the maze. She was sure they could never retrace their steps at this point, and so the only option was to continue forward.

Half-pint appeared unconcerned, and she gathered courage from the hobgoblin and smiled bravely whenever he caught her eye. Her feet were tired and her back and shoulders ached from carrying the pack, but the goblin wasn't complaining, and he took five steps for every one of hers, so she kept her aches and pains to herself. After a time, the candle guttered out, and they continued on in the small halo of green light.

"Aha," Half-pint said, startling Temerity out of her morose thoughts.

"What?" she asked hopefully. She leaned in to see what he was looking at. The walls had smoothed out and were covered with runes carved into the rock. "What do they mean?"

"I can't read ancient Gnomish," Half-pint replied, "but it's a sign that we are nearing the center of the labyrinth."

"Oh. That's good, right?" she asked.

"Very good," he said, and scurried forward.

After what felt like hours more of trudging through the dizzying sameness of the labyrinth, Half-pint stopped short in front of her.

She stumbled to a stop so as not to trip over him. Yawning before them was a black hole in the ground. The rock floor fell away into nothingness, the opening spanning the entire width of the passageway and extending across as far as the eye could see. They locked gazes, then turned around and walked in the other direction. They passed the archway they had entered through, and after following the curved passageway, they eventually came upon another black pit. Temerity was unsure if it was the same pit viewed from the other side, or a different one, but clearly their progress was halted.

"We can go back through the archway and try a different direction," she suggested.

Half-pint's ears waggled. "No, this means we must go down."

"Down?" she asked, trying to keep her voice steady. "Into that? Is this the path you took last time?"

Half-pint shook his head. "No. This is new. I told you— things change in here."

She furrowed her brow at him. "Does this mean that the labyrinth spans more than one level?"

"That's right," he said, scratching his scruffy chin. "The

labyrinth takes you up and down and every which way." His eyes glinted. "It means we're making progress. Come on." He knelt at the edge of the floor, holding the green jewel down inside the pit and peering around.

Temerity lay on her belly and hung her head over the edge to see what she could make out. A rusty wrought-iron ladder was bolted to the wall and descended into the inky blackness.

"Ugh," she groaned. "We need to climb down *that?*"

Half-pint's frown mirrored her own. "I can't hold the dragon jewel and climb at the same time. I should have made a wrist strap for it—I have no idea where my old one went to." He inspected the ladder worriedly. "Those rungs are too far apart for me. I could maybe scale the wall."

"No," she said. "That is a terrible idea. You can ride on top of my pack, or hunker down inside it, like you did as a cat."

His face wrinkled in a scowl, and Temerity could see his pride battling with common sense. It did not take him long to see the wisdom of her suggestion. She got to her knees, and he climbed up and sat on top of the pack. His stubby legs dangled over her shoulders, one hand holding onto her braid and the other hand lifting the glowing jewel.

"Find my gloves," she said, and the goblin dug into her pack and pulled out her leather work gloves.

After pulling her gloves on, she turned to face the ladder and lowered one foot until she found a rung, then proceeded to climb down into the murky darkness.

Down, down, down they went. It was deathly dark above and below, but still she descended, focusing on one rung at a time. A creak and a scrape, and the rung underneath her boot fell away, her heart dropping with it. She hung on with both hands, her toes scrabbling to find a foothold on the stone wall. She extended her arms to their full length and felt for the next rung below with her feet. She found it and hesitantly put her weight on it. It held. Half-pint released her throat that he had been clutching, and she felt with her toe for the next lower rung and continued descending.

"Where is the bottom?" Her next step landed on hard stone. "Oh, thank goodness," she said, and stood on solid ground, her legs shaking. Half-pint climbed down her pack and hopped onto the stone floor.

Temerity couldn't see anything beyond their little island of green light, and a cavernous silence enveloped them. Temerity wrapped her arms around herself and shivered.

———————◆———————

They encountered more pits they had to descend into, and ladders they had to climb up to reach ledges that led into caves and more twisting passages. Up and down, down and up. They ate as they walked, gnawing on hardtack and jerked chicken and sipping from their waterskins. She wanted to rest, but not as much as she wanted to find their way out of there.

"How come there are no other adventurers in here?" she asked.

"It's always like that," he said. "In this part, anyway."

"What do you mean, *this part?*"

"This is just the beginning of the first level of the game. This is the initial challenge. We haven't really even started yet."

Temerity's stomach fell. "Well, then, how long does this part take?"

"Could take no time at all, could take a very long time," Half-pint said gloomily.

The sudden shift in mood from his normally grumpy or alternately cheerful self was more disconcerting to Temerity than the endless maze of dark tunnels.

"It'll be okay," she hurried to assure him.

"One time," he continued, his tone dour, "I was in here for weeks. Ran out of food and water."

Temerity's heart was in her throat. "Weeks?" she managed to squeak.

Half-pint nodded and shuffled ahead.

"We don't have enough food and water for days, never mind weeks," she said, angry with herself for not packing more. "I didn't know it would be like this. What happens if we run out and then we can't find our way back to the homing spike?"

Half-pint lowered his head so she could not see his face, and he did not answer.

"Oh ..." she said, her voice trailing off. A knot of fear tightened in her belly. She didn't want to die of starvation. Not like this. Not in here.

"I shouldn't have come. You'd be better off without me," he muttered.

"No, no, no," she said. "I would be miserable without you. I swear."

"The dragons must be punishing me for some unknown past misdeed. I might have broken a rule here or there." His expression drew down in such a frown that his normally bright face transformed into that of a withered old man.

"I'm sure if you have an end-game jewel, you did not break any rules," she said quickly. "What *are* the rules, anyway?"

He shrugged. "That's the issue. The rules aren't always clear. You find out through trial and error, mostly. Nobody wants to help each other much, unless you team up. Adventurers are so competitive—the reds in particular. They won't share information. They would rather watch you walk into a trap and then steal your jewels."

Temerity tried frantically to think of some way to help. She examined the tunnel they were traveling along. It was like all the others. The tunnels went straight for a ways and then curved, or ended with a ladder up or down, leading to another level of the same endless network.

"Here," she said, tugging on Half-pint's robe. "Let's go this way." She tried to pull him towards a small tunnel that branched off to their left.

"No, the main tunnels lead to the way out," he said.

"They *used* to lead to the way out," she corrected him. "You told me everything changes in here."

He glanced up at her, and she held his golden eyes. She could see the moment he relented when his shoulders drooped in defeat. "It's against my better judgment, but carry on," he said with a feeble sweep of his hand.

He followed after her as she turned down the side tunnel. It wasn't tall enough for her to stand up straight, so she hunched over and hurried along, hoping it would open up after a short while. But the ceiling only grew lower, and soon she was crouching down and second-guessing her brilliant idea.

They continued on, and the tunnel twisted and turned and branched into various paths. Temerity figured it didn't matter which way they went, so she chose tunnels randomly. Her thigh muscles burned as she tried to hurry along in a low crouch, her pack brushing up against the rock ceiling. The little hobgoblin trudged reluctantly beside her. Her thoughts turned to her warm bed and the full larders back home.

"I've never seen these tunnels before," Half-pint said crabbily. "We'll just get more lost in here."

"How can we get more lost than we already were?" she retorted, and marched forward.

After a dozen more random turnoffs, Half-pint stopped and tilted his head, bringing his hand to his ear. "Shhh, listen."

She stopped walking and held her breath. A faint gurgling

reached her ears. "What is that?" she asked, relief surging through her. "Water?"

"Sounds like it," he said, and crept forward.

Beyond the next curve, a trickle of clear water seeped from a crack in the wall and ran down the center of the tunnel. Temerity and Half-pint followed it. More cracks and more seeping water widened the trickle to a small stream, and soon water covered the entire walkway, and they sloshed through it until it was ankle deep.

They drew to another halt as the path ended abruptly and the stream cascaded over the ledge into a pit of thick, black gloom.

"Oh, no," she said, teetering on the edge of despair.

Half-pint held up his green jewel, but it lit an empty void. Temerity groaned and struggled to light a candle, with the water flowing around her feet. She was finally able to get a spark from her steel and flint, using her slate tablet as a little table that Half-pint held up for her. She managed to light the candle, but it did not illuminate much more of the cliff than the green jewel had, so she assembled a torch, wrapping a tallow-soaked cloth around her linden branch, fastening it with copper wire, and setting it to flame with the candle. She waited until the torch was blazing before blowing out the candle and stashing away her tinderbox.

The torchlight exposed more of the gaping pit, but the bottom of the chasm remained cloaked in darkness. A cliff loomed on the other side, with a wide ledge at the same height as where they stood. It was several body lengths away, much too far to leap across. Rusted iron stakes and brackets on either side of the chasm marked where a bridge must have once spanned. There was no ladder up or down. It appeared they had reached a dead-end.

She glanced down at Half-pint. Water was rushing around the hobgoblin's bare feet and hairy calves, nearly reaching to his knees. He took the torch, and she hoisted him up to sit atop her pack. She felt him rummaging around in her pack, whereupon he pulled out her coil of rope and dangled it in front of her face.

She knit her eyebrows together. "What do you plan to do with that?"

"Throw it," he said, scrambling down and tying one end of the rope around the iron stake at their feet. He made a loop on the other end of the rope and handed it to her, motioning for her to toss it to the other side.

She saw what he was getting at, and after several failed attempts, finally looped it over a stake on the far ledge. Half-pint pulled the rope taut and tightened the knot around the stake at their feet.

"I don't know about this," she said nervously, and pressed on the taut rope to test its strength. "I don't know if it'll hold our weight." It was a thick rope, but not nearly as thick as she would have liked.

"It's as sturdy as the rope down the well," Half-pint pointed out.

She shrugged in grudging agreement. "You first," she said.

They tightened the cords and straps of their packs, making sure everything was secure. He tucked his green dragon jewel into a special bag he carried around his neck. Temerity held up the torch as Half-pint grasped the rope with both hands and edged out over the chasm, hooking his feet over the rope and hanging from all fours. She battled a wave of vertigo as she watched him inch across the bottomless pit.

Gathering her courage, Temerity clamped the torch handle between her teeth, pulled on her gloves, and followed him out onto the rope. The rope creaked and sagged under her weight as she shimmied across the gaping crevasse behind Half-pint.

The rope sagged more and more, and she glanced with alarm at the ledge they had just left as the knot came loose and the rope snaked out from around the iron stake. She hung on for dear life as the rope swung with her and Half-pint, slamming them against the facing cliff. Temerity tried to scramble up the rope, but it was slick and slippery. She clawed frantically and tried to wrap a foot around the rope, but her weight pulled her down too fast, and with a whizzing sound, her gloved hands slid along its length until she was clutching empty air. The torch went out and she grabbed it from her teeth and fell through the blackness with Half-pint screeching as he plummeted after her.

Suddenly, Temerity was plunging into ice-cold water. It swallowed her with loud gurgles as she sank down and down into the blackness and then bounced back up, the travel sack pulling her to the surface like a buoy. The painful shock of the cold water rendered her numb and sharply awake at the same time. Sucking in a panicked lungful of air, she treaded water, trying to stay afloat. More gurgling at her ears warned of the pack filling with water. The pack was quickly growing heavier, and together with her wet suede vest, boots, and the steel weapons around her waist, they threatened to pull her under. It was pitch dark, but she heard Half-pint splashing nearby. She frantically began shrugging the pack off her shoulders when the green glow of Half-pint's dragon jewel illuminated the cavern, revealing a long narrow lake bordered by a shiny rock ledge.

She slid off her pack and swam towards the stony shore, dragging her pack with her and focusing on reaching the ledge without drowning or losing her belongings. Temerity and the hobgoblin reached the rocky ledge at the same time and climbed up onto it, dragging their waterlogged packs with them.

Temerity sat on the cold stone, panting and sputtering, her heart hammering in her chest. She stretched out on her back, arms splayed and water streaming off her and forming a puddle beneath her.

"Wow," she panted. "I thought we were goners there for a minute." She turned her head towards Half-pint. He was standing up, squinting at the lake.

"What do you see?" she asked, climbing to her feet and gazing down into the black pool. A tiny glimmer of orange winked in and out of sight as ripples from the disturbance they had created bounced off the shore in tiny cross currents.

"Wait here," he said, peeling off his sodden robe and cap.

"Where are you going?" she asked, panic rising in her chest again.

But he had already dived into the murky water, taking his green jewel with him.

She clutched her hands to her chest as darkness consumed the cavern and she was left by herself on the platform. She kept her eyes on the green jewel as it descended into the depths towards the orange glimmer. Soon, both dots of light rose towards the surface. Half-pint's hand broke through the water, triumphantly clutching his green dragon jewel and a second jewel that pulsed with the fiery orange of a blacksmith's forge.

The hobgoblin swam over, snagging the forgotten floating torch stick as he went, and scrambled up onto dry ground with his prize.

"What good fortune," he said, chortling happily. He handed her the torch stick and held out the orange jewel. "You can have this one. Your first dragon jewel. Congratulations."

"Oh, no. I couldn't. You're the one who found it," she said, waving away the jewel.

"But you're the one who led us down the pathway that brought us here," he countered.

"You mean, I'm the one who led us to a cliff and almost to our deaths."

"It's always the darkest moments in this game that reveal the treasures," he said with a wry grin, and held out the jewel insistently.

"Oh, alright. Thank you." She accepted the egg-shaped jewel, her mood instantly improving. The dragon jewel was still icy cold from the water, but it glowed the incandescent orange of an ember in a hot fire. She turned it over, examining the faceted sides, which were cut like a gem. "What do the different colors mean? And where did the jewels come from?" she asked.

"Well, the qualities differ depending on who wields them. But in general, green is for healing." Half-pint held up his jewel. "Orange is usually a premonition jewel. You should feel hunches about things now, as we go along. Orange jewels come in very handy in this game."

"Hmmm," she mused, examining the glistening jewel. "So you're a healer?"

"It's not me, really," he said. "It's the jewel. But yes, it is a powerful healer. In addition, being an end-game green jewel, this one can be used one time per game to revive someone from death, so they don't have to go back to the beginning. A great advantage, indeed. Starting over can be a long slog, especially if you die near the end of the seven levels."

"Can you use it on yourself?" she asked, intrigued that a jewel could hold so much power.

"To heal myself, yes, but not to revive myself from death. I would be dead, after all. It's kind of hard to do anything when you're dead." His snarky humor was back, which was a relief to Temerity. "And it doesn't work with the final bosses," he added. "You can only resurrect someone during regular gameplay."

"Could you have chosen any color to bring out with you? Lucy said red is the best. Why did you choose the green jewel if you can't use it to save yourself?"

He peered at her quizzically, his ears lying back a bit, reminding Temerity of his cat form. "Because I value my companions," he said curtly, as though affronted that she would ask him such a question. He continued, his tone softening a bit. "Playing this game alone is very difficult. If my companions die, then I need to either proceed by myself or go back to the beginning to start over with them. Not fun at all. No, not fun at all."

She gazed with appreciation at her experienced and virtuous adventuring companion, feeling very fortunate indeed.

"As to where they came from," he said, "the jewels were first left behind by the dragons when they built the game. Apparently, they left an enormous chest filled with them at each level, as currency to level up and proceed through the game. Since then, the jewels have been found and lost, stolen, and scattered by adventurers throughout the ages."

"Why did the dragons build the game?" she asked.

Half-pint shrugged. "I heard it isn't a game to them. The mazes and challenges were built as rites of passage to ascend to dragonhood." He lifted his bushy eyebrows. "I couldn't tell you if there is any truth to that tale. I've never made it past the first game. Many who attempt the advanced games never come back, and those who do, never reveal their secrets."

Temerity wrinkled her brow, trying to piece together bits of legends she'd heard over the years.

"But at the moment, we are in a bit of a pickle," Half-pint

said, interrupting her thoughts. "We will catch cold if we stay in the caves for too long, soaking wet like this." He turned and began removing the sodden items from his pack and laying them out on the flat ledge.

She did the same, kicking off her boots, wringing out her clothing, and pulling out the other contents of her pack. The tinderbox had remained sealed, as had the jar containing the torch cloths. Everything else was dripping wet, including her bundle of hardtack, which was now a clump of soggy dough. She spread out her vest on the rock and shook out her boots. "How do we get out of here?" she asked. "How far is it to the end?"

"I don't know," he said. "But the orange dragon jewel is a good omen. Perhaps we are close to an exit."

"There's a draft coming from that direction," Temerity said, gesturing at a curtain of shadows draping the rocks behind them, where she sensed a faint stirring of air. "Maybe that way will lead us out."

He turned his long nose towards the shadows and sniffed. "I hope you're right," he said, sounding pleased.

"Then will we be done with Level One?" she asked hopefully. "Finished with the labyrinth?"

"Oh, no. Not even close, Miss Temerity," he said, chuckling. "I told you. The tunnel labyrinth is just the entryway to Level One. We'll need to keep going until we each have three jewels, not counting my green one."

"More of these cold caves?" she asked, unable to keep her voice from betraying a growing dread.

"No, not caves. We are going to a place called Dark Town. It's an endless maze of alleys and inns. Much better than here."

"Oh, good," she said, exhaling with relief. "A real town."

The little hobgoblin surveyed their belongings with his hands on his hips and his mouth turned down. "This will not do," he said. "Our things will never dry in this cold, damp cavern. We are wasting time. We should follow the draft."

And so, they packed up their things again, shouldered their heavy, wet travel sacks, and trudged towards the whiff of cold air coming from the shadows.

7

DARK TOWN

Temerity and Half-pint found the passageway, which twisted and turned and branched off into another tunnel, and then another, as they followed the elusive breath of air that came and went. They finally found its source, a steady, whistling flow of cold, dank air escaping from a narrow crevice. They squeezed through the crack in the rock, emerging into a long, curved tunnel that looked to be well-traveled. She felt hopeful as they followed the gentle stirring of air, until they came upon a shadowed archway.

Temerity's spirits fell, fearful that they had found themselves back at the very beginning, where stone archways and identical curved paths led deeper and deeper into the circular labyrinth. Had they traversed the multi-leveled tunnels over countless hours—or had it been days—only to find themselves back where they had started?

"Come on," Half-pint said, waving her forward and appearing unconcerned.

She grudgingly followed the hobgoblin through the stone

archway, each of them holding up their glowing jewels. She exhaled with relief that the path did not span from left to right. Instead, she and Half-pint stood at the base of an ancient corkscrew stairway. They began climbing the narrow stairs, hanging onto the walls to help keep their footing on the smooth, stone steps, which had been worn down to a dangerous slant.

Temerity's hose were sodden inside her wet boots, and blisters on her heels made every step a painful effort. She was hot and sweaty from the effort of climbing, so although her hair and clothing were still damp, at least she was not cold.

At long last, they reached the top, passed through another stone archway, and found themselves aboveground, at the end of a gloomy cobblestone alley that reeked of sour, stagnant sewers.

"Oh, thank the dragon gods below," she said, wiping her brow and leaning against a stone wall. "I thought we were never going to get out of there."

"Come, we cannot linger here." The goblin scuttled off and glanced furtively at the shadows flanking the narrow lane. "Hide your jewel," he hissed, and pocketed his, extinguishing the green glow.

She was startled by his sudden anxiety and glanced down at her orange jewel. Aside from the nervousness emanating from Half-pint, she felt no ominous forebodings, and slipped the jewel into a pocket, darkening the alleyway into a murky path of black stone and blacker shadows.

"Is this Dark Town?" she asked in a whisper.

"Yes," he mouthed back at her, placing his finger across his lips for silence.

A wan light up ahead indicated the end of the alley, and they hurried towards it, emerging onto a larger thoroughfare lined with stone hovels and lit by an occasional flickering lantern. The sewer smell mellowed to that of burning lantern oil and rotted refuse. Dregs of forgotten trash lay clumped and slimy in the gutters. It was not silent here as it had been in the caves, nor was it noisy. No one was about, but the occasional creak of a doorway or screech of a sign swinging on rusted hooks made her jump and search over her shoulder for unseen enemies.

Many hovels had a sign hanging over the doorway, advertising a room, a mattress, or a cold meal. They were all dark and unwelcoming. Temerity shivered and quickened her pace.

"What time is it, I wonder," she whispered, examining the ash-gray sky.

"Feels like evening, although there is no sun here, so it's difficult to tell," he murmured.

"No sun?"

"No," he said, and continued scurrying forward.

Temerity had always considered Haverly Arms to be a depressing town of muddy roads and modest cottages, and she had been embarrassed by her simple life. But compared to Dark Town, Haverly Arms was a prosperous and cheerful hamlet. A sudden wave of homesickness washed over her, and she missed her ma. She remembered how her ma had cried each time her pa and brothers had left to seek glory in the Dragon's Game, and now Temerity had abandoned her, too. For the first time, she felt her ma's heartache as her own, made harsher by the guilt of leaving her all alone. She had even taken Half-pint away, and the sting of her own betrayal made her wince.

Temerity scanned the surroundings as Half-pint turned onto another road. This one was wider, and the buildings were more substantial. She hesitated as she spotted a few small groups of men walking along a row of inns. Half-pint shed his furtive posture and stood up straight and strong, and she followed his example. They strolled slowly down the street, peering into the inns and small shops. Some windows were lit with candles, and a bright blue glow shone through one building's bay window. She slowed down to peek inside. A man sat at a long table by himself, hunched over a stack of parchments and reading by the light of a large candelabra. A sign over the door read, *The Blue Jewel. Fine Accommodations for the Discerning Adventurer.*

"This one doesn't look so scary," Temerity said.

Half-pint shook his head. "We need one with a bathhouse and laundry."

They continued down the road for several blocks. Narrow, dark alleyways branched off from the main road on either side. Noise from a brightly lit pub echoed off the hard cobblestones, and men spilled out into the empty street, holding mugs of ale and puffing on pipes and rolled tobacco leaves. Most of the men were plainly clothed and scruffy, with the exception of a dashing young man in a long, gold velvet waistcoat, red and gold slashed breeches, and a cleanshaven face. Eyes followed Temerity and the small hobgoblin as they strode by.

They turned onto another road of similar-quality inns and pubs, and from what Temerity could tell, the warren of main roads and alleyways stretched in every direction. There were no normal wagons or draft animals to be seen, but small hand-drawn wains and barrows were parked along the sides of the roads and alleys. Dark Town had the feel of late evening, when most people were safely inside, although what distinguished day from night here was a mystery to her, if there was no sun. Overhead, she could see neither starry sky nor rocky cavern. The overcast sky was low and dark, with a murky cloud cover of unknown composition.

Half-pint gestured to a building across the road, and she walked over with him and read the sign. *Avon's Grotto—Bed, Bath & Laundry.*

She pushed the door open, and a set of cowbells loudly announced their entry. A small, narrow room greeted them, made smaller by the men who lined the walls to either side, sitting or lying on thin mattresses on the floor. The ones who were awake examined them openly as they strode through the open area between the beds.

The room was warmed by an open-faced brick oven in a back corner, glowing orange with coals, and Temerity's mood improved immediately as waves of heat caressed her face.

In the other back corner, a tall woman stood behind a wooden counter, with a single lantern sitting on the countertop next to her. As they approached, Temerity realized the woman was not tall—she was rather short, in fact—but was standing on a wooden chair. She leaned her delicate hands on the counter and peered at them with bright green eyes the color of Half-pint's hidden dragon jewel. She wore a silken gray robe, and pointy ears stuck out from the sides of her head, poking through thick tangled locks of greenish hair.

"Ooh, a female hobgoblin," Temerity whispered to Half-pint.

"She is no hobgoblin," Half-pint whispered back, offended. "She is a water faery, by the looks of her."

"Ooh, a real-life nymph," Temerity whispered with wonder.

"A water sprite," the woman corrected loudly, appearing even more offended than Half-pint. "Whispering is rude, you know." The water sprite tapped her long, polished fingernails on the countertop.

"Oh, I'm so sorry," Temerity said, reminded of Half-pint's phenomenal hearing. The two little people did look like kin of a sort, Temerity observed, but she would not dare say so out loud.

Half-pint cleared his throat and looked up at the sprite. "We would like a bath, laundry, and beds. In that order. And a *private* room," he said, glancing over his shoulder distastefully at the motley collection of sprawling, snoring adventurers. "Where is your price sheet?"

"The price sheet is in here," the water sprite said, tapping a finger to her forehead. "I don't take coin. I only take trade. And what I need today is coal. One bucket of coal apiece, for each service you require. And if you'd like food, then that is an extra bucket each. Supper has been served, but I have cornbread and beans left that I can heat up for you."

Temerity and Half-pint traded glances. That totaled four buckets apiece. The water-logged pack was heavy on Temerity's back, her clothes were still uncomfortably clammy, and her stomach growled at the mention of hot food. "We don't have any coal," Temerity said.

"You can get some tomorrow," the sprite replied. "The coal mine is not far from here. However, I require a guarantee."

"What kind of guarantee?" Temerity asked suspiciously.

"One dragon jewel apiece." The sprite's tulip-pink lips curled into a smug grin.

Half-pint cast Temerity a sidelong glance, and she followed him over to the brick oven, where they held out their hands to warm them while conferring as quietly as they could.

"I cannot part with mine," Half-pint said in barely a whisper. "We'll just offer her yours."

"Can we trust her to give it back?" Temerity asked.

Half-pint furrowed his brow. "Well, she wouldn't stay in business long if she stole dragon jewels. Not in Dark Town.

Not that people don't steal jewels, mind you, just not out in the open."

Temerity weighed worry against cold and hunger, and decided warmth and food were worth more to her at this moment than losing a glowing orange jewel retrieved at the end of a nightmarish maze.

They returned to the counter and Temerity held out her dragon jewel. "This one for the both of us," she said firmly.

The sprite crossed her arms and regarded the two of them coolly. "One each."

Temerity shook her head dejectedly, then turned with Half-pint and headed towards the door, dreading the cold street beyond.

"Oh, *aaaalright,*" the sprite said with a big sigh, just as Temerity reached for the door handle.

Temerity dropped her hand and turned around, having never wanted a hot bath and reheated beans so badly in her whole entire life.

8

AVON'S GROTTO

Avon, the water sprite, showed them into the back. A central room was dominated by an enormous copper kettle over a coal furnace, with copper water pipes entering and leaving the steaming kettle. A large room to the left held a series of copper washtubs on one side and a firepit that resembled a forge on the other side, surrounded by lines of drying laundry. The room to the right held four copper bathing tubs, and the wall was lined with benches, hooks, and lanterns. Avon lit two lanterns and then stepped over to a tub and opened two water spigots, running her hand under the water until she was satisfied with the temperature. Then she handed Half-pint a linen towel and wash rag, a sprite-sized gray silk robe with a long pointy hood that matched her own, a pair of wooden sandals, a brush, and a pot of soap. She waved her fingers at him, then left the room with Temerity.

"We don't see many female adventurers in Dark Town," Avon said. "You can use my private bath." The sprite led Temerity through a door in the back.

Temerity stood inside the threshold, mouth agape. Twittering yellow birds flitted amongst thick greenery. Small fruit trees and flowering vines filled a stone grotto, floor to ceiling, their citrusy, floral scent chasing away the grit and grime and acrid stench of the outer chambers and alleyways. The grotto glowed with luminescent lemons, limes, and oranges. Phosphorescent purple wisteria, red bougainvillea, and orange trumpet vines trailed from the ceiling. Fern-covered walls dripped melodiously, and two small waterfalls fed a steaming pool of clear, emerald water. Temerity breathed out coils of tension and gratefully accepted a stack of linens and bathing supplies. Avon left her alone in the enchanted room, and Temerity peeled off her damp clothing and settled into the hot water, closing her eyes contentedly.

◆

After their long and luxurious baths, Temerity and Half-pint left their sodden clothing, leather garments, and travel sacks with Avon, who promised they would be clean and dry by morning. They followed her up a set of narrow stairs in their bathrobes and wooden sandals, carrying only their weapons, lighting supplies, and precious items. The sprite left them in a small garret room, which was clean and had two thick mattresses on the floor, mounds of pillows and blankets, two small dressers, two wooden chairs, and a small porcelain water pitcher and matching basin. Lanterns glowed from atop the two dressers. Temerity and Half-pint each took a bed and quietly polished their blades before extinguishing the lanterns and crawling under the covers.

Weak streetlight filtered in through a small window, and Temerity examined the lump in the bed across from her. The hobgoblin had been part of her household her entire life, but she hadn't had a meaningful conversation with him before this adventure. She hadn't realized how well-spoken and thought-ful he was and felt ashamed for having considered him such a strange creature. She had always thought of him as a household servant of sorts—when he wasn't being a mischievous prank-ster—though he was ferociously independent and hated to be told what to do. When he was in his cat form, he felt almost like a family pet, although of the ornery, hissing tomcat type.

"What are you looking at?" the hobgoblin snapped, star-tling her out of her reverie.

"I, um ... are you comfortable?" she asked.

"Yes. Quite, Miss Temerity. Are you?"

"Yes, I am. Thank you, Half-pint. The bed must be a lot more comfortable than your well back home."

The goblin rolled over and gazed at her with big yellow eyes. "I do not live in that well, my young Miss."

"You don't?"

The goblin rolled his eyes. "No, of course not."

"Where do you live, then?"

"Miss Lucy set me up with my very own garret room above her tavern, after your father removed the attic from the big farmhouse to create your tavern. He thought the ceiling should be tall and threw away all my belongings."

"Oh, that's awful," she said, aghast.

The little goblin shrugged. "He didn't know I lived up there. He was always throwing away my blankets, complain-ing about a racoon den and trying to figure out how they got into the attic." A coarse chuckle escaped his lips.

"Why didn't you tell him?" Temerity asked.

Half-pint sucked his tongue loudly against his teeth. "A goblin has his pride, you know. And I like my privacy. If you stupid humans can't figure out an obvious thing like the house goblin living in your attic, why should I waste my breath?"

Temerity sat up in her bed and wrapped a blanket around her shoulders. "Lucy took you in? So she knows you live up there?"

"Yes, of course she does. She cleared out the space for me and gave me a key and everything. She already knew I was cleaning her cellar. I didn't have to tell her or show my face. Not like with your family. But then again, Lucy has a touch of fae blood, which makes her much more perceptive than you dumb-as-a-rock, full-blooded humans."

Temerity broke out in a sardonic laugh. "Dumb?"

"Yes. Dumb. Blind. Deaf. You are so wrapped up in your little lives that you fail to notice an entire other world humming and swirling and glittering all around you. If you would just open your senses a little bit, you would see that you are missing so many things."

Temerity pulled her legs up to her chest and rested her chin on a knee, pondering his words. "Avon's private bath is filled with birds and fruit trees and flowers and waterfalls," she said. "And everything glows."

"See? The whole world is magical like that if you would only slow down for a moment and look around you."

"Hmmm," she hummed. "I will need to think about that."

"No. Don't think. *Feel,*" he insisted.

"Okay," she said, lying down and pulling the blankets up under her chin. "I'll try."

"*Tsk, tsk,*" he chided. "It takes no effort. It takes the *opposite* of effort."

She did not quite know what he meant but was too tired to reply, and soon slipped into a dreamless sleep.

The next morning, they found their clothing and travel sacks piled neatly outside their door, clean and dry, just as Avon had promised. They got dressed, hiding in opposite corners of the room, and went downstairs. Breakfast was served in a small dining area off the main room, and they ate the oatmeal and sausages and bread hungrily, washing it down with hot tea.

Avon gave each of them a wooden yoke that fit over their shoulders and held four wooden buckets apiece, two over each shoulder, front and back, hanging from wooden crossbars. She handed them each a sledgehammer and a pickaxe. Temerity took her tools and slung them through her belt next to her sword and knives.

"Remember," Avon said as she accompanied them out to the street, "I have your dragon jewel, and I do not take kindly to my equipment going missing."

"You needn't worry about that," Half-pint assured her, his buckets dragging and bumping along the ground.

"Fine," the water sprite sniffed. "The entrance to the coal mine is ..." And she described a route of twists and turns over streets and alleyways, and Half-pint nodded as though he was following what she was saying. "Once you get below ground," she said, "be sure to follow the path straight down the hill until you reach the mine. Do not veer off on any of the side branches along the way, or you could become lost for a very long time." She smiled sweetly and bid them farewell.

9

COAL

Temerity followed Half-pint through the maze of streets and alleyways. The neighborhood changed from lively inns to abandoned buildings and dark streets. Most streetlamps were unlit and the glass globes were shattered—long forgotten by the lamplighters—leaving the streets only faintly illuminated by a ghostly gray glow from the leaden sky. Overhanging buildings cloaked narrow side alleys in impenetrable shadows, hiding their secrets in heavy silence.

Sticking to the wider, straighter streets, they eventually reached the entrance to the coal mine: another stone arch like the one they had passed through to enter Dark Town the day before. They headed down a dark, sloping passageway, and Half-pint held up his green jewel to light the way.

A pair of adventurers stumbled out of a side passage, bleary-eyed and filthy.

"That way to get out," Half-pint said, gesturing behind him with his thumb.

The adventurers nodded gratefully and hurried up the hill.

Temerity and the hobgoblin continued down, down, down until the tunnel leveled out and a lantern cast a golden glow ahead of them. They entered a low-ceilinged cavern of black stone, with a latticework of wooden struts holding up the ceiling. A hunched-over, elderly troll sat on an upturned barrel behind a makeshift counter. He stood up wearily, soot staining his face and bald head and ringing his watery eyes like a racoon's.

"Avon sent yer?" he asked, motioning to the buckets hanging from their shoulders. "Yer can put them down, yer need a wagon," he said, nodding towards several small empty carts waiting on a junction of iron rails that split off and snaked away into the darkness in various directions.

"Why did she send us with buckets, then?" Temerity asked.

The tall, stooped troll shrugged. "She uses them to measure, I guess. Everyone comes with them, but everyone leaves renting one of my wagons. You'll see."

"We need to rent a wagon?" Temerity asked, worrying that he would demand another dragon jewel.

"Only if yer leave with one," he said in a deep, grunting tone. "If yer want to take some coal with yer, then yer need to mine four wagonloads fer me, fer every wagonload yer want to take away." He eyed the eight buckets as they shrugged off the yokes and set them on the ground. "Looks like about one wagonload thar. And yer going to need some hard hats." He pointed to a pile of dusty metal helmets. "And shovels. Them all will cost yer another wagonload. Yer got yer own lights? I'm fresh out'a lantern oil."

Half-pint and Temerity glanced at one another. She hadn't thought to bring her candles or torch. Half-pint pulled out the green jewel he'd hidden in his robes.

The troll grunted and waved them away. "Take the southern

tunnel." He pointed to one of the rail tracks. "And don't touch the ceilings. Only take coal from the walls, or I might not be able to drag yer out if the tunnel collapses."

Temerity frowned, not liking the sound of that, but she followed Half-pint's lead as they grabbed their supplies, loaded the buckets and tools into a wagon, and pulled it along the metal tracks into a pitch-black tunnel. Half-pint held up his jewel, lighting the way as they went deeper and deeper, until the hobgoblin judged they'd found a good spot to chip away at the walls.

"I didn't think we'd need to mine rock," she grumbled.

"It's a game," Half-pint said, setting the glowing jewel on a rocky ledge and examining the wall. "You have to work to progress. Nothing comes for free."

She scowled and swung her pickaxe at a small outcropping. On the second strike, a big chunk of black coal broke loose from the wall and fell at her feet, crumbling into pieces. It was easier than she had anticipated, and she continued clawing off chunks, breaking up the larger pieces with the sledgehammer, and shoveling the rubble into the wagon. The green jewel cast its light in a small circle, leaving the rest of the tunnel in ghoulish, murky shadow. Temerity continued striking at the wall, using the glinting reflections of the black rock to guide her.

She pretended the pickaxe was a battle-axe and the wall was a monster and swung ferociously. She sank into a low stance, shifting her weight with each swing.

"You'll wear yourself out like that," Half-pint commented. "I have a feeling we'll be here all day."

"I'm practicing fighting," she said, taking in a breath and swinging the pickaxe horizontally at the wall and then again from the opposite side. A chunk of coal broke loose and landed at her feet.

"Use your hips to turn, then," Half-pint said, demonstrating and striking the wall with his pickaxe. "And don't straighten your legs between swings."

She recalled her pa's footwork training, and continued hacking at the wall, her leg and shoulder muscles already burning.

After a time, the wagon was full. Her entire body hurt, and her palm was swelling with a blister, even with her gloves on. She gritted her teeth. This would make her stronger, and the blister would turn into a callus, she told herself. She helped Half-pint pull the wagon back to the troll. The hunchback nodded silently and motioned for them to unload the coal onto a large pile. They did so and then headed back into the tunnel.

After they'd brought the troll four more wagonloads, they returned with a final wagonload and filled their buckets. They were much too heavy to carry from their shoulders, so they loaded the full buckets onto a hand-drawn wain that the troll agreed to rent to them for coin.

"Bring the cart back tomorrow," the troll said, and picked through a handful of coins that Half-pint held out, taking a few silver bits and some coppers.

Half-pint pulled and Temerity pushed the cart up the long hill, her whole body aching and sore. She trudged forward, dreaming about a hot meal and a hot bath.

They made it back to Avon's Grotto and lugged in the buckets of coal. Avon nodded with satisfaction and directed them to a covered yard out back, where they deposited the coal onto a large pile of the black, shiny rock. They stored the troll's wain in a small, gated yard off the street and returned to the inn.

They were covered with coal dust from head to toe, and Avon hurried them towards the baths, promising to launder their clothes by morning. Temerity sank into the hot pool in Avon's enchanted grotto, submerging her head and letting the coal dust float away. After a hot meal, they stumbled into bed and fell promptly asleep.

———◆———

"Four more buckets for last night's meal, room, laundry, and bath," Avon informed them as they followed the water sprite into the dining area for breakfast. Eggs, bacon, fresh bread, and dishes of grapes and soft white cheese awaited them at the table.

Temerity's mouth watered as she and Half-pint loaded up their plates and sat across from each other, alone in the dining room. Mugs of hot tea sent tendrils of steam into the air.

"Looks like another day of coal mining," she said, between mouthfuls of food. "How did that happen?"

Half-pint slurped his tea, then said, "My pa always warned me against taking on debt. This is why."

"You have a pa?" she asked.

The goblin glowered at her, not deigning to acknowledge her question with a response.

She tried to put on a smile as if she had been joking. *Of course he has a father,* she thought to herself, feeling like an idiot. She dared not ask if his pa was still alive, or where he dwelled.

"We'll mine an extra wagonload today," he said, "pay off our debt, and move on."

They got ready to leave for the mine, taking a candle and the tinderbox this time.

"I require another bucket each tonight," Avon called after them as Half-pint carried one bucket—enough for measuring—through the inn's main room towards the front door. Temerity sneered over her shoulder at the water sprite, who met her scowl with an innocent smile. "Interest for providing services in advance of payment," the sprite said, holding up Temerity's orange jewel.

Temerity turned away and stormed through the door of the warm inn and out into the cold dark street. They pulled the wagon out from the yard and trod across the winding cobblestone streets towards the mine. People were out and about, hurrying towards their destinations in the morning gloom. Some carried sacks of flour over their shoulders, others pulled carts filled with firewood—grain and wood from she knew not where, in this land of darkness and stone. It seemed everyone had something to do and somewhere to go, aside from the occasional groups of young men loitering on corners and inspecting the passersby.

"Don't make eye contact with them," Half-pint cautioned, under his breath.

They turned a corner and continued on, past bakeries and blacksmiths, wheelwrights and fortune tellers. A green dragon jewel was displayed in a front window under a sign that read, *Healing and Potions.* At a fortune teller's shop, Temerity noticed a yellow jewel on display, and a red jewel glowed from the front counter of a weapons dealer.

"Wait here." Half-pint left the wain in her care and stepped inside a bakery. He emerged a few minutes later with a bundle wrapped in a linen napkin. He unwrapped it and showed her a half-dozen small meat pies, half-moon-shaped dough pockets still steaming from the oven. "For our midday meal."

"Good idea," Temerity said gratefully. She adjusted the fat waterskin that hung over her shoulder, wishing she had two, having finished all her water halfway through the day yesterday. They had brought strips of linen with them this time, torn from her dress scraps, to cover their mouths and noses against the coal dust. She felt more prepared today, although every muscle was sore and the blisters on her feet and hand hurt. The hobgoblin strutted in front of her, uncomplaining and unconcerned. She lifted her chin and followed with the wagon.

The tunnel the troll sent them down this time was farther away and the walls were harder to break apart. Her candle burned down by the time they had returned the five wagon-loads due as payment to the troll. They ventured into the dark tunnel one last time to fill up the wagon for Avon's payment. They labored in the greenish glow from the dragon jewel and finally broke off enough coal to fill ten buckets. Temerity sighed and stretched her back.

"One more bucket each," Half-pint encouraged her. "We will pay up front an additional bucket per day, and soon we will be free of our debt."

They chipped off enough for two more buckets, then trod wearily to the troll's counter. Half-pint doled out more coin to rent the cart again, and they pushed and pulled it up the incline and across the dark streets to Avon's Grotto. The water sprite graciously accepted the buckets as payment, and as they handed over the sixth bucket each, Half-pint explained that they were paying for their chamber up front this time.

"Oh, I'm so sorry," the sprite said, gazing at them with brilliant green eyes. "Another patron wants that chamber tonight and has offered four buckets of coal for it." She glanced at the men lounging on the floor, and Temerity's eyes landed on the dandy with the gold waistcoat and colorful slashed pants, whom they had seen the other day.

"Hmpf," Temerity grunted dismissively. "Him?"

"Yes, indeed. As you can see, he is not accustomed to sharing quarters with street urchins."

Temerity regarded the unkempt men lying on thin mattresses on the floor and did not much want to share quarters with them, either. Besides, she and Half-pint had become quite comfortable in their garret room, their belongings unpacked and their privacy assured.

"But I will let you keep the room for two buckets apiece instead of one. He will be disappointed, of course, but I told him the current occupants had first dibs. I will take your sixth buckets as advance payment for the extra charge, and tomorrow you shall owe me eight buckets each." The water sprite smiled her sweet smile.

Temerity couldn't figure out how that math made sense, but she grudgingly nodded, and Half-pint nodded beside her. They took their baths, then handed over their coal-black clothes to be laundered, ate a hot meal, and retired to their room.

———————◆———————

Hammering at rocks was hard work and boring. Swinging the sledgehammer used the same muscles as chopping wood, which was one of her chores back home, but rarely did she chop wood all day long. She was already tired and hobbled around on sore feet, and her back and shoulders ached. But she pushed on, telling herself that the heavy labor was making her stronger. She was thankful for the company of Half-pint as they toiled side by side, as they often had in the dairy barn and the tavern. Wanting to strike up a conversation, she asked, "So, how long have you served our family as a house goblin?"

Half-pint stopped the swing of his pickaxe mid-air, then brought it down with unusual force, knocking off a big, square chunk of coal. He set the head of the pickaxe on the ground and leaned on the long handle. "I do not *serve* anyone," he said, his long hooknose flaring with disdain. "I *manage* the *house.*"

Temerity took a step backwards, startled by his fiery yellow eyes. "I'm sorry, Half-pint. I didn't mean it that way."

He turned back to the wall, swinging the pickaxe and chipping off another chunk of coal. A few swings later, he glanced at her, the blazing fire gone from his eyes. He continued swinging while he spoke, cracking off chunks with each strike. "I was there when you and your brothers were born, and when your father was born, and his father, and his father before him." *Crack.* "I helped your great-great-grandfather build the farmhouse and the cottage and the barn." *Crack.* "So, by rights, those buildings are more a part of me than you." *Crack.*

She ignored his barbed words, more intrigued by their meaning. "Those buildings are over a century old," she exclaimed. "How old *are* you?"

He stopped swinging, huffing from exertion. "By my count, I believe I'm around a hundred and twenty human years." Her eyes widened as he continued. "But by goblin years, I'm still a relatively young man. Well, mature, at least. In my prime." He gave her a rare smile, showing his numerous teeth.

"A hundred and twenty! That's ... wow," she said. "I had no idea."

"Of course you didn't." He went back to swinging his pickaxe.

"Do you have a family of your own?" she asked.

He did not reply but struck at the rock with a loud crack, and she was afraid she had clumsily said the wrong thing again.

She picked up her sledgehammer and broke up the chunks he had knocked down, then shoveled them into the cart.

10

DANDY

One day rolled into the next. Every evening when they returned to Avon's Grotto with extra coal to get ahead of their debt, the water sprite made them an offer they could not refuse, which coincidentally always equaled the price of the extra coal. A savory, chicken-dinner special that smelled like something Temerity's ma would make. Oil for the lanterns in their room. When Temerity hesitated, Avon threw in an extra candle for Temerity's stash, the sprite insisting that they would need light later on in the game. Clean robes and towels for their baths. Scented soap and expert boot polishing. Starched sheets, scented with lemon. All things they desperately needed in the moment, but when they were away from the sprite's influence, down in the coal mine, they were sure they were being played.

"So like a fae," Half-pint grumbled as he swung his pickaxe. "That Avon is a tricky one. She's got us under her spell, clearly."

Temerity nodded, noting that most things they paid extra for had been part of their room and board previously.

But each evening when they returned to the Grotto, they could not refuse the charming water sprite and handed over the extra coal.

One day, they were in the mine wheeling a cartful of coal out to the troll. The hunched-over, bald creature had increased his cut as well, demanding ever bigger loads in exchange for the use of his carts, iron tracks, shovels, and helmets. The tunnel they were mining that day was deathly dark, and Half-pint held up his green dragon jewel to light the way. They rounded a curve and came face to face with a pair of adventurers holding up a lantern whose wick had burned down to a faint glimmer.

"Oh, hi," Temerity said as Half-pint slipped the green jewel into his robes, extinguishing its light. She recognized the two men from the inn. The pale-faced pair wore plain, humble garments—the sort of men who could have been farmers back in the Haverlies. She had noticed them at Avon's Grotto every evening, occupying two mattresses in the rear corner of the room, by the brick oven.

The adventurers nodded a silent greeting, their eyes following Half-pint's hand where it had disappeared with the jewel. The two pairs of adventurers brushed past each other, and Temerity and Half-pint stumbled along in the dark, following the faint glint of the iron rails that soon terminated at the troll's junction. They emptied their cart and chose a different tunnel to continue their mining, not wanting to run into the two men again.

Later that evening, they headed across town towards the Grotto, pulling their cart piled high with extra coal that they were sure would be more than the water sprite could swindle them out of. They passed through a market square, stopping at a trader's stall to sell a bucketload of coal in exchange for coin that they needed for their midday meat pies and to rent the wain.

They continued on, snaking through dark streets and alleyways and relying on the light of streetlamps, which flickered weakly on random corners. There were no trees in Dark Town. No grass. No birds. No squirrels. All she had seen were rats and cockroaches, scurrying into the shadows.

Temerity's legs were heavy from toiling all day in the mine, and her back and shoulder muscles were so tight, they felt like they were being pricked by pins and needles. The road ahead took a long, looping detour before it would drop them off on the street lined with inns and pubs.

"Let's take a shortcut," Temerity said, gesturing towards an alleyway that cut a straight line towards Avon's Grotto, even though the narrow lane gave her an unsettled feeling in the pit of her stomach.

"No," Half-pint said. "That's an alley."

"We walk down alleys all the time," she retorted.

"But that is an *alley,*" he stressed.

"And I'm *exhausted,*" she said. "I need food, a bath, and bed, before I collapse right here on the cobblestones." She ignored Half-pint's protests and the goosebumps on her arms, and marched down the alley, dragging the wagonload of coal behind her. She felt the load lighten as Half-pint relented and began pushing from behind, the wheels clattering over the uneven cobblestones.

They were midway down the long, murky lane, when Temerity felt a niggling at the nape of her neck and glanced over her shoulder. Two men lit by a weak flame moved towards them. She recognized the lantern and the lanky forms of the pair of adventurers they'd encountered in the mine. Half-pint dug in his heels, drawing the wain to a halt, and in front of them appeared two more men, stepping forward and blocking their way.

The gold waistcoat and red and gold pants identified the taller man as the fop who also stayed at Avon's Grotto, in the main room.

"Fancy meeting you here," the dandy said with a wide smile.

"Good evening to you," Half-pint said, and made to push the wagon past the men.

"Not so fast," the gold-vested man drawled.

Temerity's hackles rose, and she checked herself from drawing a blade.

"We'll be needing that wagonload of coal," the man said with a friendly grin. "Can't mine enough to satisfy that faery. She drives a hard bargain, that one."

"They've got a jewel," the man behind them said as the pair approached.

"You don't say," the fop said, his eyes glimmering. "So much the better. I need to move on from this cursed Dark Town. Ain't that right?" he asked, elbowing his companion, who was muscle-bound, with thick arms and legs.

His burly companion nodded.

Temerity was considering handing over the coal, when Half-pint appeared next to her and said in his scratchy, nasal voice. "We need our coal, and we ain't got no jewel. Avon has our only one."

"He lies," the man behind them said.

"Please move aside," Half-pint said, his voice steely.

The dandy placed his hand on his hip and sneered. "You think a dirty little goblin's going to tell me what to do?"

Half-pint pushed past the dandy, and in the blink of an eye, blades were bared and steel flashed all around. Temerity drew her sword and slashed wildly at figures as they leapt at her and Half-pint.

"In his cloak," the lanky man said. He grabbed at Half-pint's robes but met the edge of the meat cleaver instead and jumped back with a squeal.

Temerity charged at the cluster of men who were converging on Half-pint, but a hard hand struck her in the chest, sending her sprawling to the cobblestones. Crawling forward, she slashed at calves and knees. The attackers hopped aside and kicked her while Half-pint whirled, wielding his meat cleaver in an arc. The men stepped back a pace to avoid the blade before falling upon the goblin again.

Temerity popped up in the middle of the fray, trading her sword for two knives, slashing with both hands and meeting arms and chests and cheeks, striping skin red, and then raising her arms to protect her face as blades sliced at her in return. A yowling screech stopped everyone mid-swing. A ball of fur leapt through the air, and Half-pint the cat slashed and clawed at the nearest thug.

The gold-vested dandy was suddenly at Temerity's throat, squeezing with an iron grip. Without thinking, she sank her boning knife into his neck, the long, sharp blade meeting bone with a crunch. The dandy's eyes bulged as she pulled out the knife and blood spurted onto his white ruffled collar as he slowly sank to the pavement.

The two men from the mine gaped at them for a moment and then ran off, disappearing into the shadows. Temerity stared in horror at her bloody blade, her hands suddenly shaking violently, when a sudden blow to her skull sent her reeling, and all went black.

"Temerity. *Temerity.*"

Temerity cracked her eyes open. Half-pint was leaning over her, peering into her eyes, a green glow illuminating his skin in a sickly hue. His long goblin fingers were at her throat, feeling for a pulse, and his other hand held his dragon jewel against the side of her head, its warmth soothing against her throbbing skull.

"Ow," she said, reaching up to feel her head. "What happened?"

"That big guy hit you with a hammer," he said. "Terrible human being. We're not even officially in the alleys yet. Very dishonorable behavior."

Temerity gazed blearily around her, confused. "Are we still in the game? Did I die?"

"Fortunately, he just knocked you out." Half-pint moved the jewel to a gash on her arm. "Otherwise, you would be back in Lucy's cellar."

"You wouldn't have saved my life with your jewel?" she asked, sitting up gingerly and watching the skin on her forearm heal into a scab and then a thin white line as the dragon jewel did its work.

Half-pint *tsk'd*. "No, not so early in the game. That would be a waste. I need to save it for a higher level. Six or seven. Seven, probably. That's the most brutal level."

"Oh," she said, too exhausted to question his judgment. "Where'd the guy who attacked me go?"

"He took off," Half-pint said with a smirk, gesturing towards the dark alley behind them. "He didn't like having an angry feline slashing his face."

Temerity attempted a smile. "I wouldn't think so. What did you mean, 'We're not officially in the alleys yet?'" She glanced around at the cobblestone lane. "It seems to me we are right in the middle of one."

He moved on to her next wound, and replied, "We are not playing the alleys yet, we are playing the inns."

"Oh, that explains it," she said sarcastically.

"I mean, we are frequenting the inns and the surrounding zones, where it's safer. That way, we can upgrade our gear, get a feel for Dark Town, and gather some jewels to increase our abilities, before venturing into the maze of alleys where we risk getting killed by roving gangs looking for loot."

"Oh," she said. "Like the guys who attacked us."

"Exactly. The inn zones have inns and markets and some industrial centers, connected by relatively safe streets. The alley zones surround the populated districts, expanding outward from the centers, and are very dangerous. Where we are right now is on the outskirts of an inn zone—just on the border— but we are not in alley territory yet. Those guys were a bunch of hooligans who took advantage of the moment, in violation of an unspoken rule."

Temerity nodded, but Half-pint couldn't resist one last barb. "That's why I didn't want to go this way."

She glanced at him sheepishly. "The alley didn't feel right to me, but I was just so tired."

He squinted at her thoughtfully. "You must always pay heed to your intuition." She considered his comment and recalled her ma telling her the same thing.

Half-pint focused his attention on healing the rest of her wounds and some of his own. Temerity quickly regained her strength and alertness, the green jewel's healing effect lingering in her body with a strange buzzing sensation that gradually subsided.

When they were fully recovered, they walked over to their wagonload of coal, and Temerity retrieved her sword and knives from the gutter. Her eyes landed on a clump of gold fabric. She crept forward to examine it. Sprawled across the dark cobblestones, a familiar gold velvet waistcoat, bloody ruffled shirt, and red and gold pants covered the ground as though the body still lay there—an empty husk of the man who had worn them.

She stared down at the clothing, perplexed.

"He died," Half-pint said, leaning over and squinting at where the dandy's head should have been.

"He ... *died?*" Temerity asked in a strangled voice. "Did *I* kill him?"

Half-pint's yellow eyes flitted to hers. "Yes, I believe you did."

She inhaled with alarm, but a glint of approval shone in the hobgoblin's eyes.

"But ... but ... where is he?" she asked, her hands quivering and her heartbeat thudding in her ears.

"He went back to the beginning," Half-pint said. "From wherever he started. He'll be fine, don't worry. All his wounds will be gone."

"Then why are his clothes still here? And where are his blades?"

"He must have acquired the clothes in-game. His blades must be the ones he started with. When you die, you return to your starting point with whatever gear you brought in."

"Oh," she said, feeling a little bit better. She wiped her brow and took a few deep breaths. "That scared me for a minute. But it's not so bad, right? It's only a game."

"Well, he's not *really* dead, if that's what you mean."

She pushed aside thorns of self-recrimination. She had been defending herself, after all. He had been trying to strangle her. Looking down at the expensive clothing at her feet, a devious thought replaced lingering pangs of guilt. "Can I take his things?" She leaned over and started rummaging through his pockets.

"Yes, you can. Anything left behind is fair game. First dibs goes to the one who did the killing. But if you had permanently abandoned your kill, anyone could nab the loot."

Her fingers closed around a cool, egg-shaped stone, and she raised it up. It glowed a stunning blue. "Look," she exclaimed.

"Ah, a warding jewel." Half-pint's eyes glittered. "Those are good to have. If he hadn't attacked you with his bare hands in such close quarters, it would have been difficult for you to get near enough to hurt him. Maybe he didn't understand how to use it. Blue jewels create a barrier that's hard to penetrate, among other things. We are only in Level One, though. Jewels are relatively weak at this level."

She continued digging into the many pockets of the vest and puffy breeches and cackled with glee. She held up another dragon jewel. This one was a deep, ruby red, glowing from within like an ember, and sent a surge of warmth up her arm. A rush of adrenaline flowed through her body. She straightened up, feeling good all of a sudden.

"Ah, I suspected he had two, bragging about how he was ready to leave Dark Town," Half-pint said. "This is great fortune, indeed."

"Here, you take one," Temerity said, holding out both. "Which one do you want?"

Half-pint rubbed his chin. "Well, the red one imparts extra strength and skill, and the blue one, as I said, creates a defensive barrier. Not a very strong one at this stage, but helpful, nonetheless. You choose."

She hesitated for a moment, then handed him the blue one. "Here, you know how to use this, and I want to be stronger." She liked the surge of energy that she attributed to the red jewel.

They grinned at one another, and she continued rifling through the satin and velvet, coming up with a metallic-gold dyed leather belt and a red satin money purse. The purse was heavy and jangled with coin. She smiled and tucked it into her pocket, then gathered up the clothing. "I kind of fancy these dandy duds," she said, chuckling. "See how fine this fabric is?" She ran her fingers over the luxurious velvet waistcoat and the satin pants, the red and gold strips parting to reveal an under-layer of royal-blue satin, in the slashed style popular with wealthy city folk and nobles. "But these ruffles are bloody," she said of the overly extravagant collar that spilled over the front of the vest.

"It'll come out in the wash. Avon can work her magic," Half-pint said.

"If he took everything with him, how come he didn't take his blood, too?" she asked, considering that blood belonged to a person more than weapons did.

"He must have been here for quite a while," Half-pint replied, "and made a bunch of new blood."

"So if you're here for a really long time and have all new blood, does that mean you'd go back home with no blood?" she asked. "You'd be dead."

Half-pint stared at her as though she was asking too many questions. Or he had never thought about it before. He pursed his lips, then finally replied, "You go back with what you came in with, so you'd have a body full of old blood."

"Oh, okay," she said, satisfied with that answer. She bundled up the clothing and then pushed the wagon while Half-pint pulled, and they headed towards Avon's Grotto.

11

TAKE ONE, LEAVE ONE

They hovered outside Avon's Grotto, worried that they might run into the other three ruffians. Temerity peered in through the front window and scanned the men lounging on mattresses. The two mattresses by the brick oven were conspicuously vacant, as were two in the middle, where the dandy and his burly sidekick normally slept.

They entered the inn and approached the counter. Avon examined them, her greenish eyebrows knitting together. Temerity looked down at herself and Half-pint. The hobgoblin's dragon jewel had healed their skin, but their clothing was still torn and bloody.

"Ran into some, um ... unpleasant folks," Temerity said with a confident grin, feeling the strength of the red jewel smoldering inside her.

"Hmpf," the sprite grunted. "How many buckets of coal did you bring today?"

"The nine each that we owe you from last night," Half-pint said, "plus an extra one each."

The sprite flared her nostrils but said nothing, flashing a charming smile. "I'll be waiting here for your laundry." Avon handed them their usual stack of towels, bathrobes, and soap.

"Thank you," Temerity said, suspicious that the water sprite had not invented some new charge to wheedle the tenth bucket out of them.

Temerity and Half-pint climbed the stairs to their garret room, lit the lanterns, and looked around.

"That shyster," Half-pint grumbled.

Their belongings were stacked and folded neatly along the walls and on the dressers, but the mattresses, pillows, and blankets were gone. They frowned at one another and then turned their backs to each other and changed into their bathrobes, then tramped downstairs.

Avon held out her arms for their dirty clothes. "I suppose you would like these mended as well," she said brightly.

Half-pint and Temerity cast sidelong glances at one another as they handed over their laundry. "How much?" Half-pint asked.

"Only a bucket apiece," the sprite said.

Temerity refrained from rolling her eyes. "And what about mattresses and bedding?"

"Oh, yes," Avon said apologetically. "I meant to mention that to you, but you can see that I have more patrons than normal. I needed those mattresses for customers who can pay up front." The sprite showed them her perfectly white teeth.

Temerity glanced around. Despite the empty mattresses of their attackers, the room did seem more cramped than usual.

"However," Avon continued, "I do have my own mattresses that I suppose I could spare for one night if you can bring me two extra buckets each tomorrow."

Temerity sighed, desperately craving a hot bath, clean clothes, and a soft mattress—and she thought she smelled lamb stew coming from the dining room. Her stomach rumbled, and the scent of orange blossoms wafting from Avon's hair made Temerity long for the sparkling waterfalls and steaming turquoise pool of the sprite's private bathing grotto.

Avon went into the back and returned with her arms overflowing with rolled mattresses, folded blankets, and two pillows balanced on top. They took them from her, climbed back up to their room, and arranged their beds.

Temerity turned around to find Half-pint standing in the middle of the room. The blue jewel was in his hand, and a glowing nimbus surrounded him. A low buzz emanated from it, and he gazed with unfocused eyes at the shimmering cobalt light.

"We need to get out of here," he said in a monotone. "Now."

"But ... our baths. And dinner," she said. "And our clothing. We just gave everything to Avon to launder and mend."

"We brought enough coal to pay off our debt from last night, and then some. If we leave now, we will be free."

"But ... but," Temerity said.

"Take out your red jewel," Half-pint instructed.

She took it from her pocket and held it out in front of her. A glimmer of red radiated from her palm, and warmth seeped into her hand, up her arm, and swirled in her chest. "Yes, we should go now," she agreed. "We'll ask for our clothes back."

"No," the hobgoblin said. "She will entrap us if we try to negotiate anything further. She can have our garments."

"But they're my brother's clothes. The green suede vest. And your homespun robe."

"Seems to me you have the matching curtain in your travel sack," he said, eyeing her slyly. "Besides, I kind of like this faery-spun gray silk robe. I wouldn't be surprised if there was some sort of glamour woven into this. It could be very helpful."

He ran his hands over the smooth, shimmering fabric, which draped to the floor in folds of light and shadow.

"Well, that's fine for you, maybe," she said, noticing that he did look rather wizardly in the hooded robe. "But I'm not traipsing around Dark Town in a bathrobe." She spread her arms and glanced down at her beige linen robe, fastened only with a fabric belt.

"You have an extra set of clothing," Half-pint said, "plus the dandy's fancy pants and waistcoat. You still have your boots, at least. Besides, you will eventually need to leave something behind, equal to the new garments, if you intend to take them with you to the next level. Take one, leave one. That's the rule. If you want to trade up, the game extracts its due, one way or another."

"Hmmm," she hummed thoughtfully, holding up the gold waistcoat and puffy pants. She had given the sprite the blood-stained, ruffled shirt, Hamish's pants and work shirt, and Mathias's vest. "I liked that ruffled shirt," she said sadly.

"That shirt was ridiculous," he scoffed. "You have the golden belt, too, don't forget."

"And the money purse," she added.

"Coin doesn't count for trade," he replied. "It's unlimited in the game."

"That's good, at least," she said.

He shrugged. "It's not worth as much as you'd think. Most things require barter with like goods or crafting supplies. Anyway, hurry up and get dressed. We need to go before her spell enthralls us again."

Temerity ended up wearing her woolen hose and bell-sleeved linen shift under the satin breeches and gold velvet waistcoat. The breeches buttoned just below the knee, and she laced up her boots, wishing she had footwear other than her sturdy workboots—something more elegant to match the fop's clothing. She supposed the streets of Dark Town were too cloaked in shadow for anyone to notice the clunky boots.

She still wished she could take a bath but made do with cleaning the coal dust and dried blood off her skin as best she could with a washrag, using the small water basin. Her fingernails were still black, and her hair was coarse and ratty, no matter how many times she ran a wet comb through it.

"Ready, Your Highness?" Half-pint teased.

She sighed and nodded. "Ready as I'll ever be." She hid the golden waistbelt and money purse under the thigh-length waistcoat, stashed her red jewel in one of the many hidden pockets of the satin pants, strapped on her pa's leather belt and her blades, stuffed all her remaining belongings into her travel sack, and went downstairs with Half-pint.

Avon eyed them suspiciously from behind the counter.

"I'm afraid we must be leaving this fine establishment," Half-pint said, hopping up onto a chair so that he was eye-level with the water sprite. "We've brought more than enough coal to pay off our remaining debt. You can keep the extra as a tip." The hobgoblin bared his many teeth in something resembling a smile.

Avon narrowed her eyes at them, no doubt wondering how they had suddenly gathered their wits enough to escape her trap. "I'm afraid your clothes are already soaking in a washtub. They won't be dry until morning. Please stay another night, and you can depart in the morning. I'll take the final payment tomorrow evening."

"No bother," Half-pint said. "You may keep the clothing. I quite like this faery robe in exchange." He thumbed the gray silk lapels. "More than fair, wouldn't you say?"

Avon scowled. "Your robe is brown homespun. That is silver sylph silk," she said, eyeing the shimmering fabric.

"Sylph silk. Sounds special," Half-pint said. "But that 'homespun,' as you call it, will hide you in the shadows better than any sylph mantle." He gave her a sincere look, and the sprite's forehead furrowed in a puzzled frown.

Avon's frown quickly transformed into a simpering smile, and she said in her sing-song voice, "Oh, *aaalright*. You drive a hard bargain. I'll give you a deal for the blankets and mattresses: only one bucket of coal for each of you. Even though I'll be sleeping on the floor with nothing but my robe to keep me warm."

Temerity was beginning to think that was a fair trade when Half-pint shot her a warning glare. A faint nimbus of blue escaped the side pocket of his robe, and Temerity clutched the red jewel in her pocket, seeking its strength. She gave Avon a determined smile. "No, thank you. Very kind of you, but I'll take my orange dragon jewel now." Temerity extended her open palm.

Avon glowered at her but grudgingly handed over the orange jewel, then folded her arms petulantly.

"Thank you for your hospitality," Temerity said sincerely, tucking the jewel into a vest pocket. "I really love your bathing grotto."

The water sprite's expression softened. "It has been nice to have another female around. And one of the wee folk," she said, turning her emerald eyes on Half-pint. "Don't be strangers. Come around anytime."

"We shall," Temerity assured her.

"Indeed," Half-pint echoed, giving the water sprite a gracious bow.

They turned and headed for the door, stepping between the rows of mattresses. The two beds by the brick oven were occupied again, and the lanky troublemakers tried to hide under their covers, but she caught them peeking out and gawking at her plundered clothes and the goblin who could shapeshift into a cat. She returned their stares with a menacing grin and left the inn.

12

THE BLUE JEWEL

They returned the wagon to the troll, and Half-pint began haggling over a pickaxe and sledgehammer from the troll's collection of tools.

"What do we need those for?" she asked.

The hobgoblin threw her a veiled glance to keep quiet, and she clamped her mouth shut. He ended up trading a dagger with a ruby hilt, along with a smoking pipe he produced from his robe, for a pickaxe, and then offered to trade something of hers for a sledgehammer.

"I don't need a sledgehammer," she whispered as the troll searched among his tools for one he was willing to part with.

"Shhh. Yes, you do. Let me handle this."

She scowled but held her tongue as he traded away her hunting knife for a steel sledge.

Half-pint proceeded to trade a bundle of tobacco and her pot of hand cream for two dinged, steel hard hats. She glared at the hobgoblin as they tucked their helmets under their arms.

The troll seemed happy with the trade, rubbing the cream on his dry, cracked hands, and lighting up the pipe before they'd even left the junction.

As they climbed the long incline, Temerity turned to Half-pint. "Pa gave me that knife. And my hands get dry, too, you know. You could have at least asked me."

"I'm sorry, I should have discussed it with you first. These rock-breaker tools will help us get out of Dark Town, trust me. They're usually hard to find. We were lucky to have a source right under our noses. And we'll need helmets. These were a real bargain, and high-quality steel. I was afraid we wouldn't be able to find the mine later on if we wandered too far across Dark Town. This place is a maze, and one can easily get lost."

She sighed loudly and slid the long handle of the heavy hammer through her belt. She wanted to continue scolding the hobgoblin but decided that keeping the peace with him was more important than her hunting knife. "Where'd you get that ruby knife?" she asked.

"Lucy gave it to me. Some adventurer left it in her tavern years ago. It looked pretty, but the blade never held its edge, and the rubies were only glass beads."

They reached the surface and struck out across town, back towards the neighborhood filled with inns. The streets were mostly empty, with only the occasional passerby or noisy pub to break up the gray monotony of stone buildings and shadowed streets.

"How big *is* Dark Town?" she asked as they meandered through the sprawling web of cobblestone streets and alleys.

"As big as it needs to be," Half-pint said. "It will go on and on until we level up."

"So, we each have two jewels now," she said. "We only need two more."

"No, Miss Temerity. I told you, my green one doesn't count. That's a dragon treasure. Can't use it to level up. We only have three total, so we need three more."

"Where will we find them?" she asked. "I thought we might have found one in the coal mine."

Half-pint shrugged. "You never find them where you expect them to be."

"You can get them by stealing from other people, though, right?" she asked, casting a wary glance at a small group of men who were ambling in their direction. "Or killing someone."

"Yes," Half-pint said as they hurried past the men. "But fighting to the death is risky. You could just as easily die as kill your opponent. Only reckless adventurers play that way. Or overconfident noobs. Like that dimwit you killed. He was a first-timer, mark my words. He'll be more careful next time."

Temerity delved into her looted money purse. There was an abundance of coin in there, more than the Tin Roof brought in over a whole month. Several glints of the tiny gold teardrop coins were mixed in with the almost-as-valuable electrum, as well as the standard silvers, bronzes, and coppers.

She felt rich, and the gleeful, lighthearted feeling was so unfamiliar that she danced in the street, laughing, and drew a stern glare from Half-pint. "Don't bring attention to yourself," he warned. "That gold vest is loud enough."

She smirked at him and brushed her hands over the luxurious fabric, but she stopped dancing and returned to the shadows cloaking the walls. She paused to peer into a shop window displaying finely crafted elven boots and hats. "I need some of those," she said. "They will go quite nicely with my new outfit. We'll come back during the day when they're open."

Half-pint rolled his eyes. "I doubt they take coin. Who knows what impossible-to-find materials they'll demand in exchange for those?"

They continued down one street after another, and Half-pint rejected each inn they came upon.

"No good," he said at each of the many inns, the blue light from his pocket growing stronger as he gazed into the windows. "We need a place that won't ensnare us."

They turned a corner and found themselves on a wide street that looked familiar. Temerity recognized it as one of the roads they had walked down when they'd first arrived in Dark Town. She stopped in front of the inn with the big bay window and the sign that read, *The Blue Jewel. Fine Accommodations for the Discerning Adventurer.*

"I like this one," she said, and peered through the window at a long table strewn with books and scrolls.

Half-pint made a dismissive gesture and continued down the street towards a cluster of inns further on.

Temerity reached for the brass doorknob of The Blue Jewel and pushed the door open. The scent of fresh-baked cinnamon rolls drew her into the reception area. She stepped onto a thick woven carpet depicting elves floating on chariots in the sky. The spacious room was lit by a large brass chandelier, bright with a dozen taper candles burning with steady, yellow flames. A loud buzz emanated from the front counter, where a dragon jewel sitting atop a small velvet pillow cast a shimmering blue light in a transparent orb that nearly reached the threshold where she stood.

Temerity lifted her hand hesitantly and touched the glowing blue barrier. It gave her a small shock, buzzing louder and then quieting. Driven by curiosity, she stepped into the translucent sphere, the light brightening and stinging her skin for a moment before dissipating to a sparkly mist. A melodious chorus of jingles tinkled and faded away, and motes of blue sparkles swirled and then disappeared, leaving a fresh scent of ozone in the air.

"What are you doing?" Half-pint asked from the doorway. "Ah, an end-game blue jewel." He stepped inside and latched the door closed behind him. "This might do." He sniffed the air and gazed around at the well-appointed foyer, squinted at the orb, and then cautiously stepped into it. The same buzz and jingle filled the air and quickly faded away.

"Brilliant," he said, admiring the blue orb, which had thinned to a faint barrier as insubstantial as a soap bubble.

"I know taverns and inns," she said confidently. "I know a good one when I see one."

"Just like Avon's," he said dryly.

"That was your idea," she reminded him. "You should have seen her bathing grotto, though. I wouldn't mind going back there just for her enchanted hot spring."

A tall man appeared from the back and hurried up behind the counter. He leaned over the polished wood and peered down at them through small spectacles perched on a long nose. It was a true elf, his pointy ears sticking out from a head of fine silver hair neatly arranged in rows of tight, shoulder-length braids. Moss-green robes flowed from narrow shoulders, and wide sleeves draped almost to the floor. Gold rings and gems adorned his delicate fingers.

"Well, well," he said in a voice that reminded Temerity of a fine crystal goblet being struck lightly with a steel blade. "I rarely get visitors these days who can get past the warding jewel. A lovely young woman and a wise hobgoblin, at that. How intriguing."

The elf smiled down at them, his silvery eyebrows arching up in pointed peaks.

"Nice end-game jewel," Half-pint said, gesturing up at the glimmering blue jewel on the countertop.

"Indeed, indeed," the elf confirmed. "You recognized it. Have you won the game then, yourself?"

"I have. Once," Half-pint said, producing his green jewel and holding it up for the elf to examine.

"Ah, a healing jewel. I almost chose to keep a green one myself, but at the last minute decided on the warding jewel."

"It's a tough choice," Half-pint agreed.

"You're looking for accommodations, then?" the elf asked. "You have come to the right place. Safe and secure. Soft beds and gourmet meals. Only the finest guests allowed. You will be quite happy here."

The scent of ozone had cleared, and in its place, the enticing aroma of cinnamon reminded Temerity of honey cakes back home, and her ma. She swallowed, suddenly achingly hungry and homesick.

"What's the cost?" Half-pint asked.

"Well, I don't get many inn patrons these days, as most new adventurers are scalawags and grifters." He shook his head sadly. "As I mentioned, almost no one has been able to get past the jewel lately. That's been bad for business, in more ways than one. You see, having very few guests at the inn, I rely on my trading business, but I can't find couriers who the warding jewel will allow in. It's a very useful jewel, but very strict. So if you are open to picking up and delivering goods around town, I'm happy to provide you with the best accommodations this side of the Swamp in exchange."

"What's the Swamp?" Temerity whispered to Half-pint.

The elf's ears perked up. "The Swamp is Level Two, my dear," he said with a kind grin. "Hasn't your companion told you?"

Temerity pinched her lips together and looked askance at Half-pint, who innocently ignored her sharp glare.

"First time through for you, then, eh?" the elf asked, and Temerity nodded.

"There's a first time for everyone. You're fortunate to have an end-gamer with you."

Half-pint seemed pleased at the recognition and smiled smugly.

"Very well, then, very well," the elf said. "Name's Elvin. What do you say?"

He held out a thin hand, and Half-pint reached up and shook it.

"Jolly good," Elvin said, and turned to Temerity. "What say you, my young adventurer?"

Unable to resist his bubbling enthusiasm, Temerity returned the elf's wide smile and shook his hand.

───────◆───────

Elvin was not kidding when he called the accommodations the finest around. Temerity gazed around her spacious, private room, connected via a shared bathroom to Half-pint's room. It wasn't even in the attic, but had a high, plastered ceiling, with ornately carved crown moulding decorating the edges. Logs blazed in a limestone fireplace, chasing away the constant chill of Dark Town. A bed, bigger than any she had ever seen, dominated one wall. The mattress was so high off the carpeted floor that there was a small, embroidered stepstool to climb up onto it. The bed was covered with fluffy, white down bedding edged with lace, and matching lace curtains hung from the canopy frame and draped the leaded-glass windows. Sprigs of lavender and orange blossoms, wrapped in sheer silk and tied with a green velvet ribbon, rested on a pillow, scenting the air with their heady fragrance. She was afraid to touch anything, lest her grimy hands leave a mark.

She had removed her boots at the doorway and padded around in her woolen hose. She was left by herself while their very own porcelain tub was filling with hot water from interior plumbing. Half-pint insisted that she bathe first, and so while she waited for the tub to fill, she wandered around her room. The carpet was woven with wine-red and indigo-blue wool in a repeating pattern of birds and twining branches. Inlaid-wood furniture was polished to a warm sheen. Delicate porcelain vases and statuettes of various animals and mythical creatures sat upon the polished surfaces. Paintings of elves and faeries battling ogres and goat-headed men decorated the walls.

When the bath was ready, she sank into the pool of citrus-scented bubbles and wondered at their good fortune.

13

ᴄCOURIERS

Elvin served them a light supper of quail and mushrooms in a red-wine sauce with green peppercorns, roasted turnips and parsnips flavored with tarragon and mint, warm white bread with cold butter, and a dessert of plum cake drowning in a hot cream sauce. He gave Half-pint an extra jug of cream to take up to his room. Apparently, the hobgoblin had made some sort of deal with the elf for a jug of cream morning and night. Elvin knew how to get to a hobgoblin's heart.

Temerity fell fast asleep in the gentle embrace of the featherbed and awoke to something close to sunshine lighting the windows. She climbed out of bed, donning the thick cotton robe Elvin had provided, and peered outside. The light came from a string of small white jewels, wrapped around a railing. She pushed open the large windows, which turned out to be doors, and stepped out onto a small balcony. The hubbub of what passed as daytime in Dark Town went on in the street two stories below, while up on her private balcony, she was relaxed and serene, protected by the inn's blue jewel.

She yawned and stretched, then donned her foppish attire. Soon, she joined Half-pint out in the hallway, and they descended to the first floor, where breakfast was being served at a long table lit by a candelabra holding a dozen tapers.

They devoured eggs and sausages on fluffy biscuits with a tangy cream sauce, with roasted potatoes and red peppers, and sipped at fermented black tea with dollops of cream and honey. They chatted with the only other guest at the table, the man she had seen through the window their first day in Dark Town.

The portly, moustachioed man wore tan tweed pants and vest, a starched white shirt, and a red and gold kerchief around his neck—garb that scholars from Glistening City wore. He had filled one end of the table with stacks of parchments and rolled scrolls, which turned out to be maps. His name was Gentry. While they ate, Gentry told them about his quest to map the tunnel labyrinth and Dark Town, a nearly impossible task, he admitted.

After breakfast, Elvin gave them their first courier assignment. They were to deliver a sack of snakes to a warehouse in exchange for tanned snakeskin leather, which they were to deliver to a leatherworker in exchange for adventurer's weapon belts, which they would sell at the market out of a gnome's stall, and then they were to use the coin to purchase food-stuffs, of which he provided a long list.

Gentry showed them the various stops on a detailed map of the neighborhood. Half-pint studied the route with him while Temerity gaped at the grid of parchments that Gentry had spread across the entire table, which mapped only a small portion of the extensive town.

"The layout of Dark Town does change from time to time," Gentry said. "It makes my job that much harder when things shift all of a sudden. Please let me know if you notice an error in my maps."

Half-pint nodded agreeably, and Temerity tried not to worry.

Out in the antechamber, they stared at a large leather sack, which jiggled and heaved like a living creature as the trapped snakes searched for a way out.

"They're *alive?*" she asked with horror.

"Of course. Best quality snakes this side of the Swamp. Don't worry, the leather is too thick for them to strike through."

Temerity swallowed loudly. Half-pint was too short to carry the large sack, so Temerity was forced to. She clutched the red jewel for courage and then slung the sack over her shoulders, insisting that Half-pint assume his cat form and ride atop it to make sure no snakes escaped. He obliged her request, and Elvin smiled as though he was accustomed to seeing a hobgoblin shapeshift into a cat.

They left The Blue Jewel and headed towards their first stop while Temerity tried not to think about the creepy, crawly, slithery, slimy reptiles she carried on her back.

◆

The tannery was a long ways away—two sectors over from where they had spent all their time thus far in Dark Town. They kept to the main, lamp-lit roads that connected the inn zones, intent on avoiding the riffraff who loitered in the dark alleyways. As she walked towards their destination, Temerity kept a conversation going to distract herself from the writhing mass on her back. It was mostly a one-sided conversation, given that Half-pint was currently a cat.

His feline vocabulary was limited to a short, high-pitched *mew* for *yes,* a long, low-pitched *rrhhoowl* for *no,* silence for when he did not care to comment, and a purr for when everything was good. And, of course, the blood-curdling shriek when danger was at hand, which she hoped to never hear again. He kneaded her right or left shoulder to direct her to turn this way or that, seeing as how she had paid little attention to Gentry's map.

"Do you think we'll find my pa and brothers?" she asked, pulling out her half-locket and tucking her chin to try and see the etching of her pa. The chain was too short to see it well, so she tucked it under her linen undergarment near her heart, not wanting to lose her homing amulet.

Half-pint dug his claws into her right shoulder and otherwise gave her the silent treatment in response to her question. She turned down the cobblestone lane, having arrived at the inn sector Elvin had sent them to, and scanned the faces of the passersby rushing here and there. They were mostly men, but none were her family.

She rambled on, "I suppose, since Dark Town is so huge and it's dark here all the time and so many adventurers come and go, it might be hard to find them."

Silence.

She sighed. "But it *is* possible, right?"

Silence.

"*Right?*" she insisted.

"*Mew.*"

She huffed out an exasperated breath. "But not likely. Right?"

"*Mew.*"

She frowned, missing Mathias's dry wit, Hamish's ready smile, and Pa's quiet strength. And she missed Ma. Temerity wondered if her ma was still sore at her, or terribly sad and lonely. Or maybe she had gotten used to Temerity and Half-pint being gone and had discovered that Siobhan and Shannon were better company and harder workers. Temerity scrunched up her face, unsure whether she preferred being missed or not being missed. She sighed again, loudly. Neither condition was good. She was a horrible daughter for abandoning her ma. She kicked at the cobblestones, wondering if she should go back home.

"Do you miss home?" she asked Half-pint.

Silence.

"Don't you want to find Pa and Hamish and Mathias?"

Silence.

Half-pint the hobgoblin had never expressed much attachment to the humans who occupied their shared dwelling. He mostly seemed motivated by fresh cream. But when he was in his feline form, sometimes she would catch him curled up at the foot of her parents' bed, snuggled against her pa's legs on the warm wool blanket.

"So you grew up with Pa?" she asked.

Silence, then, "*Rrhhoowl.*"

"I mean," she corrected herself, "you knew him since he was a baby? You were already grown up by then, as you told me."

"*Mew.*"

"So you know him pretty well, then. Right?"

"*Mew.*"

"You like him the most out of all of us?"

Silence.

"You don't talk much, do you?" she asked.

Claws pricked her left shoulder.

"Ow," she said, and turned left onto a busy thoroughfare.

The snakes shifted in the sack in reaction to the noise and onslaught of smells as she entered a bustling street market—chicken manure and roasted chicory, sweet apples and spicy root vegetables, flowery perfumes and fermented bean curd.

She covered her nose and mouth with a scrap of linen and pushed through the crowd.

Looking up, she found herself face to face with a familiar visage. She stopped and squinted at the tall young man whose blue eyes peered at her, similarly trying to place her.

"Fancy meeting you here," she said, finally recalling the blond adventurer from the Tin Roof. He was holding his scythe like a walking stick. His burly, dark-haired companion appeared at his side with a wide smile, a woodsman's axe slung through his belt.

"I recognize you," the woodsman said, grinning as though he'd found a long-lost friend. "You were the serving girl in that tavern in the Haverlies. But I didn't peg you for an adventurer."

"What are you wearing?" the blond one asked, wrinkling his brow at her gold velvet waistcoat and multi-colored pants.

"Don't be rude, Keenan," the dark-haired one said. "She looks very successful. More than we can say." The two men glanced down at their peasant garb.

"You upgraded your gear already?" Keenan asked. "How'd you do that?"

She shrugged casually. "Killed someone." She put her hand to the hilt of her boning knife and gave them a crooked smile as they gaped at her. She met their surprised stares, feeling a mixture of pride and guilt. That moment in the alley had happened so fast, ending with a blow to her head, and she'd not had much of a chance since then to reflect on what she'd done. Game or not, it had felt real. "Don't worry," she said, feigning nonchalance, "he didn't really die. He just went back to the beginning of the game."

"Well, I'll be a green elf," Keenan quipped. "We could use you on our team. Ain't that right, Tomaz?" he asked, glancing at the bearded young man who was gazing quizzically at the cat perched on her carrying sack.

"We don't need a fifth," a gruff voice said as a thickset, red-bearded man pushed his way into the conversation. A thin, gray-haired man sidled up next to him, a bow and quiver of arrows sticking up over one shoulder.

Temerity ran her eyes over the older pair of adventurers she had served that day in the Tin Roof.

"So, you guys teamed up, eh?" she observed.

"Sure did," Tomaz said. "We followed them to another tavern in Haverly, which turned out to be an entrance to the game. Ain't that right, Rory?" He directed his comment to the red-bearded man, who scowled in reply. "And Ianan, here, was kind enough to agree to help us through the tunnel labyrinth. Right scary, that dungeon is."

"I told you," Rory said, sounding irritated and resting a thick, hairy hand on the hilt of the broadsword at his hip. "The dungeon is at the end. Those tunnels are just a maze. Let's get going."

Tomaz hesitated, and Keenan turned to Temerity. "Should you really be out here by yourself?"

"Leave the girl alone," Rory snapped. "Teams of four are best to beat the boss. Any more than that will draw out too many trolls. She'll never make it that far, from the looks of that frippery she's wearing. Safer for her that way, anyhow."

Rory sauntered off, stopping at a weapon vendor's stall. Ianan gave her a toothy smile and followed behind his mate. The younger men shrugged with apologetic grins.

"Sorry," Keenan said. "Rory's kind of cranky, but he's been through here so many times, he knows his way around."

"But he's never won the game, I'd wager," she said slyly.

The men's smiles faltered.

"Best of luck to you," she said. "See you at the end." She grinned broadly and stepped away, blending into the crowd and elbowing her way through the teeming marketplace.

14

SNAKE TRADE

The crowd grew thicker as they exited the street market and entered a large open square. Street cafes and shops lined the perimeter, and in the center, a stone monolith towered over the throng, the glowing blue capstone drawing her eye and her heart.

"Oooh," she said as she pushed her way closer. A bright blue spiral glowed from the center of the pillar. "We can go home through here?" she asked, coils of tension unwinding in her chest.

"Yes," Half-pint's voice replied in her ear.

The cat had transformed back into a goblin, and he crouched on her sack of snakes and peered over her shoulder, his tufted ear tickling her cheek. She gently swatted it away.

"Why do they call it a homing spike?" she asked.

"Well, it takes you home, obviously. But as for the spike, I've heard two different legends. One version says that as the worlds were splitting apart, the dragons took standing stones from our side of the world to theirs, as a way to link the two.

The other version is that when the worlds split apart, they took spikes from the backs of deceased dragons and brought them to this side. Again, to link the two worlds, and also to honor their most revered ancestors. Over time, the dragon spikes petrified into stone."

"I like the second version the best," she said, shivers rippling over her skin.

"Me too," he said.

"Should we go home?" she asked, gazing longingly after an adventurer who pressed his palm to the blue spiral and disappeared.

"Only if you want to abandon the game." Half-pint raised the long, pointed, sylph-silk hood over his ears. "Otherwise, we'll just need to traverse the tunnel labyrinth again, and we'd lose the three jewels we've collected already. Is that worth it to you?"

"No, I guess not," she said. "But I do miss my ma."

"She'll be fine," Half-pint said gently. "Those red-headed twins will keep the place tidy for her."

"I guess," Temerity muttered.

"Besides," Half-pint said, "we might find your brothers and pa in here."

"I thought you said we wouldn't."

"I didn't say that. It's just that they're probably way ahead of us, in one of the higher levels already. And the levels are vast. If the dragons don't want us to find each other, we never will."

"There are seven levels, right?" she asked, confirming if the information she'd picked up in Haverly Arms was correct.

"That depends. It changes over time. They keep adding more levels. Or sometimes they remove them. The dragons are fickle that way. Last time I went through, there were seven levels, but I heard there were as many as thirteen at one time."

"Thirteen? That would take us forever."

"Some people speed through the levels. Some people get stuck in one level forever."

"Forever?"

"Figuratively speaking. They can always return home through a blue spiral. Some people like it here, apparently. Come on, let's find the tannery. I think it's down that street." He pointed to a corner of the square.

They finally found their destination, the Two-Bit Tannery.

It was a large, run-down building, with the paint chipping on the sign, and rusty hinges on the door. They climbed up worn stone steps and entered the warehouse. Vats of noxious liquids brought the linen rag to Temerity's face, and her eyes watered as she hurried towards the back, where a fat, long-haired creature was beating at an animal hide hanging from a rod. The creature turned, and Temerity realized it was a female, though an especially ugly one, reminding her of the troll in the coal mine. Temerity tried not to stare rudely, having never imagined that female trolls existed.

The troll peered at them suspiciously through one blue eye and one brown one. She had a greenish tint to her leathery skin, a hairy wart on her bulbous chin, and a pronounced underbite.

"What do you want?" she asked in a gravelly voice. "I only sell wholesale."

Temerity tried not to stare at the troll's overly large head, flat nose, matted gray hair, and green rags that passed for a tattered dress and apron. "We brought snakes from Elvin," she said, trying not to gag at the stench of rotten eggs coming from the troll. Half-pint hopped down to the floor, and Temerity gratefully set down the undulating sack.

"Ahh, good. It's about time," the troll said, setting aside the stick. "I ordered these ages ago."

Temerity backed away as the troll opened the sack and several snake heads poked up and looked around, beady black eyes staring and forked black tongues lashing. The troll grabbed a snake behind its head and dragged it out. The snake's scales were bright red, and its length—nearly as long as the troll was tall—made Temerity recoil. The troll took the snake to a wooden countertop and hacked its head off with a cleaver, tossed the head into a bucket, and dropped the thrashing body into a large vat. Temerity and Half-pint pressed their backs against a wall as snakes slithered from the sack and glided slowly across the floor in all directions.

The troll seemed unconcerned and hunted them down one by one, beheading them and tossing their bodies into the vat and sealing it with a metal cover. She wiped her hands on her apron and motioned for them to follow her further into the warehouse.

Temerity swallowed back an upwelling of nausea and stalked after her. The troll handed them each a bundle of tanned snakeskins. Temerity stuffed the skins into the sack and pulled it onto her shoulders, relieved that it was no longer filled with slithering, squirming live snakes.

Their next stop was a leatherworker, whose small shop was crammed with belts, bags, shoes, boots, jackets, and leather armor. They exchanged the snakeskins for a bundle of adventurer's weapon belts, which were outfitted with loops, straps, hooks, holsters, pouches, and secret pockets. The shop was run by a human man, who went back to his workbench while they browsed through his goods.

Temerity was drawn to a pair of knee-high boots made from the same red snakeskin, which she thought would look very dashing with her red, gold, and blue slashed pants. Half-pint was busy pawing through the leather body armor, looking for something his size.

"How much for these?" Temerity asked, holding up the boots.

"More than you can pay," the leatherworker replied dismissively.

Temerity frowned and put the boots back onto the rack.

"Do you have something my size?" Half-pint asked, holding up a child-sized cuirass.

The man peered down at him. "No, but I can make something for you."

"Custom?" Half-pint asked. "I'd be much obliged."

"You should order some boots, too," Temerity suggested.

"Boots? Hells, no," Half-pint said. "How can I feel the ground with boots on?" He waggled his ears at her, and she bobbled her head in return, glancing down at his long, hairy toes and black toenails.

"Goblins," she muttered, under her breath.

The man took Half-pint's measurements, then she and the hobgoblin left the building, exiting into the lantern-lit street.

"How come he was so nice to you but shrugged off my question?" Temerity asked.

"Probably because he could see I am a seasoned adventurer shopping for something practical, whereas you are a noob enchanted by every shiny object."

Temerity curled her lip at him but did not argue. The red boots were indeed very shiny and would look fabulous with her fashionable attire.

Their last stop that day was the same street market, where they found the cobbler Elvin had told them about, a gnome with long braided moustaches who let them sell the belts out of his stall. The adventurer's belts were apparently in high demand, because before long, a line had formed and soon they had sold them all. The gnome asked to see Elvin's food shopping list, then directed them to the appropriate vendors. By the time they had procured everything, the market was emptying out. Exhausted, they made the long journey back to The Blue Jewel.

———————◆———————

They spent their days crisscrossing Dark Town and delivering snakes to a wide variety of customers: an apothecarist who milked venom from snakes and whose selection of potions made Half-pint more excited than when he used to skim cream off the top of the milk buckets; a snake charmer who entertained adventurers in the cheerfully-lit and boisterous carnival square; a fortune teller who lured people into her den with dragon jewels of every color and wore live snakes draped around her neck; an orc who roasted snake-meat over a grill at the night market in a part of town that was even darker than the rest of Dark Town.

One night, alone in her room after a gourmet meal with Elvin and the map-maker, Temerity emptied her pockets, set her knife on the dresser, and hung her sword over the back of a chair. She turned the orange jewel over in her hand, reluctant to put it down. Goosebumps nettled the nape of her neck. Suddenly, the jewel vibrated in her palm, sending twinges up her arm. She gazed at it, perplexed. The sharp vibrations were disconcerting, but she couldn't make sense of them and finally sighed and placed the jewel on the dresser. She stripped down to her linen shift and stoked the fire, enjoying its warmth.

She was exhausted, but a jittery restlessness made her pace back and forth. She checked under the bed and behind the curtains, stepped out onto the balcony and peered down at the abandoned street below. She went back inside, latching the balcony door shut, then crossed the room and cracked open her door and scanned the hallway. Nothing was amiss. Her skin was still prickling with a sense of foreboding, and she crept silently across her room, through the connecting bathroom, and peeked through the slightly open door into Half-pint's room. He was in his bed, snoring loudly.

She padded back into her room, leaving the connecting doors ajar. Finally, unable to detect anything out of the ordinary, she shrugged away her concerns, collapsed onto her featherbed, and fell fast asleep. She was dreaming about reaching into a sack full of snakes when a cold hand wrapped around her arm.

Temerity jerked awake and grabbed at the hand, but instead of fingers, she was clutching the cold, scaly skin of a reptile. A sharp jab pierced her arm. Panic constricted her throat and she fled the bed from the opposite side, dragging the snake with her. She stepped on its tail, stretching it to its full length from where it hung from her arm, then took her sword and hacked at the squirming snake, chopping it into twitching pieces. The head still clung to her bare arm, the jaws clamped shut and the eyes staring at her, still alive.

"Whaaaaaa," she screamed, as more shadows slithered from the bathroom and across the bedchamber floor.

"Oh, *hells* no!" she exclaimed. She ran on tiptoes over to the dresser where she had set her boning knife, then levered open the snake's jaws, flinging the severed head across the room and leaving two bloody pinpricks on her skin.

"Snakes!" Half-pint yelled from the adjoining room.

"I know!" she yelled back, and ran for the balcony, hopping over several snakes. Her arm was numb, and she felt woozy as she leapt over the balcony railing, hung from the wrought-iron crosspiece, and climbed down the iron rungs with her hands. She dangled her bare feet until she felt the railing of the balcony below and hopped down onto it, springing off and catching the lower rungs and then vaulting down to the street, landing in a crouch.

The dimly-lit street was vacant, and no snakes were following her. Half-pint was in his feline form and was scaling a trellis up to the roof, where he pranced across the cornice and gazed down at her. He jumped across to the next building, which had steep wooden stairs for an escape route, and soon he was on the street in his hobgoblin form.

The front door of The Blue Jewel cracked open, and Elvin peeked around the doorframe. "What was that racket?" the elf asked, squinting out at them. He descended the front steps, and Half-pint quickly explained what had happened while Temerity sat on a step with her head in her hands, her vision blurring as the street spun and the world grew foggy around her.

"Snakebite," she heard Half-pint say through the haze as she crumpled over.

15

SNAKE PIT

Temerity awoke in Elvin's sitting room, a warm fire blazing on the hearth. She was stretched out on a velvet settee, and Half-pint was sitting next to her, bathing her forehead with a cold, damp cloth.

"What happened?" she mumbled, her tongue as swollen and dry as a wad of cotton.

"You were bitten by a snake. I used the green jewel, and Elvin gave you an antivenom. You should be fine."

"Ugh," she grunted, feeling sick to her stomach. She turned onto her side and drifted off.

When she awoke again, Half-pint the cat was curled up in front of the fire, which had burned down to red coals. He saw her stir and stood up on his four paws, had a big cat stretch, and then transformed into a goblin again.

"Oh, good. You're awake," he said, bringing her a glass of cold water. "How do you feel?"

She sat up and drained the glass, then replied, "Pretty good."

"Great. It's still nighttime," Half-pint said with a yawn. "Let's go back to bed."

"You must be kidding me," she protested. "There is no way in the seven hells I'm getting back in that bed."

"It should be okay," Half-pint assured her. "Elvin cleared out all the snakes. Which is a wonder, since he's petrified of them. Gentry helped him and found a break in the tub's drainage pipe, down in the cellar. The snakes climbed up it and squeezed through the drains into all of the bathrooms. The other bathroom doors were closed, so they were easy to remove from those rooms. Elvin swears he and Gentry evicted all the snakes from our chambers. They changed all the bedding, beat the drapes, and even cleared out the chimneys. They've both gone to bed. Elvin said he'd make it up to us."

"He's petrified of snakes? I thought he raised them," Temerity said.

"He does, but Gentry's the one who captures them from the snake pit."

"Snake pit?" she asked, aghast. But sleep was tugging at her head, which was still a bit muzzy.

After some convincing and a fair bit of bribery, Temerity allowed Half-pint to lead her upstairs to her bedchamber. They inspected both rooms and the bathroom, and saw no signs of the creeping, crawling creatures. She held her orange dragon jewel in her palm and closed her eyes, trying to detect any warning prickles or vibrations. The jewel sat in her hand, calm and cool, and her skin felt normal. She opened her eyes and nodded at the hobgoblin.

Coals were smoldering in the fireplace, and Half-pint agreed to sleep in front of her hearth for the night, to guard her. He changed into his cat form, curled up, and kept one yellow eye open as she climbed under the covers and fell asleep.

"I'm deeply sorry. I swear to the dragon gods, it won't happen again," Elvin said, at the breakfast table while serving them peach pastries with whipped cream.

Temerity cast Half-pint a skeptical look but accepted a pastry and let the elf refill her hot chocolate.

"I have never found such talented, skilled, and honest couriers in all my years in Dark Town. You have warmed an old elf's heart."

Half-pint waggled his ears and bit into a pastry.

"Does that mean you'll stay?" the elf asked hopefully.

Half-pint replied with loud chewing, and Temerity dropped a dollop of whipped cream into her mug.

"I'll give you one snake for every five you deliver," the elf said.

Temerity cringed and curled her lip. "The last thing I want is snakes."

"Oh, no, not to keep," the elf said. "To trade. And I have an even more exciting opportunity for you." Temerity arched an eyebrow, and the elf hurried on. "The apothecarist and the meat seller both want snake eggs, but neither I nor Gentry have been able to retrieve any. Isn't that right, Gentry?"

The scholar nodded, pre-occupied with a map of the tunnel labyrinth. "You must show me which way you entered Dark Town," Gentry said distractedly, tapping on a parchment.

"Yes, yes, but first you must show them where the eggs are." Elvin turned back to Half-pint and Temerity, trying to catch their eyes as they successfully dodged his insistent gaze. "You can earn a fortune with the snake eggs. Take half the eggs for yourselves."

"Let us think about it," Half-pint finally said, to which Elvin nodded vigorously and placed another pastry on each of their plates.

Temerity and Half-pint spent the morning with Gentry, going over his extensive, multi-level maps of the tunnel labyrinth, trying to retrace their path. Gentry was aware of the entrance below Lucy's Tavern in Haverly Arms, and they found the arched exit they'd used not far from The Blue Jewel, but the path between the two could have been any of a thousand.

Temerity was intrigued by the hundreds of sheaves of paper that Gentry assured her connected in a three-dimensional grid, with only a few sections missing. The first level for everyone was the symmetrical, circular-grid labyrinth, which spread underground in every direction from Glistening City to Port Maverick and beyond. But one could not access Dark Town from that level, Gentry told them. Everyone needed to descend into the deeper tunnels, which eventually terminated in various sectors of Dark Town.

"You say you fell down a chasm into a pool?" Gentry asked, leafing through the parchments. "Perhaps it is … aha! The Dark Pool of Despair." He pulled out a yellowed vellum. "I've never met anyone who found the ancient pool. I only learned about it from an elderly cartographer. He let me copy this from his map collection. Fascinating."

"Temerity led us that way," Half-pint said proudly.

"And we found an orange dragon jewel in the pool," she added.

"Fortunate, indeed," Gentry exclaimed.

Temerity inspected the parchment laid out in front of them. It could very well have been the lake they had plunged into.

"Most people access the exit near The Blue Jewel from this tunnel," Gentry said, tracing a long, curved tunnel with his finger.

"I think we ended up there," she said, trying to find the connecting paths from the lake to the main tunnel. They

followed threadlike lines of ink branching off in various directions from the lake, until they found one that intersected the
tunnel, where they must have squeezed through the narrow
crevice. They then located the circular stairway that ended at
the alleyway. "Why doesn't everyone just use a map instead of
getting lost and scared for who-knows-how-long?" she asked.

"Well ..." Gentry sighed and sat back in his chair. "The
problem is, no one can carry a map from here back to the real
world. Some people study the maps and try to navigate from
memory. I've tried it several times myself. The problem—well,
one of many problems—is the tunnel labyrinth confounds
everyone, and you will inevitably end up somewhere you do
not expect. The possibilities are endless, and it simply boggles
the mind." He tapped a tall stack of parchments, and she was
overwhelmed just thinking about it.

"Another problem," Gentry continued, in a hushed tone,
as though afraid someone might overhear him, "is the dragons
don't much like maps. They don't seem to mind if you make
them. But using them is another matter." He shook his head
wistfully, then continued in a normal tone. "I create them
strictly for my own educational studies and amusement—the
most complicated, challenging puzzle I've ever encountered.
My doctoral thesis was in Portal Mechanics and Interfaces
Between Worlds."

"If the dragons wanted adventurers to use maps, they would
have provided them," Elvin called from the kitchen.

"Yes, yes," Gentry said, waving a hand. "That's what I said."

Temerity stole a glance at Half-pint, but he was engrossed
in the yellowed parchment. She leaned over his shoulder and
they tried to retrace their path backwards from the Dark Pool
of Despair, but soon got confused by the many branches.

They left Gentry to his maps. Temerity crouched with Half-pint by the hearth, where they discussed Elvin's offer.

"We can use the snakes and eggs to upgrade more of our gear," Half-pint whispered. "The dragon gods are offering us a safe way to do so, and we should take it."

"Safe?" she asked wryly, rubbing the arm where she'd been bitten.

She finally relented, and they joined Elvin in the kitchen and told him they agreed to his deal.

"Fantastic. Wait here." The elf scurried into the back and reappeared, handing them each a vial of antivenom and a small glass syringe. "Maybe you should each carry two," he said, disappearing again and returning with two more vials.

"Won't the green jewel take care of any bites?" she asked.

Elvin cocked his eyebrows. "If Half-pint can get to you fast enough. And if he doesn't lose his jewel."

The hobgoblin clutched the green dragon jewel to his chest. *"Never."*

Temerity turned her attention to the vial. Elvin showed her how to fill the syringe and explained how to jab the needle into the body at the site of the snakebite, then administer a second dose into the thigh and a third dose into the abdomen.

She winced, hoping she would never need to use it.

They shook hands to seal their agreement, then returned to the dining room. Gentry set aside his maps, lit a lantern, and led them all down into the cellar.

———◆———

The cellar was unfinished, with dirt walls, a dirt floor, and a large pit filled with writhing snakes. Temerity stopped cold at the sight of the snakes and then rushed back up the stairs, goosebumps rising over her entire body. She stopped halfway up and turned back around to peer down at the pit. There were many more snakes than she had thought would be down here—she had tried not to think about it, to be honest. She supposed she had expected there to be cages, at least. Some sort of organized husbandry. Instead, there were hundreds of snakes, layers deep, all squirming and squiggling and trying to climb out of the pit.

A blue flash stunned one snake that had made it up to the rim of the pit, and a blue dragon jewel in the corner pulsed until the snake fell back down into the squirming nest. She noticed a water drainage pipe that sank down into one corner of the mass of snakes. Apparently, the snakes that had broken through and climbed up inside the pipe had somehow evaded the jewel's warding powers. Sneaky snakes. She might have felt sorry for them, if they didn't make her feel all creepy-crawly and shivery.

"How did you seal the pipe?" she asked Gentry, imagining him diving into the sea of snakes wearing a steel suit.

"I capped it where it comes up into the kitchen and rerouted the drainage out the back."

"Oh," she said. "That's much more reasonable than swimming with snakes."

Gentry cast her a quizzical look, then turned his attention to the snake pit. He demonstrated using a long stick with a hook on the end to grab a snake and drop it into a basket, latching it shut. Gentry handed Half-pint the stick, and the hobgoblin succeeded in hooking a snake after the second try.

"There are eggs under the mass of snakes," Elvin said.

Gentry took back the hook and poked around among the snakes, trying to expose some eggs, but several snakes started climbing up the stick and almost reached his hand before he could uncover any eggs. He threw the stick into the pit, and they watched as it was consumed and buried by the wriggling mass.

"Sorry," Gentry said to Elvin.

"No worries. That's not the first hook the snakes have claimed. I've got more in the storeroom."

The elf went into the back and returned with two long hooks, and Gentry and Half-pint filled the basket with snakes. The basket turned out to be lined with the leather carrying sack, which they cinched closed and carried upstairs.

"I'm sorry I didn't help," Temerity said as she pulled the sack over her shoulders. "They give me the creeps."

"That's okay," Half-pint said. "You've been lugging them around town this whole time. We're even."

Elvin wrote a note for each of his customers, informing them of the cut Half-pint and Temerity had earned, and the pair of them headed off on their courier route.

16

SNAKE CHARMER

Temerity and Half-pint made their rounds, trading one extra snake per batch of five, the value of which they took in credits in the hopes of accumulating enough credits over time to exchange for something substantial.

Every evening, Half-pint tried to uncover some eggs, but the snakes were too quick and too determined, so he shook them off and lost two more hooks for his efforts. Not one to admit defeat, he rigged a long stick with two ropes connected to a jaw-like clamp on the end that he opened and closed with the ropes. The device gave him more control than the hook did for catching the snakes and dropping them into the basket, but it did not help any when the snakes swarmed the stick when he tried to dig for eggs.

On the sixth morning, he said he had an idea. The last stop that day was the snake charmer. She was a faery and reminded Temerity of Avon, whom the faery knew, although the snake vendor was a woodland nymph and Avon was a water sprite. She saw them approaching and put down her flute, then deftly picked up the snake that had been dancing for her, by gently looping a finger around its body. She let it slither into a box and then closed the lid.

They greeted one another, and Temerity handed the nymph a small bundle of meat pies she had bought for her at the market, and a cherry strudel from Elvin.

"Oh, thank you, my dear," the nymph said. "Tell Elvin that the cinnamon raisin cookies he made the other day were divine."

Temerity and Half-pint had kept the extra snakes instead of selling them to the other three vendors that day, and produced a total of four extra for the nymph. They normally traded Elvin's snakes for baubles the nymph collected in her tip basket, for Elvin loved such things—shiny objects from the pockets and purses of adventurers. Temerity enjoyed looking through the random trinkets: earrings, rings, pendants, glass beads, tiny glass animals, polished stones with runes etched into them, balls of scented resin. They took a handful in trade for Elvin's snakes, as usual, and Temerity picked out a rune stone for herself, in exchange for the meat pies. But for the four extra snakes, Half-pint asked if he could look at her flutes.

The nymph raised a moss-green eyebrow, but showed Half-pint her basket of reed flutes.

"Would you take these four snakes as trade for a flute?" Half-pint asked.

"Are you tiring of the courier business?" she asked with a friendly smirk. "Do you intend to offer me some competition?"

Half-pint returned her crooked grin. "No, I want to try and charm Elvin's snakes. They have been breeding like crazy, and his snake pit is out of control. We want to get some eggs, but the snakes are very protective of them."

"No doubt," she said, her fern-green eyes lighting up. "I would love some eggs. I can try incubating them with my pet snakes. Mine never lay any. I was thinking of creating a small forest in my back room for them, but I haven't found the time. It would be much easier to get the eggs from you. Imagine the bond I would have with them if I raised them from hatchlings?"

Half-pint nodded. "We will bring you some eggs, if we can ever get any."

The nymph selected a flute for Half-pint and spent the rest of the afternoon teaching him how to play it and which tunes the snakes liked best. "It's all about being gentle with the snakes," she said as Half-pint's long fingers pressed the various holes on the flute, the breathy melody wafting its way through the carnival square, attracting onlookers and tips, while the snake the nymph had brought out waved its head in a figure eight.

When the nymph was satisfied with Half-pint's progress, they gave her the four extra snakes for the flute and promised to bring her a clutch of eggs as soon as they had gathered some.

The next morning, Half-pint played his flute for the snakes in the pit, and soon, the myriad of snakes were swaying their heads in a synchronized dance. Temerity used the gripper to transfer one mesmerized snake after another into the basket until they had all they needed. Then she slowly and gently delved the stick down into the mass of hypnotized snakes and came up with an egg.

She carefully placed it in a cloth-lined basket. It looked like a small chicken egg, but the shell was leathery. The snakes didn't seem to notice, so she went in for another until she had a dozen.

They carried their treasures upstairs to show Elvin, who flapped his hands in delight.

"We must keep them alive for the nymph," the elf said worriedly, and rummaged around in his pantry. He brought out a picnic basket and carefully arranged the eggs in a nest of linen napkins, then Half-pint played his flute while Gentry transferred one snake from the carrying sack to the egg basket.

Elvin quickly sealed the lid. "There," he said, wiping his hands on his apron.

Temerity and Half-pint went directly to the snake charmer to deliver the eggs. The nymph glowed green with delight, and the six eggs that were Half-pint and Temerity's share went towards future credits.

The next morning, they brought the meat seller two dozen eggs, and the following day, they supplied the apothecarist with three dozen.

On the fourth day, Temerity dug around in the snake pit for more eggs and lifted out a glinting, faceted yellow egg that glowed bright like golden topaz.

"Look, Half-pint," she exclaimed, "a dragon jewel!"

He nodded happily whilst continuing to play, enrapturing the snakes with the trilling melody.

When she had the jewel safely in hand, he put down the flute and they examined it together.

"Yellow jewels are used to charm people," Half-pint told her.

"The way your flute charms snakes?" she asked.

Half-pint chuckled. "Kind of. Yellow jewels make it easier to convince people of things, easier for people to like you and want to do your bidding. Avon, no doubt, was wearing yellow jewels hidden under her sylph cloak."

"Hmmm. That could be useful. Here, you take it," Temerity said, holding it out for him. "Your flute music made it possible to find this."

He examined the glistening jewel and did not object. "Okay. We each have two now. I believe this is a sign that it's time for us to move on."

"What do you mean?" she asked.

"Once we have completed a quest the dragons have sent us on, we should not linger long, or we may miss the next sign."

"The dragons sent us here?" she asked, her eyes widening.

"It's their game," Half-pint replied. "They set all the rules and oversee gameplay. It's not a coincidence that we landed in an inn with a jewel hiding in the cellar. The dragons like the jewels to be found, they just don't like to make it easy."

Temerity sighed, not understanding, and not really believing in all the legends of dragon gods creating the Dragon's Game in order to lure humans into their den for their amusement. She voiced her doubts, and Half-pint frowned at her.

"It is not for their amusement," he said. "It is a natural progression. Anyone who beats the first game has the option to continue to the second game, and finally to the third. Or so I have heard."

"What are the second and third games?" she asked.

"Well, the *Dragon's Game* is not the actual name of the first game, it's the name of the whole thing. The dragons refer to our real world as the *Dragon's Egg*, the first phase of a dragon's development. As you know, they call the game we're in now the *Dragon's Crawl*. Think of it like the caterpillar stage of a butterfly. And like a caterpillar crossing a road filled with horses and wagons ready to crush it and birds and vermin hunting it, adventurers have to make their way safely across dangerous terrain and through a series of challenges and obstacles in order to progress. The second game is called *Dragon's Chrysalis*, although some humans call it the *Dragon's Cocoon*. In that game, the transformation is as much mental as it is physical. The third game is *Dragon's Ascension*, where you can ascend to become a dragon, if you can survive it."

Temerity stared at him, unsure what to believe anymore. It all seemed so far-fetched. "Does that mean we're all baby dragons?"

Half-pint laughed. "I suppose you could look at it that way."

"And dragons are gods?" she asked.

Half-pint shrugged. "We call them gods. They are masters of their domain, that is for sure."

"So, you beat the first game already, the Dragon's Crawl?" she asked.

"Yes, one time."

"How do you know so much about it if you only beat it once?" she asked.

He laughed again. "I *beat* it once, but I've been through Dark Town sixteen times, if I recall correctly."

"Sixteen?"

"Yes. It's hard to beat the game. It can take many attempts."

"Did you have the option to continue on to play the Dragon's Chrysalis?"

"Yes, I could have. But no one with any brains moves directly on to the second game. They try to beat the Dragon's Crawl several times to gain enough strength and skill to have any hope of beating the Dragon's Chrysalis."

She sighed again, wondering how far along her pa and brothers were in the game. "How long did it take you to run through Dark Town so many times?"

"I spent several years playing the game. A decade—or maybe it was twelve years total—before I got married and gave it up."

"Married?" she asked, her jaw dropping open.

"Yes. You find that so strange?"

"No, it's just ... I ... never ..."

Half-pint had a dreamy look in his eye that Temerity had never seen before.

He went on, "I met her in the game. She was a sight to behold, let me tell you."

"Another hobgoblin like you?"

"No, no. Males mostly take on the household tasks of a hob-goblin. No, Daphne is a woodland nymph. Same as the snake charmer. Powerful dryads, woodland faeries are. Couldn't have asked for a better gaming partner. We cleared the levels in lightning speed together." He gazed into the distance. "Those were the days."

"Why did you stop?" she asked.

"Daphne got pregnant and wanted to go home to the forest."

"Pregnant? You have children?" she asked, her bewilder-ment making her question the foundations of her world.

"Yes, one. A son. He's dedicated to the Dragon's Game still. Last I heard, Roskar had beaten the Dragon's Crawl five times and was going for a sixth so that he could move on to the Dragon's Chrysalis."

"Why six times? And where is Daphne now?"

"She lives back home in the wildlands north of Glistening City. She got tired of living in town, but that's how I make my living. So we went our separate ways and eventually got divorced. I see her on occasion, usually when Roskar comes out of the game for a spell."

He continued, "Six times is the usual number. That's because there are six colors of dragon jewels. Adventurers try and take one of each of the end-game jewels with them into the Dragon's Chrysalis."

"Six? Let me see." She counted off the colors with her fingers. "Green for healing. Blue for warding. Orange for premonition." She glanced at Half-pint for confirmation. He nodded, and she continued, "Red for strength."

"And skill," Half-pint added.

"Oh yeah, skill. What kind of skill?" she asked, crinkling her brow.

"Fighting. And weapons," he said. "It doesn't grant new skills, it only enhances those you already have. But it does allow you to learn new skills faster than normal. Good thing for you, your pa taught you since you were a child."

"I suppose," she said. Her pa had always insisted she train alongside her brothers. She had never taken the sword, knife, and hand-to-hand fighting drills all that seriously. It was mostly for fun—she hadn't expected to need those skills in real life. There hadn't been war in several generations, and the Haverlies were generally safe and peaceful, aside from the occasional drunken lout.

But she was good with a bow and arrow and had killed her first deer at the age of twelve. She and her ma had each gotten a deer the past two seasons when her pa and brothers had been away, plus she caught the occasional wild turkey, and that juvenile boar that kept breaking through the fence and rooting up their vegetable garden.

But she hadn't ever had a real fight with another person, except that one time a drunk at the Tin Roof had reached up her skirts and she had broken his wrist. Her reaction had been a reflex, and quite effective. Her ma had hit him over the head with a frying pan, and together they dragged him to the front door and tossed him out into the mud.

"What are the other jewel colors?" Half-pint prompted.

"Oh, yeah. Let me think ..." She glanced down at the new jewel resting in Half-pint's hand. "Oh," she said. "Yellow for charming. And what is the sixth?"

"White," Half-pint said. "For intelligence. Those are the rarest and most difficult to find. That's the one Roskar is missing."

"Like the white jewels strung across our balconies?" she asked.

Half-pint scoffed. "No, those are cheap imitations. Actually, not cheap, and not imitations, but that's how they are described. No, those are sprite lights. You can get some from faeries on occasion, if you know the right sprite. They are good for lighting the way, but they have no powers beyond that."

"So your son's name is Roskar, and your ex-wife's name is Daphne. What is your real name, then?" she asked. "It can't be Half-pint."

His cheeks puffed out and his eyes bulged.

She wished she could take back her words—she knew better. Hobgoblins were known to leave a household after such a prying question. Hobgoblins were weird that way. They would abandon a house they had tended to for years after the most minor slight. She bit her tongue and met his horrified stare.

"You know it is not polite to ask a hobgoblin his name," he said, his mouth pinched.

She exhaled, relieved that he had not turned on his heel and stalked away, leaving her alone in Dark Town.

"Why?" she asked. "What's the big deal? You know my name."

"A fae's name is very personal," he said, furrowing his brow at her, his face flushing. "It holds power. Daphne and Roskar are not their true names. But since it's you asking, Miss Temerity, I will tell you. My name is Haater Vapin. It means dangerous weapon." She gaped at him, and his skin darkened to a deep russet. "But please don't call me that. Half-pint is just fine."

She inclined her head in a small bow, happy to have avoided his stormy temper. "Thank you for telling me. I will not repeat it."

"Shall we go?" Half-pint asked, shifting self-consciously and tucking away his flute. "We should upgrade as much gear as we can before departing The Blue Jewel."

"Elvin will be sad we're leaving," she said.

"I'm sure he will," Half-pint replied. He helped Temerity lift the sack filled with snakes and a basket of eggs to her shoulders, then they climbed the stairs, leaving the snake pit behind.

17

GEARING UP

The evening before they were to set off to trade up their gear, Half-pint asked Temerity if she would give him her linden stick.

"But I need it for torches. You said we'll need light later."

"It's not green enough anymore," he said. "We'll find you another suitable torch holder. Trust me."

She sighed and fetched it for him. "You owe me," she said, handing it over.

He next asked her if she would let him have the brown curtain from the Tin Roof's front window. "I need it for a cloak," he explained.

"What are you going to trade me for it?" she asked, smirking slyly at him. "I kind of like that silver sylph-silk robe. I could make a nice bodice out of that fabric."

He frowned at her. "I want to keep that," he said stubbornly.

"Well, then, what will you give me for the curtain?"

He put his finger to his chin for a long moment, then dug

into his travel sack and emerged with a tiny scroll. He unfurled it and handed it to her.

It was a meticulous charcoal sketch of her whole family: her pa, her ma, her two brothers, and herself as a baby in her ma's arms. Her heart caught in her throat at the sight of them. "Ohhh," she crooned. "It's so beautiful." Then she knit her eyebrows together. The style of the sketch reminded her of the portraits of her pa and brothers that hung behind the Tin Roof's bar.

"You stole this from my ma?" she asked indignantly, fire blazing in her eyes.

"Stole it!" Half-pint retorted, his nose flaring angrily. "I *drew* it."

"You drew it?" she asked, shocked and then instantly ashamed at having wrongly accused him.

"Yes, I drew it. Does that surprise you so much? Who do you think sketched the portraits of your father and brothers on the wall of the tavern?"

Her eyes grew wide. *"You* did?"

"Yes," he said, his feelings clearly hurt.

"I'm sorry," she said, getting to her knees to be at eye level with him. "I didn't know. They're beautiful. Did you ..." She pulled out the half-locket, holding up the miniature etching of her pa.

"Yes," he said. "That, too."

"Oh," she said, finding no other words. She sat on her heels and felt horrible for holding such little regard for her talented and brave companion. "I don't deserve you." She fought back tears—she had no right to cry. He was the one who had been scorned and dismissed his whole life, just because he had been born a hobgoblin.

"Don't worry about it, Miss Temerity," he said, patting her gently on the back. "You're still young. It takes a good hundred years to develop proper sensibilities."

She chuckled wryly. "That means few humans will ever be as wise and sensitive as a hobgoblin?"

"Pretty much," he said, and gave her a big, toothy smile.

———————————◆———————————

One of the concessions she had gotten out of Half-pint when he had convinced her to stay at The Blue Jewel after the snake-bite, was that she could get a pair of red snakeskin boots, and he promised not to object to her purchase as frivolous or wasteful or offer any other criticism of her taste in clothing.

They headed out with their last delivery of snakes and eggs. It promised to be a long day, as they intended to visit all the vendors.

They stopped first at the tannery and traded a few snakes to the troll for a large batch of tanned red snakeskins, all of which they could keep for themselves today, based on the credits they had accumulated.

Next stop was the leatherworker. Between Half-pint's share of the snakes, a few snakeskins, and their credits, the hobgoblin had enough to trade for his custom-made leather body armor. The leatherworker made him try it on, fussing and nipping and tucking until he was satisfied with the fit. The armor consisted of a cuirass, the chest and back guards buckling at the sides; shoulder spaulders made with strips of thick leather overlapping almost to his elbows; hip faulds, similar to the spaulders, with overlapping strips that covered his hips and thighs; and a pair of long gloves, with runes carved into the leather.

Half-pint carefully folded up his silver sylph-silk robe and tucked it into his travel sack, wearing his leather armor proudly. It was Temerity's turn, and she showed the leatherworker her stash of red snakeskins and asked if he would make her a pair of boots like the ones that were still sitting on the rack but were too large for her.

The leatherworker lowered a gray eyebrow at her, and she thought he was going to refuse, when Half-pint rolled the yellow jewel around in his palm while the man gazed at it.

"Well ... I could, maybe ... I don't make the boots, you know. A cobbler friend of mine does. A gnomish fellow over yonder."

"The cobbler in the market square?" Temerity asked.

"No, his cousin. The cobbler at the market can direct you there. Tell him I sent you."

"Thank you very much," Temerity said. Half-pint pocketed the yellow jewel and she put her snakeskins in a burlap sack the leatherworker gave her.

"You still have a few credits left with me," he said to Temerity. "Do you want something else? No armor for you?"

"No, thanks," she said with a grin, suspecting he wanted to get her to trade the rest of her snakeskins for a full suit of armor. "I like my fancy pants."

Half-pint rolled his eyes. "I told her—" he began to say, but she cut him off with a stern look.

"Do you have any rope?" she asked. "I lost mine in the tunnel labyrinth."

"Rope? Of course," he said, disappearing into the back and returning with a coil of sturdy hemp rope. She stuffed it into the burlap sack.

"What else?" the leatherworker asked.

Temerity looked around the shop and chose two of the leather belts that the adventurers prized so much. She handed the short one to Half-pint, and they proceeded to transfer their weapons and other tools to their new adventurer's belts, which conveniently had a place for everything. They handed their old weapon belts to the leatherworker, but he would not accept them until they took some leather and suede scraps in exchange, which he insisted they would need.

"Here, take these for the remainder of your credits," he said, rifling through a crate and emerging with two suede sacks. "The experienced adventurers carry these."

They were compact backpacks, smaller and sturdier than the canvas ones they had entered the game with, and had several pockets and straps. One was sized for wee folk, and the other would fit Temerity.

"Ah, brilliant," Half-pint said, examining his while Temerity transferred her snakeskins and other items to hers.

"Seems you guys are preparing to head out. You got all your jewels yet?"

"Almost," Half-pint said. "We're about ready to run the alleys."

"Ah, good luck," the leatherworker said, and Temerity eyed Half-pint quizzically.

They thanked the leatherworker, and Temerity strapped her new pack onto the sack full of snakes, which were growing restless, by the feel of things.

They took their leave and walked to the cobbler's stall, who directed them to his cousin's workshop. The cousin, who apparently did all the shoemaking, was hidden away in a ramshackle building several blocks from the market, and the gnome led them through his shop to the back. They handed him the note from his cousin, transferring all their credits over to him.

"Hmpf," the gnome grunted, pulling on his long gray beard. "So you're the pair who've been selling the adventurer's belts out of my cousin's stall? Workin' for the elf, eh?"

"Yep, we're about done, though," Half-pint said. "Heading to the alleys after this."

"Hmpf. Brave. Well, what can I do yeh for?"

Temerity showed him her bundle of red snakeskins.

He whistled with admiration and ran his stubby fingers over the shimmering red leather. "Beautiful," he murmured.

She told him about the boots at the leatherworker's shop.

"Oh, those. Yes, indeedy, I can make yeh a pair that'll fit like a glove." He measured her feet and calves. "I'll start on 'em right away. They'll be finished by tomorrow at this time. Come by anytime after that. What're yeh gonna do with these?" he asked, tapping her workboots. She shrugged, and he said, "That's good cow leather. I'll take them in trade and make yeh a pair of snakeskin gloves as well," he said, wriggling his fingers. "They'll work together with yer new boots."

She nodded happily, and he traced her hands onto a piece of parchment and then took the snakeskins he would need for the boots and gloves.

They left the workshop and headed across the sector to the meat seller, who was just setting up his stand for the night market, which was just like a day market but busier and smellier and with extra-special deals. The orc greeted them and handed them a bundle. "Here you go, just like you ordered." They gave him his live snakes, then unwrapped the bundle. Stacked neatly together were dozens of strips of jerked snake meat. They also accepted their usual hot meat pies for their afternoon snack, and took a few extra for the nymph.

Their next stop was the apothecarist's, whose shop was in an unmarked flat off a narrow alley. The hobgoblin was unable to contain his excitement as he rushed from one potion rack to another.

"Don't break anything," Temerity whispered at him.

He ignored her and flitted over to the next rack.

The apothecarist was a female true elf with long silver hair, a pointy nose, and eyes of gold. She watched with an amused grin as Half-pint ogled every vial, vaporizer, and infuser in the place. He ended up choosing several vials of snake venom and several other vials of potions of various colors, along with a vaporizer and a large glass syringe with a long steel needle. Temerity had given him her credits, since she had no idea what all the potions were for, and she had already been the beneficiary of his healing more than once.

He wrapped his goods carefully and arranged them in his sack, nestled in his sylph-silk robe. They left the apothecarist's and walked across the sector to the colorfully lit carnival square.

Half-pint stopped and dug into his sack. He pulled out the old, faded brown curtain and draped it around himself as a cloak, then pulled out Temerity's torch stick and held it like a walking stick.

"Shall we?" he asked.

She cocked an eyebrow at him and followed him across the square.

They greeted the woodland nymph, handing over her delivery of snakes and the meat pies.

"My eggs hatched," she said cheerfully. They peeked into her snakebox, and several tiny snakes stared up at them.

"Very cute," Temerity said wryly. "Congratulations."

"We're ready to use our credits," Half-pint informed her.

"Oh?" the nymph asked. "Ready to move on, are you?"

They nodded and proceeded to trade. Temerity used her credits for several rune stones. They apparently had no value in Level One, but Half-pint and the nymph said they were very useful in higher levels, where they could be traded to craftsmen in order to enhance weapons and gear.

Half-pint used his credits to pay for another flute, and then drew out his yellow jewel as though to casually inspect it.

"Nice cloak you're wearing," the nymph said.

"Thank you," Half-pint replied.

"Linen?" she asked.

"Barkcloth, actually," he said, and Temerity examined the fabric more closely. She had never noticed before, but the threads were indeed the shiny, smooth texture of bark. The women in Haverly Arms sometimes stripped bark from the trees when they didn't have linen or wool to spin.

"Ooh, barkcloth," the nymph said, clasping her hands to her heart. "Reminds me of home."

"Yes. The forest. Too bad there are no trees in Dark Town," Half-pint said. "Perhaps you should move up to the Swamp."

"Oh, dear no," she said, making a face. "What a wretched level that is. No, it's either here or the Pastoral Lands, but they've razed most of the forests for farmland there. Besides, business is good here. The newbies don't understand the value of the trinkets they toss into my tip basket." The nymph eyed Half-pint with narrowed lids. "What will you take for the cloak?"

Half-pint scratched at his chin. "Oh, I don't know. I don't think we need anything. Unless, perhaps ... no."

"What?" the nymph pressed him.

"Oh, just that blanket you're sitting on. Could get cold in the Swamp."

"Blanket!?" she exclaimed. "I'll have you know, this is woodland sylph silk. Softer and stronger than any fiber humans or goblins spin. So rare, I'll bet you have never come across any."

Temerity had paid no attention to the blanket before, but on closer inspection, she saw that it was a shimmery green silk, thick like Half-pint's silver sylph silk, but the color of pine needles.

"Oh, yes," Half-pint chuckled. "I was married to a dryad. All of our bedding was woodland sylph silk."

"Ah, so then you understand its value," she said, still eyeing the brown robe.

"This barkcloth," Half-pint said, running his fingers over the faded fabric, "has similar qualities, if you know what I mean."

"Of course I know what you mean," she said with a huff. "But this silk is such a large piece, and your robe is so small."

"It's big enough for you to sit on," he said, waggling his ears. "Here. I'll throw in this walking stick, just for you. It's a linden branch."

The nymph inhaled sharply, her fingers fluttering. *"Linden ..."*

The deal was struck. They bid farewell to the snake charmer and left the carnival square behind, with a roll of green sylph silk under Half-pint's arm and a smug look on his face.

18

---◆---

FORTUNES

Their final stop was the fortune teller's shop. The fortune teller was a plump human woman who reminded Temerity of her aunt Ethel, who loved fresh cream more than Half-pint did. They entered the shop, which was in the below-ground floor of a dreary building. The room was a welcome respite from the dark street, festooned with colorful scarves and lit with dragon jewels of every color arranged on a shelf behind the fortune teller's head.

They gave the rotund woman the remainder of the live snakes, and she took the creatures into the back and then returned with three snakes draped around her neck. The snakes hissed at Temerity, who sneered back at them.

"This is our last day as couriers for Elvin," Half-pint told her.

"Ah, so, then you are ready to exchange your credits for a reading?"

Half-pint made a wry face that sharpened his nose and chin. "I don't believe in that stuff."

Temerity stiffened, afraid the ornery little hobgoblin had offended the woman, but she appeared to be amused. "The cards do not care if you believe in them or not."

Shivers ran up Temerity's spine, and she blurted out, "I would very much like a card reading. My ma used to always look at the tea leaves in her cup and see things there. She was strangely accurate." Temerity shivered again.

The woman nodded knowingly and invited them to sit down. Temerity tugged on Half-pint's cloak, and his pointed expression relaxed in reluctant surrender. They sat on pillows across from the fortune teller, who lit several pillar candles and settled onto a large cushion of her own.

A small, low table sat between them, covered in purple velvet. The fortune teller shuffled a deck of oversized, illustrated cards, and gazed at the two of them. "Would you like separate readings, or a combined one?"

Temerity glanced at Half-pint, but he still wore a dubious scowl.

"We are a team, so I guess a combined one would be best," Temerity said, elbowing Half-pint in the ribs. He shrugged in tacit agreement.

"Are you interested in a reading about your fortune in the Dragon's Game?"

Temerity nodded.

"Are there any questions in particular you would like answered?" the fortune teller asked, shuffling the cards.

Temerity tried to think of the most important question, but before she could say anything, Half-pint cleared his throat and said, "We're planning on running the alleys. Is it the right time? And do we have everything we need to beat the boss, aside from the additional jewels?"

Temerity glanced at him with annoyance—first he didn't want a reading, and now he was hogging all the questions.

"What is 'running the alleys?'" Temerity asked curtly.

"It's when adventurers want to speed through the first level," the fortune teller said. "From what I've gathered, you've been working the inns thus far, is that correct?"

Temerity nodded.

"Well, my dear, there are basically two ways to progress through the Dark Town level. One way is to play the inns, taking whatever jobs they give you. That is the safer, but much more time-consuming method. Then there's running the alleys. That is just as it sounds. You run up and down the maze of alleys, searching for jewels and loot and competing with other adventurers who are doing the same. First-timers who run the alleys right away usually die pretty quickly. If they return to the game, then they usually play the inns the second time through. More experienced players generally use a mix of both. The most advanced, aggressive players strictly run the alleys, in order to level up as quickly as possible."

"Oh, I get it," Temerity said.

"Well said," Half-pint added. "Couldn't have explained it better myself."

"Could've tried, at least," she grumbled, casting him a sidelong glance. "Thank you," she said to the fortune teller. "I would like to know if I will find my father and brothers. Also, we've been playing as a two-person team. Is that a good idea?"

The woman smiled and pushed the stack of cards across the table towards Temerity. "Please cut the cards into three piles."

Temerity did so, and the fortune teller stacked the cards again into a single pile and began laying out cards, face-down. She started with a pair of cards and then laid down five more in a line. She placed the eighth card in a crosswise position, and then continued in a line again, laying down six more cards until she reached the end, and then capped it with another pair of cards.

Temerity and Half-pint watched in silence as the fortune teller turned over the first two cards and gazed at the images for several long moments.

"The Elf and the Scholar," the fortune teller finally said in a sonorous voice. "These cards are where you have been—where you are starting from. The elf makes sense to me, but do you understand what the scholar represents?"

Temerity nodded, and Half-pint gazed at the cards, wide-eyed. The fortune teller inclined her head and turned over the next card.

"The Inn. I think we know what that means." She turned over the next card. "The Dark Alley. I suppose that answers your question." The fortune teller glanced up at Half-pint. "It follows immediately after The Inn, and so that is what comes next."

Half-pint nodded, and she continued with the next card.

"The Orange Jewel. This card contains a warning." The woman peered at them through narrowed lids, and Temerity's skin tingled—but Half-pint did not seem disturbed. Candles flickered, and the fortune teller laid down the next card. "Deep Darkness," she said ominously. "This card not only represents physical darkness, but darkness of a symbolic nature."

Temerity frowned at the card, which pictured a dark cave.

"I don't know what that means," Half-pint said.

"Me neither," Temerity added.

"It is another warning," the fortune teller said. The three snakes lifted their heads from the woman's ample bosom and hissed in unison, and the hairs on the nape of Temerity's neck rose with a shiver. "You should heed the warning signs." She gazed at them with solemn eyes, and the snakes flicked their tongues.

Temerity swallowed and nodded vigorously. The three

snakes settled their heads back onto the fortune teller's chest, and she turned over the next card.

"Hmmm," the woman mused. "The Doorway. However, the card is reversed. Upside-down door? No," the fortune teller murmured to herself, shaking her head. "I do not know exactly, but this is not a normal doorway, I know that much."

"Is it bad?" Temerity asked.

The fortune teller furrowed her brow. "It is not good."

Temerity was not sure she liked this 'card reading' business very much, but the fortune teller turned over the next, cross-wise card, laying it down perpendicular to the others.

"This card is what crosses you." The woman looked up at them with raised eyebrows.

Temerity looked down at the card. It was called Dark Dragon, and a tingle ran up her spine. The dragon pictured was coal-black with fiery-red eyes.

"He is not happy," the fortune teller said, and the snakes lifted their heads again, weaving from side to side. Temerity's legs started jittering. She pressed her hands on her knees to steady them, telling herself this was just a silly card game.

The fortune teller waited until the snakes calmed down, then asked, "Shall I continue?"

Half-pint nodded silently, and Temerity did not dare object.

The next card was Darkness and Light.

"Ah. A decision point. The next two cards will show the two possible paths depending on which choice you make." The fortune teller turned over two cards and arranged them next to each other. "This one is the path of darkness," she said, showing them the Death card, a devil with its throat slit and lying in a pool of blood. "And the second is the path of light." That card was called Sacrifice, and showed a man hanging upside down, his head consumed by flames.

"Some choice," Temerity said, and the fortune teller bobbled her head in a vague *it's-hard-to-fathom* gesture.

"Death is the end of the dark path," the fortune teller said. "But don't worry, death in this game is not a real death, as you know. You'll just need to start the game over. If you manage to escape the darkness through sacrifice, then the rest of this reading will show you the way of light."

The fortune teller sounded cheerful, but a heavy sense of doom sank into Temerity's bones. She felt for the orange jewel in her pocket, and the ominous feeling grew stronger. She clutched the red jewel in her other pocket and waited for the next card.

The fortune teller flipped over the card and laid it neatly in line with the others. It was called Melee and pictured a group of men skirmishing with knives drawn. That needed no explanation.

The card after that was Companions, which showed a group of smiling men.

"Are they my brothers and father?" Temerity asked hopefully.

The woman pondered the card and said, "I think not. But they are a good omen."

Temerity furrowed her brow with disappointment and tried to make sense of the image. "There are four men on the card," she observed. "So are four-person teams better than two?"

The fortune teller tilted her head. "Four is the most common number of adventurers on a team."

"For humans," Half-pint said. "The wee folk prefer pairs, or some fae even prefer to go solo."

Temerity and the fortune teller exchanged glances, and the woman said to Temerity, "I believe your question about a two-person team has been answered."

Temerity gave Half-pint a smug look, but he avoided her gaze, his face impassive.

The fortune teller offered no further explanation and moved on to the next card.

It was the Sword, which displayed a single, shiny blade with a red grip.

"Cutting through," the fortune teller said simply, and looked up at them. "The final two cards are the outcome of the path of light. Are you ready?"

They nodded, and she turned over the last two cards: the Troll and the Ogre.

"Oh, excellent," Half-pint said, clapping his hands together, and the fortune teller grinned.

"Looks as though the path of light is the best course," the woman said. "That is, if you can discover the way out of the darkness and follow the positive signs."

Temerity did not know why Half-pint was so happy to have drawn the Troll and the Ogre. Both monsters looked ferocious and were covered with green gashes. The troll carried a battle-axe, and the ogre was consumed in flames. She was afraid to ask if they had to fight the monsters—she might lose her nerve and choose the path of darkness to escape such a fate.

The candles flickered, and an otherworldly presence seemed to hover around them.

"Very interesting," the fortune teller said, climbing to her feet. "Thank you for letting me read your fortunes. Best of luck to you. Do say hello to Elvin for me. Tell him he is overdue for a reading."

They said that they would, and gathered their things.

"Here, dear," the fortune teller said, handing Temerity a fresh pillar candle. "To help light your way in the deepest darkness." The woman removed a small vial from her robes, then bent over the candle and placed two drops of clear liquid near the wick. The snakes followed the droplets with their beady black eyes, their tongues lashing. "This is oil made from an infusion of white intelligence jewel," she said, corking the vial. "There is a single dose for each of you. Inhale the scent from the candle when you first light it. Use it wisely." She peered up at them to make sure they understood.

They nodded, and Temerity looked sidewise at Half-pint. Excitement shone in his eyes. They left the fortune teller's den, and an odd sense of sharpened awareness lingered with Temerity as she stepped out onto the dark street.

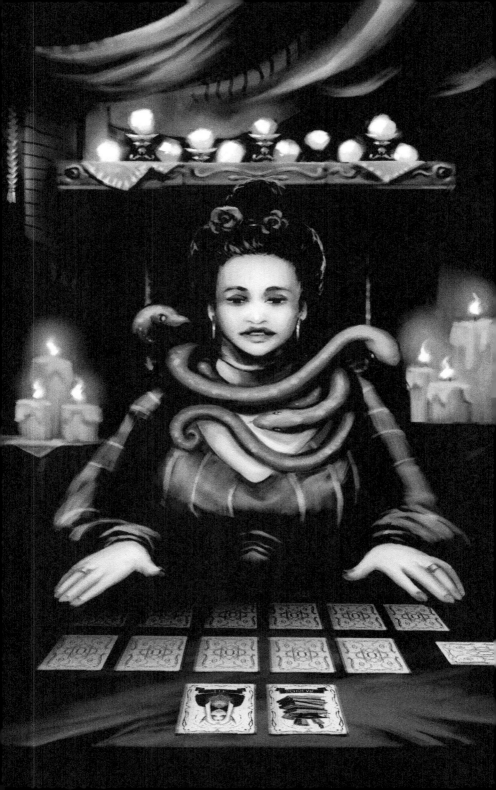

19

LEAVING THE INN

They enjoyed a late dinner at The Blue Jewel with Elvin and Gentry. Elvin asked several times if they would reconsider, but he understood that they wanted to beat the game and not play the inns forever, like Gentry had ended up doing.

She and Half-pint spent the rest of the evening upstairs in Temerity's chamber, sewing a long, hooded cloak for Temerity from the green woodland sylph silk.

"You need something to cover up those garish clothes," Half-pint told her, and she reminded him of his promise not to insult her taste in clothing. She saw the wisdom in wearing a cloak that wove into the shadows, however, and sylph silk seemed to blend into the surroundings more than other fabrics. She tried on her finished cloak, quite pleased with the flowing faery silk. Next, they polished their blades. She had wanted to polish her mining helmet, thinking it would look much nicer burnished to a bright sheen, but Half-pint pointed out that the tarnished helmets were perfect for dark alleyways.

In the morning, Half-pint gave Elvin one of the snake charmer's flutes and taught him how to play it to enchant the snakes. Being an elf, he caught on quickly, and soon the snakes in the pit were waving and weaving, mesmerized, while Temerity taught Gentry how to use the gripper to capture the snakes and retrieve eggs.

"I hope I can find another courier," Elvin said, after they had returned to the main floor for tea and pastries.

"Someone will come along," Half-pint assured him.

"What do you want in exchange for the flute and the snake gripper?" Elvin asked. "I'm sure you have something in mind." The elf gave them a kind smile. "Don't be shy. What strikes your fancy?" He waved his hands around the ornately decorated room filled with vases and figurines.

Temerity asked, "What about those faery lights on the balconies?"

"Sure, I can give you the string from your balcony," he said. "I know where to get more. You won't want to be drawing attention to yourselves however—not in the alleys."

"She likes sparkly things," Half-pint said.

She cast him a stern glare.

"Why are you looking at me like that? That's not an insult, is it? What I'd really like," Half-pint said, not waiting for a response, "is some maps." He turned his golden eyes to Gentry, who froze, holding his pastry in mid-air, halfway to his mouth.

Gentry cleared his throat and placed the pastry back on its plate. "Well ... um, h-hum. Interesting proposition." He dabbed his napkin nervously at his lips. "You understand ... as we discussed ... those maps are a scholarly pursuit. Not used for navigation so much as to detect patterns. To document the evolution of Dark Town. To try and decipher the dragons' methods and understand their awesome power."

"Surely you can spare a few parchments from your extensive collection," Half-pint said.

"Oh, no, no, no." Gentry shook his head. "They fit together like a puzzle. It has taken me years to map all the sectors. Although I am still missing some streets, to be sure. Plus, the dragons keep changing things. Very intriguing."

"How about I make a copy of a small number of parchments," Half-pint suggested. The yellow jewel had appeared in his hand, and he was turning it over and over with his thumb, as though idly fidgeting. "Not much to give in exchange for the snake flute and gripper, wouldn't you agree?"

"Elvin said if the dragons wanted us to use maps, they would have provided them," Temerity cut in, shifting her gaze between the human, the hobgoblin, and the elf.

"Yes, that is what I said, and what I meant," Elvin said, bobbling his head at Half-pint with disapproval.

"The dragons reward ingenuity and curiosity. Innovation and invention. Bravery and courage," Half-pint retorted, appearing wise in his silvery sylph-silk cloak and bearing the glimmering yellow jewel.

"They do?" Elvin asked.

"I thought we were supposed to follow the rules," Temerity pressed.

"Aha!" Half-pint said, brandishing the jewel in his raised palm as though it were a wizard's orb. "If ... and I stress *if* ... the dragons deigned to communicate the rules clearly, then we would surely follow them. However, seeing as how they prefer to teach us through trial and error, then it is up to us to discover hidden secrets of the game. Is it not?"

Temerity, Elvin, and Gentry gazed in confusion at one

another. Temerity shrugged, Elvin shook his head in consternation, and Gentry seemed to be considering Half-pint's reasoning.

"Just a few maps, you say?" Gentry asked. "You will copy them, and study them for their hidden esoteric meanings?"

"Yes, precisely," Half-pint said, looking suddenly erudite and earnest.

"Well ... um, h-hum. That could be ... yes, I think that would be possible."

With that settled, they finished their pastries and then cleared the table. Gentry produced several stacks of parchments and rolled-up scrolls and asked Half-pint what sector he was interested in.

"How about the alleys that surround the Dragon Gate?" Half-pint asked. "I always get lost there. I mean ... the dragons display their magnificence with the design of that area."

"Yes, indeed," Gentry said, leafing through a stack. "That sector is a masterpiece of obfuscation, a perplexing matrix of loops and dead-ends and interlocking octagons. It took me years to piece it together. And the dragons keep changing the shapes. One year the alleys were laid out in hexagons instead of octagons, and another year they were pentagons. I think the dragons enjoy tricking us." He looked delighted instead of frustrated, as Temerity would have been. "But last I checked, they were still octagons, so hopefully these maps are still current. Here we are." He pulled out a sheaf of parchments from the center of a tall stack.

Gentry and Half-pint selected a half dozen squares, then they sat down to copy the maps onto blank vellums while Temerity and Elvin fetched her faery lights.

Copying the detailed maps proved to be a time-consuming task, so Temerity took a leisurely bath and then a nap, happy for a day off. Late in the afternoon, she peeked into the dining room. Gentry and Half-pint were still hard at work, the hobgoblin standing on a chair and leaning intently over a parchment spread out on the table, quill in hand. Temerity and Elvin retreated into his sitting room, where he plaited her long hair into rows of elven braids and told her legends of elves sailing the heavens in sky chariots before the worlds split apart.

It took the mapmakers well into the evening to finish, so Temerity got to spend one last night in the fluffy, lacy feather-erbed. She stretched out between the luxurious sheets, afraid to ask how long it would take to run the alleys and where they would be sleeping from here on out.

◆

They sorted through their supplies, leaving their old, canvas travel sacks behind and carrying only the bare minimum of what they needed in their new adventurer's packs.

They left The Blue Jewel after breakfast—Elvin sending them off with a bundle of hard biscuits and dried fruit—and went directly to the cobbler's workshop. The gnome ushered them into the back and proudly unwrapped a pair of shiny red boots. The reptilian scales glimmered in a subtle, shadowy texture.

"Ooh," Temerity cooed. "I have never seen such gorgeous boots."

Half-pint rolled his eyes, but Temerity ignored him as she pulled off her workboots, handing them to the gnome, then pulled on the snakeskin boots. They slid on without laces or buckles, the rubbery leather clinging snugly to her calves. The soles were made of the black underbelly of the snakes, thick and rubbery.

"Good for gripping, and waterproof," the gnome said, and handed her matching gloves.

The red snakeskin gloves also had the black underbellies on the fingers and palms, and the red cuffs extended almost to her elbows. She twirled around in a circle. "What do you think?" she asked.

"Hideous," Half-pint said, as though it were a compliment, and the gnome beamed proudly.

She stooped over and gave the squat gnome a hug, the surprised creature awkwardly patting her back. "Thank you," she said.

"My pleasure," the gnome said, smoothing his beard, his face flushing a deep crimson.

They left the shop and stood outside in the dark, cobblestone street. A single streetlamp glimmered faintly on a far corner. Though it never seemed to rain here, Dark Town always had the feel of a dreary, drizzly night. The sky was perpetually overcast, blanketed by a murky gray haze that cast a faint glow, as though a moon were out there somewhere, trying to break through stormy skies. Black paving stones reflected what little light emanated from street lanterns or the occasional candle set in a window.

"Where do the alleys begin?" Temerity asked, clutching the red jewel in her pocket, the snakeskin gloves allowing tactile sensations to come through while providing a padded, firm grip. The jewel warmed her hand, and a surge of strength ran up her arm and pulsed through her body. She stood up straighter, and her muscles felt invigorated and primed for action.

"They're all over," Half-pint said, waving his hand around. "The alleys extend in every direction, surrounding the islands of inns and market squares and bordering the wide thoroughfares that connect the inn zones. If you stay on the main streets, it's pretty safe, but venture too far off into the dark side roads, and you've entered the alleys."

"Okay," she said, exhaling. "Where do we start?"

He pointed to a side street on their left. "According to Gentry's maps, this way will eventually take us to the Dragon Gate."

"What is the Dragon Gate?"

"The entrance to the Ogre's Eyes, the final challenge of Level One. The first big boss."

She was both nervous and excited, all the whispers she'd overheard in the tavern throughout the years beginning to make sense.

Half-pint opened his adventurer's pack and pulled out the silver sylph-silk robe, then shouldered the pack and draped the robe over it and his leather armor, the pack creating a small, trollish hump. He donned his coal-black helm and raised the silk hood over it, then glanced meaningfully at Temerity.

"You want me to hide my sumptuous clothes and stunning new boots?"

"You mean your excessively gaudy attire? Yes, precisely."

She scowled at him.

"What?" he asked innocently. "We survived Elvin's snake pit, so don't you think my promise has been fulfilled?"

She exhaled loudly but retrieved her forest-green sylph-silk cloak and draped it over her gold velvet waistcoat and satin pants. The long robe easily covered the small backpack and nearly reached the ground, floating just above the grimy cobblestones and concealing her velvet and satin garments and shiny new boots. She donned her helmet and pulled up the green hood, clasping the robe closed at her throat. "Happy now?" she asked.

He nodded with a satisfied smirk. "Much better."

Temerity held her tongue, searching for her red jewel through the side-slash of the robe, and strode at Half-pint's side as they headed away from the main thoroughfare, their sylph-silk cloaks blending into the shadows.

20

RUNNING THE ALLEYS

It did not take long until they found themselves in a maze of dark alleys. Abandoned tenements and shuttered warehouses lined the narrow streets. Gaping windows, their glass long gone, stared after them like hollow eyes. They padded across broken cobblestones, Temerity's snake soles making no sound and Half-pint's bare feet as quiet as his cat paws. The rank odor of urine marked shadowed stairwells, and she pressed a square of linen to her nose.

Soon, every streetlamp was dark, no one having bothered to refill the oil and light them. Only the hazy mist overhead offered a ghoulish gray glow, revealing decrepit buildings leaning over black, basalt cobblestones.

"Where is everyone?" she asked in barely a whisper.

"Hiding. Lurking. I don't know. We'll come upon fellow adventurers soon enough. In the meantime, let's keep our eye out for other opportunities. Such as this." Half-pint led her through an open doorway.

"Do you think this is a good idea?" she asked, hovering at the threshold of the pitch-dark building.

"We must take risks to advance in the game," he said. "Shush." They stood stone still, listening. The silence was deep and unbroken, reminding her of the tunnel labyrinth.

He drew out his blue jewel, casting an eerie glow. A rickety wooden staircase rose in front of them.

He motioned for her to follow. She trod carefully through the entryway and climbed the stairs behind him, keeping to the edges where the rotting wood was sturdier and hopping over steps that were missing entirely.

"What are we doing?" she asked.

"Looking for loot," he whispered, over his shoulder. They reached the top of the stairs. "People stash jewels and weapons if they have extra, hoping to retrieve them next time through, if they should die unexpectedly. Or sometimes, you come upon the remains of someone who died, like the guy you got your favorite clothes from."

He led her down a short hallway and into a room. Aside from an old, warped table, the room was empty. They explored a series of chambers, then climbed another set of stairs to the third floor. These rooms were smaller, but aside from a few pieces of dusty furniture, they were empty. Half-pint paused in the hallway and peered up at the ceiling. A square section appeared to be an attic hatch.

"Let me stand on your shoulder," he said, and she gave him a hand up. Balancing on one of her shoulders, he took the pickaxe from his belt and pushed up at the square. It moved, and he pushed it aside. Next thing she knew, he was a cat pouncing from her shoulder up into the attic. Whenever he transformed into a cat, everything he had been wearing or carrying as a hobgoblin disappeared. In this case, that included the blue dragon jewel, plunging them into total darkness. Suddenly, he was a hobgoblin again, brandishing the glowing jewel. He set the jewel on the attic floor and lay on his belly, leaning down and dangling the pickaxe over her head.

"Grab it and climb up here," he said.

She peered warily at the pickaxe, not sure he could hold her weight. She grabbed the metal crossbar anyway and tried to pull herself up, scrabbling at the wall with her toes. The rubbery soles of her snakeskin boots allowed her to easily scale the wall, pushing herself up while Half-pint pulled. Soon, she was crouching in the low-ceilinged attic. Cobwebs crisscrossed the dusty space, and the floor was littered with mouse droppings and bat guano.

"I don't see any treasure stash," she said, glancing around the empty attic and squinting up into the rafters, searching for spiders and bats.

"Patience, Miss Temerity," Half-pint said. "We just got started. Follow me."

They crept through the attic to the far wall, where a window had been removed. She peered out the square opening at a rooftop not far below.

"Come on," Half-pint said, and climbed through the window, dropping down onto the pitched roof.

She dropped down after him and stepped carefully across the slate tiles, sure-footed with her rubbery snakeskin soles. Half-pint transformed into a cat and trotted along the ridge line. They climbed in and out of more open attic windows and along a web of rooftops. This route was evidently well-traveled, littered with a trail of discarded items of little value and empty chests with broken locks hinting at past adventurers. Half-pint scampered ahead in his feline form, and Temerity held up her orange jewel to light the way.

They ended up back on the street and entered another building through a ground-floor window. The building had been grand at one time, perhaps in an earlier generation of the game when people lived in this neighborhood. Temerity guessed it had been an inn, featuring a spacious foyer leading to a wide staircase. A once-ornate chandelier hung from a crumbling plaster ceiling at the base of the stairs. Most of the chandelier's crystals and candles had been plundered, leaving bare metal loops and stubs of dusty wax.

They searched the ground-floor rooms, finding nothing of interest, then headed upstairs. The staircase was missing several steps, but the banister was intact, so Half-pint hopped up onto the handrail. Temerity climbed up onto it as well, using her rubbery boots and gloves to scale the narrow railing to the second floor. The third floor was a garret, accessed by narrow wooden stairs.

At the far end of a garret room, an open window led to the window of the next building via a plank. Temerity peered down at a narrow alley three stories below, prickles nettling her skin. She reached into her pocket for her red jewel, but Half-pint was already halfway across the plank, loping on silent cat paws. She held her breath and crawled on hands and knees across the sturdy board into the next building's attic. They crossed the small room and exited into a short hallway that led to another room, but they stopped short. Half-pint transformed into his hobgoblin form and held a finger to his lips. Orange light leaked out from underneath the door, and the faint sound of men talking reached Temerity's ears.

A floorboard creaked under Temerity's foot, and she pocketed her jewel, leaving only the slash of orange to light the dark hall.

"What was that?" a voice asked. "I heard a creak."

"It's an old building. It's probably just settling," another voice answered.

"I thought I saw a flash of light," a third voice chimed in.

"We'd better check," a fourth voice said.

Temerity and Half-pint turned around and crept on tiptoes into the first room, but boots trampled loudly behind them. Breaking into a run, they dove through the window and clambered over the plank. Half-pint slid to a stop inside the next building, and he and Temerity pulled at the plank. The heavy board swung loose and fell to the cobblestones below.

"You'll have hell to pay!" a man yelled at them from the facing window, waving a fist with a red jewel clutched in it.

Temerity and Half-pint turned and ran down the stairs and then slid down the banister to the main floor and jumped out the window to the street. Men burst through the front door of the neighboring building and chased after them, yelling curses, their voices echoing through the silent streets. The noise brought out more adventurers, and soon a pack of men were chasing them through the dark alleyways.

They pulled up their sylph-silk hoods and ducked into a narrow side street and around a corner as voices shouted at one another, splitting up in search of them. Temerity's heart was hammering in her chest, and if goosebumps were cautionary prickles from the orange jewel, then every direction was a trap.

"Here," Half-pint whispered, and hooked the pickaxe claw through a metal grate at their feet and pulled it loose, sliding it to the side. A gaping back hole stared up at them, followed by a foul odor. "You first," the hobgoblin whispered insistently.

Shouts drew closer. Temerity knelt on the cobblestones, and Half-pint's blue jewel illuminated a rusted ladder leading down into the darkness. She climbed down a few rungs and

Half-pint climbed down after her, extinguishing the jewel and sliding the grate into place above them. Footsteps ran by, and Temerity climbed further down into the hole until her feet hit water. She felt around with her toe and found hard stone not far below the water's surface, then gingerly descended into the muck.

"Is that water?" Half-pint asked, clinging to the rung at her shoulder.

"Yes, if you can call it that." She held her sleeve to her face and tried to breathe through the linen weave.

"Do you mind if I ride on your pack?" he asked, and she imagined a pleading grimace on his face. "You have those fancy waterproof boots, after all," he said in an overly sweet voice.

"You mean my *hideous* boots?"

"Your beautiful, gorgeous, exotic, *amazing* boots." His long goblin fingers and toes clasped onto her shoulder and helmet until he found a perch on top of her backpack.

She felt her way along the sewer until Half-pint dared unveil the blue jewel, shielding most of the light with his hand. It cast enough of a glow to see that they were in a long stone tunnel with sewage meandering slowly down the center. She tried to keep to one side of the passageway, where there was less of the stinky muck, and crept along, turning onto side branches until they determined they were far enough away from their pursuers to brave the surface roads again.

They found another ladder and sewer grate and climbed out onto a dark street. All was quiet. They replaced the grate and snuck along the walls of buildings, clinging to shadows with their sylph cloaks drawn tightly around them. They wandered aimlessly, looking for a place to hide out and rest. Nothing looked appealing. Minutes stretched into hours, and the alleys and buildings all began to look the same.

"Can't we take a break from this alley nonsense and find an inn?" she whispered.

"We could," he said, "but look."

They had rounded a corner, and Temerity followed his gesture. It was the same decrepit inn they had escaped from earlier.

"We must have gone in a big circle," she said, under her breath.

"That happens a lot here," he replied.

They skulked slowly down the alleyway. "Look," he whispered. "The plank is back." Sure enough, the two small garret windows were connected again by the plank. "Those guys must be back in their attic hideaway," Half-pint murmured. "That's one of their escape paths, so that they don't get trapped up there."

They continued stalking down the alley past the building where the men were hiding out and located the window of the attic room where they had found them last. The window was not accessible by any roof or facing window, since the building stood on a corner overlooking a wider street.

"I have an idea," Half-pint whispered, pulling her into the shadow of an abandoned wagon. "I'll go in and distract them while you climb up that drainpipe to their room and see what loot you can grab."

She scowled and inspected the outer wall of the building more closely. A rusted drainpipe descended from the roof, passing next to the attic window. "That's a terrible idea," she whispered. "I can't climb up there."

"Why not?" he asked. "I'll bet those sticky snake boots and gloves will let you scale that wall, no problem."

"I don't like this 'running the alleys' game," she whispered. "Why can't we go back and find another inn? I like playing the inns a lot better."

"How long did we spend doing that? Weeks," he said, answering his own question. "Besides, we need to practice fighting and evading enemies or we'll never get past the mobs, never mind beat the boss."

"How long do we have to spend in the alleys?" she asked, longing for Avon's fern-grotto pool and the featherbed in Elvin's guestroom.

"As long as it takes to get two more dragon jewels. It'll be a lot faster than working another inn, I can guarantee that."

"If we survive," she muttered.

"As I told you, we have to take risks to progress in the game. Running and hiding won't get us anywhere."

She sighed. "Okay, have it your way."

Half-pint nodded confidently. "Hide under the wagon until I lure them out of the room."

"How will I know when that is?" she asked.

"You'll know," he said with a crooked grin. "Meet me back here after." Then he ghosted into the shadows and was gone.

21

LOOT

Temerity crouched under the wagon, clasping the orange jewel in her pocket. It was pulsing in her hand. What was the point of a premonition jewel if she was going to defy its warning? She scowled, annoyed that Half-pint was so insistent on finding trouble—perhaps she would be better off by herself. She immediately dismissed that vagrant thought. Without him, she would probably have taken a few turns around the beginning of the tunnel labyrinth and given up before even finding the runes and ladders, never mind making it all the way to Dark Town. She would be safely back home right now, working at the Tin Roof and serving adventurers braver than herself.

She waited in the darkness, listening.

A faint trampling of boots came from the open window three stories overhead. Then silence. She waited for the clatter of the plank hitting the pavement, but it did not come. A feline shriek split the air, then banging and thumping. A streak of fur shot along the pavement. Four adventurers raced after it at a full run. A few more adventurers appeared out of neighboring buildings, sprinting after an unknown quarry. Footsteps faded into the distance, and Temerity peered around at ground level. The streets were empty and silent.

She crept out from under the wagon and grabbed the drainage pipe, pulling herself up by her hands and finding toeholds on the stone wall. The gloves and boots were as the cobbler had promised—good for gripping—and she quickly scaled the building and climbed in through the window.

The attic was dark—there were no dragon jewels for her to loot. She pulled the orange jewel out from her pocket and scanned the room, her heart thudding. Packs and belongings sat where the adventurers had left them. Temerity rifled through them, but they only contained a few articles of clothing and some food. She grabbed a bundle of meat pies and a full waterskin, shoving them into her backpack, then inspected items scattered on a makeshift table, finally finding something interesting. A small, spike-like dagger sat next to a leather sheath, a pair of thin straps, and a whetstone. She sheathed the blade and shoved it all into a pocket, then examined a small shield hanging from a wall hook. It was a simple steel buckler, round with a central handle on the concave side. She strapped it to the outside of her pack and searched for anything else useful. Finding nothing, she peered out through the window to make sure the way was clear, then climbed out the window and used the drainpipe to clamber down to the street.

She hid under the wagon, eating meat pies. After some time, adventurers began straggling back to their hideouts, disappearing into dark buildings. The four adventurers she had looted from strutted by, and she feared by their demeanor that they had been successful in catching Half-pint. Panic gripped her throat. Did they kill him? Was he suffering in some dark alleyway? Maybe she should strike out and search for him, but how would she find him? She hunkered down and waited. If he was still alive, he would make his way back here eventually.

A minor fuss erupted up above when the adventurers discovered they'd been duped and robbed, but silence soon returned and no one came out to the street to search for her.

Worry crept in as time passed and still no Half-pint. What would she do without him? She could end up lost in the alleys for ages, chased by gangs of adventurers. Could she find a homing spike before she was killed? She tried to calm her racing pulse, not ready to give up yet. Minutes ticked by, then hours. She clung to her red jewel for strength, trying to recall Gentry's maps and the nearest town square with a homing spike. She vaguely recalled several of the landmarks scattered across various sectors of Dark Town, placed at the center of town squares and serving as central hubs of inn neighborhoods, which in turn were surrounded by alleys that expanded out in concentric webs until they merged together in a random network with no discernible pattern. She should have paid more attention to the scholar's puzzle of parchments.

She twisted herself around under the wagon, trying to find a more comfortable position, when her elbow scraped against cold metal. It was a sewer grate. That would explain the stench. Happy for a distraction from her worries, she spent the next few minutes trying to lift the grate while crouching under a wagon, with no tools. She finally tied the rope around a bar of the grate, looped the rope over the wagon's rear axle, and managed to lift the grate enough to push it aside with her foot.

The sewer was dark and she dared not bring out a jewel, so she stashed her rope and felt around for a ladder. Finding a rusted rung, she climbed down into the hole until she reached the bottom. The sewer water was not deep, and she felt along the wall until she was far enough away from the entrance to produce the orange jewel from her pocket, illuminating the dank space.

Only a steady *drip drip drip* broke the heavy silence. She followed the tunnel, hoping to find some loot for her efforts. Not finding anything after several twists and turns, and afraid of getting lost, she turned back and headed for the ladder.

Movement up ahead froze her in her tracks. She reached for her boning knife, and a squat shape stepped into the light of her jewel. It was Half-pint, motioning for her to stay silent and glancing furtively over his shoulder.

"You scared me," she hissed, her fright quickly turning to joyous relief at the sight of the disheveled little creature.

"A pair of adventurers are after me," he whispered. "Good thing you found this tunnel. Come on."

They hurried through the sprawling sewer network, startling a pack of rats who ran down a side branch and scrambled up an ancient set of steep stone stairs.

They followed the rats towards the murky gray of aboveground and pushed through a grate and into an enclosed yard where the rats scattered and disappeared into a crumbled stone building. It was an old warehouse that had once been mainly windows and was now a skeleton of wooden beams and mounds of debris.

The building creaked and moaned. Hoots and howls of a band of adventurers sounded from beyond the warehouse, reminding her of a pack of coyotes baying over a kill. She fled across the yard and over a stone wall, with Half-pint fast on her heels. They ran down a narrow lane and burst onto a main thoroughfare. A street fight sounded from around a corner—screams and jeers and the clang of blades. Temerity and Half-pint sprinted across the road and into another neighborhood of abandoned shops and inns and what had once been grand homes. They slowed to a creep, clinging to silent shadows. Temerity led the way over a stone wall, through a courtyard, and over another wall.

She leaned against the stone wall and slumped down to the ground, winded. Half-pint collapsed beside her, panting loudly.

They were in the back courtyard of a dark building. Her orange jewel was cold and still, and she trusted that the building was empty. The yard was paved with slate and had a carved marble bench and table, still intact and relatively clean. She climbed to her feet and explored the yard. It had once been a garden, with trellises and dirt, but no sign of living plants. A little shack stood in a corner, and she opened the door on squeaky hinges, holding up her orange jewel. It was a proper outhouse, musty and unused in recent times, with a smooth wooden seat and a cover painted with faded roses. It made her unduly happy—much better than squatting in an alleyway.

Back outside, she lifted the handle of a well pump and pushed it down. A spurt of brown water splashed into a small ditch with a drainage grate. She continued pumping until the water ran clear. She smelled and tasted it—it seemed to be clean. She proceeded to wash her face and hands with her pot of soap, rinsed off her boots and gloves, and drank her fill.

"What did you find in the attic?" Half-pint asked, finally rising and tasting the water for himself.

"Attic? Oh, yeah," she said. They sat together at the table, and she pulled out the dagger and buckler. "No dragon jewels," she said, disappointed that she had not found much, but his yellow eyes gleamed as he inspected the buckler.

"This is great," he said, practically purring. "Everyone needs shields. We need to find one for you. But this is perfect for me." He stood on the bench and held up the buckler. It was nearly as big as he was tall. "What luck," he exclaimed. "You normally don't find shields this early in the game. Good haul. And what's this?"

She handed him the blade. "A dagger."

"Not just any dagger," he replied, slipping it out of its sheath. "This is a sleeve dagger. Brilliant. Give me your arm."

She stretched out her arm and he tightened the straps around her forearm and wrist. The bone handle had a little knob on the end that she was able to grab with her fingertips to unsheathe the blade single-handed. She practiced until she could draw it out in one smooth motion, brandishing the narrow dagger at the hobgoblin.

"Very handy for close-quarter combat," he said. "From your weapons so far, looks like you're headed to become a Melee fighter. A Blade."

"Really?" she asked, shaking down her sleeve so that it hid the dagger. "And what are you?"

"Probably a Healer, seeing as that's the end-game jewel I carry. Not sure what type of Healer yet, exactly. But I'll need to do a bit of everything—play Attack and Shield, as well as Heal."

"Do we need to leave something behind for the dragons, if we want to take these?" she asked, unsheathing the dagger again.

Half-pint shook his head. "No, I don't think so. We left stuff behind at Elvin's, so we have some dragon credit, I think. I left behind my good carrying sack, a garden trowel, and a hammer and nails. Should be enough for this shield." He lifted the buckler again, examining its dings and scratches. "What did you leave behind?"

"I left my big backpack, my pa's cap, my serving apron, my work gloves, and a tin of tea."

"More than enough for that dagger," Half-pint said. "Elvin will make good use of an apron and tea, I would imagine."

"Oh, and I got these," she said, showing him the meat pies and waterskin.

"Great," he said, and quickly gobbled down a pie.

She put away the food, and Half-pint continued admiring his buckler. Temerity unrolled her blanket, lay down on the bench, and fell fast asleep.

22

THE CHALLENGE ROAD

They ventured deeper and deeper into the maze of alleys and came upon a noisy, raucous strip with bands of adventurers crowding the wide street, a jarring contrast to the silent, slinking shadows of the alleys.

"Is this an inn sector?" Temerity asked, her jaw dropping at the fearless display of dragon jewels and weapons as a parade of adventurers swaggered down the center of the crowded street, chests and chins jutting out and glowing jewels adorning them as though it were a New Year's festival.

"No," Half-pint said, pulling her back into a shadow and drawing his sylph cloak closed. She did the same and stared at the circus-like displays. Some adventurers juggled dragon jewels, while others showed off with backflips and synchronized sword forms. A group of four women were outfitted in steel armor and carried a collection of sharp, pointy weapons, and glared at anyone whose gaze lingered on them for too long. One group of ten were walking slowly down the lantern-lit street in a pyramid formation, standing on each other's shoulders, with four stocky men holding down the base of four tiers. The lone adventurer at the top was a diminutive dwarf, balancing on the raised palms of two fine-boned elves below him.

"This is a Challenge Road," Half-pint explained. "People get tired of all the sneaking about and gather like this to challenge each other to fights. The victor takes the spoils. It's a quick way to get your dragon jewels, or to die."

Behind the pyramid, strutted a band of four men, displaying their jewels openly. One wore two red jewels strapped to his wrist on his sword hand. One wore two blue jewels on his shield hand. One wore an orange jewel fastened to a scarf wrapped around his forehead, and a second orange jewel hung on a leather sling near his heart. The fourth man carried a green jewel in each hand.

"Why are they wearing their jewels like that?" she asked.

"Dragon jewels are more powerful when held or worn close to the body, as opposed to carried in loose pockets or in backpacks. Also, you can only use a maximum of three. If you happen to collect more than three, you need to wear the ones you want to activate and stash the others so that it's clear to the dragons which you intend to use. If you try to be tricky and use more than three or switch jewels mid-fight, all your jewels become de-activated until the fight is over and you decide to play by the rules. Switching mid-fight is not allowed."

"So everyone is limited to three activated jewels per fight," she said, and Half-pint nodded. "What about your green end-game jewel?"

"That doesn't count. I can use my end-game jewel anytime, in addition to the three."

"What if you had more than one end-game jewel, like your son?"

"Then I'd be very powerful, indeed. You are allowed to use as many end-game jewels as you can collect. But don't worry, it's rare to encounter advanced players in Dark Town. They generally speed through the lower levels to get to the Tower as soon as possible.

"Those four men are working as a team," Half-pint pointed out. "The one with the blue jewels is acting as the Shield. The red one is playing Attack—a Melee Blade, from the looks of his swords and knives. The green one is the Healer. The orange one is a Scout, which is a waste in a situation like this. Orange is useful if your main tactic is evasion, or if you're in total darkness or enemy territory, or something like that. But in a place like this, everything is out in the open."

"How come they're only carrying two jewels each, instead of three?" she asked.

Half-pint peered sideways at her. "Because, Miss Temerity, anyone with three jewels is headed towards the Dragon Gate to level up. It's risky to linger in the alleys any longer than necessary. You could die at any time and lose everything you've worked so hard to get. It's a vulnerable time when you have three jewels. You become a prime target for looting."

"Oh," she said. "What if they are staying together, though? Maybe not everyone has three yet."

He shrugged. "You have a point. Some members could have three jewels already but are trying to outfit everyone else on their team, to level up together."

"Together, like us," she said with a grin.

"Correct," he said, returning her smile.

"But wait. Why would you ever have to show the dragons which three you're using, if you only have three?" she asked, confused.

"Sometimes you end up with more than three, out of sheer luck. Or greed. Or because you want a certain color. Or you want options. But you can only use three in any fight. Once we move up to the other levels, we'll start upgrading our jewels. Selecting three you want to specialize in from the beginning will get you the most powerful jewels, although some people diversify as they go. I'll explain more when we get there."

Another band of four men marched into the street behind the pyramid, blocking the path of the bejeweled band. The two groups stood facing one another.

"Alright, a challenge," Half-pint said, rubbing his palms together. "The challengers will win."

"How can you tell?" Temerity asked, examining the new band, who looked very sure of themselves.

"Because of the wasted guy with the orange jewels on the other team," Half-pint said. "The challengers have chosen an aggressive formation."

Those men wore their jewels on their belts. One man wore two blue jewels and carried a sword in each hand. The second and third men each wore two red jewels, and together they brandished a sword, battle-axe, halberd, and war hammer. The fourth man wore one green jewel and one red jewel and carried a sword and a bottle of potion.

The challenger with the blue jewels and swords stepped forward, drawing in the Shield and the Attack from the first crew. The blue-jeweled swordsman struck first, and a fight broke out with a roar and clatter, steel flashing and sparks flying as metal met metal. Soon, metal met flesh, and the second band was on the first like hounds to a fox. The Healer from the first band was frantically trying to heal his bandmates, when he fell to the battle-axe. His head rolled away from his body, blood splattering the cobblestones, and soon it was all over.

Temerity had barely taken two breaths before the winning band began pillaging the dragon jewels of the dead men, who disintegrated into shadows and left the game before her eyes.

The victorious crew claimed their prizes and pranced about, holding up their glowing jewels and howling at the sky before running off into a dark alley. The onlookers fell onto the remaining gear of the deceased like vultures, the dwarf tumbling down from his perch and the elves flipping through the air to join the mass of adventurers in the street picking through clothing and weapons. Scuffles broke out over loot, and soon skirmishes were flaring up all around.

Half-pint grabbed Temerity by the cloak and pulled her into a side street, and they fled.

23

YELLOW JEWELS

This sector of alleys was crawling with adventurers, more than the others they had crossed. It was not uncommon to encounter marauding bands at every turn. Temerity and Half-pint nimbly avoided them by ducking into doorways or standing stone-still in their sylph cloaks, or running away and climbing walls, then racing over rooftops and through warrens of attics.

One neighborhood was infested with archers and crossbowmen staked out in busted-out windows overlooking the streets, raining down arrows and bolts on anyone who dared enter their territory. Temerity and Half-pint quickly reversed course and fled the area, not wanting to serve as target practice for a bunch of overly enthusiastic Range Attacks. At least with Melee fighters, you could look them in the eye and anticipate their next move. Fortunately, most adventurers preferred swords or other close-range weapons and to engage with their adversaries face to face.

They came upon one such group after Temerity's orange

jewel warned them to turn back but Half-pint insisted that they confront whatever lurked around the next corner.

"We have to practice," he stressed, for the third time that day.

"You mean, *I* need to practice," she said wryly.

"You've done well so far, to be honest. But you're new," he said. "I failed the first level twice before I was successful. You've already made it farther than I did the first time."

That did little to quell the anxiety that made her jump at every shadow. The orange jewel didn't help, stinging her hand and vibrating insistently whenever she held it. It seemed every street held some danger the jewel wanted her to avoid.

When they turned the corner, they nearly bumped into a band of four. Both groups drew up short and stepped back a pace. She quickly assessed the jewels carried by the members of the opposing band—two each, worn strapped to their forearms—and the roles they played. A double-red Attack, a double-blue Shield, a double-green Healer, and a red and blue combo, which made a lot of sense to her, for strike and parry.

She and Half-pint were woefully outmatched and still carried their jewels in pockets—or if they held them in their hands, it did not allow them to wield a weapon in that hand. And their assortment of jewels was not good. They had one red, one orange, one blue, one yellow, and the end-game green jewel. What good was healing if they both were killed? What good was premonition when the threat was right in front of them? What good was charm against a steel blade?

But Half-pint was not deterred—neither was he fighting or running. Temerity stood behind him, waiting to see what he was up to.

"Jolly good evening to you," the hobgoblin said, giving the

foursome a little bow. He held the yellow jewel in one hand, blue in the other.

"How do you know it's evening?" one of the adventurers growled. "It's always hella dark in this cursed town."

"It is indeed," Half-pint agreed pleasantly. "That's why we must all make it to Level Three, the Pastoral Lands, as soon as the dragons allow. There, the fertile land is bathed in golden light, day and night. So bright that you might long for these dark, soothing streets."

"I highly doubt it," another adventurer said. "Hand over your jewels, and we'll be on our way to those Pastoral Lands you speak of. But first there's the Swamp, right?" he asked, and Temerity began to suspect they were first-timers.

"What's the Swamp like?" another asked, lowering his axe.

"Brighter skies than this, but still overcast," Half-pint replied. "Instead of cobblestone alleys, there are endless waterways and bogs you can sink into and never climb out of. Instead of buildings, there's a tree canopy. Instead of only other adventurers, you'll find frightful creatures who slither out of the water or down from the trees."

The expressions on the adventurers' faces went from curious to gloomy.

"But that's how you'll learn what you need to know to beat the big boss in Level Two. A fearsome serpent."

"Give us your jewels and stop yapping," a heavyset man with a war hammer and two red jewels said.

"Our jewels won't help you," Half-pint replied, in a conversational tone. "To beat the final challenge, you need strength and intelligence. You already have plenty of red jewels, but what you lack are white jewels. For cunning. You must outsmart the trolls and ogre if you hope to beat them."

"We don't have a yellow one," another of them remarked, pointing his hairy chin at Half-pint's yellow jewel.

"Yellow dragon jewels will do you no good against trolls and ogres," Half-pint said. "They're only good against faeries, and you won't run into any faeries in the wild, until the Swamp. But you can't get there unless you kill the ogre. The best thing is to go to the Challenge Road. Train against other fighters as strong as yourselves, and maybe you'll be lucky enough to win a white jewel."

"We've been to the Challenge Road, early on, but we can't find it again," one of them said. "Where is it?"

"There are several of them. The one we just came from is several blocks that way," Half-pint said, pointing over his shoulder.

"Give us your jewels, and we'll let you go without killing you," the oafish man with the war hammer said. He squinted at Temerity. "What is a young lady doing in a town like this? And what in dragon's name are you wearing? Never mind. Show me your jewels."

"She doesn't have any jewels yet," Half-pint said, rolling the yellow jewel around in his palm. "She's a newbie."

Temerity let go of the jewels she had been clutching in her pockets and withdrew her hands, showing them her empty palms.

"But she does have fresh meat pies, although I'm sure you're not hungry." Half-pint eyed the burly man and a tall, husky farm lad whose belly spilled over his belt.

The burly one licked his overhanging moustache and exchanged glances with his bandmates.

Temerity dug into her pack and held out the bundle of meat pies. Greedy hands reached for them, and the pies went directly into four hungry mouths.

"Best of luck to you. See you in the Swamp," Half-pint said with a parting bow, and ushered Temerity into an alleyway. They took off at a run, dashing into a haphazard array of narrow streets, turning this way and that before finally stopping to catch their breath.

"A hobgoblin with a yellow dragon jewel is not to be underestimated," Half-pint said with a proud smirk, and Temerity had to agree.

24

MATCHED

They hid out in an attic and fastened the red and blue jewels onto leather bands to wear around their wrists. The yellow and orange jewels worked fine handheld, for now, they determined, but the battle jewels needed to be worn properly if she and Half-pint were going to go up against teams of adventurers. Temerity fastened the red jewel around her right wrist, and the sleeve dagger was on her left. Half-pint wore the blue jewel on his left wrist, the hand he used for his shield, leaving his right hand free to wield his meat cleaver.

"The next adventurers we meet, we will fight," Half-pint said firmly. "No more running."

"No more charming?" Temerity teased.

"Well, charm is warfare of a sort, is it not?" he asked with a glint in his eyes.

"I don't think this ogre creature that you keep warning everyone about will be hypnotized by a fast-talking hobgoblin with a yellow jewel."

"No, I suppose not," Half-pint agreed, and began sharpening his blades.

Later that day, they stumbled into a dead-end—the sort of dead-end they normally avoided. But this time, they were unlucky, or perhaps Temerity had been ignoring the orange jewel at their peril, because when they reached the end of the alley and turned around, two strapping fellows were standing there, smiling in an unfriendly way.

"Well, well. What have we here?" one of them drawled, twirling a knife in his hand. "A wench and her pet rat."

Temerity traded glances with Half-pint and then peered from the corner of her eye at the wall at her shoulder, wondering if she and Half-pint could scale it. Then she recalled their agreement to fight, and returned her attention to the adventurers, who were smirking cockily. One had two blue jewels strapped to his wrists and lunged at them with a sword and shield.

Half-pint easily deflected the sword blow with his buckler, and Temerity kicked at the adventurer's kneecap. The man swung his shield at her, but she ducked and got up under it and went for his throat with her sleeve dagger. He was quick, however, and struck her wrist with the side of his sword hand, jarring her bones and sending the dagger flying. Half-pint hacked at the man's thighs, but the adventurer met the blade of the meat cleaver with his sword, and Temerity turned to confront the second man, who came at her with a knife in one hand and brass knuckles on the other. A red jewel glinted from each of his forearms, and he swung his brass fist at her head. Half-pint leapt up with his buckler, intercepting the blow. She and the hobgoblin traded places, and she took the Shield warrior, who, despite his bulk and fancy sword, had a weak arm. She tightened the helmet strap under her chin as she danced away, then lunged in for an attack. She could not get past his shield but easily parried his strikes with her sword, anticipating his feints and thrusts. As much as she tried, she could not get past his defenses to land a blow on him, the blue jewels on his wrists glowing brightly at every clash. She switched to her sledgehammer and started pounding at his shield, driving him back a pace. Half-pint was spinning and kicking at the shins of the Attack, who was unable to connect with the whirling goblin.

The four of them battered at one another until Temerity's arms became wooden and the two adventurers were grunting and cursing. Half-pint hopped back and forth, still kicking at the Attack's legs, playing with him.

"Call it a draw," Half-pint said, leaping back a pace and throwing a crossbow bolt, which stuck in the man's bicep.

"Ow! Stop that!" the man yelled, pulling it out as another bolt bounced off his leather body armor.

"Where'd you get those bolts?" Temerity asked, backing away from her sweating opponent.

The two adventurers took a step back, and the Shield wiped at his brow while the Attack dabbed at the spot of blood on his sleeve.

"I picked them up from behind that trash bin yesterday," Half-pint replied. "Remember?"

"Oh," Temerity said, stooping to retrieve her sleeve dagger and Half-pint's bolt. "I thought you meant *bolts,* as in, you know, like *nails.*"

"No. Look, I got half a dozen." He showed her a handful of stubby metal arrows.

She peered at the metal shafts, and the Shield leaned in for a look.

"You need a crossbow for those," the Attack said.

"Yeah, I know," Half-pint replied. "But if I had one, that leather armor you're wearing wouldn't have stopped it. Not at this range."

"Who're you to criticize my armor?" the man asked. "Yours is the same as mine."

Half-pint glanced down at his leather chest guard and shrugged. "Mine was custom made."

They continued bantering as they walked out of the alley together.

"Nice sparring with you," Half-pint said, holding his yellow jewel in one hand and extending his other for a handshake.

"Likewise," the Attack said, returning the other bolt to Half-pint.

They shook hands all around.

"You fight pretty good, for a girl," the Shield said, gripping her hand gently. "You take care out there, now. You hear?"

"Yes, sir," she said with a grin. "You need a red jewel," she added. "Your sword arm is weak."

"I know," he said sheepishly, rubbing his shoulder. "Some brute nearly tore my arm off a few days ago. It ain't been right since. You hear that?" The adventurer attempted to rotate his arm, and Temerity detected a grating, crackling sound.

"That doesn't sound very good," she said. "Hey, Half-pint, this guy has a hurt shoulder. Could you maybe ... you know ..."

"Huh?" Half-pint asked, breaking off his conversation. "Injured shoulder, you say? Let me see." The man lowered himself onto one knee at Temerity's encouragement, and Half-pint kneaded the man's shoulder and then pressed his green jewel to it. The man's face, which had been twisted in a permanent sneer, relaxed into a broad smile.

"Well, I'll be," the man said, rolling his shoulder. "That is ... wow ... the pain is completely gone. Look, Lucas, I can move my arm again." He stood up and grinned at his partner, swinging his arm in a large circle. The man moved his arm every which way and then unsheathed his sword, slashing and thrusting at empty air and playfully challenging Temerity to a rematch. After going on about how it was a miracle, he leaned over and vigorously shook Half-pint's hand with both of his until Temerity was afraid the hobgoblin would start bouncing across the cobblestones.

They parted ways with promises of sharing a pitcher of ale back in the real world, and Temerity and Half-pint went in search of a hide-out to take a rest and have a meal of dried snake meat and hard biscuits.

25

RED JEWELS

"How could you defend against the guy with two red jewels if you only had one blue one?" Temerity asked Half-pint. They were sitting in a garret room on the top floor of an abandoned tenement. Half-pint's green jewel was perched on top of an empty wooden chest, casting its light throughout the filthy room.

"Because I had the equivalent of two blue jewels," he said, peering at her through narrowed eyelids.

"How is that?" she asked.

He pulled out a small blue vial from his backpack, uncorked it, and placed a drop of blue oil on his meat cleaver blade, then held out his hand for her sword. She unsheathed it and he placed a blue dot on it and said, "Infusion of blue dragon jewel. One drop gives your weapon one dose of blue jewel, enough for one fight."

"Oh?" She watched the oil soak into the metal, leaving a blue sheen. "No wonder you were so excited in the apothecary."

"It's frightfully expensive, and very rare, to be honest. We were fortunate to have met that apothecarist and built up so many credits. Snake venom is rare as well, so working at Elvin's inn and trading venomous snakes was a big boon for us. I got red jewel infusion, too." He pulled out a small red vial and placed a drop of red oil on the same blades.

It soaked in and the steel shimmered with color.

"No infusion of white jewel?" she asked.

Half-pint shook his head. "No, sadly. She didn't have any, and even if she did, we wouldn't have been able to afford it."

"If we put five drops on our blades, will we have five jewels worth of power?"

Half-pint shook his head. "No, only one dose per color per fight. That's the rule. I found that out the hard way and wasted an entire vial one time."

The hair on her arms stood on end, and she reached for her orange jewel as she often did. It was vibrating again. She crept over to look out the open window, which was their escape path, while Half-pint cracked open the door to the hallway, peered out, and then latched it and braced it shut by wedging a piece of slate roof tile underneath it.

"I don't see or hear anything," he said.

They returned to sharpening their blades, accustomed to bands of roving adventurers in the alleys below triggering the orange jewel.

"Uh-oh," Half-pint said, hopping to his feet and brandishing his meat cleaver as he stared intently at the ceiling.

Temerity sprang to her feet and followed his gaze up to the dark rafters. A large black bat stared down at them, its eyes glinting red.

"We'd better go," Half-pint whispered, grabbing his buckler and backing away towards his green jewel and their pile of belongings.

Temerity pulled up her sylph hood and backed away with him.

The bat dropped from the ceiling and landed on Temerity's face, pain lancing through her. Wings flapped madly, and talons slashed her skin and scrabbled for her eyes. The room erupted in a storm of flashing blades and spiked wings as Half-pint jumped at the bat and tried to pry it off Temerity, who was stabbing at it with her sleeve dagger as needle-sharp talons sank into her cheeks and adrenaline flooded her body in a chaotic rush. The chisel end of the pickaxe pried the bat loose, the creature's hooked talons ripping at her skin as it turned on Half-pint. The bat and the goblin rolled to the floor, and with a piercing shriek, the bat shapeshifted into a small, hairy creature clothed in a black cloak and boots, with five red jewels strapped to its forearms. It slashed at Half-pint with knife-like claws and a mouth full of fangs. Temerity crawled across the floor towards the squirming mass of fists and blades and stared in horror as the long claws raked down Half-pint's chest, rending his leather armor in two.

Temerity swung her sword at the creature's hunched back, but it turned and grabbed the blade with a clawed hand, wrenching the steel from her grip and turning it back on her. The beast slashed at her leg, her jewel-infused blade flashing red and slicing cleanly through her thigh muscles. The five red jewels gleamed menacingly on the creature's forearms. She staggered backwards as it whirled back to Half-pint and tore the hobgoblin's belly wide open with a single swipe of its claws, splattering blood in a wide arc. Stumbling to regain her balance, Temerity's heel rolled off her hammer haft and she fell backwards, her feet flying in the air and her skull striking the floor. The room spun for a moment but the grunting sounds of a struggle turned her head, and she saw that the black-clad creature was still on top of Half-pint and blood was pooling underneath them. She rose awkwardly to her knees, blood welling from the deep gash in her thigh and dripping from her face onto the floor.

Time slowed down as the clarity of the moment chased all distractions from her head, and she regarded the two hairy little creatures vying for dominance. The bat creature was winning, and life was seeping away from Half-pint.

Half-pint's backpack was open in front of her, and she instinctively reached for a black vial of snake venom and the syringe. Deftly unwrapping the linen sheath from the long steel needle, she uncorked the snake venom with her teeth and stuck the needle into the vial, filling the entire reservoir. She turned to the creature, whose back was to her as it crouched over Half-pint's motionless body. Its jaws were at Half-pint's throat when Temerity crossed the room with two silent strides and jabbed the needle deep into the muscle of the creature's rear end and pushed the plunger.

The creature turned on Temerity, but she was ready this time and met its hairy palm with her sleeve dagger and then sliced the back of its elbow with her boning knife. The creature grabbed at her with its other hand, claws dripping with blood and eyes red like burning coal, but she ducked, dodging its twitching fingers as it swayed and slowly fell onto its side, green bile dripping from its open mouth.

She let the venom do its work and looked down at Half-pint, his entrails sitting in a pool of blood in his open belly. Her mind was sharp, her emotions icy, as she crossed the room and returned with his green jewel, pressing it to his belly above the gaping wound. She felt his chest rise and fall with a labored breath, but his belly was still a pulpy mass of entrails. His mouth opened and shut silently, and his hand reached weakly for hers.

The jewel.

She pressed the green jewel into his palm, and he held it to his chest. She sat back on her heels and watched as his wounds

slowly closed and the color returned to his face. After countless minutes, he regarded her with alert eyes and sat up.

"Whew, that was close," he said in a raspy voice. "Nasty
gremlin." He glanced over at the mound on the floor—an
empty pile of black clothing and three red jewels. "What happened?" he asked.

"I used your snake venom on him," she replied.

"Ah, quick thinking. How much did you give him?"

"A whole vial," she said, picking up the large syringe from
the floor.

"No wonder he died so fast," Half-pint said.

"Sorry. Did I waste some?"

"No, you did the right thing. We had no time to lose.
I'm glad to be alive. But come here, let me see your leg. That
doesn't look good." He pressed the green jewel to Temerity's
thigh, which she had wrapped tightly with a strip of linen. She
cut away the blood-soaked bandage and watched as the gash
slowly closed over. Half-pint moved the jewel to her cheeks,
and she shut her eyes until the lacerations on her face healed
and the pain disappeared.

"It's a good thing you handed me that jewel," he said. "If
anyone other than the owner holds an end-game jewel, it only
has the power of a normal jewel. You gave me enough energy
to remain conscious, but you never would have been able to
heal my abdomen with a Level-One jewel. Nasty, vile creatures, gremlins." His mouth turned down in a sour grimace.

"He had five red jewels," she said, noting that only three
remained on the floor.

"Like I said, a vile, wicked creature. Only an evil, selfish
soul would collect three jewels and continue to lurk in the
alleys and prey on fellow adventurers. Gremlins love to
cause pain and create mayhem. And of course, he was only

collecting red ones, to inflict the most damage. Plus, he had two red end-game jewels, apparently." He shook his head in disgust. "Horrid."

"That was scary," she said, her muscles suddenly weak and trembling. "But in the worst moment, I was calm, cool, and collected."

"Like a true warrior," he said, gazing at her with golden eyes. "You are a good Dragon's Game companion, Miss Temerity."

"Thank you, Half-pint. That means a lot to me." She held his gaze, and her heart was full.

26

BLUES

There was little loot to plunder from the gremlin's belongings, aside from its jewels. Half-pint unlaced waxed hemp cords from the dead creature's boots to stitch together his torn leather armor. Temerity nabbed a full waterskin, which she used to rinse the blood from her satin pants and gold velvet waistcoat.

Sitting across from one another, they each took one of the gremlin's red jewels, conveniently fitted with wrist straps. Temerity placed hers on her left forearm above her sleeve dagger and was shot through with a surge of raw power. Suddenly hot and jittery, she hopped to her feet, ready to run or fight. She breathed in and out, growing accustomed to the influx of red-jewel energy.

When she had settled down, she sat and regarded her two red jewels, one on each arm. Holding her orange jewel in her palm, she considered what it would be like to wear three reds.

She put down her orange jewel, strapped on a third red

one, and was overcome by a dizzying rush. She closed her eyes, waiting for the disorienting vertigo to pass.

"You'll get used to it," Half-pint said.

She opened her eyes, her heart pounding and her forehead beading with sweat.

"I don't like it," she said, removing the third red jewel. She popped it out of its strap and set the orange one in it instead. A burst of clarity sharpened her senses, her vision clearing and far-off noises suddenly distinct. "Ahhh," she said, exhaling as the grounding orange energy calmed her racing heart. "Much better."

Half-pint was watching her and said, "Even though the orange jewel doesn't repel attacks, it does have the warding property of alerting you to imminent threats, if you pay attention to it."

She nodded and pushed the extra red jewel towards him.

One by one, Half-pint picked up the yellow, blue, and two reds. They discussed his options and decided that his yellow jewel had proven its worth more than once. They needed the blue shield jewel, so he kept that one, plus a red jewel. He packed away the extra red in case they changed their minds later on.

Half-pint fashioned a wrist strap for his yellow jewel from their scraps of suede, then washed and mended his burlap undergarments while Temerity mended her pants.

"Are we allowed to trade jewels with other adventurers?" she asked as she pulled thread through a strip of red satin.

"Yes," Half-pint said, "but only in exchange for other jewels. There's an active black-market jewel trade, if you can find a dealer, that is. But the dragons frown upon hoarding and trading jewels for such purposes, and those merchants often die peculiar deaths."

After they finished sewing, they left the garret through the window. Each story of the building had windows with prominent lintels and decorative cornices, which they dropped down onto until they reached the ground.

It did not take them long to stumble upon a pair of adventurers slinking through the shadows towards them. The orange jewel barely registered their presence. Temerity and Half-pint stepped forward with blades bared and lunged in for the strike.

The two overweight, pampered-looking men parried half-heartedly with brand new blades that appeared to be cheap knock-offs from Glistening City. The men were dressed in tweed vests, white shirts, neckerchiefs, and new suede traveling cloaks over their scholarly attire. Soon, the men were winded and backed away, then turned tail and ran off.

Temerity wiped off Pauly's sword and sheathed it, and they continued on. It was an hour later that the orange jewel drew her to a halt, sending shivers up her spine.

"Stop," she said to Half-pint. "Someone is stalking us."

"More bands of sorry adventurers, no doubt," he said flippantly, but frowned when he saw the look on her face. "Where are they?"

"Up ahead," she whispered, "and behind us." She knelt down. "Give me some of that red jewel oil." She held out her blade, and he placed a drop of red dragon jewel infusion and a drop of blue infusion on Pauly's sword and the meat cleaver.

Her orange jewel was nearly burning her skin, and she focused on drawing energy from her two red jewels, wishing they imparted courage as well as strength. She crept forward and scanned the walls for something they could climb. When she lowered her gaze, adventurers were blocking the narrow lane, two at each end, their silhouettes black against the endless twilight of Dark Town. The four ambushers closed in slowly and looked to be neither scholars nor pampered. Temerity's hackles rose, and she unsheathed her sword. Her two red jewels were hot on her wrists, and a shimmer of red glowed on her blade.

Two men were in front of them, and a man and woman came up from behind, stepping forward slowly and confidently. The pairs split up and encircled them on all sides, blocking the escape route Temerity had been eyeing—the uneven stone wall of a shuttered inn that led up to a flat roof.

Temerity and Half-pint crouched, back-to-back, circling slowly and assessing the threat. Blue jewels glinted from the four adventurers' wrists and waist belts, and Temerity noted with surprise that blue was the only color they carried. The woman was taller than her three companions and did not appear to notice or care that Temerity was a woman as well, rare as their gender was in the Dragon's Game.

Soon, the adventurers were within striking distance and brandished blades and blunt instruments but did not attack. They drew closer, and Temerity jumped forward, swinging her sword at the nearest man, her red jewels pulsing power through her blood. The man casually raised his sword, and the jarring impact of his blade meeting hers threw her backwards with such force that she landed on her rump, embarrassed and confused. She jumped to her feet and charged him a second time, and again was thrown backwards. Half-pint was having similar results, flashes of blue limning the blades of the foursome as they parried strikes with little effort.

"Blues," Half-pint grumbled, and ran forward with his meat cleaver and buckler, only to be launched backwards, tumbling head over heels and landing at Temerity's feet.

Unsure of what else to do, she kept attacking, growing more and more frustrated with each deflected blow. It was clear that the four adventurers were playing with them, engaging just enough to get Temerity and Half-pint to attack, intent on wearing them down little by little.

"We need to run," Half-pint muttered to her, and she agreed. "Now!" Half-pint said, and they ran in the same direction towards the largest space between their assailants.

The man and woman whose defenses they were trying to pierce extended a sword and axe out sideways, closing the gap. The proximity of their blades to one another sent a shimmer of blue through the air. Temerity bounced against the translucent shield and fell back.

The four attackers had the discipline not to laugh, focused instead on Temerity and Half-pint and jabbing at them enough to keep them fighting. Temerity made another run for it, springing off the ground to leap over the shoulder of the shortest man in an effort to make a mad scramble up the stone wall, but he blocked her with a wooden shield. She fell flat on her back in the center of the circle of attackers, the wind knocked out of her. She struggled to her feet and kept fighting.

It was hopeless. The blue-bejeweled adventurers had them trapped. Half-pint tried negotiating with them, brandishing his yellow jewel and complimenting their ingenuity and prowess. He may as well have been talking to stacks of stones, for they paid him no mind at all. Apparently, one yellow jewel was powerless against a bunch of blues.

Having exhausted their prey, the four adventurers strode forward, slashing and thrusting in earnest. Blades impaled Temerity's torso from all sides, and she fell to her knees, steel burning like hot pokers in her ribs. Liquid rose in her lungs, and she was unable to breathe, choking and drowning in her own blood. She slowly collapsed onto the ground, her face striking the cobblestones and blood gurgling from her mouth. Her eyes cracked open enough to see Half-pint transform into a cat and dash between a pair of legs and flee down the alleyway.

Boots approached and kicked at her.

"Is she dead?" a male voice asked.

"No," the female voice said. "She's still trying to breathe. Give me your dagger, I'll slit her throat."

Temerity gasped for air—a fish out of water—and tried to push away, but she was in a gutter, blocked by a high stone curb. A boot planted on her back, and the crushing weight forced the last air out of her lungs.

The ringing sound of a blade being unsheathed was interrupted by the loud clatter of an overturned trashcan and the trampling of many boots.

"It's those reds again," a voice said, alarmed.

"There's more of them this time," another said.

A cat streaked across Temerity's line of sight at ground level, and hot on his tail came a group of men, hooting and hollering, "We found you, you dragon-cursed blues. Let's see how you do against eight triple reds."

Menacing laughter and guttural yells followed, and the band of blues sprinted away. Temerity watched through bleary eyes as men thundered past her, a forgotten clump in a shadowy gutter.

The alley was suddenly quiet, and she pushed herself up onto her hands and knees and tried to cough her lungs clear, spewing blood and bile and snot out of her mouth and nose.

Her lungs were burning and her vision clouded over. The street started tilting around her, and all she heard was her heart thudding in her ears. She fell over and thought of her ma, wishing she'd had the courage to say goodbye in person.

Warmth burned in her chest, then cool water, then air rushed in through her mouth and filled her lungs. Her eyes popped open, and Half-pint was at her side pressing his green jewel to her ribcage.

"Good thing you had that backpack on," he said softly as he moved the healing jewel to the next puncture wound.

She gasped for air, reminded of nearly drowning that time when she was a child and got caught in the river current. She lay there on the cobblestones, taking deep, life-giving breaths, while Half-pint moved from one wound to the next and then finally helped her to her feet.

"We need to get out of here," he whispered. "They'll come back, looking to steal your stuff."

He tugged at her sleeve and led her into a dark side street. She hobbled after him and crossed her wrists so that each hand could rest on a red dragon jewel, drawing strength from them. Soon, she was running at his side, and he was a cat, loping down one narrow alley after another, putting distance between them and the blue and red raiders.

They turned a corner and came face to face with another band. Four startled male faces gaped back at them. Fresh off the farm, by the looks of them. Temerity unsheathed her blades and hacked a path through the clumsy men, who barely put up a fight and backed away to let them pass. She and Half-pint fled down the alley, in search of a hideaway where they would be left in peace.

27

MAPS

"We're ready to get out of here," Half-pint said, from the dank cellar of a crumbling hovel they were hiding in. His green end-game jewel lit the cramped space with a ghoulish glow.

"Out of where?" Temerity asked.

"We're done with the alleys," he replied.

"Oh, good." A rush of relief flooded through her, immediately replaced by anxiety. "To go where?"

"To fight the boss, of course, and leave Dark Town."

"Our last street fight convinced you that we're ready?" she asked in disbelief. "The one where I almost died?"

"Those wounds weren't deadly," he assured her. "At least not right away."

"I could have died of fright," she said. "You think being scared to death makes me ready to fight a monster?"

He nodded, grinning impishly. "It does. You did not actually die from fright. You got up and ran away, then immediately beat another band of adventurers. That means you're ready."

She rolled her eyes, trying to hide the nervous twitch of her hands. She didn't argue with him. After all, she did want to leave Dark Town behind, as soon as possible. The Swamp sounded idyllic after the endless maze of dismal cobblestone streets, abandoned buildings, and stinking sewers.

Half-pint pulled out his copies of Gentry's maps and laid the parchments out on the dirt floor in a grid, displaying a sector of dense alleys around a central circle with a star drawn on it.

Temerity lit a taper candle, placed it in the candleholder, and perched it on a stack of bricks, adding a cool white light to the green glow.

"This is the Dragon Gate," Half-pint said, pointing to the star. "That leads to the boss fight of Level One, the Ogre's Eyes. But finding the gate can be just as confusing as navigating the tunnel labyrinth. It took me weeks to find it one time. Drove me nuts. These maps should save us a lot of time and effort."

She was distracted by the orange jewel, which kept vibrating on her wrist. They scanned the floorboards overhead for bat gremlins, checked dark corners of the cellar, crept through the ground floor, second floor, and roof of the hovel, then finally went back down into the cellar and cracked open the hatch that led directly to the street. Temerity peered down the alley. A small band of adventurers skulked past the end of the narrow lane and disappeared behind a building, but the jewel kept vibrating. This neighborhood was crawling with adventurers. They lowered the hatch and wedged a chunk of broken brick underneath the door at the top of the steep wooden stairs leading up into what had been the living area. Unless there was an invisible bat hiding between the floor beams, they were as safe down here as they could be. She finally took the orange jewel off her wrist, to stop its incessant shuddering, and stashed it in her pocket for the time being.

They turned back to the maps, and Half-pint set a small black sliver on the ground near the grid.

"Is that coal? Charred wood?" she asked, taking a closer look, assuming he was going to mark up the maps as they traveled across the sector.

"Neither," he said, peeking up at her through bushy eyebrows.

"What is it?" she asked.

"It's a bone shard," he said cagily, and she furrowed her brow at him.

"A burnt bone? From where?"

"It's not burnt," he said in a rasping whisper. "It's a dragon bone."

The breath caught in her throat. "A *dragon* bone? Wherever did you get that?" Goosebumps prickled her arms. "Are you even allowed to have that?"

Half-pint shrugged and spoke in a more normal tone. "Gentry gave it to me. It goes with the map. You see, the problem is that we don't know where we are, so the map won't help us until we can locate our position."

He placed the bone shard on the center star, then held up a second bone shard. He walked slowly around the map grid until he was at the western side, when the center shard suddenly spun and pointed at him.

Temerity jumped, startled, and Half-pint cackled gleefully. He knelt and placed his shard on the edge of the map, but it shot off the parchment and out onto the floor. He placed it on the parchment again, with the same result.

He sat back on his heels, rubbed his chin, and said, "As I guessed, we are not in the Dragon Gate Sector. We are west of it. So we just need to head east until we get on the map." He pointed towards the hatch. "That way is east."

"Do you have a normal compass?" she asked with a frown.

Half-pint shook his head. "No, and there's no sun or stars in Dark Town. We'll just need to start walking in that direction and check the bone shards and map to orient ourselves occasionally."

It seemed like a reasonable plan. Before heading out, they took turns sleeping and standing watch. When restlessness grew stronger than fatigue, they strapped on their jewels, hiding their light under sleeves and sylph cloaks, then gathered their things and left through the hatch.

They headed east, ducking into doorways or behind trash bins whenever they encountered other adventurers, their sylph cloaks blending into the shadows. The orange jewel gave her a jolt before they saw anyone, which was helpful, but it continued vibrating at a low level at all times, inducing a constant state of anxiety in Temerity. She gritted her teeth and tried to remain alert, scanning every broken window and dark alcove for lurking enemies.

They crouched in the dark entryway of an abandoned tenement to check the map. They had gotten a little off course and adjusted their trajectory, striking out again and clinging to shadows. A large gang of rowdy adventurers appeared around a corner, and she and Half-pint slipped into a side street and huddled behind the skeleton of a carriage until they passed.

"This is a critical time," Half-pint whispered. "We have all of our jewels, and if we get attacked now, we could lose everything. Once we get to the main road leading to the Dragon Gate, we'll be safe. Orcs and dwarves patrol the queue and don't put up with any shenanigans."

They moved on, and the next time they checked the map, the center shard pointed north. They had traveled way off course this time, heading north instead of east. They reoriented themselves and kept going.

"I want to at least get on the map before we take a break," Half-pint said.

"Okay," she said, her feet aching, "but how do you know those dragon-bone shards really work?"

Half-pint's face stretched into a grimace, but he offered no other reply. She sighed and kept pace with the knee-high hobgoblin.

They consulted the map a few minutes later, and the bone shard in the center pointed due south, the opposite direction from the last time they'd checked.

"That can't be," Half-pint said. "Unless we entered the sector already."

He laid out all the parchments in the full grid, but the center shard still pointed south and shot the second bone shard off the map and onto the cobblestones.

"Those things don't work," Temerity said.

"Or the map shifted," he said darkly.

"You mean the town shifted?" she asked.

"Could be," he said, waggling his ears. "Gentry said it happens sometimes. Well, everyone knows that, but this is a pretty big shift. Those dragons are up to their tricks again."

"Maybe they don't like us using a map," she said.

Half-pint snorted. "I think they have bigger things to worry about than a couple of adventurers navigating their puzzle. No, I think they just like to mess with everyone. Keep us on our toes." He sighed. "Let's take a break and then try again."

"Well, my orange jewel has been vibrating this whole time, so something is wrong."

"There are adventurers everywhere," he said, gesturing towards a pair of shadows flitting between buildings a block away. "The closer we get to the gate, the more people there will be."

They took a break and then headed north. Temerity hoped they would reach the edge of the map soon. She was tired from jumping at every shadow, and although the snakeskin boots didn't cause blisters, her feet and legs ached—and her shoulders and back, too. She longed for a hot meal, a hot bath, and a soft bed.

They knelt on the cobblestones in the shadow of an old inn and checked the map again, and this time the dragon-bone shard pointed clear in another direction—due east.

"This is not good," Half-pint said, shining the light of his red jewel over the parchments to make sure he had not mixed them up.

A loud creaking and swaying shook the street and surrounding buildings. Temerity pressed up against the inn's exterior wall, and Half-pint hurriedly gathered his parchments and stuffed them into his pack. The ground rumbled, and Temerity grabbed the hobgoblin by the collar and dragged him to the middle of the street as dark cracks snaked across the walls. Stones fell from crumbling façades, crashing onto the cobblestones where they had just been standing. The street began to slowly rotate around them, and the ground opened up under their feet.

Temerity scrambled for a foothold, but she slid on hands and knees into a growing sinkhole, and Half-pint tumbled down after her.

28

ᏣBLACK JEWELS

Down and down she slid into the pitch-black hole, then hit flat ground with a painful thud. Rocks rolled down after her, then with a mad flurry of claws and fur, Half-pint the cat landed in her lap.

"Ouch," she said, and he hopped off, followed by the familiar rustling of sylph silk as he changed back into his hobgoblin form.

"What in the seven hells!" he exclaimed, his voice rasping in the dark. "Are you okay, Miss Temerity? What happened to our jewels?"

Temerity pushed up her sleeves, but her jewels were dark.

"I don't know," she said. She could not see a thing. She removed her pack and felt around inside for the string of white faery jewels. She pulled them out of her pack, and they began to glow, casting a dim light.

The dragon jewels on both their wrists were black, and the orange premonition jewel had stopped vibrating.

"Black jewels," Half-pint said, bewildered. "I've never heard of such a thing."

"They're dead," Temerity said.

"They were never alive," Half-pint replied. "But their magic is definitely gone." He wrinkled his brow, examining all the jewels.

"I think this is a bad sign," she said.

"Very bad," he said gravely.

They looked around, taking stock of their predicament. They were in a deep pit, and the only way out was up. The top was not visible from where they had landed, and the absence of any air stirring overhead offered them little hope that the top was within easy reach. They attempted to climb, but the walls were slick with mud that slid down with them as soon as they got a hand or foothold. They tried climbing with their blades, but that just brought down more mud. Half-pint attempted climbing as a cat and rolled down in a ball of fur. After several tries that resulted in them being covered in mud from head to toe, they tied Half-pint's pickaxe to Temerity's rope and tossed it up, hoping to hook it on something. That brought down another cascade of mud and rocks. After multiple failed attempts, they sat on their haunches and tried to figure out what to do.

All out of ideas, they ate a few mouthfuls of food, drank some water, and stared at their muddy prison.

❖

"I hate dungeons," Half-pint muttered.

They had been in the pit for what Temerity estimated to be the equivalent of two days, and their food and water was running low. They had screamed for help for a few hours, and now her throat was sore.

"You think this is a dungeon?" she asked. "I think it's just a sinkhole and we were very unlucky."

"There is no such thing as luck in this game," Half-pint said despondently. "Nothing happens by chance. The dragons control it all. They trapped us here on purpose."

"I thought you said they wouldn't concern themselves with two pathetic adventurers—that they had more important things to worry about."

"I lied," he said, and stared sullenly at the muddy walls surrounding them. "I wanted to keep using the maps, even though Gentry warned me not to."

"What do you mean?" Temerity asked, the hairs rising on the nape of her neck.

"I think we're being punished," Half-pint said. "We'll die a slow death and get sent back to the beginning. I wonder if they'll let me take my green jewel out with me."

She had never seen Half-pint so depressed. Cranky, yes. Irritable. Bored. But never depressed.

"You never give up on anything," she said. "How can you give up now?"

"Who's giving up?" he asked. "But who am I against dragons? You break the rules, you pay the price. That's how the Dragon's Game works."

"What rules?" she asked.

"No maps," he said simply, meeting her gaze. "Maps are not allowed. If the dragons had wanted us to have maps, they would have provided them. Everyone knows that. But I thought, since Gentry had been able to map the entire tunnel labyrinth and Dark Town, that I had been mistaken. Perhaps maps were allowed all along, and only those smart enough would get to use them. But Gentry told me that his maps were strictly a scholarly pursuit—an effort to study the godlike qualities of the dragons. That using maps to progress through the game was strictly prohibited."

"So, then, why did he let you copy them?"

"I think he wanted the snake-charming flute and the gripper. He hates snakes. He told me so—almost as much as Elvin does. Besides, I used the yellow jewel on him. That probably wasn't fair."

"What about those black dragon bones?" she asked. "Do you think the dragons like us using their bones?"

His face grew ashen. "Oh, seven hells," he muttered, and sank his head into his hands.

"What's wrong, Half-pint?"

"Relics. Bones are dragon relics."

"And ...?" she prompted. "What about them?"

He gazed glumly at her and made a slashing motion across his throat.

"Prohibited?" she asked.

"Strictly," he said, lying back in the mud with his head on his pack. "We're doomed."

◆

"I apologize, Miss Temerity," Half-pint said, kneeling in front of her. "I don't know how long it will take us to die of thirst and starvation, but it will be slow and painful, I fear. I am the worst hobgoblin the world has ever known." Tears were brimming in his eyes.

"Don't cry, Half-pint," she begged. "It's not your fault. Besides, having dragon relics can't be that bad, if Gentry had them."

Half-pint shook his head. "He told me he had recently procured them from a black-market seller in the main square, that it was going to make his map-making so much quicker.

But then he told me that when he went back to get more the next day, the merchant had died a grisly death just that morning. I should have put two and two together. Trying to take shortcuts in this game always ends up leading you the long way around. I should have learned that by now. Gentry is probably dead already."

"But we're not dead," she said stubbornly, unwilling to believe that Gentry had died.

"No, we're not," Half-pint agreed. "The dragons want us to die a slow death to teach us a lesson."

The more he talked, the heavier was the sense of doom permeating the mud pit.

"There must be a way out," she said, searching frantically for a solution. "Think, Half-pint. We need to think."

She sat on her pack and reviewed in her mind everything they had done since they'd passed through the doorway in Lucy's cellar. She felt for the locket hanging from her neck. She hadn't thought about her pa in days, yet he had been here this whole time, resting close to her heart. She wondered how he and her brothers were faring in the game this time around, if the dragons were so unforgiving. Perhaps they had died already and were back at home with Ma, worrying about Temerity. She was so selfish, leaving Ma like that. Fancying herself an adventurer. Now here she was, stuck in the bottom of a mud pit, suffering the dragon's wrath.

She forced herself to set aside her self-pity and recalled the tunnel labyrinth, the Dark Pool of Despair, Avon's Grotto, the coal mine, The Blue Jewel, the snake trade.

Think, think!

The female troll tanner, the gray-haired leatherworker, the orc meat seller, the gnome cobblers, the woodland nymph snake charmer, the elven apothecarist, the rotund fortune teller.

She thought back on the reading the fortune teller had given them. The cards she had drawn. The candle she had given her.

Temerity slid down off her pack and searched for the candle and tinderbox.

"What did the fortune teller say about this candle?" she asked Half-pint, who was squatting next to her, curiosity glinting in his eyes. "She put some drops on it. One for each of us."

"Infusion of white intelligence jewel," Half-pint said excitedly. "That's what we need, intelligence!"

She lit the candle, and they leaned over the flame, inhaling the scent of wax and wick and ... something indescribable. Something bright and crisp, clear as a cold and sunny winter's day.

"To help light your way in the deepest darkness," they said in unison.

Temerity was filled with a sudden sharp clarity of mind and purpose. Despair was replaced by curiosity. Dead-ends, traps, hopelessness—they were all simply challenges to be overcome. Life was a puzzle, and the Dragon's Game was a puzzle inside a puzzle. Solving their current problem was a matter of tenacity and ingenuity.

They stood up, and she raised the candle, gazing up at the walls of their mud prison. Perhaps they had missed something obvious. A hidden ladder. A secret passageway. Half-pint stood on her shoulders and peered up into the darkness, looking for a clue. They tried everything they had tried before, with the same muddy results, and wracked their brains for the missing piece of the puzzle.

Temerity turned in a circle, seeing no way out. She gritted her teeth in frustration. *It could not end like this.*

"The infusion will wear off soon," Half-pint said bleakly, and Temerity gazed down at him, hope slowly slipping away.

"Pa always said that the simplest solution is the best and is usually staring you right in the face." The candle flickered, reflecting back at Temerity from Half-pint's glassy eyes. "Maybe ..." she said slowly, "we just need to get rid of the source of the problem." Her heart pounded. "Give me those maps. Hurry."

He understood, and soon they were feeding the parchments into the flame. Temerity lit the other candles, and before long, all the maps had burnt to wisps of black smoke that rose in dark tendrils up into the gaping hole.

"And the bones," she said. "Burn the dragon bones."

"No," Half-pint said, clutching the two bone shards. "It's not our place to burn the relics. We should bury them. Return them to the Dragon's Game." He rushed to his pickaxe and began hacking at the ground until he'd made a good-sized hole.

"I hope we're doing the right thing," she said as he dropped the bone shards into the hole and covered them with dirt. They placed the flickering tapers in a circle around the mound, and Temerity raised the fortune teller's pillar candle.

"Oh dragon gods," she called up into the void. "We're sorry. We're horrible, stupid humans."

"Hobgoblins," Half-pint corrected her, shouting up to the dragon gods. "Stupid, selfish, utterly ridiculous hobgoblins."

"Human and hobgoblin," Temerity called. "A terrible pair. Horrible judgment. It's a wonder we survived at all."

She lowered the candle and exchanged fraught glances with Half-pint.

They sat on their packs and waited for the candles to burn down. The flames guttered out one by one, leaving only the string of faery lights shining weakly from where she had hung them from the dagger she'd stuck in the wall.

"Half-pint," she said breathily. "Pull up your sleeves."

He raised his arms, his robe's sleeves falling around his elbows. His dragon jewels glowed yellow, blue, red, and green. Temerity shook the sleeves away from her wrists, and her orange jewel and two red jewels winked back at her, the orange jewel humming happily against her arm.

They laughed with jubilation and relief, then looked up at the hole they had fallen down, and their laughter trailed off.

Silence filled the pit. There was still no way out.

A rumble shook the ground, and Temerity turned helplessly in a circle, afraid the walls would crumble around them, burying them alive.

A crack appeared in the wall, growing ever larger. A black abyss opened in front of them. Two fiery-red eyes peered out at Temerity, and she took a step back, the air frozen in her lungs. Was it another gremlin? No, it was too big to be a gremlin. Black scales and a snout glinted in the jewel light, and a large head poked out of the crack in the wall, rising above them and peering down. A huge clawed foot reached out, and then another.

Temerity's heart jumped into her throat, and she and Half-pint fled to the far side of the pit and pressed their backs against the mud wall, trapped. Visions of her life flashed before Temerity's eyes, and she took small comfort in the thought that when she awoke back at home after a gruesome and violent death by dragon, she would have one hell of a story to tell.

The dragon, thrice the size of a cow, with scales glittering like black diamonds, stomped out from the crevice and swept aside the circle of candle stubs with one swipe of its enormous front foot. The long, lizard-like creature, with spikes along its spine and tail, and spiny wings tucked neatly against its sides, dug into the mound with knife-like talons and pulled out the two black bone shards, then glared directly at Half-pint.

The hobgoblin shrank into a smaller version of himself, peeking out from his sylph-silk cowl. "Sorry?" he squeaked, then continued in a trembling voice. "That was thoughtless of me, and selfish. I knew better."

The dragon's ruby eyes held his gaze and then turned and rested on Temerity. A rush of hot and cold, fire and ice, washed over her. She was immobilized—held prisoner under the dragon's red-jewel eyes. Her limbs felt pinned to the wall by taloned feet, even though the dragon stood several paces away. Her heart thundered wildly in her chest, and she wondered grimly if looks could actually kill.

The dragon finally released her, then stalked gracefully back into its hole, wings folded primly at its sides and its long, spiked tail swishing back and forth before snaking into the crevice and disappearing from view.

Temerity stared after it. Her legs suddenly grew weak, and she sank to the floor, trembling violently. She was overcome with awe and terror, as though having just seen a god she had always thought was a faery tale. Or a monster—who had let them live.

When they recovered enough to stand and walk, they hurriedly gathered their things and, by the light of their jewels, crept into the crevice and followed the newly revealed tunnel to wherever it would lead.

MAP OF DARK TOWN

DRAGON GATE SECTOR

29

THE GAUNTLET

They followed a long and twisting underground passageway, seeing no further sign of the dragon. At long last, the tunnel narrowed, and they squeezed through a gap and found themselves in a sewer. This one had low stone ceilings and did not stink as badly as it could have. Temerity crouched down and they crept along, taking random turns in the warren of underground drainage tunnels until a dim light led them to a grate overhead.

Temerity pushed up the iron grate and they climbed out onto the cobblestones. They were in an abandoned alley, but a distant hubbub lured them forward.

They soon found themselves in a large, vibrant square, lit up like the carnival square and lined with merchant stalls. At the center of the bustling crowd, the pyramid-shaped capstone of a homing spike glowed like a beacon. At the sight of it, Temerity's anxiety unwound in the span of a single, shaking breath. Home was but one touch away, and this whole nightmare would be behind her.

"Ah, the dragons have smiled upon us," Half-pint said with a relieved grin. "This is the entrance to the gauntlet."

"The gauntlet?" she repeated, still distracted by the pulsating blue monolith.

He saw her intent gaze and asked gently, "Are you considering going home? If you want to, this is the place to do it. This is the last homing spike before entering the Dragon Gate."

She reflected on her many conflicting emotions: guilt at leaving her ma alone, a longing for her safe and boring life, a lingering fright from the dragon encounter, fear of the unknown, and excitement for what lay beyond.

"No," she said, squaring her shoulders. "We've come this far. Might as well see what's around the next corner."

"That's the spirit," he said. "I wouldn't know what to do without you."

That made her smile, and she glanced gratefully down at her companion. He smiled warmly back at her, then they turned their attention to the excited adventurers who filled the square. It was the usual assortment of men and the rare woman, interspersed with the occasional wee folk, all either sorting through their packs, gazing thoughtfully into the distance, or jabbering excitedly with their bandmates. No one was leaving via the blue spiral.

The mood of this square was different from the others they had passed through. Here, almost everyone displayed the easy confidence of having survived the inns and alleys while collecting the required jewels. Now, they were replenishing their supplies and getting ready to embark on the final challenge.

Temerity and Half-pint followed the aroma of meat pies and found a row of food vendors. They bought a variety of hot foods with coin and sat on a stone curb to eat, washing it down with hot tea. They took some time to purchase foodstuffs they could eat on the move, then filled their waterskins at the pumps.

Half-pint assured her that they would be spending the next unknown amount of time standing in a queue in the gauntlet, waiting for their turn to pass through the Dragon Gate, and wouldn't want to lose their place in line to buy food— although some enterprising vendors walked up and down the queue, selling food at exorbitant prices. "Then, it will take us another unknown period of time to get past the packs of troll mobs and beat the ogre boss. We'll need to eat to keep up our strength as we go."

"Do we really have to fight trolls and ogres?" she asked, her gaze wandering to the homing spike.

"Yes. The ogre is the boss for Level One, and a tribe of trolls guards the passageways leading to the ogre's arena. What did you think?"

"I don't know," she said weakly, pulling her gaze away from the glowing pillar. "We've only been fighting other humans this whole time. How can we possible beat trolls and an ogre?"

"You killed a gremlin," he reminded her. "The tanner was a troll, and so was the coal-mine tender. They weren't so scary, were they?" She shook her head, and he continued, "We also outsmarted a water sprite—that's a trick in itself. And we beat plenty of other adventurers. But, regarding fighting, you'll come to find out that humans are the most treacherous creatures in the Dragon's Game, and in the real world as well."

She lifted an eyebrow. "You think so?"

"Yes," he said, rolling his eyes as though it were obvious. "Who can be trusted less than humans. Huh?" he challenged.

She made a face at him. "Lots of creatures."

"Who breaks promises more than humans?" he pressed.

She shrugged, starting to dislike this conversation.

"Who kills for the sport of it?" he asked, unrelenting.

"Cats," she said pointedly, and he clamped his jaws shut.

She tried not to gloat at her witty comeback and asked, "Why is it called the gauntlet?"

He blew out a loud breath, as though he had been about to counter her very accurate point with another accusing question, and said, "It's just the name of the street where you need to wait to enter the Dragon Gate. It used to be a real gauntlet, back before my time. You know, the kind you need to run through, not my gloves," he said snidely.

"I know what a gauntlet is," she said icily.

"Anyway," he went on, "supposedly, the street was lined with gangs on either side, trying to kill anyone who wanted to reach the Dragon Gate. It got so out of control that the orcs and dwarves finally took it upon themselves to impose order. Now, we just have to make sure not to anger the guards, or they'll yank us out of line and send us to the end of the queue again."

She nodded that she understood while scanning the faces in the crowd, on the off chance that her pa and brothers might be in this very square at this same moment in time. At the very least, they had most assuredly passed through here on more than one occasion. It felt good—and weird—to be standing where they had stood. In all her years of imagining where her pa and brothers had gone off to, wondering what had been so enticing as to take them away from her and her ma for months at a time, she had never imagined this. Endless mazes of dark tunnels, abandoned alleys, quirky inns, and market squares were not where she had imagined dragons dwelled.

The pictures she had painted in her mind had been of mystical, magical faerylands, where dragons reigned over sparkling castles and fertile lands of ripened grains and fruit. Dragon lairs, yes, but her imagination had conjured grand caverns with mountains of gold and gems, not muddy pits and sewers. Adventurers had been shining, mythical knights, serving their dragon masters and embarking on brave conquests to vanquish foes and bring glory. Not getting lost in a pitch-black labyrinth and plunging nearly to their deaths into a cold pool. Not being entranced by a water sprite, or mining coal, or catching venomous snakes. Nor had she imagined skulking around in dirty cobblestone alleyways, killing a man and stealing his clothes, or fighting off bat gremlins. She shook her head at her naivete. If she had known the truth, would she have come?

The one thing that had vastly exceeded her expectations was the black dragon. A part of her had always doubted that dragons really existed. She still could barely believe she had actually encountered one—that it had stared her in the eyes, and let her live. It was the most powerful, beautiful creature she had ever seen, and that alone made it all worth it.

"Ready?" Half-pint asked, breaking into her musings.

She took in a big breath and let it out before answering. "Ready as I'll ever be."

They turned towards the far end of the square and joined the stream of adventurers headed to the Dragon Gate.

———◆———

The gauntlet was exactly as Half-pint had described it—a wide cobblestone street with a very, very long line. They entered through a simple stone archway, then not too far down the street, they came upon the Dragon Gate itself. It was a massive white stone archway, covered with carvings of fire-breathing dragons slaying hordes of men. The gate was heavily guarded by several gray-skinned orcs, their horn nubs poking up through greasy hair, and dwarves, clothed in fur and scowling at everyone. The guards let through a team of four adventurers, then assumed a wide stance and folded their arms, blocking anyone else from passing.

The queue extended down the street as far as the eye could see. Temerity and Half-pint walked alongside it, away from the gate, looking for where it ended. Adventurers stood two and four abreast, yelling idle threats to passersby, or standing in bored silence. Some sharpened blades, while others stood facing the neighboring wall and gutter, pissing or squatting to do their business in full view of everyone, adding to the overpowering stench of too many adventurers gathered closely together. Temerity was suddenly more thankful than ever for her long, green sylph cloak.

Tall, grisly orcs leered at the loud-mouthed adventurers until they shut up. Short, stocky dwarves patrolled the line, swinging war hammers and battle-axes, with bones and feathers braided into their long hair and beards. More dwarves dumped buckets of water into the gutters to send the human waste into the sewers. As Half-pint had said, food and beverage vendors paced up and down the line, calling out their goods and prices. Unlike the party-like atmosphere of the square, the gauntlet was thick with nervous tension.

Temerity walked next to the hobgoblin, block after block, along the seemingly endless queue, which appeared to not be moving. If they only let in one band of adventurers at a time, it could take them days to get to the head of the line.

"Why do they only have one gate?" Temerity whispered loudly.

"Only one boss," he said. "I guess this game is more popular than they had anticipated. Seems they let anybody in these days."

Temerity regarded the multitude of adventurers—a crosscut of society, from nobles to scholars, craftsmen and farmers, beggars and thieves. And tavern wenches and hobgoblins.

She looked down at herself and Half-pint, suddenly feeling self-conscious in her satin-and-velvet finery. She drew her dusky-green cloak across her chest and raised her hood over her helmeted head. Likewise, Half-pint cloaked himself in his silver sylph silk. She lifted her chin. She had worked hard and fought bravely to make it this far, as had Half-pint, who could outwit most of these sorry-looking adventurers.

They finally reached the end of the queue and jostled against other arriving adventurers for their place in line. They ended up behind a foursome of middle-aged men, the sort who might have sat at the bar of the Tin Roof all day, every day. She ignored their curious glances and sour smell and settled in to wait.

"Why are most people in groups of four, and we're only two?" she asked Half-pint worriedly.

"Small groups are more nimble. Fewer adventurers for the trolls and ogre to kill, and they draw smaller packs of mobs. Some brave souls even go in solo."

"So this could be the end? We're likely to die in there?" she asked.

"No, the final boss fights are special instances of the game. When you die in final challenges, you only get kicked out of the boss fight, not the whole game, and get sent back to the Dragon Gate to try again. If you fail three times in a row, then you need to stand in line again."

"What happens if three people in a band of four die, but the fourth kills the ogre?" she asked.

"Then the whole band succeeds. That's the upside of having more people. If they are strong, that is. If your companions are weak, more people can be a negative."

"So you think the two of us can kill a bunch of trolls and an ogre?" she asked, trying to keep the doubt out of her voice.

"Confidence, Miss Temerity. Confidence. We haven't died yet, have we?"

"No, I guess not," she said, kicking at the cobblestones and hoping she didn't die too many times in there and force Halfpint to go to the back of the line again.

30

SHIELD AND ATTACK

By Temerity's estimation, they had spent two days in the queue before finally getting within throwing distance of the Dragon Gate. Temerity and Half-pint ate and drank a fair bit, but not too much, and Temerity kept checking to make sure her weapons were sharp.

A commotion at the gate drew their attention. Instead of the next band of adventurers entering the gate, a band of four was being thrown out. The orc and dwarf guards shoved the scraggly band along, and an oversized orc pushed one of them to the pavement. The barrel-chested, bearded adventurer climbed to his feet, glowering at the orc who had pushed him.

"No need to get huffy," the adventurer said, brushing off his tunic. "We'll just wait here to get back in."

"End of line," the orc grunted, his beady eyes glaring down at the man.

"End of the line?" the man protested. "Again? We already went through this line-from-hell twice."

"Come on, Rory," a thin, gray-haired adventurer said, tugging at his companion's arm and slinging a quiver of arrows over his shoulder.

Temerity peered at them. The red-bearded man and gray-haired archer were the adventurers she had served at the Tin Roof and had seen again in the market square. The two younger adventurers were still with them and straggled behind the older pair as they shuffled along the line past Temerity and Half-pint.

The red-haired adventurer turned to one of the young men. "I told you to keep the trolls away from me," he snapped. "If the Shield dies, we all die. You're supposed to deal damage, not take it, you useless hoe-swinging hedgehog."

"It's a scythe," the lanky youngster said, shouldering his long, curved blade.

The huskier young man jumped to his mate's defense. "The Shield is supposed to draw in the trolls and distract them, like Ianan told us, not pull the whole stinking horde and then leave us behind to be swarmed by them."

"You guys need to keep up," the burly man retorted, his cheeks turning a deep crimson.

"You're supposed to fight too, you know," the husky one said, and then caught Temerity's eye and stopped walking. "Hey. Aren't you that ... and your sidekick, the mini-troll."

"I am a *hobgoblin,*" Half-pint said, puffing out his chest and lifting his long nose.

"Temerity," she said.

"Tomaz," the smiling young man said, holding out his calloused hand. His hair was black and wild, his full beard was the same, and his large brown eyes were warm and friendly.

She shook his strong, thick hand, and then the hand of the one with the scythe, Keenan. He was tall and lean, more bone than muscle, and had fine, dirty-blond hair and a scraggly goatee. His hands were narrow but as strong as Tomaz's. Both of them were clearly farm boys, used to working with their hands all day long. They were still wearing the roughspun clothes they had been wearing at the Tin Roof, and Tomaz still had his woodsman's axe.

"Keep up!" the red-haired man bellowed.

"We'll be right there," Tomaz said, waving away the two older men, who turned on their heels and stalked down the line.

"What a blowhard," Keenan muttered, glaring after the men and pushing tangled blond hair away from his sweaty forehead.

"You've been kicked out twice?" Half-pint asked, to the embarrassed nods of the young men. "Did you make it to the ogre, at least?"

They shook their heads sheepishly.

"You guys haven't upgraded any of your clothes or weapons, either," Temerity observed. "You're wearing the same rags you wore in Haverly Arms."

Keenan shrugged. "We didn't have time. Rory and Ianan rushed us through the alleys. Said we just needed jewels."

"They took all the good loot," Tomaz added. "They said they needed it because Rory was the Shield and we were just playing Attack."

"The fourth guy was the Healer?" Half-pint asked.

"No cutting in line," a man behind them interrupted angrily.

"We're just talking," Temerity said, casting him a stern glare.

Tomaz glanced at the adventurers in line, who were eyeing them threateningly. "Ianan was supposed to heal us, but he only had one green jewel and he kept getting killed. He said he preferred to play Range Attack. Archer. But arrows don't kill trolls very easily, turns out."

"Move along," a dwarf guard said, slapping a heavy iron hammerhead onto his thick palm.

"Alright. Good luck," Keenan said, nodding farewell and stepping away with Tomaz.

"Wait," Temerity said, stepping out of line.

"What are you doing?" Half-pint asked, and Tomaz and Keenan turned around.

"We need companions," she said, holding Half-pint's yellow eyes. "Remember? The fortune teller's card said so. I know good guys when I see them. And I don't want to face a horde of trolls and an ogre by ourselves."

"But they haven't upgraded anything," Half-pint said, regarding the two farm boys dubiously.

"We can help them," she said.

Tomaz and Keenan took a step closer.

"Get in line or get out of line," the dwarf said to Temerity. She shifted her attention from Half-pint to the young men, who were looking at one another and shrugging.

"Would be nice not to be yelled at constantly," Keenan said.

Tomaz smiled and said, "Yeah. Rory's like my bull, Grapenut, who runs at you and then when you say, 'boo,' he shits all over himself."

Keenan laughed. "Yeah, like my red rooster, Raspberry, who claws at your leg and then gets all uppity when you kick him across the yard."

"And Ianan's like my old gran," Tomaz said with a wide grin, "who would rather sit by the fire all day, knitting."

"Alright, alright," Temerity said to the dwarf, who was poking her shoulder with the butt-end of his hammer haft.

She looked over her shoulder at Half-pint. The hobgoblin

had left the line, and adventurers had already closed up the gap where they had stood, folding their arms and staring straight ahead.

"To the end of the line," the dwarf said, his eyes stony.

"Yeah, yeah," Half-pint said, waddling along next to the three young humans as they headed back down the gauntlet.

31

A BAND OF FOUR

They neared the end of the line and walked past Rory and Ianan.

"We're going with these guys," Tomaz called out, waving at them.

Rory's eyes bulged and his cheeks grew red.

"You'll be better off without us," Keenan said, over his shoulder, "like you told us a hundred times."

Ianan looked stunned, and Rory sputtered and spat and yelled after them, "Yeah, sure, a tavern wench and a dirty gremlin will surely be better than two expert adventurers. Good luck, you sorry pig farmers."

"We ain't pig farmers," Keenan grumbled.

"We're wheat farmers," Tomaz called back to Rory.

"Gremlin!" Half-pint muttered under his breath.

They ignored Rory's continued rantings and soon reached the end of the line and kept walking. They had decided they needed to go back into the alleys to get Tomaz and Keenan better gear, and so they headed towards the sector of alleys that stretched beyond the gauntlet to look for some likely adventurers to challenge.

Before leaving the gauntlet, they huddled inside the stone archway to take stock of their jewels and weapons.

Temerity had her two reds and an orange. Half-pint had his blue, yellow, red, and end-game green jewel, which the two young men had never heard of, plus their extra red one. Tomaz had yellow, orange, and red. Keenan had green, blue, and red.

After much discussion, they began trading amongst themselves, deferring to Half-pint's guidance.

"You take the two blues and a red," Half-pint told Tomaz. "You will be the Shield."

"Me?" the young man asked, pressing his hands to his broad chest. "Why me?"

"Because you're the biggest," Half-pint said simply. "And you already have an axe, although you need a battle-axe instead of that woodsman's axe. And a shield, ideally. What have you got to leave behind if we find a shield?"

"Why do I have to leave something behind?" Tomaz asked, his wide, bearded smile puckering into a pout.

Half-pint rolled his eyes. "Didn't those 'expert adventurers' teach you anything? Anyway, what else have you got? I hope you knew enough to bring three weapons in with you."

Tomaz unsheathed a small knife and showed it to Half-pint.

"That's *it?*" the hobgoblin asked.

Tomaz dug into his pocket and held out a set of brass knuckles. "I like to play Melee," the big man said in a small voice. "I want to be a Fist."

"Shields *do* play Melee, as well," Half-pint assured him. "But the 'Battle-axe' class of Melee. If you get close enough to use those brass knuckles, you'll be so tangled up with a troll, you'll be dead before you can ever land a punch."

"Yeah, they kept putting me in a headlock while another one pummeled me," Tomaz said with a wince.

"Or buried a blade in his belly. He died three times like that," Keenan said, and Tomaz shot him a pointed glare.

Half-pint smirked knowingly and added, "And the ogre will pick you up and eat you sooner than you can say 'brass-knuckle sandwich.'"

The three youngsters stared at the hobgoblin.

"*Eat* you?" Temerity asked. "As in, put you in his mouth and chew?"

"And swallow?" Keenan asked, his pale face growing paler.

Half-pint's mouth turned down. "That's exactly what I mean. Happened to my ex-wife one time. Was horrid."

Temerity exchanged glances with Tomaz, who closed his fingers around his brass knuckles. "I suppose I could part with these, even though I won them fair and square playing dice."

"Good for you," Half-pint said. "You'll win yourself a shield in the alleys, unless you want to be an ogre's supper. And Keenan, you'll play Attack, with Temerity. She's got a good sword, a half-okay knife, a sledgehammer, and a dagger. We should get better weapons for you, as well," he said to Temerity.

"Now you tell me," she said. "How were we planning to survive before?"

"The way we survived in the alleys. Stealth. Evasion. Trickery. But that was with just the two of us. We'll need to change tactics now," he said with an arched eyebrow.

She pressed her lips together, and the hobgoblin turned back to Keenan. "That scythe will serve you well, but somebody needs to play Range, if we can find some proper long-range weapons. I have bolts but no crossbow. It'd be hard to kill a crossbowman, and even if we did, what are the chances they won the weapon in the game? I've never looted a crossbow in

Level One. Bow and arrows are easier to come by, but they don't deal much damage to trolls. There's no spell casting in Level One." He rubbed his chin and mused, "The sledge-hammer and pickaxe will be good against the rock trolls, but swords won't do anything."

"Rock trolls?" Tomaz asked. "I didn't see no rock trolls."

"They defend the ogre," Half-pint explained.

"Rock trolls?" Temerity repeated, accusingly. "You said trolls were friendly."

"Did not," Half-pint said. "I said the few we'd met were not very scary. Rock trolls are another thing entirely." She scowled at him, and he shrugged. "I didn't want to frighten you. In any case, we'll see what weapons we come across. See what the dragons see fit to bring our way. Keenan, what other weapons do you have?"

The young man pulled out a knife.

Half-pint frowned at the hunting knife and felt the blade's edge. "At least it's sharp. What else have you got?"

Keenan lifted his shoulders and shook his head.

"Nothing?" Half-pint pressed. "Surely you knew the basics."

Keenan lowered his head into his shoulders, like a turtle, then pulled out a metal tool that looked like pliers, but instead of teeth it had a circular wheel with small metal spikes.

"What in the seven hells is that?" Half-pint asked. "A *leather* punch?" He turned his yellow eyes onto the young man.

"That's all I had," Keenan said meekly.

Half-pint sighed. "That's okay. We'll find a leatherworker and trade it for something useful. In the meantime, I'll teach Tomaz the finer points of playing Shield. Don't worry, it's easy," he said to the bearded young man, "once you get the hang of it. I'll play Healer. Here, take my blue." He handed Tomaz his blue jewel, then turned back to Keenan, eyeing the jewels on his wrists. "I'll need your green jewel, and you can have our extra red. And take Tomaz's orange one for your blue. Yellow jewels won't work very well with trolls, not with the big packs of mobs we're going to pull with the four of us, so we'll stash Tomaz's extra yellow one for now."

Jewels changed hands, and the foursome ended up with a respectable jewel configuration for two Attacks, a Shield, and a Healer: Temerity still had her two reds and an orange, and Keenan had the same; Tomaz had two blues and a red; and Half-pint had his end-game green, plus a second green, a yellow, and a red. The regular green jewel appeared dull next to the end-game jewel, which glowed and glimmered and cast a globe of light around them.

Half-pint bobbled his head, saying, "I'd rather have blue than yellow in the final challenge, but yellow is useful in the alleys. Let's try to find another blue for me, and maybe a blue for Keenan instead of orange."

The hobgoblin's jewel strategy was making Temerity's head spin. She let him rattle on about different color combinations. She was content to feel the power of the reds surging through her blood while the orange jewel sent subtle waves along her skin, teasing of things to come.

When Half-pint had finally exhausted his monologue, they arranged their things and headed into the alleys.

32

RAIDING

Unlike when it was just the two of them and they did a lot of sneaking around and chatting up their opponents, now Half-pint led them on full frontal assaults. Well, technically, he sent Tomaz out front and directed from the rear while scrambling about and healing the three of them as they engaged in fights with random adventurers, blades slashing and blunt instruments swinging.

Temerity thrust and dodged, switching fluidly between sword, dagger, knife, and sledge, and using an elbow or her teeth or a well-placed head-butt with her steel helmet when all else failed.

"Ho!" she yelled as their latest adversaries cornered them in a dead-end. She and her companions had been trailing the band of four but had lost them, only to turn into a dark alley and discover too late that it was an ambush.

"Where's your orange jewel?" Half-pint yelled to Temerity as he swung his meat cleaver at an incoming blade, the two hunks of metal clanging together with a spray of sparks.

"I felt it buzzing," she yelled over the cacophony, "but I ignored it."

"If you ignore it in the trolls' tunnel" —*clash*— "we'll be dead!"

"Yes, Half-pint." She ran up the wall with her snakeskin boots and lunged down into the fray, swinging her sledgehammer.

Their opponents dodged and covered their heads as she flew in from above and Half-pint shapeshifted into a shrieking cat, clawing at necks and faces.

Tomaz and Keenan had managed to switch positions with the assailants, hemming them in and blocking the exit. One of the men was on his knees, covering his bloody head. Another was battering at Half-pint the cat with gloved fists, and the other two were crouched in defensive stances, eyeing them warily.

"You give?" Tomaz asked.

"Go to hell," one of them spat back.

"Yes, we do! We give!" the one fighting Half-pint yelled. "Get this mangy tomcat off me!"

Half-pint pounced away and turned into his goblin form, smoothing a finger down the flat edge of his meat cleaver's blade and flicking off drops of blood.

Three of the men exchanged glances, while the fourth was still on his knees, holding his head.

"Give us two blue jewels and I'll heal your friend here," Half-pint proposed, baring his green and yellow jewels and glancing at the kneeling man. "And your face," he said to the one with cat scratches crisscrossing his cheeks and forehead. "I stayed away from your eyes on purpose."

"Mighty kind of you," the adventurer grumbled, wiping away blood with his sleeve. "But we only have one blue jewel."

"I'll take it," Half-pint said. "What else you got?"

He handed Half-pint the blue jewel, then conferred quietly with his companions.

"Just show us your weapons," Keenan said impatiently. "We don't have all day."

"Heal us first," the man with the scratched face said, and gestured to his companion, who was lying on the ground, moaning, with blood pooling under his head.

Half-pint pulled out his green jewels and went to work.

The four men were in a much better mood after Half-pint healed their injuries, but they still grumbled as they laid their weapons in a line on the cobblestones. It was a sorry collection of weapons, even to Temerity's untrained eye. There was a pitted and rusted sword that Pauly would have melted down; another sword that was halfway decent—but hers was better; a collection of random hunting knives; a small hatchet; and a wooden club.

Temerity examined the men—another lot of first-time adventurers from a small village, by the looks of them.

Temerity and Half-pint shared wry glances with Tomaz and Keenan.

"I'll trade you my brass knuckles for that sword," Tomaz said, pointing his chin at the nicer sword.

"Those knuckles ain't worth this sword, not by a long shot," the man replied.

"Listen, here," Tomaz said, his perennial smile curling into something resembling a sneer. "You lost and we won. Hand it over."

"Will not," the man said.

"These knuckles have broken many noses in their time. Good for a Melee fighter, if you have the balls."

"Oh, I have balls, bigger than you can ever imagine."

Tomaz spat on the cobblestones. "I can think of nothing more disgusting than imagining such a thing. Come on, it's a fair trade."

The man folded his arms and set his jaw.

"I'll sic the cat on you," Tomaz said, darting a glance at Half-pint, who was sharpening his cleaver.

The man scowled but made the trade, trying on the brass knuckles and polishing them on his sleeve while Tomaz demanded the scabbard. With that transaction completed, Keenan stepped forward.

"I'll trade you this here leather punch for that hatchet."

The four men stared at the leather punch.

"Are you shittin' me?" the one with the hatchet scoffed. "What, do you think I'm gonna get into a fist fight with a deer hide?"

The others broke out laughing, and Keenan's neck and cheeks grew red. "Here, take my knife, then," Keenan said, holding out his hunting knife.

It was not a bad knife, and a fair trade. They made the exchange, and each foursome went their separate ways.

Temerity and her band strode down a street lined with abandoned inns, keeping an eye out for other roving bands of adventurers.

"Aren't you going to wear the blue jewel instead of yellow?" Temerity asked, nodding at the yellow jewel that was still on the hobgoblin's wrist.

"No," Half-pint said, taking the new blue jewel from his pocket and admiring it. "Not yet. Level One players are so easy to manipulate with yellow jewels. They don't understand the yellow's charming power. It gives us a big advantage." He slipped the blue jewel back into his pocket and turned to Keenan. "What are you going to do with a hatchet?"

"You said somebody needs to play Range," he said. "Watch this." Keenan held the hatchet in front of him, then cocked it over his head with both hands and threw it.

Temerity followed the glinting blade as it turned end over end and landed with a thunk in an old wooden sign hanging from a post, in front of what looked to have been a pub at one time.

"Not bad," Temerity said, walking with the others to retrieve it. Keenan jiggled it free from the thick oaken sign that was in the shape of a shield. The painted lettering had mostly worn off, but carved into the wood was the name *The Dragon Shield.*

"Well, I'll be," Half-pint said. "Give me a leg up there."

He looked up at Temerity, and she knelt on one knee while he climbed onto her shoulder. She stood up, and he hopped onto the horizontal arm of the signpost, balancing easily on his bare hobgoblin feet. "Give me a hand with this," he said, tugging at the sign's rusted hooks.

The two young men lifted the sign from below while Half-pint guided the hooks loose from the metal eyes, saying to Temerity, "We're supposed to follow the signs, remember?"

"Ha ha," she said as they lowered the sign to the ground and Half-pint climbed down the vertical sign pole.

"I think I know where you're going with this," Tomaz said as he unscrewed the hooks from the top of the sign.

"You're pretty quick for a pig farmer," Half-pint said with a wink.

"*Wheat* farmer," Tomaz said blithely, lifting the sign and admiring it. "It's pretty heavy," he observed, not unhappily. His thick arms and broad shoulders were plenty strong enough to carry a slab of wood, Temerity reckoned. It was quite large, reaching from his shoulders to his knees, and was shaped like a kite—triangular with a flat top and two curved edges. "Now I just need a handle."

"I have some extra leather," Temerity said, digging out scraps the leatherworker had given them.

"I shouldn't have left behind my hammer and nails," Half-pint said, wrinkling his brow.

"I have nails," Keenan said, producing a handful of wrought-iron nails from his travel sack. He used the flat side of his hatchet as a hammer and attached a short gripping handle, a second strap to brace Tomaz's forearm, and a third, longer strap for carrying the bulky thing on his back.

Tomaz carried it proudly, and the band of four strutted down the dark alley, searching for their next victims.

33

CRUSHERS

They came upon their next band of four right out in the open. Temerity and her crew were walking down a street, and the four men were walking towards them. All at once, the four men charged, running at them at full speed and with no warning, not even from the orange jewel, whose constant, nervous vibration was not helpful.

Temerity and her bandmates hesitated for a moment too long, hovering between running away and meeting them head-on, until they had no choice but to fight—and these guys were not playing. Nor were they newbies.

It was not a fair match. The men were all outfitted with heavy steel weapons, thick leather armor, and no sense of humor. First, Keenan went down with a longsword blow to the head. Next was Tomaz, whose shield was yanked from him by a halberd. He was tackled to the ground from behind, then suffered three lightning-fast strikes from a battle-axe, spewing arcs of blood from his thigh, arm, and back. Temerity parried a sword slash but turned her head too late, meeting a heavy iron mace with her helmet. The steel helm clanged like a bell, and the sky exploded with stars.

❖

"Oh, good," Half-pint said, kneeling next to her with the glowing green jewel pressed against her heart. "I thought you'd died there for a second."

"What?" she asked, her head muzzy. She rubbed her eyes and sat up. "What happened? Where'd those crushers go?"

Half-pint was already at Tomaz's side, healing his back wound. The hobgoblin lifted his green jewel and said, "Crushers? They ran away."

"Why'd they run away?" she asked.

He ignored her question. Tomaz was still groaning from the pain of his other injuries, but Half-pint rushed over to Keenan, who was sprawled motionless on the cobblestones. Temerity bandaged Tomaz's arm and leg, trying to staunch the bleeding, while Half-pint leaned over Keenan. It took several minutes for Keenan to come around, but he finally sat up, bleary-eyed. Half-pint staggered over to Tomaz and worked on closing up his other gashes.

"How come they didn't kill you?" Temerity asked as Half-pint held the healing jewel to Tomaz's leg. "Or at least gravely injure you, like the rest of us?"

"I turned into a cat. They screeched and hightailed it out of here."

"Those crushers are afraid of cats?" she asked skeptically.

"Not afraid of cats," Half-pint said. "Afraid of shapeshifters. Scares some people." He smiled and waggled his ears.

"Did you revive Keenan from death?" she asked.

He didn't answer until he was finished healing Tomaz's

thigh wound, then he looked up and said, "No. He was just unconscious."

"Would you have revived him if he had been dead?" she asked.

"I don't know. It's very early in the game, so probably not." He moved on to Tomaz's arm, not at all concerned about what he had just said.

"If I had died, then I would go back to the beginning, right?" Keenan asked, more curious than troubled that Half-pint might have chosen to let him perish.

"That's right," the hobgoblin said. "Hold still, Tomaz."

"What would I have done, then?" Tomaz asked, rubbing his leg with his good hand. His pants were torn and bloody where the battle-axe had sliced through the woven fabric.

"That would be up to you," Half-pint replied. "You could find a homing spike and meet Keenan back at the beginning, if you wanted. You two should figure out a plan, in case one of you dies."

The two young men glanced at one another while Half-pint finished healing Tomaz's arm.

"We'll meet back at Temerity's tavern," Tomaz said with finality.

Keenan smiled and walked over to Tomaz as Half-pint stood up, the healing complete. The two farm boys clasped hands in a pact, and Keenan pulled Tomaz to his feet.

"If you do, tell my ma I'm fine, and that I miss her."

"We sure will, Miss Temerity," Tomaz said, adopting Half-pint's name for her. The big man shook out his limbs and felt around to his back, regarding the hobgoblin gratefully. "Good as new," he said with a wide grin. "Thank you."

"My pleasure," Half-pint said, then slowly collapsed onto the paving stones, lying on his back and staring up at the gritty sky. "Water," he croaked.

Temerity rushed to him with a waterskin, held up his head until he drained the whole thing, then fed him dried snake meat and dried fruit. He chewed slowly, then turned his mouth away when she offered him more.

"Hand me my pack," he said weakly. "That was a lot to heal all at once."

Temerity found the pack on the ground nearby and brought it over. "Give me a drop of the red jewel infusion," he whispered hoarsely.

She fumbled in his pack and found a red vial, then held the dropper over his open mouth.

"Are you sure you're supposed to drink this stuff?" she asked warily, but he grabbed her wrist and brought it closer, and she squeezed the dropper until a single red drop fell onto his tongue.

He swallowed. "I hope so," he murmured, then closed his eyes and moaned.

◆

Half-pint recovered quickly. They were still sitting in the middle of the empty street, preparing to leave, when Temerity glanced around and patted at the cobblestones behind her. "Where's my sword?"

"And where's my shield?" Tomaz asked, climbing to his feet.

"And my scythe?" Keenan added, displaying a rare flash of anger.

"They grabbed them before they took off," Half-pint said, gesturing towards a dark alleyway.

Temerity pushed back her sleeves, exposing the glow of her double-red and orange. "They didn't take our jewels."

"Well, they can't have my scythe," Keenan said, hopping to his feet and pacing back and forth.

"Or my shield. We should go after them," Tomaz said.

"What, and almost die again?" Temerity asked.

"Sure," Tomaz said with a big toothy grin. "We have a Mage Healer." He patted Half-pint's head.

"Do not touch my head," Half-pint said, standing up and pulling on his helmet. "You do not touch a goblin's head."

"Sorry," Tomaz said, backing away with his hands in the air. "Didn't mean to offend."

"I'm older than the three of you combined," he said stiffly, picking up his sylph robe from the ground and flapping it with a loud snap, sending up a cloud of dust, then swinging it around his shoulders. "Show some respect."

"My apologies, oh Mage Master Half-pint," Tomaz said with a deep bow.

Temerity shook her head, her expression somewhere between a wince and a grin.

Half-pint stalked off down the street, and the three of them hurried to catch up.

"Where are you going?" Temerity asked.

"We need to take a break," Half-pint grumbled. "We need to find an inn sector and a town square, and get some proper food and rest."

"I second that idea," Temerity said.

"Me too," Tomaz said.

"Me three," said Keenan, and the two young men and Temerity fell in step behind the hobgoblin.

◆

"How are we going to find a town square?" Temerity asked as they passed one dark alleyway after another.

"The straight roads eventually lead to an inn sector and a square," Half-pint said. His mood had improved, and he strode at Temerity's side, with the two young men walking behind them.

"We never found one before," she said. "Not since we started playing the alleys."

"That's because we never found a road that ran straight for more than a few blocks. Am I right?"

She shrugged and squinted at the road ahead of them. It did extend in a very straight line, fading into the murky distance. "I suppose."

"They've always twisted and turned," Half-pint affirmed. "This means the dragons are leading us to our destination."

"Really?" Keenan asked. "I never knew any of that."

"Me neither," Temerity admitted.

"There are things you learn after visiting this town a dozen times," Half-pint said.

"You've been here a dozen times?" Tomaz asked. "That means you've played this game a dozen times?"

"Sixteen, to be exact," Temerity answered for Half-pint. "He won the whole game, that's how he has that end-game jewel and saved us from the brink of death."

"Wow, that's impressive," Tomaz said, whistling. "Why'd you come back?"

Half-pint glanced up at Temerity. "For her sake," he said softly.

She gazed back at him in surprise.

"For Temerity?" Keenan asked. "That's friendship."

"It's called loyalty, my good man," Half-pint replied. "I made a promise, and I always keep my promises."

"What promise?" she asked.

Half-pint's yellow eyes gleamed up at her. "When you were born, your father asked me if I would promise to always protect you."

"He did? You did?" Tears sprang suddenly to her eyes, and she reached under her collar for the half-locket, clasping it between her fingers and then pressing it to her beating heart.

34

ᴄCOMPANIONS

J ust as Half-pint had said, the straight road led to an inn sector with a town square in its center. They found a clean-looking inn that accepted coin instead of barter and rented a private room with four straw mattresses, complete with scratchy wool blankets and flat feather pillows. It was on the second floor and looked out over an alleyway with an easy exit, if it came to that. They tossed their belongings to the floor, claimed their mattresses, and took turns washing up at the water basin, ladies first.

"That was good practice," Half-pint said, peeling off his leather armor and stretching out on his bed. "If you think those crushers, as you called them, were bad, you should try trolls."

"Oh, we know, believe you me," Tomaz said, and Keenan nodded as he gargled and spat out the window.

"Those crushers were like baby trolls," said Keenan, filling his mouth again from his waterskin and swishing the water around in his mouth.

"Exactly. We're going to find those baby trolls," the hob-goblin said, rolling himself in his blanket and turning onto his side. "First, we're going to kill them, then we're going to get your weapons back."

"Kill them?" Temerity asked.

"They have a battle-axe," Tomaz said, his eyes glittering.

Keenan spat again and asked, "How are we going to find them in the first place, never mind stay conscious long enough to kill them?"

"We'll figure it out tomorrow," Half-pint said, and two seconds later, he was snoring.

◆

"Where are you guys from?" Temerity asked. She was sitting on her mattress, and they were across the small room, on theirs. Half-pint was snoring in a steady, buzzing cadence.

"Bristle Flats," Keenan said, pulling his fingers through his long, tangled blond hair.

"Where's that?" she asked. "Want to borrow my comb?"

"You brought a comb?" Keenan asked, accepting it gladly.

"She's a girl. Of course she brought a comb." Tomaz turned his brown eyes to her. "Young woman, sorry." He grinned, and went on, "Bristle Flats is out in the boonies, a few hours' horse ride northeast of Glistening City."

"Have you ever been to the city?" she asked.

"Keenan has. His cousin studies there."

"Is it nice? I hear everything glitters," she said, recalling paintings she had seen of the magical capital city.

Keenan shrugged. "It's okay, but I wouldn't want to live there. It's all polished stone and metal and glass. No trees except at the university and the rich areas. Lots of rules and snotty people. I like Bristle Flats better."

Temerity examined the two young men sitting across from her. She had met a few travelers from Glistening City, who had stopped at the Tin Roof on their travels. They talked and smelled funny and treated her as though she were their servant instead of the daughter of the owners of the establishment. As though book learning and gold were more important than working with your hands and earning an honest living.

She much preferred the company of these two men, whom she could well have grown up with. They had the rough exterior and honest hearts of most everyone she knew from the small villages and farming communities around Haverly Arms.

"Why'd you come all the way to my town to enter the Dragon's Game?" she asked. "I thought there was an entrance in Glistening City."

"There are two entrances in the city," Keenan said. "Far as I know. And two in Port Maverick. And one in the caves in the northern reaches. I heard about the one in Haverly Arms from my pa. He said it was the safest one. Not very many people use it, and it's not infested with thieves and murderers, like some of them are. Or so he told me."

"You left your pa on the farm?" she asked.

"No," Keenan said. "Both our fathers are in the game somewhere. We hope. They've been gone for two years now. We waited until our little brothers were old enough to help our mothers and sisters with our farms, then we took off. And here we are." He smiled and worked at another knot in his hair.

"Have your fathers ever won the game?" she asked.

Tomaz answered. "No. They made it to the last level once, but died. Two guys on their team stabbed them in the back. Literally. They went back in to find those guys and finally beat the game."

"Were there seven levels last time they tried?" she asked. "Half-pint told me the number of levels can change."

"Yeah, there were seven," Keenan said, counting on his fingers as he listed off the levels. "Dark Town, the Swamp, Pastoral Lands, Feudal Feuds, the Secluded Islands, Palace Intrigue, and finally, the Tower."

"I thought the last level was dungeons. Real dungeons," she said.

"Yes. There are dungeons below the Tower, supposedly. That's where our fathers were killed."

"Your fathers never told you about the end-game jewels, or the take-one-leave-one rule?" she asked.

"Well, they might have mentioned something about it," Keenan said. "I didn't really know what they were talking about, most of the time. Plus, that would have been a long time ago. Last time they came out, they went right back in. They were mighty pissed off. My pa spent most of his short stay eating and drinking and sleeping, and spending private time with my ma. She was not happy he was going back in so soon. He told me to take care of her, then he was gone."

She listened to their stories of home, chewing on her lip and thinking of her ma, and the rat terriers, and the cows. And the two young bulls in the back pasture that must be growing fat by now. And even the chickens. What she had considered a dismal existence did not seem so bad, after all.

"So the dungeons are under the Tower," she said. "What are they like? And is the Tower really in Glistening City? Have you seen it for yourself?" She wanted to get as much information from them as she could, seeing as how Keenan had first-hand—or second-hand—knowledge. Much better than the rumors and yarns she'd heard in Haverly Arms.

"You have to get through the dungeons first, before you can enter the Tower," Keenan said. "Real dungeons, with cells and torture chambers. Sounds horrifying. And the Tower is supposedly in Glistening City, but I've never seen it. It's inside a city within a city. Someplace you can't get to directly from the real world, only by passing through all the levels of the game. I don't really understand it, myself. It's the dragons' seat of power, supposedly."

"But how is there an entrance there, if you can't get there from the real world?" she asked, trying to puzzle out the dragons' nebulous world.

"There's an entrance to the Level One tunnel labyrinth under an ancient castle with a tower keep, on the outskirts of the city," Keenan said. "I've seen that with my own eyes. But the Tower in the game, well, I guess it's in the same location, in another dimension or something ... but they say it reaches up so high that you can't see the top from the ground."

"I hope our fathers aren't stuck in the dungeons again," Tomaz said.

"Me too," Keenan agreed.

"My pa, too," Temerity said. "He's in here somewhere, with my two brothers. Look," she said, pulling out her locket and crossing the room to show them the miniature portrait. "Have you seen him in Dark Town, by any chance?"

They examined the tiny likeness and shook their heads. "No," Tomaz said. "I don't think so. I hope all our fathers and your brothers are climbing the final Tower as we speak."

"And Half-pint's son. He's in here, too," Temerity said. "He won the game five times and came back in for his white end-game jewel."

"No way," Tomaz said, casting a respectful glance at the snoring hobgoblin. "Here's to all of us." He raised his water-skin in a toast.

"Hear, hear," Keenan said, handing Temerity her comb and raising his waterskin.

She fetched her waterskin, and they drank to their success.

35

BARTER

They headed into the market square, devoured hot food from various street vendors, stocked up on their food supplies, and then went in search of a leatherworker. They found a dwarf selling leather goods, and he directed them to the craftsmen's district a few blocks away. There, they found a strip of leatherworking shops and tanneries, and entered the one he had recommended: *Dwarven Fashion Creations.*

It was a dwarf's delight—combination workshop and wholesaler, with racks of dwarf-sized leather armor and other gear. A husky dwarf was browsing the wares and another dwarf wearing an intricately tooled leather vest was tending the shop. A rhythmic pounding and the whistling of a happy tune came from the back workshop area.

"Do dwarves play the Dragon's Game?" Temerity whispered to Half-pint.

"Only for fun," he whispered back. "Same as elves. Both

races live on this side of the worlds. If they die here, they really die. There is no other home to go back to."

"What about faeries, nymphs, and sprites?" she asked.

"Well, there are many types of fae. But nymphs, sprites, and the smaller goblins like me were inhabiting the forests and valleys when the worlds split apart, eons ago, and we got stuck on the same side of the rift as humans. And gremlins too, unfortunately, and other such wicked imps and fiends. That's our only home, same as you."

"We all used to be together?" she asked, gesturing towards the dwarves.

"Yes. The dwarves dwelled deep underground at the time, so they ended up in the dragon's land after the split, and the true elves lived higher up, so to speak, so they also landed in the dragon's side of the worlds. Only the surface dwellers got stuck on our side, the place we call the 'real world.' Ours is the best side, in my opinion. To the dwarves and elves, plus orcs and trolls and ogres and many others, this is the real world, and we are thought of as outsiders."

"What can we do you for?" the shopkeeper asked, interrupting their whispers. The dwarf eyed Half-pint's leather attire. "You've got some nice body armor, there. Where'd you get that?"

"A sector over yonder," Half-pint said, waving vaguely towards the door. "Had it custom made."

"Dwarf?" the shopkeeper asked, inspecting the stitching. "Gnome?"

"No, a human. Tall. Gray hair. Nice chap."

The dwarf's brow raised in recognition. "Oh, yes. I thought the handiwork looked familiar. He learned everything he knows from my uncle. What happened here?" he asked, pointing to the rough stitching down the front.

"Gremlin," Half-pint said with a dark scowl.

"Ugh, nasty creatures, gremlins." The two little people shook their heads in rueful commiseration. "I can have my cousin fix that up for you, if you'd like. Won't take but a few minutes. He can straighten it out and add a protective flap, and sew on some leather straps, so that you can tighten or loosen it in the front."

"That would be great," Half-pint said, patting his belly. He removed his cuirass, and the dwarf disappeared into the back, reappearing with an armful of human-sized leather cuirasses and piling them on a table.

"Looks like you thin-skinned humans could use some adventurer's garb," the shopkeeper said, regarding the young men's homespuns with a critical frown. His gaze slid to Temerity's foppish attire.

"I like my pants and tunic," Temerity said, wrapping her arms around her velvet-clad torso. "They have lots of pockets."

"They're, um, very colorful," the dwarf said, inspecting her outfit with an appraising eye. "Nice boots and gloves, though. That red snakeskin is impossible to get."

Temerity and Half-pint exchanged knowing glances.

"How much do these cost?" Keenan asked, furrowing his brow as he held a cuirass up to his chest.

"Oh, a pretty penny," the dwarf said, smoothing his fluffy beard. "But I don't take gold. What have you got to trade?"

The four of them looked at one another, then Keenan reached into his pocket and withdrew his leather punch.

The dwarf's wizened eyes narrowed as he took the leather punch and inspected it. "Human tool, eh? What's this fancy wheel for? This for punching holes in leather?" he asked, inspecting the various sizes of steel punches and squeezing the handles. "Hmpf," he grunted. "Ingenious, I must say. My cousin might want this. What else you got?"

The four of them shrugged, and Tomaz fished a woolen cap out of his travel sack.

The dwarf shook his head. "I'm sorry, I can maybe give you a belt in exchange for the tool."

Disappointment scored Tomaz's and Keenan's faces.

"Wait," Temerity said, and delved into her pack. From the very bottom, she pulled out the bundle of snakeskins left over from their final courier run. She didn't even know how many there were.

The dwarf licked his lips as she unrolled the bundle and peeled the long red skins apart. "Let me see. I have, how many? Six? Seven. I have seven," she said, lifting her eyes to meet the dwarf's greedy gaze. Snakeskins were worth a lot, and he knew it.

"You still have all those snakeskins?" Half-pint asked, staring at the stack.

"Yes, why?"

"We could have gotten more jewel infusion oil," he whispered sharply.

"Oh," she said, clutching the snakeskins to her chest. The dwarf's gaze followed the snakeskins that had nearly been in his grasp. "We can go back there and get more," she said to Half-pint.

"We'll never find that place again," he said under his breath. "We'll get lost in the maze of alleys for another eternity."

"We can find it." She raised her voice from a whisper and asked the dwarf, "You know how to get to the human leather-worker's shop, right?"

"Yes, of course I do, I grew up here. You just go ..." and he started describing streets and alleys, corners and streetlamps, left turns and right turns. He stopped talking when he noticed Temerity's and Half-pint's eyes glazing over. "Sorry. It's a little confusing," the dwarf said. "I think that's the way, but I'm not sure I told you exactly right. I know it by sight, but I could have missed a couple of turns here and there. I wish there were street signs in this darned place, it would make things so much easier. Although the streets do change from time to time. That workshop is quite a ways across Dark Town. I only got as far as telling you how to navigate this sector. Where you want to go is seven or eight sectors over and three down. Wait, let me try and draw you a map," he said, turning towards the back.

"A map?" she asked in a high-pitched voice.

"A map?" Half-pint squeaked, and the dwarf turned back around.

"No, no," they both said, waving their hands.

"We c-c-can't ..." Temerity stammered. "No maps. No, no. No maps. We'll just ..." She turned to Half-pint. "We'll just outfit our friends here as best we can. Right, Half-pint? They're our companions. The dragons would like that, right?"

"Yes, yes," Half-pint agreed, nodding vigorously.

"Fine, good," the dwarf said, eyeing the snakeskins with a relieved grin. "Let's have a look, then, shall we? Are you playing Shield?" he asked Tomaz, who nodded. "Figured as much. You'll want this thick armor then."

He selected two cuirasses, and Tomaz tried on both. The dwarf went into the back and brought out more until he found one that fit just right.

"You'll want shoulder guards too, and elbow guards, and gauntlets. And hip faulds."

Tomaz nodded and smiled, accepting everything the dwarf handed him and trying on the various pieces.

"And here, try on these buckskin pants and this barkcloth shirt," the dwarf said, directing Tomaz to a curtained area.

"See? Barkcloth," Half-pint said, waggling his ears at Temerity.

"The best," the dwarf said. "Stronger than silk."

"But not as shadow-sensitive as sylph silk, which is nearly as impenetrable as metal, I might add," Half-pint said, showing the dwarf his sylph-silk robe. They debated the merits of various materials until Tomaz came back out.

"You look good," Temerity said as he turned around to give them the full effect. "Like a real adventurer."

He grinned and flexed his thick arms, and Temerity laughed. He donated his torn and bloody homespuns to the trash bin, then began preening in front of the full-length mirror and examining the complex knot motif carved into the leather cuirass and gauntlets. The detailed tooling would announce to other adventurers the high-quality dwarven craftsmanship, and Temerity wondered if the pattern also contained some sort of warding spell.

"Now, that'll be, let's see," the dwarf said, scribbling on a parchment with a sliver of charcoal. "Five snakeskins for everything."

Temerity and Half-pint frowned at one another. Half-pint rubbed his yellow jewel and talked him down to three.

"Okay, then," the dwarf said, seeming pleased with the trade but still eyeing the four remaining snakeskins. "Do you want me to outfit the two of you as well?" he asked Temerity and Keenan.

"No, not me," she said. "My clothes are already perfect." She didn't even need to bother looking at Half-pint to know that he was rolling his eyes.

"Oh, yes, so you said. Are you playing Range, then?" he asked.

"No, Melee. I'm playing Blade," she said confidently, though she glanced down at the sledgehammer hanging from her belt, wondering if she should try and trade it for another sword.

The dwarf cocked an eyebrow and followed her gaze, then said, "Blunt instruments come in handy for Melees. Especially against those thick-skinned trolls. Although their skulls are hard as rocks." The dwarf choked out a gravelly laugh and then turned to Keenan. "You're playing Range?" he asked, and Keenan nodded. "You're playing Archer, then, are you?"

"No," Keenan said. "I mean, I can shoot, but I didn't bring my bow and arrows. I had thought everyone used blades here."

"In any case," the dwarf continued, "to play Range, you'll want mobility. Something lightweight and flexible. Let me see what I can find."

He disappeared into the back and came out with another pair of buckskin pants, a barkcloth shirt, and a thigh-length, dark-brown leather vest. "Try these on." The dwarf handed the items to Keenan.

Keenan went into the changing area and came back out, turning in a circle to show off his new gear.

"Wait," the dwarf said, glancing at the snakeskins, anticipating that he would be out-haggled again. "There's a dwarven metalsmith next door. Hang on, don't go anywhere." He rushed into the back. A door slammed, and Temerity and her companions shrugged their shoulders and waited.

He returned with a bulging burlap sack, took out two conical steel helmets and plopped one on each of the young men's heads, then pulled out a shirt of chainmail with long sleeves. Keenan held it up to his shoulders, and it reached nearly to his knees. "Good," the dwarf said. "You can wear this under your vest."

Keenan put it on and stretched his shoulders. "It fits, and it's not too heavy," he said, examining the interlocking steel rings.

"And for you, young lady with the flashy clothing." He handed her another chainmail shirt, and she held it up. "Go ahead," the dwarf said. "Put it on under your gold tunic. No one will even see it. Except for the sleeves, and a bit hanging down over those, um, interesting breeches."

She did as he suggested, pulling it on over her linen shift. It was not half bad, and if it would save Half-pint from having to heal her so often, it would be worth it.

"Okay, deal," she said. "Three snakeskins for the helmets, chainmail, buckskins, shirt, and vest."

The dwarf tried to negotiate the last snakeskin into the deal, but he was no match for the yellow jewel, and he disappeared into the back once again. He returned with four leather collars.

"What in dragon's name are these?" Tomaz asked, snapping his on. It covered his throat, neck, and collarbones.

"They're gorgets," the dwarf said, handing one to Temerity.

She tried it on. The gorget reached nearly to her chin and was not too terribly uncomfortable. She tucked the long leather collar piece under her gold velvet lapels.

"Knives to the throat are deadly," Half-pint observed as he put his on. "Thank you."

"That should do it for the last snakeskin," the dwarf said firmly.

Half-pint rolled the yellow jewel around in his palm. "I don't know ..." he muttered, scanning the display racks.

Keenan was in a back corner and turned around, holding up several long-handled brooms. "Can we get these?" he asked.

"Brooms?" Temerity asked.

"Brooms?" the dwarf echoed. "Well, I suppose ... sure, why not?" He shrugged and glanced at Temerity.

"Okay, if you want them," she said, casting Keenan a bemused look.

"Do you have any sinew?" Keenan asked. "And that belt you promised for the leather punch?"

"Sinew?" the dwarf asked, rubbing his bearded chin. He left and returned with a spool of sinew and an adventurer's belt and handed them to Keenan, then turned a hopeful gaze onto Temerity.

She glanced at Half-pint, who returned the yellow jewel to its wrist strap. She turned to the dwarf with a smile. "I think we're all set, then. Thank you kindly."

The dwarf grabbed the snakeskins and whisked them into the back, then returned with Half-pint's repaired cuirass.

The hobgoblin fastened the side straps, then tightened the front straps until it fit just right, while Tomaz and Keenan took turns in front of the mirror, admiring their gear.

They thanked the dwarf and left the building, with Temerity's newly outfitted young companions strutting like a pair of roosters who had finally learned to crow.

36

RANGE ATTACK

"Brooms?" Temerity asked as they walked towards the square.

"Not brooms," Keenan said. "Spears. Or, more precisely, javelins. Now I just need spearheads."

"Ahhh," she said. "Yes, sharp pointy objects are required for spears."

Tomaz quirked a smile. "Keenan's an expert knapper, aren't you Kee?"

"I can make a sharp pointy object if I have to," he said, casting a sidelong glance at Temerity.

Half-pint inspected a broom. "Good solid wood. Straight handle. Can I have the bristles?"

"Sure, they're all yours," Keenan said.

They reached the market square and browsed through the stalls, looking for a suitable material for spearheads. They came upon a rock dealer, and Keenan purchased several chunks of black obsidian.

When they returned to their room, Keenan began walking

in a circle and grumbling. "I forgot I need copper for knap-ping. Did you see any copper at the market?"

"I have some copper wire," she said, digging into her pack. "This was for my torch, but I can spare a bit."

"I don't need much," he said with a grateful smile.

"I traded away my torch stick," she said, eyeing Half-pint, who was stripping the bristles from a broom.

"For a very helpful shadowy sylph-silk robe," he reminded her.

"I know," she said. "But maybe you can cut one of those broom handles in half and we can have two torches?"

"Or a torch and a hobgoblin-sized javelin?" Half-pint suggested.

They made the trade, and work began. Keenan went outside with a broomstick and his hatchet, then returned with two halves of a stick and a stout sliver of wood. He gave Temerity one half of the stick, then he wrapped the wire around the tip of the sliver and began chipping away at a chunk of obsidian.

Temerity gave Half-pint some thread and watched as he carefully wove tufted bristles in with the wooden fletching of his metal bolts.

"What are you up to now?" she asked, to which he simply shrugged and gave her an impish smile.

Keenan was indeed good at knapping, and after Temerity had sharpened her knives, mended some clothing, and dozed off twice, he was done. He used the sinew to fasten the long, narrow spearheads onto four full-sized shafts and the half-sized one, handing each of them a javelin and keeping two for himself.

"You can't keep two," she said.

"Why not?" he asked. "I offered two of my weapons to the dragons: my scythe and my leather punch."

"Hell of a weapon, that leather punch," Half-pint teased.

Keenan pointedly ignored him, and Temerity hefted her javelin. The balance was good.

"I don't know how to throw a spear," she said, "but I can hit a bullseye with a tavern dart."

"It's not the same thing at all," Keenan said with a frown. "I'll show you later."

"What happens if you keep more weapons than you should?" she asked, turning to Half-pint and picking up her sledgehammer.

"Every level has a limit," the hobgoblin said. "But it gets murky later on. You can come in with three. I know that for sure. And you're not supposed to hoard things; you're supposed to contribute your castoffs to the available pool of weapons for others to find.

"What I've learned over the years is that you are allowed to loot, trade, or craft an extra weapon in Dark Town and enter Level Two with four weapons, then add one more at each level. The full rule is, 'leave one, take one, plus one.' But that means 'plus one per level.' People stopped saying the 'plus one' part because greedy adventurers thought that meant plus one for every transaction, and then they walked around with weapons and gear hanging off them like a tinker's wagon. One guy I fought was so loaded up with steel that he could barely move. I felled him with a knife to the back of the skull.

"Anyway, when you start counting potions and other power objects, I still get confused about the rules. Just be assured that you will lose items along the way, and remember that you should always try to trade up and not carry around useless weapons that will only weigh you down. The dragons will extract their due, one way or another."

Temerity tried to count everyone's weapons—which ones

they had started with, which they had left behind, and why. She lost track and started over. After the third try, her head started to hurt, and when Half-pint said, "Same general idea with armor and clothing," she abandoned the effort altogether and lay down for a nap, vowing to write it all down on her slate tablet later and figure it out.

———————◆———————

"You three stay here," Half-pint said, strapping on his weapons.

"Where are you going?" Temerity asked.

"I'm going to find those murderous thieves. Can I borrow your orange jewels?"

Temerity and Keenan raised their eyebrows quizzically but had learned better than to question Half-pint's wisdom. They exchanged their orange jewels for Half-pint's yellow and red ones.

"Be ready to move out the moment I return," Half-pint said, then he climbed out the window and was gone.

They passed the time practicing their throwing technique, launching javelins into the bedding and scattering straw and feathers everywhere.

Some time later, Half-pint climbed in through the window, out of breath.

"Bring me your weapons. Hurry up. And give me back my yellow and red jewels."

They complied, taking back their orange jewels and presenting him with their weapons.

Half-pint placed a drop of red oil on an obsidian spearhead for each of them, a blue drop on another of their weapons, and a blue drop on his steel buckler.

"Follow me," he said curtly, and climbed back out through the window.

They scurried to sheathe and holster their remaining weapons, then hung from the window ledge and dropped down to the alley. Keenan tossed them their javelins and climbed down last. Half-pint shapeshifted into a cat, dashed around a corner, and took off at a loping run, with the three of them on his heels. They jogged at a steady pace for several blocks, navigating twists and turns, then stopped at a corner and peered around a building and down a street that stretched in a straight line into the gloom.

Half-pint transformed into his hobgoblin form, pulled his sylph-silk hood up over his helmet, and skulked along the edges of buildings. The others followed him, flitting silently from shadow to shadow.

Half-pint stopped, pressed his back against the wall, and cocked his chin in a forward direction.

Temerity spotted the silhouettes of four men walking abreast down the middle of the street, away from them, with the casual, confident gait of practiced killers. Shapes of weapons loomed over their shoulders: hilts of swords, a scythe, a mace head, a battle-axe.

Temerity and her companions pressed against the wall with Half-pint, who made a throwing motion. He brandished his javelin, and in a crouching run, hurried silently forward, trailed by his three shadows. When they were in range of the four crushers, Half-pint crept out onto the cobblestone street. The others followed his lead, and Temerity and her bandmates spread out side-by-side, stalked silently forward, and then at Half-pint's gesture, cocked back their javelins.

Temerity threw with all her might, her javelin flying through the air alongside three others. She watched as the javelins hit their marks with red flashes, lodging in a back, a shoulder, a thick neck. Temerity, having realized at the last moment that her target carried Tomaz's shield across his back, struck the man in the calf. Keenan's second javelin followed in the next breath, hitting her target in the back of the skull, which was left arrogantly unprotected. The adventurer stumbled to his knees. Tomaz's axe flew through the air, striking the biggest man in the back again. The four crushers fell forward and hit the ground with grunts and garbled curses, then two of them staggered to their feet, turning to see who had attacked them, while the other two lay in motionless heaps.

Temerity and her mates ran forward as the two men prepared to confront their assailants. Keenan and Half-pint each threw a blade, glinting in deadly arcs. They landed with a crunch and a squelch as the hatchet met a startled face and the meat cleaver lodged in the other man's throat, a grotesque grimace stretching his lips as blood spilled from his mouth and he crumpled to the ground.

The man who'd taken the hatchet to the face yanked the javelin from his mate's calf and threw it with a practiced motion, the javelin glancing off Half-pint's buckler, which emitted a blinding flash of blue, and the javelin skidded across the cobblestones.

They sprinted forward and converged on the hulking man as he pried loose the hatchet from his face and threw it at Keenan, who ducked and laughed. Enraged and bleeding from a crushed eye socket, the man swung his battle-axe, slicing through empty air. They beat him down with sledge and pickaxe, sword and knives, until he moved no more. Tomaz quickly finished off the other man, who had been twitching on the ground.

Temerity stood in a pool of blood, every limb shaking.

"That was horrible," she said, blood dripping from her sledgehammer.

"What was horrible?" Keenan asked. "Killing?"

All she could do was nod, nausea welling up in her throat.

They watched as the four adventurers slowly faded away, leaving nothing but a smattering of blood on the paving stones, along with the weapons they had taken from Temerity and her crew, and a yellow and orange jewel.

"That's it?" Tomaz asked, lifting his arms in exasperation. "All that for two jewels we don't need? Where's the battle-axe?"

"He must have come in with it," Half-pint said, glancing around with fiery eyes. "They couldn't have been here very long—they left little blood. Must have all had end-game jewels, too. How else would they have been so strong?"

"And cocky," Keenan said.

Half-pint nodded and picked up his javelin. "End-gamers can get overconfident and forget to watch their backs."

"They must not have been carrying an orange end-game jewel," Temerity said, feeling much better now that the dead men and pools of blood were gone. She picked up her sword and the orange jewel from the cobblestones. "Otherwise, they would have felt us coming, right?"

"My guess is they were all carrying red end-game jewels," Half-pint said. "Aggressive types tend to choose red. Works for some, I suppose, but not very smart for a team of four. But who ever said adventurers were smart?"

They retrieved the rest of their weapons and the yellow jewel and headed back to their inn.

"Are orange jewels any good?" Keenan asked skeptically as they strode down the dark street, his scythe strapped across his back along with his two javelins.

"If you know how to use them," Half-pint said. "They helped me track those guys down. They're good for scouting. But not only that—some of the fiercest foes I've met carried only orange. One such man I befriended in the dungeons described the premonition power in battle. He said he could anticipate every move, and that time slowed down so much he could dodge or parry every blow and go in for the kill before his opponent even finished his swing."

"Wow, I could use that skill," Temerity said, reconsidering her jewel choices.

"What about yellow?" Tomaz asked, using his javelin as a walking stick.

"Ah, the yellow. Beware the sorcerer. Or sorceress," Half-pint said with a faraway look. "That was my ex-wife's color. They can talk you out of—or into—anything. Hypnotize you and bend you to their will." He shook his head. "Never under-estimate the Yellow Mage."

37

ᗡRAGON GATE

"With this javelin, I have five weapons," Temerity said, back at the inn room, showing Half-pint her sword, sledgehammer, sleeve dagger, boning knife, and javelin. "Was I supposed to leave my javelin on the street?"

"I have more than four as well," the hobgoblin said, showing her his meat cleaver, hunting knife, pickaxe, half-javelin, and buckler. "And if you count the bolts, then I'm way over. But without the crossbow, I'm not counting them. A bow and arrows only counts as one weapon, after all."

"Shields shouldn't count as weapons," Tomaz said.

Half-pint shrugged. "I think they do, but I could be convinced otherwise."

"They are defensive gear, like chainmail," Tomaz argued.

Half-pint waggled his ears. "I don't make the rules. Anyway, you don't have to worry too much about it right now. You'll have to discard any extra weapons before entering the Swamp.

The guards will make sure you only take four. They will let you know if a shield is a weapon or not."

Tomaz's grin flattened into a thoughtful frown.

"How did that halberd rip away your shield so easily?" Keenan asked Tomaz.

Tomaz grimaced sheepishly. "I didn't use the arm brace. It's not in the right place."

"Why didn't you tell me?" Keenan demanded, getting to his feet and grabbing the shield.

"I didn't realize it until I really needed to use it," Tomaz said as Keenan took his hatchet blade and dug at the nail heads, pulling out the nails one by one. They figured out the right spot for the strap, and Keenan hammered it in again.

"What else haven't you told me?" Keenan asked. He playfully punched at the shield while Tomaz tested the straps.

"That your javelins were a brilliant idea?" Tomaz quipped, laughing as Keenan threw kicks at the thick wood.

"You're welcome," Keenan said, pivoting into a flying kick.

They continued roughhousing until Tomaz tackled Keenan, battering him with the shield. Keenan lay motionless on the floor, his face pale and eyes closed. Temerity rose to her knees on her mattress, where she had been watching them play-fight. He wasn't breathing, and Tomaz leaned over him. "Hey, Kee," he said, shaking his friend's shoulder. Keenan popped upright with a ghoulish grin, startling Tomaz and earning a cuff upside the head.

"Alright, young men and young lady. We're ready for Ogre's Eyes." Half-pint stood up and slung his adventurer's pack over his shoulders. "Let's check out of here and vamoose."

"Already?" Keenan asked with a slightly stricken expression. "We'll just get killed again."

"Yeah," Tomaz seconded. "Those trolls are mean."

"Gotta go back in sometime," Half-pint said. "Now is as good a time as any. We have our jewels. We traded up some of your gear and got some practice in. We work well together as a team." Half-pint examined the reluctant expressions on Tomaz's and Keenan's faces, and continued, "We risk dying if we linger in the alleys too long. As you may have noticed, the stronger we get, the stronger the adversaries we attract."

"But I don't have a battle-axe," Tomaz pointed out.

Half-pint shrugged. "Can't wait for perfection. Besides, some of the trolls carry battle-axes. Loot an axe from one of them."

"But first I'd have to kill one," Tomaz said, fear flashing in his eyes.

"You never killed any trolls?" Half-pint asked, lowering his bushy eyebrows skeptically.

"Well, yeah. A couple. But that just made the others even madder and then they attacked me even harder. I had no opportunity to loot anything. Especially with Rory sprinting through the tunnels like a crazy person."

Half-pint smiled, showing his many teeth. "Trolls are always angry. It'll be better this time around, without that jackass Rory, I assure you."

"So, I'm supposed to play Shield?" Tomaz muttered, not sounding very confident. "That means I have to go first."

"Yes, just like you've been doing all these days," Half-pint said. "Stop whining and get your stuff. You'll do fine."

And with that, they gathered their things, left the inn, and headed down the straight street.

After three days of crossing several sectors and circling back again, with Half-pint cursing the complex maze of alleyways, they finally found the central square that led to the Dragon Gate. They stocked up on food and water again and ignored the bands of adventurers who wandered around the square puffing out their chests and intentionally knocking shoulders as they strutted by.

"Reds," Half-pint muttered.

They all pretended not to glance back at the glowing cap-stone of the homing spike as they passed through the archway and entered the gauntlet. They found the end of the interminable line and waited. And waited. And waited.

———————◆———————

They decided to go in with nearly the same mix of jewels: two blues and a red for Tomaz; two reds and an orange for both Temerity and Keenan; and a red, blue, green, and end-game green for Half-pint, the hobgoblin swapping out his yellow for the extra blue.

"Now, don't go dying unnecessarily," Half-pint said with a warning scowl. "If you get injured, run to me and I'll heal you, or lie down and play dead and I'll get to you as soon as I can."

They nodded mutely, and Temerity's heart thudded in her chest. She regarded her companions. They looked like seasoned adventurers: Half-pint and Tomaz with their scuffed leather armor and dinged shields, and Keenan with his chainmail. Temerity glanced down at herself. She shrugged. She looked fabulous in her velvet-and-satin finery. And she had genuine dwarven mail underneath her extravagant attire.

A team of adventurers strolled by, looking for the end of the line, and their gazes landed on her. She struck a dashing pose, flipping her green sylph-silk cloak over her shoulder to expose her gold waistcoat and colorful satin pants, and dared them with her eyes to say something. Their eyes flitted to her chainmail sleeve and Pauly's sword, and they clamped their mouths shut and continued on.

When they finally progressed to the head of the line, they showed the orc guards their three jewels each, and were allowed to pass through the Dragon Gate.

The din of the gauntlet faded away as the four of them walked through a long stone passageway. It was lit by torches, and the stone walls curved overhead to form a barrel-vaulted ceiling, every inch carved with detailed scenes of dragons. Some were like those on the outer gateway: fire-breathing dragons chasing hordes of fleeing men, whose weapons were no defense against the flaming inferno. But other scenes depicted humans curled up in the curve of a dragon's tail or sitting happily at a dragon's feet, as though depicting a mother with her children. Still others were of dragons soaring through the sky, free and joyful.

Unlike the streets and buildings of Dark Town, which were made of dreary, black or gray stones, these walls were a soft, shimmering white, which caught the torchlight and reflected it back, illuminating the passageway in a comforting glow.

They reached the end of the archway and entered a massive stone cavern, and Temerity felt as though she were stepping into another world. The noises from the street had disappeared entirely, replaced by a deep silence that reminded her of the tunnel labyrinth. The white stone of the archway had transitioned to a wavy, red-and-white-striped stone, like ribbon candy. The stone was luminescent, lighting the space without the need for torches. The walls soared up to a jagged ceiling of the same glowing rock, with stalactites hanging down like chandeliers.

Half-pint gestured for them to gather around him. Temerity tore herself away from the wonder of the cavern and knelt on one knee next to Tomaz and Keenan to listen to what he had to say.

"This is an ancient salt mine," Half-pint told them, in a hushed tone. "The dragons' lair. They allow us in here to test us and see if we are worthy of proceeding to the next level of the game. The dragons do not deign to fight us themselves. The trolls and ogre do the dragons' bidding, and their job is to winnow out the weak. The trolls may appear one at a time, or more often, they appear in packs.

"Tomaz," he said, "sometimes it is best to sneak past them, but once they have sensed us, they will chase us until we beat them back. They are very difficult to kill, as you know, but weakening them is often enough to leave them behind.

"Now, I will apply a drop of red oil and blue oil to the weapons of your choice, one drop of each per person. It will last for one fight. This is to get you accustomed to the trolls' fighting style, but I don't have enough to use for the whole challenge. So, the first troll fight will be the easiest, then they will get harder after that. Do you understand?"

The three of them nodded, putting on brave faces, and offered him their weapons. He applied the jewel infusion oil, then motioned for Tomaz to lead them out of the chamber.

38

THE RED GATE

Tomaz looked strong with his shield and armor, but Temerity could see his sword trembling. He held the blade in one hand and the shield in the other and led them across the cavern. His javelin was strapped to his pack; they all carried their packs, unsure if they could retrieve them later were they to stash them somewhere. Temerity had fastened slings out of twine for her and Half-pint's javelins, to carry the long weapons over their sylph cloaks.

The space widened, and the back of the cavern split off into several tunnels, forcing them to choose a path. The tunnel directly in front of them was broad and straight. Others curved off into narrower passageways, and the one furthest to the left was of red stone, its glow muted by the rich color.

"Let's try this way," Tomaz said, heading for the red tunnel.

"I think Rory always went straight," Keenan said.

"Yeah, and we always died," Tomaz retorted.

"I think Keenan's right," Half-pint said. "We should go straight."

"I agree," Temerity said, her orange jewel vibrating on her wrist.

"I'm the Shield, and the Shield takes point," Tomaz said stubbornly. "Isn't that what you've been training me to do, Half-pint? Come on." His tone grew more conciliatory. "We're adventurers, right? Let's see what's down there."

He broke away from their scowling gazes and entered the red tunnel, and the three of them reluctantly followed.

The red tunnel was similar to the entry archway, only smaller and blood-red, its walls and barrel-vaulted ceiling carved with fire-breathing dragons and fleeing humans, and other humans bowing in supplication at the dragons' feet.

"What's this?" Keenan asked. They stopped in front of a closed, wrought-iron gate, which had rusted red and whose bars were twisted and curved to form the shapes of flames.

Tomaz pushed the gate and it creaked open. They stepped through it, and Temerity's orange jewel juddered in a silent warning, raising the hairs on the nape of her neck.

"I don't think we're supposed to be in here," she said.

Tomaz ignored her, swaggering along as the tunnel descended in a spiral of red-and-white-streaked stone.

"Tomaz, stop!" she said, but he disappeared from view around the corkscrew turn. Temerity hurried to keep pace with him, growing irritated. "He's stubborn as a goat," she griped to Keenan, who nodded in agreement.

Around and around they went until the passageway straightened out. The tunnel continued to slope downward, leading them deeper underground. The hollow silence was unsettling, and every scrape and rustle made Temerity jump. They came upon a juncture, the single tunnel branching off into four.

Tomaz glanced over his shoulder at Half-pint, who shrugged. Temerity glared at Tomaz. "We're supposed to go *that* way," she said, pointing back the way they had come.

"You're too timid," he replied.

"I'm *smart,* and you can't take it," she said, her hands on her hips.

He scoffed, blowing air noisily through pursed lips, and turned back to consider the four tunnels.

"Pig farmer," she muttered.

Tomaz ignored the insult and led them into the leftmost tunnel, which continued in a steep decline. Temerity's orange jewel vibrated painfully, and she stopped.

"Psst," she hissed, and Tomaz and the others halted. "This is *definitely* the wrong way," she whispered, fear nettling her skin. "We need to turn around."

Tomaz lifted his nose, testing the air. "I don't feel anything. I think this way is as good as any."

"I don't think so," she said, glowering at him.

He pressed his lips together, his smile gone. "I'm the Shield. I lead."

She folded her arms across her chest, reminded of her stubborn older brother, Mathias. "Then you should carry an orange jewel," she snapped.

"Half-pint told me to carry two blues and a red." His normally friendly demeanor had turned dismissive and cocky. He brandished his sword and strode down the tunnel.

Temerity flared her nostrils and stalked after him, walking abreast with Keenan, who was pressing his hand to his orange jewel. "I don't feel anything," he whispered.

"You haven't been wearing yours long enough. It's hard to detect at first. Or maybe you're not sensitive enough."

"I'm sensitive," he said with a serious frown, his gray-green eyes meeting hers.

"Shush," Half-pint whispered. "Noise attracts trolls."

They stopped talking and continued forward, with

Half-pint taking up the rear. Tomaz strode several paces ahead, without even looking back to make sure they were with him.

When they approached a sharp curve, the orange jewel practically leapt off her wrist. Tomaz was strutting out in front, walking fast and not appearing to be listening to the heavy silence around them, so she nudged Keenan and slid her javelin from its sling, crouching as she crept forward. Keenan did the same.

They rounded the curve, and Tomaz drew up short, raising his shield, and then turned and charged at them. *"Run!"* he bellowed.

Over his shoulder, a red snout and golden eyes nearly filled the tunnel. Red-scaled shoulders and a spiky back came into view as the enormous, clawed feet of the dragon moved at a surprising speed.

Temerity screeched, then turned and ran with the others as a deafening whoosh and fiery heat pushed at her back, red and orange flames funneling through the tunnel behind them. Panic propelled her forward, and Half-pint shapeshifted into a cat and raced at her side.

When they reached the juncture, Tomaz headed down another of the four branches. They ran pell-mell over a gradually rising path, running blindly and following the tunnel as it twisted and turned. Tomaz finally stumbled to a halt, and Temerity stopped with him, panting and holding her side. She glanced over each shoulder, not knowing from which direction the next dragon might emerge.

Half-pint changed back into his hobgoblin form and adjusted his sylph cloak. "I've never met a dragon in here before," he said, his eyes bloodshot with alarm. "What in dragon's name is going on?" He glared at Temerity, as though it were her fault.

"Don't look at me," she said, glaring back at him. "You're the one who said things always change in this game. And you!" She turned on Tomaz. "Next time the orange jewel gives me a warning, you will *listen* to me."

"Yes, ma'am," he said, his cocky smile gone. He rested his heavy shield on the ground and leaned back against a candy-striped wall. Pulling off his helmet, he pushed his shaggy black hair away from his eyes and peered around the tunnel. "Do you think the dragon will follow us? Are we going to get lost in here?" He turned to Half-pint. "Is there a certain way we're supposed to go?"

"Now you ask me? I told you to go straight," the hobgoblin said. "I don't recognize these tunnels. In fact, I never noticed the red archway before. But who knows what they've done to the game since I was last here? Or, perhaps the dragons are playing with us."

"Maybe we messed things up when we met the black dragon," she ventured, meeting Half-pint's eyes. "Opened another dimension, or something."

"You've seen dragons before?" Keenan asked nervously. "I've never seen a dragon. I didn't even think they were real. What have you guys done?"

Temerity and Half-pint bobbled their heads helplessly. "Broke a rule," Half-pint said. "It was my fault."

"Uh-oh," Temerity murmured, raising her sleeve and showing them the orange jewel strapped to her forearm.

Keenan reached out and rested his fingers on it, and his mouth fell open. "Uh-oh," he echoed, and they all circled around in a defensive crouch, weapons ready, looking for the dragon.

Temerity felt the pounding of dragon feet trampling up the tunnel. She turned with her companions and bolted uphill, expecting a stream of fire to scorch her back at any moment. They ran straight and then up the corkscrew path and slid to a stop at the iron gate. Temerity feared they had walked into a trap and were locked in, but Tomaz pulled the gate open. They ran through the red arch and emerged into the main cavern, shaking and out of breath.

Temerity looked behind her to make sure they weren't being followed, and squinted. The entrance to the red archway was wavering and shimmering, then gradually closed up, leaving only a jagged crack in the red-and-white-striped wall. The crack slowly disappeared, and she stared at the unbroken rock-salt wall, mouth agape. Half-pint was staring at it as well, but their two companions seemed oblivious, arguing between themselves about which way to go now.

"Straight ahead," Half-pint broke in. "The way everyone always goes. It's the way to the end."

"That's where the trolls are," Tomaz said. "Maybe we should try a different path."

"The trolls *are* the way out," Half-pint said, waving his hands in exasperation. "That's the point. We need to beat the trolls to get to the ogre. Then we need to beat the ogre to leave Dark Town. What is so complicated about that?"

"Dying is what's complicated," Tomaz snapped back.

Half-pint rolled his eyes. "Move along, or I'll take the Shield position."

Tomaz's eyes bulged, his mouth pinching into a knot. "Fine. If the trolls kill me, don't say I didn't warn you." He turned on his heel and walked stiffly towards the middle path, and they left the cavern behind.

39

TROLLS

This path was more like an extension of the cavern than a tunnel, cutting a tall, wide swath through the salt mine. The striped walls and ceilings were carved in places with spirals and wave patterns. Other sections had glyphs carved into the rock, depicting four-legged stick-figure dragons walking in a line from small to large, as if recording the growth of a dragon from a baby to a monstrous adult, with wings unfurled and infernos spewing from gaping maws.

The ground had the same stripes and swirls as the walls and ceiling and was littered with red and white boulders large and small, some big enough for a troll to hide behind. In some areas, the walls tapered into dark caves on either side, offering multiple hiding places.

Temerity's skin prickled as she trod silently over the rock-salt floor, her anxiety worsened by a constant low-level pulsing of the orange jewel. She imagined bands of trolls crouching in the wings, watching and waiting for the right moment to strike. She and her companions were just another team in a long line of adventurers, and attacking them was all in a day's work for the monsters. They probably kept score, keeping a tally of how many adventurers each one had killed and honoring the most prolific killers. Probably they looted weapons, armor, and jewels from their victims, the trolls growing ever more powerful over time.

The orange jewel jolted on her arm, and from the corner of her eye, she detected movement. She jerked to the side, bumping into Keenan, who followed her startled gaze. A bald troll with sickly greenish skin and small horns curving up from the sides of its head crept out from behind a boulder. Its shoulders were wide and hunched, and its beady green eyes tracked their movements. Its hands were larger than her head, and its feet were bare and hairy, with clawed toes. It wore a collection of rags and animal hides, crisscrossed by leather straps with various blunt instruments and a collection of bones hanging from them.

"Troll," she hissed at Tomaz and Half-pint, who had taken the front and rear positions.

She and Keenan broke into a trot, and Tomaz turned to look for the troll, a scowl hardening his features.

"It's a scout," Half-pint whispered loudly. "Keep going. We want to pull more of them for our first fight, to not waste the oil."

Tomaz faced forward again, and the four of them matched pace at a slow jog, scanning the boulders and shadows flanking them, weapons drawn and anticipating a surprise attack. Temerity glanced over her shoulder, but the scout was gone.

Her nerves had heightened from prickling anxiety to hyper-alertness, her attention fully absorbed in the moment and fears forgotten. Her sword was in one hand, and she had exchanged the javelin for the sledge in the other—ready to bash some ugly troll heads.

The trolls came at them from behind. It was a band of five, running on bowlegs and bare, clawed feet, with long, thick arms wielding clubs and maces, swords and battle-axes. Skulls hung from their belts, and necklaces of teeth clanked around thick necks.

Terror rushed up through Temerity's body like a geyser breaking through brittle ground, and every fantasy of bravery and heroics evaporated in a flash of panic. The grotesque monsters were broader and taller than any human and built of solid muscle.

She turned and ran.

"Tomaz!" Half-pint commanded. "Turn around and take the point; meet them with your shield." The hobgoblin barked orders as Temerity and Keenan ran past Tomaz, who had stopped in his tracks and was turning around with his shield raised and his eyes closed.

Temerity and Keenan skidded to a stop and wheeled around, crouching behind Tomaz. Half-pint stood next to Tomaz and threw his javelin, hitting a troll in the chest, the obsidian point buried in muscle and the short haft sticking out. The troll didn't miss a step, his feet pounding on the rock-salt floor and his mouth opening in a rasping roar, long fangs bared.

Temerity and Keenan followed Half-pint's lead and threw their javelins, hitting trolls as they bore down on Tomaz and Half-pint. Stone clubs smashed into the wooden shield and buckler, and steel clashed with steel, flashes of light flaring from oil-imbued weapons.

"Half-pint, get back!" Temerity yelled, pulling him behind her and taking his spot as a mace swung down at her. She dodged the flanged mace and parried a sword blade with her own sword, then, with a rush of red-jewel energy, swung her sledgehammer with all her strength, striking a troll on the elbow.

The monster winced, dropping its weapons to grab its elbow, then barked a coughing laugh, its fetid breath making her gag. Another troll swung a club at her, with the reach of a grotesquely long arm. The arm met the arc of the scythe, the long, curved blade severing the hand and sending it and the club flipping through the air. The first troll grabbed her around the throat, squeezing with an abnormally strong grip, its sunken eyes leering at her. The giant hands crushed her windpipe, cutting off the air flow. She tried frantically to breathe, but she could not.

Pain blurred her vision as she dropped her heavy weapons and unsheathed her knife and sleeve dagger and buried them in the belly of the growling troll. The point of a pickaxe fell upon the skull of the monster, and its eyes rolled up into its head. Half-pint hopped down from Tomaz's shoulder just as Tomaz swung his shield, catching one troll under the chin and sending it stumbling backwards, then jabbing another in the abdomen with the pointed base of the dragon shield.

Temerity pulled at her crushed throat and fell to her knees. Half-pint was in front of her, pressing his green jewel to her throat while Tomaz and Keenan fended off the remaining trolls, beating them back with axes and brute force.

She sucked in a lungful of air and nodded at Half-pint, then took a series of deep breaths to recover while the hobgoblin turned and helped battle the trolls. The big brutes swayed and stumbled under axe blade and meat cleaver, green blood spraying and oozing. Two monsters turned and hopped away, crawling under a dark overhang, and Temerity and her companions spun with their weapons, ready to fend off the next attack, but none came.

Three trolls lay on the ground, groaning.

"Come on, let's get out of here," Half-pint said to Tomaz, who was bashing a troll in the skull with his shield as the monster tried to stand.

The troll crumpled to the ground, and Half-pint said insistently, "We're done here. We need to go."

Temerity stepped forward and yanked her javelin out of a troll's hip, and Keenan retrieved both of his. Everyone scrambled for their weapons, and Half-pint quickly healed their worst wounds.

"That one's got a battle-axe," Tomaz said, creeping towards a bloody troll who was rocking back and forth on his chest, as though trying to roll over. An enormous, double-headed axe glinted from under the monster's shoulder.

Temerity watched warily as Tomaz reached for the metal haft. He grabbed it and started jiggling the battle-axe out from under the troll's body, when a massive hand shot out and engulfed Tomaz's ankle.

"*Argh!*" Tomaz yelled, trying to kick loose the troll's grip.

Temerity jumped forward and arced her sword over her head with both hands, then swung it down, cutting off the troll's hand. The troll roared and lurched to its knees, green blood spurting from its wrist stump.

"Leave it! *Run!*" Half-pint yelled, and the three of them obeyed, overtaking Half-pint, who was sprinting away from the troll as it staggered to its feet and limped after them.

They ran deeper into the salt mine, racing past looming boulders and dark crevices, putting distance between themselves and the crazed troll.

"That was the easy fight?" she yelled to Half-pint as they ran.

"Yes," he said, slowing to a loping gait, and the others fell in step beside him.

40

MOBS

The next pack of mobs had eight trolls, which came from behind with no warning other than the constant throbbing of the orange jewel. Chaos erupted, and suddenly Temerity was battling two trolls at once, their putrid stench overpowering her more than their clumsy attacks. She took a breath between sword swings, the two trolls likewise taking a moment to examine her as she hopped back a pace and reconsidered the wisdom of playing Melee while Keenan crouched safely behind a boulder lobbing javelins.

The trolls were big and strong, but not particularly fast, she realized, once she had channeled her panic into focused combat. But they stank like rotting carcasses. The two of them lunged at her, and she dodged a club and parried a mace with her sledgehammer, then stepped to the side, letting one of the huge monsters run at her. The troll, a particularly ugly specimen with bones piercing its flat nose, charged and swung its mace. She ducked and rolled at the last second, extending her sledgehammer behind her and tripping the lumbering beast.

314

Momentum sent it crashing to the ground. She jumped to her feet as the second troll barreled towards her with its club held high. It looked intent on crushing her skull, but she sprang forward and shoved her sword blade up into its armpit before it could get its wish. Green blood spurted out at her, and she backed away as the monster stumbled and staggered in a circle, blood coursing down its side. The first troll got to its feet and started after her, but she ran off to join Tomaz and Half-pint, who were embroiled in battle with four trolls.

"You need to distract them all," Half-pint was yelling at Tomaz, between swings of his meat cleaver. "Turn them away from us."

"What?" Tomaz yelled back, ducking behind his shield. Keenan had left the cover of his boulder and was swinging his scythe and trying to retrieve his javelins. Temerity's legs were quivering, her muscles suddenly like jelly, but she willed her body to move, pulling her javelin from its sling and launching it at the approaching troll she had just fled from. The javelin landed in the troll's midsection, and its steps faltered for a moment while it stared down at the haft protruding from its belly. It lifted its head and resumed running at her. On instinct, she grabbed the javelin's haft and swung the beast around. Keenan tripped it from behind, sending the troll to the ground with a musical clatter as steel weapons and bones hanging from its belt hit the rock floor. Temerity pulled her javelin free and rammed the spearhead under the monster's jutting chin, using her body weight to push it up into its skull. The troll shuddered and grew limp. Temerity planted her boot on its chest and yanked the javelin free.

She stared down at the troll. It was definitely dead, and her eyes ran over its oily bulk. It looked like a freakish caricature of a human, with over-developed muscles, distorted facial features, nubby horns, and skin the color of a frog. The fact that trolls and humans had once shared the same world, before the rift had torn the worlds asunder, made her shiver with disgust.

"Get them all in a group, attacking you," Half-pint was yelling, trying to instruct Tomaz.

Temerity left the troll's side and rushed to join her companions. Tomaz was on his knees with his shield over his head under a flurry of blades and clubs. "What do you think I'm doing?" he yelled back.

Half-pint turned into a cat and leapt through the air, landing on the bald head of the largest troll, and Temerity and Keenan jumped at the others from the rear, slashing and pounding, until the remaining monsters were prone and twitching on the ground, some motionless and bleeding out with green puddles forming around them.

"Come on," Half-pint said, a hobgoblin again. He retrieved his short javelin from the ground and meat cleaver from the skull of a glassy-eyed troll, then pressed his jewel to Tomaz's bleeding forehead and then his arm, which Tomaz claimed was broken.

While Half-pint tended to him, Temerity stood to the side, dabbing at a gash across her palm with a scrap of linen and warily regarding the half-dead trolls, one of which was feebly attempting to rise. One of her eyes hurt, and a laceration on her cheek dripped blood down her jaw and onto her collar. She tried to staunch that as well, vaguely recalling taking a blow from a troll's elbow, though she had no idea how she had cut her hand.

Half-pint finished with Tomaz, then they grabbed their weapons from the mass of green bodies and trotted further into the tunnel. Temerity wrapped the bloody bandage around her hand and hurried to keep up.

Half-pint called out instructions. "Keenan, you take rear guard. You have an orange jewel—use it. Warn us if any trolls come at us from behind again. Temerity, you and I will take the center. You scan the left flank, and I'll scan the right. We should not be surprised again. We know they're here, waiting for us. Tomaz, wherever the next attack comes from, you need to get in the front, attract all the trolls to you, and then turn the pack away from the rest of us, so that we can attack them from the rear. You got that?"

"All of them?" Tomaz squeaked.

"All of them," Half-pint said sternly. "You're the Shield—you can take it. The blue jewels will blunt the impact of their blows. You need to keep them away from us, and you need to fight them head-on. And try not to take too much damage. And stay alive."

"Rory didn't do any of that," Tomaz complained.

"And we all kept dying," Keenan reminded him.

"Rory is an idiot," Half-pint said. "Only idiots pretend to know what they're doing when they don't, while getting people killed in the process. But, then again, not many noobs have someone on their team with an end-game jewel. In any case, Tomaz, you take the point, attract all the monsters, and turn the pack around so their backs are to us. Temerity, you should be engaging the mobs up close, taking down as many as you can, as quickly as possible. Keenan, you should be picking them off from a distance, as I will be. If someone gets hurt, the others should try and draw the trolls away from them so that I can jump in and heal that person. Then resume as normal. Understood?"

Everyone nodded. Temerity's hand throbbed, her head and

legs ached, and she was breathing heavily, already exhausted and wondering how she was going to survive this.

————————◆————————

They found a small grotto to huddle in, and Half-pint tended to Temerity's injuries. "You should have told me about your hand," he scolded, *tsking* at the blood that was still welling up in her palm. The wound closed up, and he moved the green jewel to her cheek and eye. He went on to heal Keenan's cuts and bruises, and those he had suffered himself. Then they spent a few minutes drinking water, eating a few bites of food, and checking their weapons.

"Can we get more jewel oil?" Temerity asked.

"No, not until the ogre," Half-pint replied.

"How many more packs of trolls will there be?" she asked, trying to sound curious instead of whiney.

Half-pint shrugged. "A half-dozen? A dozen? I can't remember exactly. Depends on how many trolls we attract each time before engaging them."

"This place is infested with them," Keenan remarked, cleaning green blood off his scythe.

Temerity tried to keep her spirits up, reminding herself that she had chosen this path voluntarily.

They took off down the passageway again, and before long, another pack of eight trolls appeared up ahead, swinging battle-axes and war hammers and looking unamused.

"Remember what I told you," Half-pint said.

They nodded, and Tomaz struck out in front while the three of them hung back.

The trolls converged on Tomaz, who crouched with his shield raised, fending off attacks and lashing out with his sword. Keenan lifted a javelin, but Half-pint gestured for him to lower it. "Not yet. We don't want to draw their attention. *Turn them around, turn them around,"* the hobgoblin muttered under his breath at Tomaz, who seemed to be doing all he could just to deflect incoming blows.

Tomaz came to his senses, dodging and weaving through the pack while hooting and hollering. "Come get me, you moldy-cheese-breath slugs. You sheep-dung-covered rats. You festering pus-filled pimples. You fiendish elven-spawn bastards!"

They turned en masse and chased after Tomaz, who had climbed up on top of a large boulder and was dancing, gyrating his hips and waving his weapons in the air, and singing, *"When the trolls dropped their drawers, and the girls shrieked in horror, at the tiny dwarfish pricks, and the acorn-sized bits."*

"Now!" Half-pint said, and changed into a cat, dashing towards the mobs. Keenan threw his javelins, striking trolls who were trying to climb the boulder while Tomaz kicked their heads and smashed them with his shield. Temerity jumped into the fray, slicing limbs with her sword and bashing bald heads with her sledgehammer. Half-pint clung to a troll's face, scratching at its eyes, and Tomaz sank his axe into a skull, then yanked it free and hopped down, pulling the mobs after him and exposing their backs to Temerity, Half-pint, and Keenan, who continued attacking from the rear.

Soon, the trolls lay maimed and bleeding on the ground, and Temerity and her companions dashed down the pathway, leaving them behind.

"That worked great," Tomaz said, holding out a bleeding arm for Half-pint to heal.

"That's what I've been trying to teach you all along," Half-pint said, "but we didn't fight enough big groups in the alleys to really practice that. Plus, trolls are kind of dumb, so it's easy to trick them."

They rounded a curve and skidded to a stop. The path ended abruptly at a cliff, overhanging a gaping chasm. Temerity inched forward and peered over the edge. The cliff plunged down in a sheer sheet of rock salt that transitioned from red and white stripes to solid red and finally to black, the salt's luminescence dimming with the darker rock until the glow faded away completely, far below them. Huge steps were carved into the side of the cliff at their feet, descending in six-foot drops.

"What is this?" Half-pint asked.

"I guess we're supposed to go down," Temerity said.

"I've never seen this before," he said.

"Me neither," Tomaz said. "This wasn't here last time we were here."

"Another dragon's lair?" Keenan asked, pressing his hand to the orange jewel on his wrist.

Temerity traded glances with him, pressing her orange jewel to her cheek. "I hope not. The jewel is pretty quiet."

"Well, it's either down there or back the way we came," Tomaz said.

Half-pint frowned. "If we turn back, we'll just end up where we started. This must be the way. Those dragons—you learn one thing and they throw the next challenge at you."

"They like to torture us like that," Tomaz said.

"Or they want us to keep learning," Keenan mused, peering over the edge. "Let's see what's down there. Shield goes first."

Tomaz sneered at his friend but dropped down onto the first giant step and looked up for the others to follow.

41

GIANT STEPS

Temerity hugged the cliff face as they descended, staying away from the outer edges of the six-foot-square steps, so as not to trip and fall into the void. She crouched and swung from the tops of the steps with her gloved hands to drop down to the next level, followed by Half-pint, who used her shoulder as a step. The stairway descended for a ways, then turned back in the other direction, zigzagging down along the cliff face below them. They reached the red band of rock and continued towards the black.

The further down they went, the darker it became. The glow of the white and red rocks up above dimmed as they descended deeper, until they relied on their jewels for light, which only faintly illuminated a couple of steps above and below.

Temerity pulled out her torch supplies and quickly wrapped a torch cloth around her new stick, used her wire cutters and pliers to wrap a length of copper wire around the tallow-soaked cloth, and lit it. The torch flared yellow and orange, illuminating several of the giant steps. The light made her feel better, even though the abyss yawned ominously not a pace away.

Her orange jewel vibrated, the throbbing growing stronger, and she stopped, cocking her head to listen.

"What's wrong?" Half-pint asked.

"Shhh," she replied.

Tomaz and Keenan halted on the steps on either side of Temerity and Half-pint and brandished their weapons.

Shuffling sounds and grunts followed by a foul stench announced the presence of trolls. A few moments later, several of the monsters came into the circle of light, closing them in from above and below.

Temerity's blood surged through her veins, a torrent of pent-up anxiety escaping the dam of self-control. Various deaths flashed before her eyes: crushed under a troll's fists, beheaded by an enormous blade, smashed by a war hammer, flung over the edge of the cliff.

The trolls stalked forward, pinning them on three steps. Temerity counted six trolls on either side. Tomaz held the line below, fending off the trolls who were trying to climb up onto his step. On the step above, Keenan threw his two javelins and hatchet at the trolls looming over him, hitting one in the eye and sending the monster stumbling over the edge and into the chasm. Keenan swept the scythe across thick, bare-skinned legs while Temerity and Half-pint threw their javelins to aid him. Temerity feared Keenan would soon be overrun and was about to climb up to help him when more trolls clambered down the steps to reinforce the initial wave.

Temerity changed tactics and shrugged off her pack, pulling out her rope and frantically trying to figure out what to use as a stake. Half-pint guessed what she was doing and swung his pickaxe down into the outer wall of their step. He managed to drive it into the rock, and she pounded it in with her sledge-hammer, wedging it tightly in place. Half-pint held the torch while she quickly tied a knot around the metal spike.

She went down first, shimmying to the end of the rope, which dangled a few feet above a step. She dropped onto it and looked up, needing everyone to get down before the trolls descended the stairs and reached her. Half-pint was already halfway down the rope, holding the torch between his teeth, and Keenan and Tomaz had moved to the step she had just left, battling to keep the trolls from climbing onto the six-by-six platform. Keenan went down the rope next, and the trolls clambered onto the step with Tomaz.

He ducked and dodged and grabbed the rope after Keenan, and they both slid down and landed on the step where Temerity and Half-pint anxiously waited, while trolls rapidly descended the rope and stairs.

Temerity grabbed the torch from Half-pint and lit the rope on fire, then hoisted Half-pint onto her back, passed him the torch, and the three humans hopped down the man-high steps, bounding from one to the next. Trolls roared and chased after them from several levels above. Two dropped from the burning rope, hit the step, and tumbled over the edge.

Temerity and her crew raced down the stairs, back and forth, and suddenly hit bottom. It was a dark trench, and they turned to the right and ran along it, torchlight wavering and casting moving shadows as they hopped over the sprawled corpses and fled the other trolls, whose angry battle cries were drawing closer.

"This place reminds me of the tunnel labyrinth," Half-pint said, from his perch by her ear. "The tunnels and the chasm. Remember? There's another section there that is kind of like this, which I encountered a few times, with cliffs and stairs carved into them. I never considered that they might be connected, but now I'm wondering."

Or maybe we've somehow torn open a magic veil, she speculated silently as she ran, *exposing the dragons' secret passageways and intruding on their private territory.* It felt too arrogant to voice her thoughts, that she and her companions had shifted the configuration of the game, nudging it into a new formation. *No, it must be the dragons' intentional manipulation, to keep adventurers on their toes, to keep them guessing.*

"Cockroaches!"

Keenan's yell jerked Temerity's head up.

Emerging from cracks in the walls, thousands of cockroaches launched into the air and fluttered towards them, chittering and hissing.

"Red carapace cockroaches," Half-pint said in a strangled voice. "They're attracted to yellow light." He tried to swat out the torch's flame as the cockroaches flew towards them, but the tallow-soaked cloth was blazing too strongly.

Temerity gritted her teeth and ran faster, but she could not outrun the swarm. They landed in clumps on her shoulders and helmet, cloak and gloves, and soon she was covered with the reddish-brown insects. Shivers of disgust rippled through her as she frantically tried to swipe them away while still running, but their spiked legs stuck to her clothes. Some were trying to climb up her hair and under her helmet, and she grabbed a handful of the armored creatures and flung them to the ground.

"They won't hurt us," Half-pint said, clinging to her shoulder with his clawed feet.

"I can't see," she said, swiping a cluster away from her eyes. Cockroaches carpeted the ground and crunched underfoot as she ran. She cleared her vision in time to see a mass of black swooping down from the cavern's towering heights.

"Bats!" Tomaz yelled.

Shot through with a fresh spike of panic, Temerity ducked as a multitude of chirping bats descended upon them, darting and dancing around her head as they picked off the flying insects. She kept running, with Half-pint crouched on her shoulder, charging through droves of the mouse-sized bats. Their shiny, spiked wings flapped noisily as they carved expertly through the air.

"Ahhhh!" she yelled as more bats swooped in, filling the space around them and dodging one another as they hunted.

Cockroaches dropped off her and flew towards the cliff faces to evade the bats, while Temerity and her band kept running. The insects and bats cleared out as suddenly as they had appeared, and Temerity slowed to a trembling walk, gasping for air. Half-pint hopped down from her shoulder and held up the flickering torch. The chasm was silent again, and Temerity squatted down to catch her breath and steady her thundering pulse.

Keenan's face was ashen gray, and he swiped repeatedly at his shoulders. Tomaz removed his helmet and hung his head down, raking his fingers through his thick hair and beard. A pair of cockroaches fell from his head and flew away.

Temerity stood up, and she and her companions checked each other for any remaining insects. Afraid of trolls and whatever else might emerge from the darkness, they gathered their courage and staggered forward.

Not long after, they came upon an expanse of cliff on their left with horizontal grooves carved into the wall, stacked on top of each other. Keenan stuck his fingers inside a groove.

"It's a ladder," he said, feeling for handholds and toeholds. He pulled himself up a few rungs and peered down at them.

"I should go first," Tomaz said.

"I'm already here," Keenan said, and kept climbing.

Half-pint took his perch on top of Temerity's pack, and she went next.

She felt for the narrow grooves and started climbing, hastened by the shouts of approaching trolls. Tomaz was not far behind. They climbed onto a ledge, took a few breaths, then climbed to another ledge and looked down. The trolls were at the base of the cliff, just visible in the outer nimbus of torchlight. They didn't appear to be climbing up after them, and she hoped that their big hands and feet and hefty bulk wouldn't allow them to scale the ladder.

She and her companions kept climbing. The black rock transitioned to red, then finally to glowing red and white stripes. They made it to the top and looked around, checking for trolls. There were none in sight. She glanced down into the dark chasm and then regarded the path before them.

The passageway was similar in nature to the one they had traveled before, when it had ended abruptly at the cliff. Just like that one, this was wide and long, with luminescent candy-striped walls, the rock-salt floor littered with boulders, and the path bordered by deep shadows. It was as though a great earthquake had split the ground and slid the two cliffs laterally away from one another. It appeared they had picked up the trail where they'd left off.

Half-pint climbed down from her back, extinguished the torch, and carried it like a club. They resumed their formation, with Tomaz in the front, Temerity and Half-pint walking abreast behind him, and Keenan taking up the rear.

42

MELEE

"I lost my javelins and hatchet," Keenan said, propping his scythe on his shoulder.

"We lost our javelins, too," Temerity said, "and my rope."

"And my pickaxe," Half-pint added.

"Looks like you'll be playing Melee with me, Keenan," she said.

He brandished his scythe and sliced the curved blade through the air, then rested the shaft on his other shoulder. "I told you it would make a fine weapon," he said to Tomaz, who looked back with a smirk but did not argue.

The next pack of mobs they encountered had only four hunched-over trolls, but they were larger than the others they'd fought. They appeared like green wraiths behind them, stepping silently from the shadows and skulking after them. The orange jewel knew they were there and alerted Temerity to their presence. She glanced over her shoulder at the lurking trolls, and Keenan hooked his thumb back towards the monsters and then patted the orange jewel on his wrist with a big grin.

She gave him the thumbs up, then jogged to Tomaz's side.

"Trolls," she whispered, pointing her chin behind her.

Tomaz stopped and turned around to face the oncoming pack of mobs, raising his shield, while Temerity, Keenan, and Half-pint got into position behind him.

The two bands clashed, steel sparking.

The trolls were big, but Temerity and her friends were quicker and more agile, dancing away from heavy swings, then striking before the muscle-bound creatures could recover. Few of them wore armor, and many wore little clothing at all. Their oily skin bled from green gashes as blades slashed and tore and gutted the roaring, stinking monsters, whose rancid breath was a lethal weapon all on its own.

She found that if she dodged a blow and dashed to the flank of her opponent, she could land a sword slash to the side of the ribcage, then dart to its rear and wallop the troll upside the head with her sledgehammer, and finally slice the ligaments behind the knees, making the big hulk crumple like a rag doll. With the boost of two red jewels, her heavy weapons felt as light as wooden practice swords, and her technique was honed to a fine edge.

Soon, the four trolls were on the ground, bleeding out or groaning and clawing at the rock. Keenan darted into the sprawl of bodies and emerged with a mace, holding up his prize like a trophy.

"Of course, none of those green globs are carrying battle-axes," Tomaz said sulkily as they left the trolls on the ground and trotted down the path, looking for their next victims.

The next group of trolls was the same. Five instead of four, but large and plodding, and making big swings with blunt weapons that were easy to dodge. Temerity practiced her positionals and attack rotation on a massive troll with a pronounced underbite. The troll came at her, baring long, yellowed canine teeth that curved up from his lower jaw, reminding her of a boar.

Dodge, dip, spin. Flank, rear, rear. Sword, sledge, sword.

She severed the ligaments behind the troll's right knee and leapt away as the beast twisted around with a piercing yowl, swinging a war hammer as it stumbled to the ground. She ducked and rolled and then ran off with her companions, leaving the fallen trolls behind.

A ways further on, another group of four trolls appeared behind them. She alerted Tomaz. He glanced over his shoulder as the two of them ran side-by-side in an easy gait and Half-pint loped next to them in his cat form.

"Not a big enough group," Tomaz said with a cocky smile. "They're just slowing us down. Let's wait until there's more." And he picked up his pace.

Temerity's jewel vibrated insistently, but Tomaz had already sprinted ahead. Glancing behind her, the trolls disappeared behind a bend, and she hurried to catch up to Tomaz.

They continued down the rock-salt corridor as it curved to the left. When they came out of the curve, eight trolls stood across their path, slapping clubs against enormous palms. The one in the front licked the blade of a massive broadsword with a tongue that was long and black. Bile-green blood dripped off the blade.

"Yuck," she muttered, crouching behind Tomaz as he slid to a halt and brandished his shield.

"This'll do," Tomaz said with a sideways grin.

She didn't smile back, but traded glances with Half-pint, who was a hobgoblin again. He lifted his meat cleaver in response.

"Trolls," Keenan said from behind them, his voice pinched.

Temerity glanced over her shoulder. Four trolls were stepping out from the shadows of boulders, hemming them in from the rear.

"Uh-oh," she said. "Tomaz!"

He glanced behind him and made a face at her while shaking his sword and shield at the oncoming pack of eight in a *can't you see I'm busy here* gesture.

She looked at Keenan again, who was facing the four trolls. "Oh, for dragon's sake," she muttered as the four they had bypassed appeared around the bend, running on heavy feet to join the other four at their rear.

Hemmed in by eight trolls in front and eight behind, Temerity hesitated, unsure of which group to confront. Half-pint had joined Tomaz, and so she stood at Keenan's side, sword and sledgehammer out.

A troll behind her let out a piercing, yodeling yell, and both packs charged.

Bedlam broke out. Any illusions she'd had of her skill with rotations and positionals was reduced to mad scrambling as clubs and swords rained down on her from every side. She ducked and dodged and dove as blades cut her legs and arms and a club struck her in the chest, forcing the air from her lungs and slamming her onto her back, her breasts screaming and helmet ringing as her head snapped back and struck the ground.

Clanging and yells battered her eardrums, and a troll loomed over her. A broadsword came down, point first, and impaled her through the chest, her chainmail crunching and giving way to the heavy blade. Her body seized in a stunned spasm as the troll's face leered down at her, and her vision blurred red.

43

SECOND CHANCE

Temerity opened her eyes and gazed blearily up at the candy-striped ceiling. The air was motionless as a tomb, and she wondered if she was dead. She moved her hand to her chest but felt no blood, only the soft velvet of her golden tunic and the twine of her javelin sling. In fact, the javelin shaft was uncomfortable under her shoulder, and her pack was hard and lumpy against her back. She rolled to her feet and stood up, peering around. She was in the cavern just inside the Dragon Gate. The red gate to the dragon's secret domain wasn't visible—the rock-salt wall was smooth and unbroken.

She examined her body—no damage. She dug into her pack—her rope was neatly coiled and tucked in next to her spare clothing and food.

She took in a deep breath, realizing that she had died and been sent back to the beginning of the final challenge. She turned in a circle, confused as to what she was to do next. Was she supposed to run through the passages herself, braving the tribe of trolls, and catch up with her companions? Would the trolls they had beaten back still be injured and groggy, the way they had left them? Or would the monsters have recovered, ready to attack her again? She recalled the packs of trolls they had evaded on the giant stairway. She didn't think she could survive that part on her own. Nor did she want to run through the swarms of cockroaches and bats again.

She stood with her hands on her hips and decided to wait. For what, she was not sure. Her companions would either die eventually and meet her here, she supposed, or was it possible they could beat the ogre without her? Then what? Would she still have to run through the tunnels and meet them at the end—and how would she know if they had won? Or would they come back and get her? Half-pint had not explained how it all worked, and the options were unsettling.

She peered down the length of the carved Dragon Gate, beyond which lay the teeming gauntlet, and beyond that, the town square with the homing spike. She could walk out of here right now and be home in a matter of minutes. She would go directly to the Tin Roof, beg for her ma's forgiveness, and forget this whole misadventure.

But then she would be abandoning Half-pint, Keenan, and Tomaz. Or maybe they would abandon her first, beating the ogre and moving on to the Swamp without her. Regardless, in that event, she would definitely return to Haverly Arms, where life was enticingly normal. But then, when her pa and brothers eventually showed up at home, she would have proved Mathias's claim that women weren't cut out to be adventurers, and her pa would be disappointed. He had always told her that she could do anything she set her mind to. He had taught her everything he'd taught his sons: how to raise cattle and chop wood and build things. How to wield a sword and shoot a bow and arrow, and how to hunt and field dress a deer. Just as ma had taught her brothers how to cook and clean and sew, and how to rock a baby and change diapers. "You never know if you'll need to raise a family on your own, so you need to learn to do everything," their parents had said.

Temerity turned to a flicker of movement on the ground. It was Keenan, yawning and rubbing his eyes, and Temerity's uncertainty fell away.

"Wow, that was brutal," Keenan said, slowly climbing to his feet and examining his arms. "Oh, good. I'm all here. That big ugly one with the battle-axe chopped my hand off." He raised his left arm and caught Temerity's eye. "Those trolls were not playing around."

"No, they weren't. Sorry you died," she said, though that was a lie. Relief and joy at seeing her companion made her want to run over and hug him. But she stood her ground and merely smiled, tempered with a measure of guilt for being so happy that he had died.

"We got our javelins back," she said.

"Oh, yeah," he said brightly, pulling both of his from the strap across his back and examining their tips. He felt around his belt and unholstered his hatchet, frowning at it. "But my mace is gone. This game is good and bad that way—how everything starts over when you die." He picked up his scythe and examined its blade.

Temerity checked her sword and sledgehammer, boning knife and sleeve dagger, and the jewels strapped to her fore-arms. They were all where they should be. She was outfitted just as she had been at the start of the challenge.

"Where are the others?" she asked.

At that moment, Tomaz appeared, lying flat on his back, hands raised defensively and a grimace on his face.

"Oh," he said, starting when he saw them. He felt his throat and gazed around at the large cavern, then climbed to his feet and shook out his limbs. "I almost had him." He removed his helmet and brushed his shaggy hair away from his eyes, then glanced at Temerity and Keenan. "Those trolls were tough. I think the earlier ones went easy on us, just to make us soft so the big pack could wipe us out."

"We met those guys before," Keenan said.

"Yeah, but there weren't so many of them."

"That's because Rory knew enough to pick off a few at a time, not pull a huge pack all at once," Keenan said, glaring at his friend, who winced and turned up his hands sheepishly.

"Where's Half-pint?" she asked Tomaz.

"Last I saw, he was sitting atop a big bald head, slicing the troll's throat with his meat cleaver. He'll be okay."

"But what if he doesn't die?" she asked.

The two young men gazed at her with blank looks.

"I don't know," Keenan said, shrugging. "We all always died when we were here with Rory and Ianan. Even if Half-pint beats all the trolls, I don't think he can survive the ogre on his own. He'll be here eventually."

They sat in a circle and polished their blades, and waited.

———◆———

A full hour later, Half-pint appeared, slouched over on his chest and knees, his cheek plastered to the ground. He slowly unfolded himself and struggled to his feet, gazing at them with his big yellow eyes ablaze. He was still panting.

"I made it all the way to the ogre's arena," he said with a proud waggle of his ears. "But one of the rock trolls snuck up behind me and stomped on me. His foot is bigger than I am."

He tilted his head to the side with a loud pop. "Whew, that was fun. You guys ready to go again?"

She smiled at him with relief and asked, "What would have happened if you had beaten the ogre? What were we supposed to do then?"

"Oh. Yeah. Sorry, I should have explained that better." He removed his silvery robe and shook it out, then swung it back around his shoulders and clasped it at his throat. "In the final challenges, either everyone dies and meets back at the starting point, or if anyone beats the big boss, then everyone will immediately be transported to the end point—in this case, the ogre's arena, and we will all proceed into the Swamp. If you come in as a team, you win as a team."

"And if we all die three times in a row, we get kicked out to the street and have to wait in line all over again," Tomaz said, and Keenan nodded.

"So, then, if you killed the ogre on your own, I would never have to fight it?" she asked, unsure if she was more relieved or disappointed at the prospect.

"That's right," Half-pint said. "Happened once to me. I died, but Daphne killed the ogre with a pitchfork through two eyes in one blow. It was a sight to behold, I tell you, seeing that giant with a pitchfork jutting out of his enormous head. She was a wonder, that nymph. *Is* a wonder. I'm sure she's causing all sorts of mischief in her hidden hamlet up north. Anyway, shall we prepare to go?" They stood up and gathered around him. "No jewel oil this time—you know what we're in for now. Tomaz, let's try some sneak attacks. Go on the offensive and try to flush out the trolls instead of letting them ambush us. Temerity, use your orange jewel more." Half-pint cast her a stern glare.

"What do you mean?" she asked.

"Pay attention and let it help you," he replied.

"I *am* paying attention. Tell Tomaz he needs to listen to my warnings." Heat rose to her face. "Ever since he became the Shield, he's become intolerable."

Half-pint turned his eyes on Tomaz, who pretended not to be listening.

"We are a team," Half-pint said to Tomaz. "We are stronger if we all play our roles and respect each other's powers. Temerity is wearing orange, and her perception is enhanced. We have a better chance at surviving if you would stop acting like a tyrant."

"Yeah," Keenan said. "Listen to Temerity. A team of horses needs to pull together. If one hardheaded gelding takes the bit, they all could get injured."

"I am not a gelding," Tomaz said, puffing out his chest.

"You will be, if you don't knock it off," Keenan said, pointing to Temerity's boning knife, which she was twirling threateningly.

Tomaz made a childish face. "First you tell me to take charge," he said, directing his comment to Half-pint. "Now you tell me to take orders from Temerity. Make up your mind."

"How about you act like a serious adventurer?" Half-pint asked, his voice suddenly somber. "I want to make it out of here alive."

That brought the conversation to an end.

The hobgoblin gestured towards the back of the cavern with his meat cleaver, and they followed Tomaz to the troll's trail.

This time, they crept between the scattered boulders on the left side where the caves bordering the passageway were darkest, moving stealthily from shadow to shadow. It was slower going, but when they approached the area where they'd encountered the first small group of trolls, Temerity and Keenan crouched behind a boulder while Tomaz and Half-pint the cat crept forward.

Temerity gazed at the orange jewel on her wrist, trying to interpret its vibrations. It felt like the hum of a cat purring on her arm, but then she noticed a subtle twinge.

She looked up, and the troll scout crawled out from under the overhang, stopping suddenly on hands and knees and staring at them before scurrying back into its hole. She forced herself to march forward, anxiously scanning the shadowed border, where she caught glimpses of yawning crevices and a myriad of black holes, which she assumed led to a cave system where the trolls dwelled.

She and Keenan caught up with Tomaz and Half-pint and reported that they had spotted the scout. Half-pint nodded, appearing unconcerned. Temerity's nervousness subsided somewhat as she stayed close on the heels of the burly Tomaz and sprightly hobgoblin. Even with her brave companions, walking down a path that cut through troll territory felt unwise, if not downright stupid. The things they did for glory, she reflected half-heartedly. But her pa and brothers must have traversed this very path, several times. With that thought, her posture straightened and her steps grew lighter.

They continued creeping forward as a team, Temerity and Keenan keeping an eye out for anyone following them. With no warning other than the incessant nagging of the orange jewel, the pack of four trolls emerged from the caves on their left flank, with the scout flitting behind boulders to join the others. She and Keenan split up, each going for a troll, and Tomaz and Half-pint climbed up onto a large boulder and battled the other three. It was soon over, and without sustaining any serious injuries, Temerity's team crept forward again.

The orange jewel felt suddenly like a shower of tiny embers stinging her skin. She tried to decipher the new sensation, and the only conclusion she could draw was that a group of enemies lurked nearby. She appreciated the dragon jewel trying different ways of communicating with her, hardheaded as she was. She poked Tomaz with the butt end of her javelin. He turned around, and they crouched behind a boulder, peering into the shadows. Not seeing or smelling any trolls, they darted to the next boulder, then the next.

Their last time through, they had been attacked by a pack of eight from the rear, but this time they found the trolls squatting behind an extra-large boulder, sharpening weapons. Temerity and her band pounced on the surprised monsters, disabling three of them and luring the remaining five into the open area. Temerity practiced her positionals and managed to fell two trolls herself.

Half-pint healed any injuries, and they slunk between the scattered boulders again, looking for the next pack of eight. The orange jewel stung her arm again, and she spotted the trolls strutting down the center of the passageway towards them, like before. Temerity wondered if the trolls actually learned over time, or if they repeated the same moves over and over again. She and her bandmates stayed hidden and let the trolls pass, then attacked from the rear and wiped them out in short order.

Soon, they reached the cliff and began their descent into darkness. The jewel was quiet. Temerity lit her torch and gestured when she felt her orange jewel tremble. It was not subtle this time. The trolls were likely gathering to hem them in from both sides again. Tomaz stopped on a step, and Half-pint sank the pickaxe into the side of the rock. Temerity lashed the rope onto the crossbar, coiled and ready to drop, then they waited, listening. The stink of the monsters hit her nose before she heard or saw anything. The jewel throbbed. She traded glances with Half-pint, who cocked his long ears, glancing at the steps. A soft rustling. A single clink of metal. They nodded at one another, and Half-pint took the torch, held it between his teeth, and dropped the rope.

The four of them scrambled down and had already lit the rope on fire by the time the trolls converged on the step up above and glared down at them, shaking swords and axes.

They left the rope to burn, and Temerity and her companions hopped down the giant stairs. She extinguished the torch, and they ran by jewel light along the dark trench. The cockroaches appeared anyway, followed by the dive-bombing bats. Temerity gritted her teeth, ducked her head, and ran as fast as she could, with Half-pint on her shoulder. They left the flying mayhem behind and hurried to the ladder, scaling it one after another and pausing briefly at the top to prepare for the next stretch of larger, meaner trolls.

They employed the same stealth tactics and managed to surprise and beat the next two small groups without too much trouble.

Next up would be the pack of sixteen that had killed her, Keenan, and Tomaz, which everyone advised Tomaz they had to fight in smaller groups.

"I know," Tomaz said. "You think I'm stupid?"

Temerity exchanged glances with Keenan and shrugged.

"Yeah, yeah," Tomaz muttered, with a half-grin. "Come on."

They did not find the first pack of four where they expected them—the four Tomaz had bypassed the first time. So they backtracked, crossed the path, and searched the boulders on the right flank, where they found the trolls crouched under the overhang, staring out at them with surprise. Tomaz jumped at them, and the trolls responded by teaming up on him, only to be destroyed by Temerity, Keenan, and Half-pint, who worked together to pick them off one by one from the rear. The monsters lay scattered on the ground. One looked dead, and the other three were merely incapacitated in one manner or another. They retrieved their weapons, and Tomaz gazed longingly at a battle-axe pinned under the chest of a groaning troll.

They continued on between the boulders, searching for the next pack of four.

The trolls were waiting for them, standing in the middle of the passageway, wearing angry scowls and brandishing their oversized weapons. These were the largest trolls so far—great hulking creatures, half again as tall as Tomaz and twice as wide. Goosebumps prickled her arms and the nape of her neck. Her instinct was to flee in the other direction, but she forced herself to stand with her companions and face the creatures. She spotted the broadsword that had killed her, and the leering face of its owner. She glanced down at her puny weapons. A sledgehammer—big by human standards, but a toy for a troll. Same with her sword, though she would never tell Pauly that. He had advised her to trade up and leave it behind. Now she understood why.

She turned her focus to her red jewels, strapped side-by-side on her right forearm. Her strong hand. She consciously set her intention on harnessing the power of the jewels, imagining them amplifying her energy. Were they glowing brighter? Her arm was hot, as though she were standing in front of Pauly's forge, and she curled her hand into an iron fist. Maybe she should have put one red jewel on each wrist. Too late. She decided she would strike with her right arm and parry with her left, orange-bejeweled arm.

It was a four-on-four match, and Temerity stared across the space at the massive troll with the broadsword. The monster was focused on her like a fox fixated on a mouse. Its broadsword was in one humongous hand, and a stone club was in the other. So ... the same troll had delivered both the crippling blow and the killing blow.

She remembered her pa telling her when she was twelve, in the back pasture watching an ornery bull, that when something was stronger than you, you could either run away or outwit it. Going head-to-head with a beast with horns and a temper was a losing strategy.

So, she had taken the darts from the dartboard in the tavern and tied garlands of flowers to the fletching. Then, she went out to the pasture and tormented the bull by pelting it with rocks, from the safety of the rail fence, to get the bull all riled up, until it charged her and swung its horned head back and forth, stomping and blowing dust from its nostrils as it glared angrily through the rails. She ran back and forth along the fence, getting it to turn its flank to her, then she jabbed two darts into its thick hide, one from each hand, and hopped away as it bellowed and wheeled on her. It kicked and bucked and then stormed around the pasture, garlands of flowers trailing behind like tail feathers.

Her pa came at the distressed call of the bull and sternly put a stop to her cruel pranks. The bull was practically his pet, and although he said its hide was thicker than his thumb, he scolded her for torturing it and sent her to clean out the tavern's latrine. He butchered the bull later that season. He said it was fast and painless, but Temerity could tell that it made him sad.

Temerity examined the troll glowering at her. Not so unlike the bull, with two nubby horns jutting up from the top of its head, and wide snorting nostrils. The trick was to stay beyond the range of its swing, she determined, or get right up close.

Tomaz crept forward, and Temerity followed on his heels, her eyes fastened on the snarling bull of a troll. She could try her positionals, but that hadn't worked the last time they'd confronted this pack, although she had panicked and been overwhelmed at the time. Now she was calm and cool, her warrior brain taking over, chasing stray thoughts from her head and putting her heart and hands in control. The lizard brain, her pa called it—the one in the heart that worked on ancient instinct and knew things before the brain ever did, and reacted faster. Her hands and feet were alert, responding by reflex to the lizard brain's impulses to fight or take flight.

Flight was not an option, and so she crept forward, her weapons at the ready and her jewels pulsing. Tomaz bellowed his version of a battle cry, then yelled, *"You stink like an outhouse, you grub crawling dung heaps. Didn't your ugly mothers teach you how to wash? Do you roll in your own shit, or what?"*

She didn't know if they understood the words, but they understood the mocking tone, and stomped towards Tomaz and his wooden shield. A javelin flew over her shoulder and landed in the neck of a troll—the one who had killed Keenan, judging from its battle-axe. The monster dislodged the javelin and tossed it to the ground. Temerity aimed her own javelin, eyeing her bull, and let it fly.

She had aimed carefully, and it hit the mark: the top of the troll's bare foot, in between the bones, where it really hurt. The troll screeched and hopped on one clawed foot, dropping its sword and yanking at the shaft. She lunged forward, slipped behind the monster's back, sliced through the ligaments behind its knee and elbow, and had her boning knife ready when it whirled on her, the club whooshing through the air. She ducked and rolled and then popped up, sinking her knife into its groin and rolling away again. The troll fell to its knees and then onto its side, curling into the fetal position with its hands between its legs. She dashed in and grabbed her javelin and the troll's broadsword and dashed back out, the blade dragging along the rock-salt ground.

The blade was monstrous—she could barely lift it with one hand—but she slung her javelin across her back and then hefted the sword and swung it through the air with two hands, needing to engage her whole body to manage it. The added force of the red jewels drove her next swing as she delivered a blow to the troll still fighting with Keenan, connecting with the monster's buttocks. The blade lodged in the thick muscles, eliciting a garbled roar—but the monster continued battering Keenan. She yanked the blade free and turned back to the troll she had cut down. The boning knife was clutched in its hand, covered in green blood, and the poor beast was moaning and rocking back and forth. She glanced up, and Keenan was clinging to the back of his troll, trying to draw the blade of the scythe across the monster's throat.

Temerity lifted the broadsword, point forward, and with the long handle braced against one hip, she ran at the staggering troll. It was busy slapping at Keenan and trying to grab the scythe. "Jump!" she yelled at Keenan, who leapt free as she rammed the blade through the monster's abdomen, twisted the heavy steel, and then pulled it out with a wet, sucking sound. The monster lurched back a step, two steps, and then fell onto its rear end with a pitiful mewl. Temerity retrieved Keenan's javelin while he wrenched the battle-axe from his foe's grip.

The troll let the weapon go and clutched at the entrails spilling from its open belly wound.

"Let's go!" Half-pint called, waving at them from atop a boulder, below which lay a motionless troll. Tomaz was still bashing his troll with his shield, but the monster was already flat on the ground, bleeding from a head wound.

They turned and ran, leaving the gasping mobs behind.

44

ROCK TROLLS

They encountered the pack of eight trolls around the next bend. The broadsword worked surprisingly well. Temerity severed the spine at the neck of one troll who was not fast enough to keep up with her spinning maneuvers, first stumbling when she severed the ligaments behind its knee and then falling under her death stroke. The heavy troll lay motionless on the ground, eyes staring straight ahead, unblinking and glassy.

Fast and painless.

She spun to parry the next attack but danced away as a troll swung a ball-and-chain flail at her head. Tomaz tackled him from behind, and she tossed aside her heavy sword and crushed the troll's skull with her sledgehammer. Tomaz grabbed the flail and pivoted in a circle, shield raised, while she retrieved her broadsword, looted a shoulder strap from the troll, and hung the giant sword across her back.

Half-pint was busy healing Keenan, who was lying on the ground, so Tomaz and Temerity taunted the four trolls who remained standing, buying time until their mates could rejoin the fight.

A blood-curdling yowl announced Half-pint's arrival, and the tomcat landed on the face of the nearest troll, who roared and grabbed at the slashing feline. Keenan swung his battle-axe, taking out the troll, and Half-pint leapt onto the next one.

The trolls seemed terrified of the cat, reminding her of bulls with mice in the barn. Bulls hated mice, stomping and snorting in terror as the little rodents ran up their legs, over their backs, and hopped into the hay manger. She had witnessed it firsthand and laughed so hard she had fallen onto the ground. That's when her pa had gotten the rat terriers. He loved those bulls.

Half-pint the cat distracted the trolls long enough for Temerity, Keenan, and Tomaz to kill or maim them.

They encountered two more groups of eight and handled them in a similar manner.

———————————◆———————————

"That's the last of them," the hobgoblin announced as they ran away from the final pack of half-dead trolls.

After putting some distance between them, they huddled in an alcove of glowing white rock. They took a short break, drinking water and gobbling down dried snake meat, and then cleaned and sharpened their blades.

Half-pint sorted through the items in his pack, and they took inventory of their weapons.

Temerity had her javelin, Pauly's sword, the troll's broadsword, the sledgehammer, and the sleeve dagger. The troll still had her boning knife.

Half-pint had his buckler, meat cleaver, javelin, his old hunting knife, and a troll's double-edged dagger, which was the size of a short sword for a hobgoblin.

Tomaz had his shield, sword, woodsman's axe, a hunting knife, his javelin, and the troll's flail, which had an iron handle and a chain that was thicker than a dog chain, attached to a solid-iron mace head covered with spikes.

Keenan had his two javelins, the scythe, and the battle-axe. He had left his hatchet buried in the skull of a troll, who had fought on with the weapon still lodged in its head.

"I need a battle-axe," Tomaz said, eyeing Keenan's looted weapon.

"Really? Then you should have taken one," Keenan retorted. "Every second troll had one."

Tomaz frowned petulantly at his friend. "You're supposed to be playing Range. I'm right up there in the thick of things all the time. I need it more than you."

"I have no range weapons except the javelins," Keenan said defensively. "None of the trolls carried range weapons. What do you want me to do, throw rocks?"

"That's not a bad idea," Tomaz said, rubbing his overgrown beard and earning a scathing look from Keenan. "I'll trade you my flail for it. And my javelin."

Keenan grew thoughtful, considering the offer. "Plus your woodsman's axe."

"That's not a fair trade," Tomaz said dismissively, but he removed the single-headed axe from the hook on his belt and held it lovingly, then shifted his gaze to the battle-axe Keenan brandished with both hands. The woodsman's axe was a nice tool, with a long handle and a blade fashioned for felling a small tree. The battle-axe was another thing entirely. Double-headed, with wide crescent blades and a metal handle, it was clearly made for combat. The troll-sized weapon dwarfed the woodsman's axe by comparison.

"My grandpa gave me this axe," Tomaz mumbled.

"Your grandpa told you to beat the game," Keenan countered, arching his eyebrows at his friend.

Tomaz frowned, but reluctantly agreed.

They made the trade, and both men gloated.

"None of those are going to do much good against rock trolls," Half-pint said. "We should have taken one of their war hammers. Blades glance right off those monsters."

"Now you tell us," Keenan said, stepping away to practice swinging the flail.

"How are we supposed to defeat the rock trolls if our weapons won't work on them?" Temerity asked.

"Wit and wile," Half-pint said with a toothy grin.

<hr/>

They strode down the wide passageway, approaching the ogre's arena. The threshold was demarcated by a knee-high wall of black basalt leading into an even blacker tunnel that stood in stark contrast to the luminescent red and white rock salt.

They stepped over the wall and passed through the dark passageway, then emerged into a bright, dome-shaped hall of white rock salt, with a high rounded ceiling, jagged walls whose edges were piled high with mounds of boulders, and a large circular floor. Marring the luminescent white space were several black smudges in the center of the floor, which appeared to be soot or scorch marks.

Temerity whispered to Half-pint, "Where is the ogre?" Her breathy voice was amplified and reverberated loudly back at her from the rounded ceiling.

"He will show up after we kill the two rock trolls," he whispered back, gesturing to a large opening at the opposite end of the chamber.

"Only two?" she asked, relieved. Her relief evaporated as a rumble shook the chamber.

Tomaz stepped out in front as the ground trembled and the rumbling grew louder.

Two creatures made of black rock emerged from the opening, each clomping forward on massive legs. Although the monsters each had two legs, two arms, and barrel chests, the resemblance to the green trolls ended there. They were twice the size of normal trolls and resembled stacks of rocks more than living beings. Each of their heads was a squarish block with no eyes, mouth, nose, ears, or features of any sort. The only way Temerity could distinguish their fronts from their backs was by the bend of the knees and elbows, and the weapons held in front of them. They each carried a massive stone hammer and a stone club, and nothing else.

She instinctively backed away, the orange jewel jumping against the leather strap on her arm.

"I know," she hissed at the jewel, wishing it would stop jolting her every second. It seemed to hear her, for it calmed down to its normal nervous quivering.

Tomaz bravely yelled and shook his battle-axe at the animated stone creatures while crouching behind his shield, attracting both rock trolls to him. The monsters did not stop plodding forward and looked ready to stomp right over Tomaz, whose head barely reached the top of their tree-trunk thighs. Tomaz turned and ran, then huddled with the three of them as they looked to Half-pint for direction.

"Hit them between the segments," he advised, throwing his javelin and hitting a troll in the gap between the torso and upper arm, but the monster kept coming.

Temerity could see that the trolls were indeed stacks of rocks, their segments connected together like string puppets.

She and Keenan threw javelins at the same troll, two out of three javelins hitting the mark. Wooden hafts stuck out of the creature like porcupine quills, but the troll barely seemed to notice.

"Attack them from the rear," Half-pint yelled, then turned into a cat and dashed around the edge of the chamber and ran at the trolls from behind, changing back into a hobgoblin and swinging his meat cleaver at the ankle of the second troll.

The trolls were almost within striking distance of Temerity, Tomaz, and Keenan, and raised their huge stone hammers and clubs. The three humans split up and darted around the edge of the chamber and circled back, and the trolls slowly wheeled to meet them.

Temerity leapt to the side of one, striking at a knee joint with her broadsword. It bounced off with a jarring shudder. She jumped to the rear of the stone creature, who was swinging its hammer at Tomaz, striking the wooden shield and sending him back several paces to land on his rump, then clomping after him.

"No!" she yelled, not willing to let the troll crush Tomaz. She scaled its legs and back with her snakeskin gloves and boots, easily finding finger and toeholds between the seg-ments, and the rubbery soles sticking to the rough black rock. She mounted its shoulder and beat at its head with her sledgehammer, but she was too late. The troll swung its great hammer, splintering the wooden shield and then stepping on Tomaz's chest with all its weight. She watched in horror as the stone club descended in a heavy arc and connected with Tomaz's head, his helmet spinning off and his skull splitting like a watermelon.

She blinked, and Tomaz was gone, the troll standing on bare rock and turning towards Keenan, who was likewise frozen in horror, staring at the spot where his friend had just been crushed.

Half-pint was on the shoulder of the other troll, wedging the blade of his meat cleaver into the narrow gap where the blockhead met a short stone neck, wiggling the blade back and forth. She didn't know what good that would do but tried the same maneuver on her troll, jamming the broadsword into the gap where a throat would be. Keenan was keeping her troll busy by striking the spiked mace head onto a round river-rock kneecap and then dashing away, only to leap in and strike again.

The troll reached up with a stony hand and yanked her blade free and flung it across the arena, then reached back for her, but she was already gone, scaling down its back and climbing up its other side, like a mouse on a bull, where she perched on its shoulder.

Half-pint was not so fortunate, and she caught the moment from the corner of her eye when the troll closed a giant hand around Half-pint's little body and squeezed. She heard the crunch of bones and saw the dying light in the hobgoblin's yellow eyes before he vanished.

Her heart jumped into her throat, but the danger of the moment swept aside the rush of emotion. It was only her and Keenan left, and she had no idea how a human could kill a monster made of rocks. If Half-pint couldn't do it, then they were doomed.

Her rock troll was swatting at her, and she hopped to the ground again as the other troll turned and marched towards her.

"Run away. Make him chase you!" Keenan called, waving frantically to get her attention.

She was happy to do so and fled across the circular chamber. Both trolls' heavy footsteps pounded behind her. She reached the edge and climbed up onto a jumble of boulders and turned around, preparing to hop along the perimeter.

Keenan swung his flail, and the chain wrapped around a stone ankle. The troll hitched forward on one foot, then tottered and fell towards her, its head crashing to the ground. Keenan attacked the second troll, trying the same move, while she jumped down onto the back of the prone monster and struck it with her sledgehammer, over and over again, hitting its black head as though it were a clump of coal. Her blows sent spidery cracks blossoming across the skull, while the troll's massive arms slowly unfolded, pushing its chest up off the ground. She struck again, widening the cracks, but the monster kept rising.

Temerity gathered her wits and focused, taking a deep breath, then channeled her energy through the red jewels, raised the sledgehammer over her head with both hands, and swung it down with all her might. Energy seemed to flow like a river of fire up from her feet and through her torso, rushing through her heart and lungs and then channeling out through her arms and hands. A shimmer of red light flashed down the haft of the sledgehammer, then steel hit stone with a shower of crimson sparks.

The head split and crumbled, and the troll collapsed onto the floor with a thump and a deafening clatter. She hopped off and ran to Keenan, who was frantically trying to trip up the other troll, but it was onto his tricks and was kicking at him, lashing out with a stone foot the size of Keenan's chest.

She grabbed the scythe while Keenan was busy with the flail, and she tried to hook one ankle while Keenan attacked the other. The scythe's blade was long and curved, but the troll twisted its leg and the steel slid off. She tried again with the same result. She needed her rope, but she didn't have it anymore. She shrugged off her long robe and flung it around the troll's ankle, then grabbed each end and pulled. The troll twisted and kicked, but the sylph silk would not give. She and Keenan both gave a heave and a haw at the same time, and the troll's feet slid out from under it. The rock troll executed an impressive acrobatic split and then just sat there. Had it had a face, she imagined it would have looked stunned.

She and Keenan each hopped up onto a stone shoulder. Keenan flailed at the troll's featureless face, and she hammered the back of the stony skull, every other swing hitting rock hands that scrabbled weakly at them. The head slowly split the way the other had, and it soon fell apart in a cascade of fist-sized rocks. Temerity and Keenan hopped off as the torso fell to one side and hit the floor with a loud thud.

"Are you okay?" Keenan asked, wiping sweat from his brow.

"Yes," she said, breathing heavily. "Are you?"

"Yes," he said, then peered warily over his shoulder at the opening at the far end of the chamber.

"What now?" she asked.

He shrugged. "I don't know. We never got this far before. The ogre, I suspect."

She retrieved her sylph cloak, smoothing the shimmering silk with trembling hands, and sat on a rock to rest. Her blood sang a shrill song in her veins as she waited for the big boss to appear. The orange jewel vibrated insistently, stinging her arm.

"I know," she murmured to it. "I know."

45

RING OF FIRE

The ogre did not come from the back as Temerity had expected, but rose up out of the rock-salt floor, like a spring bulb pushing up through the snow. It was enormous, larger than the rock trolls, and with skin that was bright blue instead of the pond-scum green of the other trolls. It was obese and sat in the center of a ring of fire.

The flames surrounding the ogre were blue and yellow and burned in a thin perimeter line, flaring up only a few inches off the ground. It would be easy to step over, and Temerity wondered if it was there only for dramatic effect, to create a grand entrance. She examined the giant more closely. It was bald, like the green trolls, but instead of boasting a body of solid muscle, it had corpulent, fleshy cheeks and jowls that hung down over a thick neck, a drooping chest, and an enormous belly. Tusk-like fangs protruded from its upper and lower jaws, and its thin, pale lips curled in a sinister smile. It was clothed in a long tunic that appeared to be made of gray orc skin sewn together with sinew in irregular patches, with a thick leather belt around its substantial girth. Strands of teeth hung from its neck, and skulls, bones, and skeletal hands and feet hung from its belt. A large bowl filled with flames sat at its side. It carried no weapons.

And it had three eyes.

Two were normal eyes—or normal for a monster. One was yellow and one was blue, and they were proportional to its face, though set back in the skull. Centered above the two eyes was a third. This eye was smaller, and blue, and shifted back and forth between Temerity and Keenan, as though taking their measure.

Keenan whispered, "It looks pretty lazy. Let me try to hit its third eye." He cocked back a javelin and threw it across the open space.

The ogre's arm shot up and snatched the javelin out of midair, stopping it inches from its face and sticking it through its belt.

"What in dragon's hell?" Keenan muttered.

"Let's go around," Temerity whispered, and they crept along the edge of the domed chamber.

The ogre followed them with its three eyes, then a fourth, which watched them from the side of its head, and a fifth and sixth eye that were set into the back of its head, and then a seventh, which was on the far side of its round skull.

They stopped behind the two rear eyes, trading a bemused expression, and the small blue eyes inspected them smugly.

"Creepy," Keenan said with a shiver.

"It's just like a troll," she whispered back. "A big fat one with seven eyes. On the count of three, we'll attack."

At that moment, the ogre leaned to the side, reached into the bowl of fire, cupped a ball of flames in its beefy palm, and tossed it their way.

Temerity jumped to the side, and the fireball struck her on

the shoulder, bouncing off the sylph-silk cloak and guttering out at her feet.

"Hey," she cried, slapping at the cloak. There was no burn mark or blemish whatsoever, and she thought back on the snake charmer and how much the nymph had revered her silk.

The ogre was leaning down to gather another ball of fire. Temerity and Keenan charged, running side by side and brandishing broadsword and scythe. The giant hopped to its feet, surprisingly agile, and turned to face them, fire cupped in each of its hands.

At the very instant that Temerity and Keenan hopped over the ring of fire, the ogre lobbed the fireballs at them. The blobs of flame hit their chests as the burning ring below their feet sprang up and met the hurled flames, and the fireballs exploded.

◆

Half-pint was leaning over her, peering into her eyes.

"Wake up, Miss Temerity," he said.

She gazed into his golden eyes, remembering him as a cat when he used to stare down at her, purring, when she was in her small bed as a toddler. Her ma used to say that the cat was the only thing that could get her to stop crying in the middle of the night when she and Pa were exhausted and wanted to sleep. The tomcat always got a bowl of fresh cream in the morning for his efforts.

"What?" she asked, then felt smooth fabric under her fingertips and lifted her head to regard her outfit of silk, velvet, satin, and snakeskin, and she remembered where she was.

"How far did you get?" Half-pint asked, sitting back on his heels as she rose to sitting.

"Oh," she said, rubbing her eyes and glancing at Keenan, who was still lying on his back and yawning. "We got as far as the ogre."

"The ogre! Wow!" Half-pint said, waggling his ears at Tomaz. "I told you they were gone too long to have been killed by the rock trolls. What happened?" he asked, returning his attention to Temerity.

"Fire," she said, trying to recall. "There was an explosion."

"Ahhh," he said, nodding. "You crossed the ring of fire. *Tsk tsk,*" he said, shaking his finger. "You must not do that."

"Why didn't you tell us?" she asked crossly, reaching into her pack for her waterskin.

"I was going to, after we killed the rock trolls," he said, lifting his long nose.

"Lot of help that did us, when you went and died on us early."

"Sorry," he said, bobbling his head back and forth, but he had a proud gleam in his eyes. "Well done, you two." He nodded at her and Keenan, who propped himself up on one elbow and smiled at the rare praise from the hobgoblin. Half-pint went on, "It's always better to learn things through experience, anyway. If I had told you not to cross the ring of fire or else you would explode, you wouldn't have believed me."

"Oh, we would have believed you," Keenan assured him, sitting up and examining his weapons. "Dragon's bones, I lost my flail."

"And I lost my battle-axe," Tomaz said.

"And I lost my broadsword," Temerity added. "I liked that sword."

"And I lost *my* sword," Half-pint said.

"Sword?" Keenan asked. "Oh, you mean that dagger?"

"Yes, my sword," the hobgoblin said with a huff.

"We need to get them all again," said Tomaz, getting to his feet. "Ready?"

"No, we just got here," she said, and dug into her pack for food.

46

LAST CHANCE

"We can't die this time," Tomaz said as they laid out their weapons. "I don't want to wait in that line from hell again." Everyone agreed with that.

Half-pint had fought the rock trolls many times, and he shared his secrets. "You can dismember the rock segments if you get a wedge in the exact right spot, in the gaps between the joints, and then lever them off. Pickaxes work great for that—they're also great for busting heads. The head is the most important part. Their bodies can still run around without their heads, but then they run amok, like a chicken. If you break their heads, they'll die. Easier to bash it when it's separated from the body." He continued in a conspiratorial whisper, and they leaned in to hear him. "The trick with the ogre is to blind it. In order to do that, we need to take up precise positions. It's much simpler to accomplish with four adventurers than with just two."

"The ogre is too fast for us," Temerity said. "It grabbed a javelin out of midair."

Half-pint nodded knowingly, and replied, "If four weapons target the eyes all at once, the ogre sometimes can only grab two."

"Sometimes? And sometimes it can grab more than two?" Tomaz asked.

"If we don't throw at the exact same instant, then, yes. I've watched it grab several at once. Various techniques work against the ogre, but let's try the four cardinal directions method. Miss Temerity, may I please borrow your writing tablet?"

"My writing tablet?" she asked, finding the slate tablet and soapstone pencils in the bottom of her pack.

"Now," Half-pint said, sketching a circle on the tablet. "This is the ring of fire." Then he drew a round blob in the center, with a head and seven eyes. Then he drew four lines radiating outward at right angles to one another. "If we stand in these spots," he said, marking X's, "and we aim for the eyes at the same time, we can potentially shoot out two of its eyes with each volley."

"Is that a map?" Temerity asked warily.

"A map?" the hobgoblin asked, flashing his yellow eyes at her and then staring down at the diagram. "Hmm. I don't think so. I've made sketches of boss fights before and never met any angry dragons."

"Okay," she said. "I hope you're right."

Half-pint continued drawing and assigned each of them positions, then discussed the signals they would use in order to loose their weapons simultaneously.

Temerity asked, "How many weapons do we have? How many chances will we have to shoot out all its eyes?"

They examined their inventory, counting weapons that could be thrown: five javelins, one hatchet, one woodsman's axe, four knives, including her sleeve dagger—if they could keep them all while fighting off the trash mobs. Assuming they would land half their shots, they still did not have enough weapons, even if they included Half-pint's meat cleaver, unless they threw the swords and heavy weapons in a last desperate attempt.

"How did you beat it in the past?" Temerity asked.

"Daphne was an archer. Plus, the ogre is susceptible to yellow jewels."

"You could have told us that," Tomaz said.

"We could have looted bows and arrows in the alleys," Keenan added.

Temerity said, "Maybe I should switch out my orange for yellow."

Half-pint considered that idea for a moment, then shook his head. "No, keep the orange—it's useful for detecting trolls. One regular yellow won't do anything against the ogre. Daphne had three, plus an end-game yellow. And she was a nymph."

"I see another long queue in our future," Keenan said dourly. "Maybe we should go back into the alleys and look for bows and arrows."

"I have these," Half-pint said, pulling out his six crossbow bolts.

Temerity regarded the metal bolts, each about one foot in length—twice the length of a tavern dart and half the length of his hobgoblin-sized javelin, but not terribly small for wee folk. "I guess you could throw them like tavern darts," she said.

Tomaz shook his head. "They're not made for that. And what's with the straw fletching?"

Half-pint was too busy inspecting his bolts to reply.

"Could still maybe take out an eye," Keenan said, not very convincingly.

It was all they had, and so they packed up and headed back into troll territory.

───────────◆───────────

They knew where most of the trolls hid by now, and they easily beat them back and made it to the cliff. Tomaz picked up a battle-axe along the way with a joyful whoop, and Half-pint secured another dagger-sword.

They did their same maneuver with the pickaxe and rope, and Temerity counted on her suspicion that the trolls were not very bright and would fall for the same trick again.

When they heard the trolls approaching, Half-pint went down the rope first, and she gestured at Keenan and Tomaz to climb down before her. They both stood there, staring at her.

"Where's your torch?" Tomaz asked.

"Go!" she said, pushing their shoulders. "Hurry."

They scowled but did as she said, and as the rustling footsteps and stink of the trolls drew closer, she climbed down over the edge of the step, hanging from the rope, and felt for finger and toeholds in the rock face. Her snakeskin boots and gloves clung firmly to the side of the cliff, and when Keenan and Tomaz had reached the bottom, she tugged frantically at the pickaxe, levering it loose moments before trolls came into view on the giant steps. She stuck the pickaxe through her belt and scrambled down the cliff face, the trolls scowling down at her from above.

She reached the step where the others were waiting. Keenan had coiled the rope as she descended, and she handed Half-pint his pickaxe with a smug smile and stashed the rope in her pack.

"Hmpf," Half-pint grunted appreciatively, holstering his pickaxe and casting an appraising eye over her red boots and gloves.

Temerity and her companions ran for the trench, baring their arms to expose the light of their dragon jewels. Hopping down the giant steps, they were nearly at the bottom when another pack of trolls glared up at them from the dark trench, jewel light flickering off their glassy eyes with ominous glints of color. She could hear the trolls up above grunting and growling as they descended the zigzag steps, threatening to hem them in.

Temerity and her companions exchanged worried glances, then did the only thing there was to do. They leapt down to confront the waiting band of trolls. Swords and battle-axes split the air, cracking on shields and helmets and thick troll skulls. Temerity stopped her two-handed sword swing mid-air, and the trolls froze with her, eyes and ears alert. The ground shook, and the unmistakable, thunderous footsteps of a dragon approaching set everyone crouching in a moment of indecision.

The trolls broke ranks and scrambled up the giant steps. Temerity and her companions traded frantic expressions, then turned away from the approaching thunder and ran as fast as they could down the trench towards the ladder. Temerity barely noticed the cockroaches and bats as the dragon stomped after them. A loud roar was followed by a stream of dragon fire—blue and yellow flames licking at their heels and backs. Cockroaches burned to a crisp and fell in black cinders around them, and bats squealed and darted away, the smell of singed fur filling the air.

Temerity and her band reached the ladder and scaled it, quick as spiders, as the dragon skidded to a stop below them and blew a burst of flames at their rear ends to hurry them on their way. Temerity clung to the side of the cliff face and glanced down over her shoulder. A luminescent green dragon with red smoldering eyes met her curious gaze. It bared its fangs at her, smoke curling from wide nostrils. The glistening, scaled creature was bigger than the other dragons she had seen, and she wondered if it had been attacking them or protecting them.

She did not waste time pondering the dragon's motivations, but scrabbled up the rock face, with Half-pint clinging to her shoulders, and then hoisted herself up over the cliff's edge onto safe ground.

She sank to her knees, trembling in the glow of the red and white rock salt. Half-pint hopped down, and Keenan and Tomaz sat sprawled on the rock next to her, trying to catch their breath. Temerity peeked over the cliff's edge and caught a glimpse of the dragon's spiked tail as it disappeared down the dark trench, back the way it had come.

━━━━━━━◆━━━━━━━

They had established their cadence as a team and picked off the next packs of four and five trolls without any grave injuries. Tomaz pulled the next two packs of four together, and they fought off the monsters, having become familiar with the various trolls' favorite moves. Temerity won back the same broadsword she'd taken before, nabbed another shoulder strap, and managed to hang onto her boning knife.

The next pack of eight was still the toughest, but they were able to beat them and finally fled the mound of dead and injured trolls. Keenan nabbed the flail, and Half-pint dragged an oversized war hammer behind him. Tomaz scooped it up, and they ran until they met the next pack of eight. They dispatched them quickly, as well as the final pack of eight, and soon they stood at the black boundary of the ogre's arena.

They huddled there with nervous excitement, taking time to heal their wounds, sharpen blades, and exchange advice about the rock trolls and ogre. They had managed to keep all their weapons this time, plus they had looted the broadsword, flail, battle-axe, dagger-sword, and a war hammer. They gripped fists in a central star, then entered the black tunnel.

47

OGRE'S EYES

The domed arena was glistening white, with no sign of the blood that had spilled there before. A shivering tension hung in the air, like the foreboding silence between a blinding lightning strike and the rumbling wave of thunder that rolls in to proclaim the displeasure of the dragon gods.

Rupturing the silence, the massive rock trolls stomped into the arena, shaking the ground and brandishing stone clubs and monstrous hammers.

Temerity eyed the nearest troll and its raised hammer—a simple block of stone on a long metal haft—which could crush her skull with one blow. She did not want to suffer such a gruesome fate, and pulled her sledgehammer from its holster, gripping it with trembling hands. On Half-pint's cue, she and her fellow adventurers surged forward, going straight for the trolls' blockheads. Temerity and Half-pint took one troll, and Keenan and Tomaz took the other. She had thought the two tall men would have the advantage, but her and Half-pint's agility proved more beneficial as they quickly mounted the troll's shoulders.

Half-pint levered at the gap below the rock skull with his pickaxe, and Temerity clobbered the head with her sledgehammer, fear transmuting into force through the alchemy of the red jewels and her raw desire to live. Besides, she had no time to be afraid, only to react and dodge the rock troll's angry swings of its club and hammer. She dodged a wild blow by jumping off the shoulder and hanging from its neck as the troll struck itself in the head, the great hammer cleaving the squarish rock in two. The two halves slowly split apart, falling to either side and bouncing off its shoulders and then tumbling to the ground.

She and Half-pint leapt free and crossed the room to help their mates. Tomaz was dashing this way and that, distracting the second rock troll while at the same time calling for Half-pint's help.

Keenan was trying to drag himself across the floor away from the stomping troll's enormous feet, blood streaming from his head. Half-pint knelt down to heal him while Temerity darted behind the troll and climbed up its back, taking her position on a shoulder and whaling away at its head.

Half-pint and Keenan rejoined the fight, and Half-pint climbed up onto the other shoulder. This time, he worked at the shoulder joint with his pickaxe and cheered triumphantly as the arm holding the club popped off and fell clattering to the ground. Tomaz wielded his gigantic new war hammer, the haft as long as he was tall, and swung it at the rock troll's knee. It made contact, and the rounded kneecap cracked in a spiderweb of lines and fell apart.

Tomaz leapt to its other leg and swung at the second kneecap, but the troll dropped its hammer and swept him up in a great, stone-clawed hand and started to squeeze.

Temerity frantically swung her sledgehammer at the troll's head, and Half-pint scrambled beside her and wedged the pickaxe into the other shoulder. Keenan clasped the troll's busted leg in a bearhug and began dragging it backwards, pushing and pulling and twisting it, to the shrieks and gurgles of Tomaz.

The rock troll teetered and swayed, then hopped on one foot while Keenan continued tugging at the injured leg. Half-pint popped off the second arm, and Tomaz and the dismembered arm fell one way while the troll's body fell the other way and crashed to the ground. Half-pint and Temerity jumped onto the troll's prone torso and swung at its head with their mining tools, and Keenan rushed over to Tomaz to pry apart the stone fingers.

Half-pint and Temerity pounded away at the troll—*thwack* with the hammer, *ping* with the pickaxe—until the head broke and crumbled into a pile of rubble.

With both trolls out of commission, Half-pint tended to Tomaz, then the four of them huddled against a pile of rocks at the edge of the room. Half-pint applied red and blue jewel infusion oil to their chosen weapons, then they took up their four cardinal positions and waited for the ogre to appear.

◆

"Don't die," Tomaz warned, from his position opposite Temerity, where he perched on a pile of rocks at the edge of the large round chamber. He spoke at a normal volume, but she heard him as though he were standing next to her, his voice amplified by the domed ceiling.

Not only did she have no desire to wait in the gauntlet's queue again nor disappoint her teammates by failing, but the very act of dying was a troubling experience. The violent deaths she had suffered were not particularly painful—they had been too quick for that, and she had little recollection of the final moments. It was the sensation of being yanked from her body that she found disconcerting—a shocking violation; the most precious thing forcibly taken from her.

The ground opened up, interrupting her thoughts, and the blue ogre rose, surrounded by fire and sneering at them with its long, curved fangs and its grotesque assortment of eyes. Temerity was positioned in front of the giant's face, and the three eyes gazed at her steadily. While trolls seemed to be dull in the head, Temerity had the distinct impression that the ogre remembered her very clearly.

She swallowed and cocked her javelin over her shoulder.

"Ready?" Half-pint asked.

"Ready," they replied in unison.

Half-pint called out slowly and evenly, *"One ... two ... three ... throw!"*

Temerity launched her javelin at the third eye set into the creased forehead above the mismatched blue and yellow eyes. The ogre never took its gaze off her as it reached out and plucked the javelin from midair. With the same monstrous hand, it grabbed Half-pint's javelin while simultaneously catching Tomaz's and Keenan's with its other hand. Keenan's obsidian spearhead had already lodged in an eye socket, however, and the ogre pulled the javelin out with a yowl, the eyeball popping out with it and dangling from a slimy membrane.

Temerity and her companions called out the hit and three misses, and the ogre tucked the four javelins in its belt, glowering at Temerity as though she had thrown them all.

"Does that count?" Keenan called across the room, gesturing at the dangling eyeball. "It's still attached."

Half-pint scurried along the perimeter to look. "I think so.

I'm pretty sure that eye is blind now," he said, then returned to his position.

The ugly creature leaned forward and began lobbing fireballs at them while Keenan moved closer to Tomaz and they prepared for the next volley. Temerity ignored the fireballs, one of which hit her sylph-silk cloak and fell sputtering to the ground as she cocked back her boning knife and waited for Half-pint's countdown.

On *"throw,"* she flung the knife, wishing she had spent more time throwing knives at targets with her brothers—something they had liked to do and she had found boring. The blade lodged in the ogre's flabby cheek, and the monster caught Half-pint's knife in midair. Tomaz's woodsman's axe and Keenan's second javelin both hit their marks with flashes of red. Three eyes blinded so far, and four to go.

The ogre got to its feet and began stomping, and the ring of fire flared up angrily.

The two rear eyes and the side eye near Keenan were all blinded, so Keenan and Tomaz joined Temerity, facing the three front eyes as fireballs flew at them.

"One ... two ... three ... throw!"

Temerity threw her sleeve dagger at the same moment the ogre ducked and turned away. Her dagger flew over its head and the giant grabbed it out of the air. Half-pint's meat cleaver nicked the top of the ogre's round skull and clattered to the ground at the monster's feet. Tomaz's knife also missed completely, and the ogre snatched it from midair, but Keenan's hatchet caught the remaining side eye, the blade sinking into the eye socket. The giant yanked out the blade and then hopped and spun in a fury, the ring of fire blazing and seeping out across the room like an expanding lake of fire. Blue, acrid smoke curled up from the encroaching flames, stinging Temerity's eyes and throat.

Half-pint scrambled across the perimeter of rocks and joined them, raising his buckler against a fireball. "The front three eyes remain," Half-pint said, catching his breath. "What weapons do we still have?"

They took stock of their weapons as fireballs flew at them, hitting their backs and helmets and catching Keenan's long ponytail on fire. Temerity swatted out the flames, and they crouched behind the wooden shield and steel buckler and continued inspecting their weapons. Aside from their heavy troll implements, Temerity and Tomaz had their normal swords, Temerity had her sledgehammer, Keenan had his scythe, and Half-pint had his pickaxe, dagger-sword, and crossbow bolts.

"Here, you throw this," Half-pint said, handing Keenan the dagger-sword, then he turned to Temerity and Tomaz. "You two can throw your swords, like we discussed." They hefted their swords, practicing the spear hold Keenan had shown them. "And I'll throw a bolt," the hobgoblin said, inspecting the metal shaft.

Temerity tested the balance of her sword, cocking it with an inverse grip over her shoulder. *This will never work,* she grumbled to herself, anticipating a slow death by fire. But she cast aside her doubts and stood tall—her father's daughter, strong and brave.

They spaced themselves out, betting that the ogre would turn away again.

"One ... two ... three ... throw!"

The ogre easily caught the two swords. The hand-thrown crossbow bolt bounced off the giant's skull, but the dagger-sword sank into its yellow eye with a satisfying burst of red light.

"Four for four!" Keenan yelled out with glee.

"That's great," Tomaz said enviously, deflecting a fireball with his shield and joining Temerity on her pile of rocks. The fire lake expanded past the mounds of fallen rock trolls and approached the outer ring of boulders where the adventurers stood.

"Now what?" Tomaz asked, turning to Half-pint, who hopped up onto a boulder at Temerity's shoulder and blocked a fireball with his buckler.

"Time for my secret weapon," Half-pint said, pulling out his fae flute.

"What, are you going to charm the ogre?" Temerity asked skeptically.

"You'll see," he said with an impish grin.

"I'll throw this," Keenan said, holding up his flail.

"Lot of good that'll do," Tomaz said glumly, swatting away another fireball as the ogre stomped and threw handfuls of fire in a tantrum. "I can't very well throw these," Tomaz said, lifting the troll-sized war hammer and battle-axe. "I guess I'll just throw a rock. Wish I had my slingshot." He stooped to pick up an apple-sized rock.

"I want to try something," Temerity said. She dug into her pack, wrapped a torch cloth around her half-broomstick, and lit it.

Her companions glanced her way but were too busy worrying about their own inadequate weapons.

They spaced themselves out and waited for Half-pint's count.

"You count this time," the hobgoblin said to Tomaz.

Tomaz shrugged, and Temerity lifted her torch.

"One … two … three … throw!"

Temerity launched her torch into the ring of fire, and to her delight, the torch exploded with a loud boom and a blinding flash.

"What was that?" Tomaz asked, squeezing his eyes shut and raising his shield.

Temerity waited for the blue dots to fade from her vision and then peered over at Half-pint. The hobgoblin was lowering the flute from his mouth, where he had been blowing straight through the primitive instrument. His fingers covered all the finger holes, and he was squinting at the ogre. Temerity followed his gaze. A dart stuck out from the side of the giant's neck. The creature pulled it out and inspected it, sniffed it, and then tossed it into the flames, casting Half-pint a scathing look. Keenan's flail and Tomaz's rock lay harmlessly at the giant's feet.

Half-pint scrambled over the rocks, crouched behind Tomaz's shield, and took out another bolt and a vial.

"Ah," Temerity said, nodding. "Snake venom."

"A blowgun," Keenan said, regarding Half-pint curiously.

The three humans watched the hobgoblin as he stuck the tip of the bolt into the mouth of the vial and then turned the vial upside down and shook it. He turned it right side up and removed the bolt, sealing the vial. The bolt's tip was wet with a sticky yellow coat.

"That can't be enough to kill such an enormous beast," Temerity said as the ogre made screeching noises and stomped in a rage inside its circle of fire.

"No, but it might slow down its reflexes," Half-pint said. "Let's go again. You use your fire trick to distract it, and I'll give it another dose."

"I don't have another torch stick," she said.

They searched their belongings for something else to use and came up with Half-pint's pickaxe. Tomaz hacked off the pickaxe's wooden haft with his battle-axe, and she attached a torch cloth and lit it. Tomaz and Keenan found rocks to throw, and at Tomaz's count, they launched their volley.

Her torch exploded in the ring of fire, and the blast blinded her for a few seconds. When her vision cleared, she saw another bolt sticking out of the ogre's bare calf.

"Good job," she said to Half-pint. "How many bolts do you have left?"

"Three," he said. "There are two eyes left. Should I give the ogre another dose of venom, or should I go for the eyes now?"

They looked at one another, and just then, a loud horn blast split the air.

The ogre was blowing through what looked like a human thigh bone, and a loud rumbling shook the chamber.

"Oh, no," Tomaz said. "More rock trolls."

"Uh-oh," Half-pint said, sticking another bolt into the vial. "I'll do both, venom and aim for an eye. Temerity, try knotting up a length of rope and setting fire to it. Tomaz and Keenan, you distract the trolls. Once the ogre is blinded, it's easy to kill, and the rock trolls will flee. Go!" he yelled as two rock trolls thundered into the chamber, heading straight for them and oblivious to the flames licking at their stony ankles.

Temerity ran one way with Half-pint over the jumble of rocks while Tomaz and Keenan went the other way and threw stones at the trolls.

Temerity hurriedly cut off a length of rope, knotted it a few times to give it some weight, dunked a frayed end into the jar of torch tallow, then frantically lit it, waiting for the fire to catch. The rock trolls were chasing Tomaz and Keenan around the perimeter, and the young men dashed back and forth to keep the trolls away from Temerity and Half-pint.

At the count of four, she and Half-pint threw their projectiles. The rope exploded in a small burst, and the bolt hit the ogre's temple, missing the eye but further enraging the giant. The beast swayed and staggered from the venom, pulling out the bolt and then grabbing handfuls of flames and hurling fireballs at Half-pint and Temerity.

They ducked behind a rock and prepared another volley. The flame lake blazed hotter, and more balls of fire hit the boulder they were crouched behind.

"Hurry up!" Tomaz yelled at them, and Temerity peeked over the rock. The trolls were throwing small boulders at the two men, who were leaping out of the way.

"Hit the eye this time," Temerity said anxiously, her hands trembling as she tried to light her rope.

"I'm trying," Half-pint said, corking the vial and stuffing the bolt up the end of the flute. "Ready?" he asked.

Her knot had barely caught fire, but they had no time.

"One ..." she said. *"Two ..."* Half-pint lifted the blowgun to his mouth. *"Three ..."* She raised the burning knot. *"Throw!"*

The bolt shot through the air, and the knot hit the ring of fire and exploded.

"Good shot!" Keenan called out, and Temerity could see the bolt sticking out of the small third eye in the ogre's forehead. The giant was staggering drunkenly around in its circle, grasping at flames and tossing them weakly into the fire lake.

"Good," she said. "One more. Hurry." A rock troll was beating on Tomaz's raised shield with a stone club, and the other was swinging a humongous hammer at Keenan, who danced away, hopping from boulder to boulder.

The ogre was jumping up and down, pounding the floor with its bare feet. The floor shook and quaked, throwing Temerity off balance. She grabbed onto a boulder to steady herself when a thunderous crack resounded in the chamber. Rocks broke loose from the walls and came crashing down.

Temerity and Half-pint dodged rocks that tumbled onto the perimeter, adding to the mounds of boulders that ringed the room, while chunks of the ceiling broke off and smashed into the lake of fire. Temerity's heart was hammering, and sweat streamed down her brow, blinding her.

She rubbed her eyes, and another crack split her eardrums and shook the ground. She peered through blurry eyes as Half-pint yanked hard at her sleeve. They stumbled away from a giant boulder, which had broken loose from the wall and rolled slowly past them, coming to a stop in the blazing fire.

She hopped onto it, calling for Half-pint and looking to see if Keenan and Tomaz were okay. They were scrambling away from the rock trolls, who were grabbing newly fallen rocks and lobbing them at the pair of young men.

"Hurry!" she said, panic clutching at her throat. Half-pint knelt next to her on the boulder and shoved a bolt into the end of the flute. The ogre was staggering around inside the fire circle with its fists clenched and fangs bared, seeming to be gathering its strength for another quake.

She lit another knot and at the count of four, they launched their projectiles at the frenzied ogre.

The knot's explosion had barely cleared when the ogre wobbled and fell, the ground shaking as it hit the floor, its last eye sprouting a crossbow bolt bristling with straw fletching.

Tomaz and Keenan ran around the edge to join them as the flames slowly died and the rock trolls retreated into their cave.

"We need to finish him off," Half-pint said, and leapt over the smoldering floor onto the island of a fallen rock troll, then turned into a cat and leapt the final distance over the guttering flames and into the circle where the giant was breathing heavily and clawing at the floor.

Temerity and the young men followed behind Half-pint, who, as a hobgoblin again, pulled his meat cleaver from the ogre's belt and began hacking at the thick blue neck. The ogre shook and grunted and squealed as Keenan joined in with his scythe, and Tomaz with his battle-axe.

Temerity leaned on her broadsword and watched. She should help, she thought dully, but her limbs were suddenly leaden. Now that they had beat the boss, the brutality of the long challenge rendered her stunned and numb, and her red jewels emitted barely any light at all. The blind creature struggled weakly, then spasmed and grew still. She thought of the never-ending line of adventurers waiting for their turn to kill the ogre and wondered if the giant ever got used to dying.

48

TAKE ONE, LEAVE ONE, PLUS ONE

The ogre lay in a lifeless heap. The flames were mostly gone, and the floor was scorched black. Temerity watched as Half-pint crept towards the mountain of a corpse.

"What are you doing?" she hissed.

"Collecting our trophies," he said.

"What trophies?" Keenan asked, creeping after him.

The four of them gathered around the corpulent monster, collecting the rest of their weapons as Half-pint poked at the ogre with his javelin. It was definitely dead.

"We get trophies from every boss," Half-pint said. "Very valuable. I usually take a tooth. Aha!" He lifted the beast's pale blue lip with the tip of his javelin, revealing its long fangs and a mouthful of discolored teeth. "Lend me your pliers."

Temerity handed him the pliers and watched as the hobgoblin reached back into the monster's mouth, his goblin head nearly disappearing inside the gaping maw. He emerged with a large gold molar clamped in the jaws of the pliers. "Ha ha ha. I got the gold tooth," he said, laughing and dancing around. "Worth five rune stones, if you can find the right craftsman. My meat cleaver will become the deadliest blade in the Swamp."

"What about us?" Tomaz asked, peering inside the ogre's mouth.

"There's only one gold tooth," Half-pint said, "but the troll's teeth on his necklaces are pretty good. Worth two or three rune stones. Not a bad take."

Tomaz scowled but sliced through the sinew necklace and pulled a long curved canine tooth free, examining the fang with a disgruntled frown.

"We can take anything?" Keenan asked, poking at the ashes in the ogre's fire bowl.

Temerity looked more closely at the yellowish bowl. "Is that a skull?" she asked.

"Looks like the top of a troll skull," Keenan said. "A skullcap." He turned to the ogre, examining the skulls and bones hanging from the monster's belt, and cut loose a globe-shaped bone. He twisted it with both hands, and the halves came apart—two skullcaps, smaller than human skulls. Temerity stepped back as flames sprang up from one of the halves.

"A fire bowl," Half-pint exclaimed. "Well, I'll be. I always wondered where those things came from. I've seen a few in higher levels but never knew they were spoils from the ogre boss. Good find."

"Is it magic?" Keenan asked, gazing into the blue and gold flames.

"Yep," Half-pint said. "Burns forever. Grab some."

Keenan glanced up and then dipped his gloved hand into

the bowl and scooped out a handful of fire. A broad smile split his face, and he lobbed the fireball at Tomaz.

"Hey, cut that out," Tomaz said, dodging the flames and laughing with his friend. "That'll come in handy. No more need for flint," he said to Temerity, and she nodded happily.

"Wait, let me try something," Keenan said. He set down the flaming bowl and dipped a spearhead into it. The tip of the javelin caught fire, and Keenan threw the burning spear into the ogre's corpse, where it flared up, singeing the skin garment and causing the air to reek of scorched hair. Keenan tamped out the flames and retrieved his javelin, which was unmarred by the fire.

"What should I take?" Temerity asked. There were more fire skulls hanging from the belt and more troll fangs on the necklace. She examined the long bone the ogre had used for a horn, and the skeletal hands and feet that dangled from the monster's girth. A straight bone pierced the ogre's bulbous nose, and a polished stone earring hung from its fat ear lobe. Temerity's gaze shifted to the small blue eye that still hung by a strand from the side of its bald head.

She pushed down a queasy feeling, then sliced through the slimy strand and cupped the eyeball in her snakeskin palm. She examined the blue eyeball, rolling it around and poking at it with her sleeve dagger while the others leaned over her shoulder, looking on.

"It's rock hard," she said, touching it with her fingertip. "Feels like a marble."

"I don't know what it's good for," Half-pint said, leaning in and poking at it. "I never saw anybody with one. But maybe you can see what a craftsman will trade for it."

She shrugged and trimmed the rest of the slimy strand off, then pocketed the eyeball. "I guess I'll find out," she said with a sideways grin. "What's next?"

"We need to choose our weapons," Half-pint said.

They gathered at the far end of the domed chamber, near the arch that would lead them out of the ogre's arena.

They lined up their weapons on the floor.

"Take one, leave one, plus one," Tomaz said. "That means we can each take four weapons with us."

"You can count," Keenan said with a smirk.

Tomaz shoved his friend playfully on the shoulder, then quickly turned his attention to the assortment of weapons.

Temerity considered her choices. Her new favorite was the troll's broadsword, so she set that on the ground at her side, wishing she had a proper scabbard for the razor-sharp blade.

Even though Pauly had insisted she leave his sword behind, she saw no reason to do so yet, so she sheathed the blade and hung it from her belt. That left the boning knife, sleeve dagger, sledgehammer, and javelin.

"Knives are easy to get," Half-pint said, pointing to the boning knife.

"But that's Ma's," she said plaintively, suddenly hit with a wave of homesickness.

"That knife sat in the back of the drawer for years," he said. "She'll never miss it. Now, the sleeve dagger, that's a useful weapon."

"But it's so small," she said, examining the needle-sharp, double-edged blade.

"That's the point. It's easy to hide. Perfect for when some orc has you in a chokehold," he said, waggling his ears.

"If you like it so much, you take it," she said, but she was already sheathing it on her wrist and hiding it in her sleeve. "What do I need a sledgehammer for?"

"You're playing Melee," Keenan said. "You need at least

one blunt weapon. What have you got now, two swords and a sleeve dagger? You definitely need the sledge."

"But I'm playing Blade. What about the javelin?" she asked, examining the spearhead Keenan had expertly crafted.

"I'm playing Range. I could use that," Keenan said with a sly grin.

"You already have two," she replied.

"Now I'll have three. I'll trade one up for a bow and arrows when I find them."

"Okay," she said, handing him her javelin and setting the sledgehammer next to her boning knife, still undecided.

"Knives are easy to get in the Swamp," Half-pint repeated. "Sledgehammers are not."

She blew out a breath. "What do I do with this, then?" she asked, holding up the boning knife.

"There's a place at the end for extra weapons," Half-pint said, gesturing towards the exit tunnel.

She reluctantly set aside the knife and holstered the sledge-hammer, liking its weight and recalling how effective it had been at smashing troll heads.

"Now, what do I need?" Half-pint mused, examining his stash of weapons. "Donation bin," he said, tossing aside the head of the pickaxe. "Ogre-killer," he said happily, placing the flute and bolts into his backpack. "Sword," he said, hanging the troll's dagger from his belt. His eyes flitted between his remaining weapons: knife, javelin, and meat cleaver.

"Knives are easy to get," she said with a smirk. "And that meat cleaver's been sitting in the back of the drawer forever."

Half-pint cast her a flat look.

"And shields are weapons," Tomaz teased, unhooking the buckler from the hobgoblin's pack and placing it with the other three weapons.

Half-pint's frown deepened. He finally chose the meat cleaver and buckler, setting aside the knife and javelin.

"Well, somebody's got to have a decent knife," Tomaz said, sheathing his hunting knife.

"Knives are easy to get," Temerity and Keenan said together, giggling.

"You can only take four weapons," Half-pint said, pointing to Tomaz's knife, battle-axe, war hammer, woodsman's axe, javelin, sword, and shield. "That's seven."

Tomaz glared at his weapons. "I suppose you want my javelin," he said to Keenan.

"Nope, three's enough. I'm taking my scythe."

Tomaz scratched at his beard and gave a deep sigh. "Shields are really considered weapons?"

Half-pint shrugged. "Ask the orcs."

"Well, I'm definitely taking the battle-axe. And the war hammer. And my shield." He set the sword and javelin to the side. "And my axe," he said, lovingly cradling his woodsman's axe.

"Trade up," Half-pint said, poking the woodsman's axe and the great battle-axe with its crescent blades and runes carved into the metal handle. "Take one, leave one."

"I can have two axes," Tomaz said petulantly.

"You'd really rather have a knife than a sword?" Keenan asked. "Here, take my hatchet and flail, too," he said jokingly, pushing his extra weapons towards Tomaz.

Tomaz exhaled loudly. "Fine." He set down his knife, sword, and woodsman's axe, then picked up the flail and twirled the spiked mace head around. A wide grin split his face. "Happy now?"

"Seems like a good set of weapons for someone playing Shield," Half-pint said, nodding.

Tomaz patted the wooden shield at his side, then ran his fingers over the carved letters: *The Dragon Shield*. He then arranged the three troll-sized weapons in front of him: battle-axe, war hammer, and flail. "I guess these are good," he muttered.

"More than good," Half-pint affirmed.

"You look happier than a pig in mud." Temerity smirked.

"Yeah, I know," she said as the two farm boys began to open their mouths. "You're wheat farmers."

Keenan flared his nostrils at her, then turned to Tomaz. "You look like a troll now, with those weapons."

"Shut up," Tomaz said, but a satisfied grin crept across his face.

"Now, here is the most important part," Half-pint said as Temerity, Keenan, and Tomaz stood up to leave the ogre's arena. "Sit down. We're not done yet."

They sat back down and looked expectantly at the hobgoblin.

"We can each take only three dragon jewels with us to the next level. Not counting my end-game jewel, of course. It's a big decision, because each of these jewels will double in power when we enter the Swamp and will double again at every level. If you hang onto the same jewel for all seven levels, it becomes insanely powerful."

Everyone gazed down at the jewels on their wrists. They arranged themselves in a circle and laid their jewels on the floor in front of them, then set the extra ones in the center: three yellows and an orange.

"Why wouldn't we hang onto the same ones the whole time?" Temerity asked.

"Do people steal them?" Tomaz asked.

"They can be stolen, yes," Half-pint said. "Plus, we'll find more in the Swamp, and you might decide you want to power-up a different combination. Remember, they all do different things. Some combinations are good together or suit you better. And some people specialize in one color and need to collect three of the same. But you'll want to settle on your colors pretty early on—by Level Two, or Level Three at the latest. Unless you find an intelligence jewel, then that could change all your plans."

"Are white dragon jewels really that special?" Keenan asked.

"Yes," he said, nodding somberly. "Intelligence is a rare trait in this game."

Tomaz snickered, and Temerity asked, "If you pick up a new jewel in the Swamp, will it be twice as powerful as the ones we found in Dark Town?"

"No," Half-pint said. "They all start out at the same base level, no matter when you acquire them. It's carrying them while you pass through the portal to the next level that bonds them to you and imparts extra power. If you trade it away later, it reverts to its original power level."

Temerity turned to the jewels and pondered her options. She had two reds and an orange. She valued the amplification power of the red jewels and liked the surge of strength and confidence she felt when wielding her weapons. On the other hand, she was beginning to form a connection with the orange jewel. She gazed down at it, and it glimmered back at her. She took a thoughtful breath. If she was going to continue growing into her role as a Blade, then she would need strength and skill.

She turned to Half-pint and asked, "Can I play Attack as a triple orange?"

He cocked his head at her. "I told you about my friend. He played all orange and swore by it. I never tried it myself, though." He squinted thoughtfully. "It's a rather unusual choice. An acquired skill, I believe. If you think you'd be good at it, you could try. But I'm afraid you might die before you mastered it."

"That's what I'm afraid of, too." She gnawed at the inside of her cheek and examined the jewels. Keenan had an orange, and there was an extra orange. She could go all orange right now, if she wanted. Or, she could go all yellow, though she had no experience with that color. What would it be like to be a Yellow Mage, like Half-pint's ex-wife, or an Enchantress, like Avon? She sighed. "What are you going to choose, Keenan?"

He glanced up at her. "I don't know. I'm thinking of playing all red. If I could get another one." He eyed her two red jewels, then met her eyes again. "Want to trade one of your reds for my orange?"

He gave her a winning smile, and she chuckled. He could be charming when he wanted to be. "I'm not sure yet," she said. "Let me think about it."

Half-pint leaned forward. "I'm going to play my two greens and two yellows. He took two of the extra yellows and placed his red and blue in the center. "You can have my red," he said to Keenan.

Keenan snatched the red jewel, then placed his orange in the center and cast Temerity a sidelong glance.

"Good for you," she said dryly, gazing at the remaining yellow, blue, and two orange jewels sitting in the middle of their circle. She caught Tomaz's eye.

"I'm staying with two blues and a red," he said, shrugging.

She pursed her lips and stared at her remaining choices. She could stay with two reds and an orange and focus on strength and skill, with a little premonition. Or she could play two oranges and a red, trying out the power of the orange but still keeping a little bit of red boost. Or she could go all in on orange and trust that the sensitivity of the premonition jewels would more than compensate for the loss of enhanced strength and skill. It was a hard choice.

In the end, she dismissed her better judgment, ignoring the arguments of her rational mind, and trusted in her heart. She placed her two red jewels in the center and took the two oranges, meeting the surprised and dubious expressions of her companions.

She felt suddenly deflated as the enhanced strength of the red jewels drained away. She immediately began to second-guess her decision, but at the same time, ripples of knowing feathered over her skin and a sharpened awareness heightened her senses. Colors were brighter, and the gruff conversation of two orcs from the tunnel beyond the arena reached her ears. The orange jewels were warm and pulsating, and as she inserted them into her wrist straps, hints of things to come flickered at the edge of her consciousness. A sense of calm enveloped her, even as images of snakes and flying monkeys flashed across her vision.

"If I die, will you meet me back at the Tin Roof?" she asked, gazing at each of them in turn.

One by one, they smiled and extended a hand towards the center, and the four of them clasped hands in a loyalty pact.

───────◆───────

"Are you ready?" Half-pint asked, standing under the exit arch.

Temerity stood up, hung Pauly's sword and the sledgehammer from her belt, then picked up the troll-sized broadsword. The monstrous blade was suddenly heavy as a bag of rocks, and she struggled to sling it across her back. Not wanting to admit that choosing orange jewels over red might not have been the wisest decision, she nodded confidently and followed the hobgoblin from the ogre's arena.

At the end of the long tunnel, she and her three companions entered a large, white rock-salt cavern with towering ceilings. Curtains of stalactites dripped water from high above, landing on stalagmites of various heights that studded the floor. Temerity gazed around in wonder at the sparkling formations, reminded of icicles hanging from the Tin Roof in winter. Between the stalagmites stood stone tables filled with weapons, barrels holding more weapons, and open chests overflowing with dragon jewels of every color—except white.

They were met by several orc guards who stood with arms folded, appearing bored and grumpy. Beyond the cavern, a faint din and bustle reached Temerity's ears, and the air was tainted with the rotten-egg stink of a swamp.

Temerity hesitated for a long moment and finally placed the two extra reds, the blue, and the yellow onto a mound of glittering dragon jewels, then turned to her companions, putting on a brave smile. *Would she be strong enough to survive without any reds?*

She realized with a start that those were the thoughts and fears of her companions. Rather than indulge further misgivings, she focused her attention on the mental image that popped into her head of floating across a waterway on a little boat. She glanced up as Tomaz shuffled forward in front of her, and she knew with certainty that he was going to try and sneak extra weapons past the guards. She smirked to herself, looking forward to watching Tomaz challenge the hulking orcs. She knew who would win.

They moved further into the chamber and lined up to surrender their extra weapons, filing past a large stone table heaped high with blades and blunt instruments of all kinds.

Tomaz placed his knife on the table and then stepped away. An oversized orc held out a long arm to stop him.

Temerity stood to the side, arms folded across her chest and a grin curling her lips.

"Only four weapons," the orc growled, tugging on Tomaz's thick wooden shield.

"A shield is not a weapon," Tomaz said stiffly.

"Sword, tree-axe, battle-axe, war hammer, flail, shield. That's six." The orc tapped each weapon as he counted, then reached out with a massive hand and grabbed Tomaz by his leather chest guard and lifted him off the ground.

"Okay, okay," Tomaz said, squirming free and landing on his feet. "You don't have to get all huffy." He straightened his cuirass and then added his sword and woodsman's axe to the pile of weapons. Temerity was sure she saw tears in his eyes.

She shed no tears leaving the boning knife behind, but she did wonder if there would be a homing spike at the entrance to the Swamp and if she shouldn't pop back home to make sure her ma was okay. She reached for the half-locket, pulling it out from where it had been tucked safely under her gorget and chainmail, and held the etching of her pa between her fingertips, then pressed it near to her heart.

They finally passed the orcs' inspection and filed through a stone archway towards a murky green glow.

THE END

To be continued in Level Two, The Swamp

THE SWAMP

LEVEL TWO OF DRAGON'S CRAWL

TALES OF TEMERITY

COMING SOON

Also from Palmer Pickering

Moon Deeds

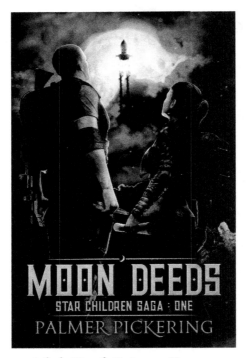

Adult Dark Science-Fantasy

Twins Cassidy and Torr must save Earth from a ruthless enemy at a time when the only force more powerful than alien technology is magic.

> *"There is so much to love about this book, from its complex and intricately woven plot filled with tension, strife, and discovery, to the personal attachment you begin to build with the characters."*
>
> **- K.J. Simmill**

Also from Palmer Pickering

Heliotrope

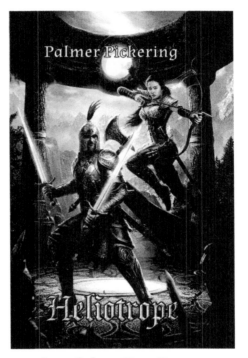

Standalone Epic Fantasy

A retired soldier turned stonemason finds himself in the middle of a coup. Choosing duty to a dead king, he adopts two orphans and launches a journey to heal old wounds and rediscover ancient magic.

"Heliotrope was the epic fantasy I didn't know I needed. It is a beautifully written, slow-burn story full of heart."

– Quinn

Printed in Great Britain
by Amazon

42778797R10233